LIGHT IT UP

Nick Petrie received an MFA in fiction from
the University of Washington, won a Hopwood
Award for short fiction, and his story 'At the
Laundromat' won the 2006 Short Story
Contest in the *The Seattle Review*. His first
novel, *The Drifter*, won the International
Thriller Writers Award and the Barry
Award for Best First Novel.

By Nick Petrie

The Drifter
Burning Bright
Light It Up

NICK
PETRIE
LIGHT IT UP

HEAD
of ZEUS

First published in the US in 2018 by G.P. Putnam's Sons,
an imprint of Penguin Random House LLC

First published in the UK in 2018 by Head of Zeus

9 7 5 3 1 2 4 6 8

A catalogue record for this book is available from the British Library.

ISBN (HB): 9781788542517
ISBN (XTPB): 9781788542524
ISBN (E): 9781788542500

Book design by Meighan Cavanaugh

Printed and bound in Germany by CPI Books GmbH

Head of Zeus Ltd
First Floor East
5–8 Hardwick Street
London EC1R 4RG

WWW.HEADOFZEUS.COM

This one's all for Margret. She knows why.

The woods are lovely, dark and deep,
But I have promises to keep,
And miles to go before I sleep,
And miles to go before I sleep.

—Robert Frost

LIGHT IT UP

1

The chain-link fence was ten feet tall with razor wire at the top. It began at the front corner of the repurposed cement-block warehouse in North Denver, wrapped in a neat rectangle around the side parking lot and the rear loading dock, and continued to the opposite corner of the building.

Peter Ash stepped down from the back seat of Henry Nygaard's big four-door pickup to pull open the rolling security gate. He kept his head on a swivel, eyes chasing from the street to the fence lines to the windows and flat rooftops of neighboring buildings.

He wore a decent secondhand armored vest and one of Henry's spare pistols strapped to his leg, neither one exactly hidden under an untucked flannel shirt, but not particularly visible unless someone was looking for them. Which was more or less the goal.

He could feel the warmth of the blacktop through the soles of his boots, and the late-September sun was hot on his shoulders and the back of his neck. The waistband of his pants was damp from the sweat trickling down his back.

Peter didn't mind. He'd been in hotter places, wearing and carrying a lot more shit.

Deacon, the driver, pulled Henry's truck through the gate. Peter closed it behind them, waved to the camera mounted high on the warehouse wall, and waited to hear the magnetic lock clang shut. It wasn't a perfect system, but it wasn't bad, either.

He hopped back in the pickup for the sixty-meter run to the back of the warehouse, where it became clear to every member of the Heavy Metal Protection team that their schedule was shot.

As it turned out, it was the grow manager's thirtieth birthday, and the cultivation workers had gotten stoned out of their gourds at lunch. Someone had brought takeout tacos and a chocolate layer cake and things had gone downhill from there. The workers sat on cheap vinyl chairs, leaning back against the white-painted block wall, eyes closed, faces raised to the afternoon sun like potted plants.

"You got to be kidding me," Deacon said. "Nap time? Ten to one says they're not ready for us."

He hit the horn and the grow manager popped out of his chair like a jack-in-the-box, standing even before he was fully awake.

In the front passenger seat, Henry looked at his watch. It was big and sturdy and dependable, just like Henry. "We're okay," he said. "We'll make up time on the freeway."

"Y'all are dreaming," said Banjo, the youngest. "Rush hour gonna kill us."

The other men wore sidearms, too, and armored vests under light shirts. Each man also had an AR-15 semiautomatic rifle, the civilian version of the M16, magazines in place but the chambers cleared, butt-down in the footwell. They left the long guns in the truck unless absolutely necessary, because they attracted too much attention.

Peter didn't say anything.

He had only worked for Heavy Metal Protection for a few days, doing a favor for Henry.

None of them wanted to do the job in the dark.

They were all thinking about what had happened the week before.

Peter was tall and rangy, muscle and bone, nothing extra. He had wide, knuckly hands and a lean, angular face, his dark hair long enough to cover the tips of his slightly pointed ears. He had the thoughtful eyes of a werewolf a week before the change.

Even out in the parking lot, he could smell the heady green funk of the growing plants.

Henry said it was bad form to call it marijuana unless you were talking about medical marijuana, which was a legal term. For many people in the industry, the word "marijuana" had racist undertones from the first attempts to regulate the plant in the 1930s, when officials tied its recreational use to Mexican immigrants.

The Latin name for the plant's genus was *Cannabis*, the industry's preferred term.

And it was definitely an industry.

Call it weed, ganja, bud, or chronic, it made billions of dollars each year.

And Heavy Metal Protection was part of it. The company provided secure facility consulting, uniformed static guards for at-risk sites, and armed mobile protection for moving cash and product from point A to point B.

The mobile protection arm was nothing like an armored-car service. An armored car was a giant rolling strongbox, painted in bright colors, and made an excellent target. Heavy Metal's invisible, late-model civilian rides had no logos. The two-person teams were armed and wore ballistic vests but no uniforms. They looked like accountants or electricians, anyone but who they were: highly trained former military personnel with a job to do.

Most cannabis-related crime occurred at grow facilities, because they were usually located in neglected or industrial areas where the rent was cheap and traffic minimal, and also because you could find them with your nose.

Growers told their employees not to be heroes. Even if cured product was as good as cash, worth more than a thousand dollars a pound wholesale, two or three times that broken down for retail, nobody needed to die to protect a pound of weed.

But when security was done properly, with hardened facilities, visible security measures, and varied delivery schedules, robberies were rare.

Problems generally happened for one of several reasons. A security lapse, like a door left open at the end of the shift because somebody's magic brownie kicked in earlier than planned. A nighttime smash-and-grab on a small new facility that assumed, incorrectly, that nobody knew where that funky smell was coming from. Or something as simple as a guy walking in like he belonged, grabbing a pound or two of vacu-packed product, tucking it under his arm like a football, and taking off like O.J. at the airport.

What had happened the week before was different, a new and much larger problem.

Heavy Metal had lost an entire vehicle, its crew and cargo.

Literally, lost.

As in, could not be found.

Two men and a Dodge Dakota. One of the men was the company's cofounder, Henry's son-in-law. The other was the company's operations manager. Their cargo was three hundred thousand dollars in cash, gross profits headed for the client's cash stash in the mountains. The vehicle's GPS tracker had dropped off-line somewhere on I-70 headed west. The men's phone signals had disappeared.

No sign of any of them since.

Peter had asked the question his first day on the job. "Did they get hit? Or just run with it?"

Henry didn't comment. He glowered darkly out the windshield, as if all his suspicions about his son-in-law had been confirmed.

"They could have run with it," said Deacon, shrugging a thick shoulder. "Maybe I got a dim view of human nature."

Banjo shook his head. "Had to be a hijacking," he said. "Three hundred grand isn't enough to fuck up your life and turn yourself into a fugitive."

With no evidence either way, what had happened was anyone's guess. The state police had been looking into it for a week. Officially it was considered armed robbery and a possible double homicide.

But it wasn't going to happen again.

Today, they had another big payload. Henry had brought the heavy crew, four capable men, their heads on a swivel in the Mile-High City, sweating behind razor wire under the hot September sun.

Henry stepped down to get the grow manager moving. Deacon stayed with the truck. Banjo jogged back to the gate, where he had a view on three sides. Peter jogged forward to the opposite corner of the building, where his own three-sided view completed the perimeter.

They'd all had duty like this before.

Peter hadn't thought the work would be a problem for him. He'd been the tip of the spear for eight long years, a Marine lieutenant with more combat deployments than he cared to remember. He'd been done with his war for a while now, but the war wasn't quite done with him. It had left him with a souvenir. An oddball form of post-traumatic stress that showed up as claustrophobia, an intense reaction to enclosed spaces. He called it the white static.

It hadn't showed up until he was back home, just days from mustering out.

At first, going inside was just uncomfortable. A fine-grained sensation at the back of his neck, like electric foam, or a small battery inserted under the skin. If he stayed inside, the feeling would intensify. The foam would turn to sparks, a crackling unease in his brainstem, a profound dissonance just at the edge of hearing. His neck would tense, and his shoulders would begin to rise as the muscles tightened. He'd look for the exits as his chest clamped up, then he'd start having trouble catching his breath. After twenty minutes, he'd be in a full-blown panic attack, hyperventilating, his fight-or-flight mechanism cranked into overdrive.

He'd been working on the static pretty steadily since spring. He'd joined a veterans' group, had been talking to a shrink. His friendship with Henry was a big part of that. He'd been making progress. He could be inside for more than an hour now.

But there was something about sweating inside the armor again, strapping on a sidearm, the familiar feel of the AR-15 in his hand. He was losing ground. He'd been having trouble sleeping since he'd gotten to Denver. He told himself it was just the noise of the city, but he knew better.

He'd told Henry he could give him a week, maybe two. No more than that.

Peter had other plans. Better plans. There was a woman he needed to see again. There was something between them, he hoped. Something real.

Heat floated up from the parking lot, turning the chain-link fence into a shimmering abstraction. Peter kept his eyes moving, searching the roads and driveways, the windows and rooftops of the neighboring buildings.

Out of habit, the way another man might tap his pockets for his keys and wallet and phone before leaving the house, Peter touched his fingertips to the butt of the pistol Henry had loaned him for the job.

It was a Sig Sauer .40, an older high-performance weapon unremarkable except for its pristine condition. Everything Henry owned had the patina of long use and meticulous care. His truck was from the late nineties, but it looked like new, except for the creases on the leather seats.

Henry was over seventy years old, although you'd never think it to look at him, standing tall, his shoulders broad and square, a stubby Honduran cigar unlit in the corner of his mouth. His voice was a hoarse whisper, but it just made the other men lean in closer to hear him.

By the time Henry signed the paperwork, carried ten cardboard boxes with labels and security tape out of the facility, and loaded them into the heavy steel toolbox bolted to the bed of his pickup, they were more than an hour behind schedule.

Peter saw Henry pat his chest over his shirt pocket, as if making sure his pen was still there, before waving Peter and Banjo back to the truck.

"Mount up," he called, his hoarse whisper somehow still carrying across the parking lot in that thin mountain air. "We're burning daylight."

_____

The Heavy Metal team rolled onto the streets of North Denver, Henry's pickup looking like a hundred others around them. Their next stop was Denver's Finest Kind, a recreational cannabis retail shop in Curtis Park.

Peter had always thought of Denver as a mountain city, but it stood on the High Plains, straddling the Platte River, nothing but dry farmland to the east for five hundred miles and more.

To the immediate west of Denver, though, was the whole of the Rocky Mountains, rising to the sky like white-tipped teeth. They gave the city a definite flavor. Peter could see the Front Range and its foothills from many parts of the city, just looking down the broad avenues. Denver had a busy, frontier feeling, a growing city constantly reinventing itself like the rest of the Mountain West.

A block out from Denver's Finest Kind, Deacon drove a recon route, looking for trouble and finding none. He parked out front like any other customer. Peter and Henry got out while Deacon and Banjo stayed with the truck. Peter kept his hands free and his eyes on the move while Henry climbed up into the bed of the truck, removed a cardboard box from the big orange toolbox, hopped down with the box under his arm, and walked the quarter-block to the retailer's front door.

Peter followed Henry inside. He felt the white static get louder in the back of his head.

But he'd been practicing. He was doing fine.

The security vestibule was a small room with a vase of flowers on a tiny table, a spotless bulletproof glass window, a closed-circuit camera, and a slot to pass the customer's ID to the cheerful receptionist. There was also an ATM in the vestibule, because the cannabis industry ran almost entirely on cash. Henry had texted ahead to the Heavy

Metal guard on-site, so the man was expecting them and buzzed them through immediately.

The interior of Denver's Finest Kind was sleek and modern in glass and chrome, like an Apple store or a high-end boutique, although the verdant smell of the product was strong. Behind a long, elegant display counter stood three attentive salespeople, chatting with customers about particular cannabis strains and their effects. Did you want to be energetic and creative, or calm and relaxed?

Henry walked into the back room with the manager while Peter monitored the progress of the static, watched the exits, and glanced at the inventory. He loved the names of the various strains.

Purple Haze, Buddha Sativa, Skywalker, White Rhino, Gorilla Glue, BrainBender, Agent Orange, Green Crack, Trainwreck, Blue Lightning, Ass Hat, Chocolope.

Who came up with this stuff?

Stoners, presumably.

Or people trying to appeal to stoners.

In addition to the attractive glass containers of fat green buds, the store sold hashish, THC-infused oils, and edibles, everything from the traditional pot brownie to cookies, chocolate, and hard candy.

Peter had only been in Colorado for three days. He still couldn't quite believe selling weed was legal. But once he started looking for them, he noticed cannabis retailers and the green cross symbol of medical marijuana everywhere. He'd stopped for gas in Aurora and found four retail stores in his line of sight from the pump.

It was like a whole different country.

Peter wasn't particularly interested in getting high himself. He liked good scotch, and was happy to crack a cold beer on a hot day. But he'd found that more than one or two drinks made it harder to handle the static.

On the other hand, some of the veterans Peter worked with smoked weed on their time off, and they said that certain strains really helped with their post-traumatic stress. The medical in marijuana. If it worked for you, Peter figured, what was the harm?

Henry walked out of the back room with a new cardboard box, this one full of cash. He nodded to the receptionist and Peter led the way outside, white static forgotten, his eyes moving and his hands open and ready.

The cash was the whole problem.

Although recreational marijuana was legal in a few states, and medicinal marijuana was legal in many, the production, sale, and use of any kind of marijuana was still illegal on the federal level, which made commercial banking relationships problematic.

Medical dispensaries were allowed limited privileges, but a bank that knowingly provided a recreational cannabis business with anything from a basic checking account to a commercial loan to credit card processing was breaking federal law and could face serious consequences.

Which meant this industry was run almost entirely in cash. Employees, suppliers, and landlords were paid in cash. Businesses paid their state, local, and federal taxes in cash. The industry was uniquely vulnerable to crime, but also provided a very real opportunity for people with certain skills.

"How much will we end up carrying today?" asked Peter when Deacon pulled away from the curb.

"Bad question," said Deacon, brown hands steady behind the wheel. Deacon's father was a preacher in the Mississippi Delta country who'd had great hopes for his son's religious calling. Deacon told Peter he'd only heard the call of the Army, one of the few ways for a black man to find his way out of the Deep South. He hadn't looked back since. "Don't ask that question."

"Why not?" Although Peter already knew the answer.

"We don't guard it because of its value," Henry said over the seat-back. "We guard it because it's our honor to do so."

"Plus," Banjo said with a grin, "y'all ain't tempted if y'all don't know what you're carrying."

Banjo was the youngest of Henry's crew, maybe twenty-five. He had a thick Appalachian drawl, and took a lot of good-natured shit for being from Kentucky. His real name was Dave, he'd told Peter when they'd met. "But all these assholes call me Banjo." He'd smiled when he said it, not minding the nickname, glad to belong in this group of capable men working together.

Peter was, too.

He didn't miss the war, but he did miss his guys.

And part of him, although he didn't like to admit it, really missed suiting up and rolling out with his platoon every day, armed to the teeth and looking for a fight, scared shitless and thrilled to his bones at the same time. Trusting your guys with your life, while they trusted you with theirs.

There was nothing else like it.

But he was hopeful that he'd found something different. He had an invitation to visit June Cassidy in Washington State. An invitation he'd worked hard to get.

No way in hell he was going to miss it.

Working their way through the metro area, Henry's crew made ten more stops, the last in Lakewood. The delay at the grow had put them into afternoon traffic, where they'd lost even more time. Now the sun blasted directly through the windshield when Deacon pulled onto I-70 heading west, leaving Denver's High Plains for the foothills of the Front Range.

The big orange metal toolbox on the back of Henry's truck was now filled with boxes of cash.

Each client, Henry had explained, did something different with his money.

The lucky clients, those with a history in medical marijuana, could put their earnings in the bank, or at least in a safety-deposit box. These were straightforward deliveries, set up by the client with a phone call to the bank manager, so the tellers didn't hit the silent alarm when a pair of armed men came walking in.

The cannabis clients didn't have legal access to a bank, so they put their money someplace else.

Grandma's attic, Henry called it. The company nickname for any secret stash spot.

Which might be the client's actual grandmother's actual attic, or a giant safe in the client's basement, or a pair of Rubbermaid bins under a trapdoor in the floor of his cousin's backyard shed, or just a sheltered spot out of sight of the security cameras behind the King Soopers on Evans, where the boxes of bills were transferred to someone the client trusted more than his hired security company.

This particular client's money was going to the mountains.

The grower, who ran two big facilities and sold wholesale to dozens of retailers, also owned a legacy parcel deep in the steeps of the Arapaho National Forest. According to Henry, the small cabin was set way back in the tall pines off a long gravel road, itself turning off a narrow winding paved county highway cut into the sloped side of a creek drainage.

Henry said you could usually get there by car until sometime in October. After that it was snowshoes from the county highway.

It seemed a safe place for a cash stash, the roads empty enough that it was easy to tell if someone was tracking them, although it was more difficult at night. The county highway didn't have guardrails, just tall rocks on one side and a long drop on the other, with a gravel turnoff for slow-moving vehicles where the mountain allowed.

The light was fading. Deacon had the pedal down, pushing the limits of the truck and the road. Henry sat in the front passenger seat, Banjo in the seat behind him, with Peter behind the driver because he was a lefty. The sun had dropped behind the serrated horizon and they were all ready to be done with this long day.

When Deacon powered through a pothole with a thump that rattled Peter's teeth, Henry said, "Jesus, take it easy. I just got new tie rods."

Banjo gave his high, cheerful laugh. "Dammit, Deacon, this is why we can't have nice things."

Henry raised a middle finger to the critic in the back seat, and Banjo laughed again. Henry had promised cheeseburgers and beer on the way home.

A half mile ahead of them on the highway, a boxy ambulance grumbled slowly up the grade. The red-and-white paint seemed dim in the fading light, or maybe the ambulance was just old. The diesel rattle of its engine got louder in the thin air as Deacon came up fast behind.

The mountain rose hard and lumpy on their left. On their right the slope fell away steeply, disappearing into treetops, the highway too narrow for passing. Deacon took his foot off the gas.

"Our turn's up here," said Henry. He pointed with his stubby unlit cigar. "Gravel road, just past the next switchback."

The ambulance driver glanced in the side mirror and picked up a little speed. Mountain driving etiquette, thought Peter. Speed up or get out of the way.

He looked out at the shadowed pines, wondering what June Cassidy was doing at that moment. Maybe microwaving her dinner, he thought, or riding her bike down the trail that wound through the orchard.

He'd know soon enough. He hadn't seen her in almost five months, but he could still picture her face, those bright, shining eyes, that wide sarcastic mouth, the brilliant constellation of freckles spread across her cheeks. He had her letters in his day pack on the floor at his feet.

He felt his momentum shift as Deacon started the truck around the tight curve. The diesel sound of the ambulance changed ahead of them, getting softer. Slowing. Coming to a stop at the wide spot just before the intersection.

"Man, get out of my way," said Deacon. "That's my damn turn." He shook his head, then tapped the horn, hit the gas, and swung wide to get around the big boxy van. Peter figured the other driver had thought it was a good place to let them by.

Until the ambulance pulled forward sharply and Peter saw the red wrecker roaring toward them down the gravel road.

Too fast to stop.

Too late to miss.

He knew immediately. The impact was inevitable.

He didn't have time to brace himself or call out to the others.

The wrecker's heavy front grille was suddenly huge in the passenger-side window.

Then it T-boned them hard enough to knock Henry's big four-door pickup across the oncoming lane and off the road into the drainage ditch.

Peter was on the far side of the impact, in the rear seat behind the driver. He was thrown forward and toward the wrecker, yanked by his seat belt like a dog on a leash, then bounced back hard against his seat and the door. He was trying to hang on to his rifle when the side of his head hit the window hard enough to star the glass.

The truck's nose dug into the back side of the ditch with a rending crunch and Peter was thrown forward again. The rear of the truck bucked and slewed around until the tailgate angled toward oncoming traffic.

He blinked off the sparkles and tried to move, but was trapped by his seat belt. He fumbled for the button. He could see the white puffballs of the air bags inflated in the front seat. All the while his mind was trying to picture the geometry.

The wrecker had come at them from a side road at high speed.

It would have been hard enough to do on purpose, nearly impossible to do by accident. Especially with what they were carrying.

There would have to be another vehicle. Somebody ahead of them, or behind. Or both.

"Hey," he called to the other men.

His voice sounded odd. He wondered how hard he'd hit his head.

"They're coming. Get ready."

2

FOUR MONTHS EARLIER

The first time Henry Nygaard saw the Marine, he stood balanced on a steep slope beside a washed-out section of the Pacific Crest Trail in the Willamette National Forest, pounding long sections of heavy galvanized pipe deep into the mountain with a twelve-pound sledgehammer.

It was mid-May and the Marine had already been in the mountains for a month, working alone on the south-facing slopes where the snow had melted early. He wore expensive high-tech trail pants, but his heavy leather hiking boots looked like they'd walked ten thousand miles, and he swung that big rusty sledge like he'd done it all his life.

Their first night together as a trail crew, he was quick to smile or make a joke, but there was something going on underneath.

Henry could see it, even if the others couldn't.

Henry didn't know the guy was a Marine until later.

He didn't have the tattoos, didn't wear the T-shirt. But Henry thought he might have guessed it from the way the guy went after that galvanized pipe.

Each ruthless swing an attack.

Pounding them down like it was personal.

Henry understood something about that himself.

The galvanized pipes were the first part of the washout repair. Set deep into the rocky soil, they stabilized the slope and provided support for the second part of the repair, wind-fallen logs laid against the metal stubs. Then rocks and dirt to fill in the fallen trail for the next generation of hikers, and on to the next little landslide.

They were an eight-person crew, all volunteers, camping rough in the backcountry while rebuilding trails for the summer. Their primary tools were double-bladed axes, shovels, sledgehammers, and a two-man pull saw. They worked a two-week cycle, ten days on the mountain, four days in town. Two young high school teachers, four college kids, the Marine, who wasn't much past thirty, and Henry, who was over seventy but could still hold his own.

The Marine, whose name was Peter, looked like he was made mostly of ax handles and shovelheads, bound together with thick rigger's rope at the joints. He didn't seem to notice that the crew's three young women stopped work to elbow each other silently when he took off his shirt to rinse himself in a creek.

The man was also never still. Even sitting, some part of the Marine was always in motion, a leg bobbing or fingers tapping time to something only he could hear. And he didn't sleep in the tents under the sheltering trees with the rest of them, either. Instead he hiked off the trail to one exposed rocky outcrop or another, where he slept in a

17

hammock under the windblown stars, with only a tarp for shelter from the rain.

The man was moving even while he slept, thought Henry. That hammock swaying back and forth in the high mountain breeze.

Henry had spent his life in motion, too. He was a farm boy from southwestern Minnesota, got his growth spurt in middle school, six feet four by the ninth grade. His pop had eyeballed him like he was a new John Deere, talking about expanding the acreage, but Henry just saw a long dull future of driving the same old machines across the same old ground, every goddamned day for the rest of his life.

Which was why he'd signed up for the Army the moment he could convincingly lie to a recruiter about his age. He'd left his pop's truck in the bus station parking lot with the keys under the seat and never looked back.

He was old enough now to see that day as the start of a pattern that would last most of his life. Any threat of boredom was enough to make him cut his tether and move on to something new. After two tours in Vietnam, he cowboyed in Wyoming until the big ranches started using dirt bikes instead of horses. He worked as a utility lineman all over the West, climbing poles and stringing wire, then built pipeline from Canada to Texas, all of it difficult, dangerous work that kept the landscape changing around him. That's how he'd always liked it.

He'd tried to be a good man. He never pretended to be someone he wasn't. He'd been married three times and loved them all boundlessly, until he didn't. With a hundred girlfriends in between, it was a wonder he wasn't dead of syphilis or an angry husband, but somehow he'd survived it all.

His third wife once told him that the West was built by men like him, working men on the move, and it seemed to Henry that she was the first one who'd really understood him. But they were standing on the courthouse steps in Durango at the time, divorce papers folded neatly in her purse, the ink still wet from her signature. So that was that.

If he could start it all over again, he liked to think he'd have done it differently. But he wasn't sure he could have. The older he got, the more clearly he saw himself, for better or worse. Not someone who floated, he was planted where he was planted. But not rooted there, not for good.

He was trying now, though. At this late stage in his life, he was trying to do right by his grown daughter, born from a woman he'd kept company with for just a few months, twenty-five years before. Eleanor was his chance to break the pattern, to dig in and root himself in that relationship, if he could.

When she started this new protection business, Henry saw his chance. Ellie's idiot husband, Randy, was supposed to provide the combat expertise that clients would pay for, but it was Henry who walked sites and drove routes with Randy to find the weak points, Henry who took out a loan on his Denver house to help buy the first round of weapons and armor, Henry who helped find and interview the experienced veterans who would become the first real employees.

It wasn't exactly what he thought he'd be doing in his retirement.

The wartime skills came back almost without conscious thought, as he'd somehow known they would, but he wasn't crazy about the baggage that came with them. The dreams came back, too. But it wasn't about him. It was about his daughter.

Ellie didn't make it any easier, she was a rose with some thorns. No surprise, given at least one of her parents.

He'd hoped she might call him Dad, but she didn't. Henry didn't blame her. He wasn't there when she was small, when she needed him. To be fair, he didn't even know she existed until she was already married.

But it all turned out okay. After fifteen months in operation with the business turning an actual profit, Ellie hired Randy's recently retired sergeant, a twenty-year veteran with a shitload of combat experience, to carry the tactical weight. Leonard was the real deal, Ellie said. She could take it from here. Henry was free to keep his volunteer gig in Oregon.

Henry was ashamed to admit that he jumped at the chance for some new scenery.

Maybe he was too old to change, he thought.

Maybe it was the war that had made him this way, had ruined him for a regular life.

Everyone who'd died, everyone who'd come back ruined in one way or another, they'd given up everything they had for nothing at all. Even those like Henry, who'd made it home with only a little shrapnel, occasional nightmares, and a lifetime of regrets, were changed forever. War never left you, not really.

So there was something about that younger guy, the Marine, that Henry recognized. The restless motion, the way he carried himself. The thoughtful, deliberate ferocity of his work. The way he'd stare, for a long moment, at something in the distance only he could see.

And maybe Peter the Marine saw something in Henry. On the crew's third day, they came to a giant downed spruce lying across the trail. With an easy smile, Peter handed one end of the six-foot pull saw across the trunk to Henry. "Let's see what you've got."

Henry took hold of the wooden handle and set his feet in the dirt. "Don't kill me, okay? I'm old."

Peter the Marine caught Henry's eye. "Like hell," he said.

That big spruce didn't stand a goddamned chance.

3

Peter had adjusted to the claustrophobic white static by moving his life outside. Trying to reset his fight-or-flight reflex, he'd spent more than two years in the mountains, sleeping out in the open, or in a tent, or in the cab of his truck, where the big windshield kept the static at bay.

Part of Peter loved living out in the weather, free to go wherever he chose. The stars for his rooftop.

Another part knew the static was only making it harder for him to get back to something like a normal life. He just hadn't cared enough to really try, or so he told himself.

Until he met June Cassidy.

Smart, profane, hilarious, bossy, delicious.

They'd met in a redwood tree, and the rest of their time together had been just as strange. Some bad guys had been bothering her, and he'd helped her with that. She'd helped him, too. He'd never felt about anyone the way he felt about June Cassidy.

She'd told Peter to get it out of his system, whatever it was that kept him outside. She'd told him to come back when he could sleep inside, in a real bed.

When he put it to himself like that, it sounded like June had just told him to get over it.

He didn't think that was really what she meant.

It wasn't that easy, for one thing.

He wasn't over it. He'd probably never get over it.

But he was working on it.

He was making progress.

Which was, he figured, what June had really wanted.

For Peter to make the effort.

For her.

His cheap phone had died before the other volunteers arrived, fell out of his pocket and the casing cracked wide open. He didn't mind. Cell service was lousy in the mountains. He didn't even bother replacing it. Peter had never really liked the telephone anyway.

Instead, he'd started a letter to June his first night on the trail, had added to it every night after that, and put it in the mail when they got down to Eugene.

You could write a pretty long letter in ten days.

He told her how the mountains looked in the first light of day, and about the deep dark blue of the evening sky, and how the stars appeared, one by one at first, then in clusters, then somehow all at once.

He told her about the people he worked with. The college kids on their Oregon adventure, passing a joint between them when the workday was done, and the schoolteachers on summer break, having a beard-growing contest. But he found himself writing most about Henry, the Vietnam vet, who was becoming a real friend.

You'd never know how old the man was, watching him clean a log of its branches with the double-bladed ax, then use the adze to flatten the round to make a walking surface for a simple footbridge. He'd stop every few minutes to sharpen the tool with the file he carried in his back pocket, then relight his big Honduran cigar.

Henry was old-school in some ways. In other ways he was more modern than most. When he found Peter doing yoga one morning— Peter's shrink had told him that yoga's focus on mindfulness was supposed to help with post-traumatic stress—Henry had asked Peter to show him some poses. He'd confessed that he was a little worried about keeping up with his new girlfriend in Eugene, a tech consultant twenty years his junior, who'd put herself through business school working as an exotic dancer.

In that first letter, Peter asked June to write him back, care of General Delivery at the Eugene post office.

By the end of his next ten-day rotation, he'd written a second letter, but he wasn't sure he wanted to send it.

He mentioned his reluctance to Henry, who had already volunteered himself to drive Peter back to town. Henry just shook his head in disappointment at Peter's general character, then drove directly to the post office.

June had sent him a picture of the little teardrop-shaped valley where she lived, taken from the top of the waterfall, along with a nicely designed lightweight backpacker's hammock and rain fly that Peter never would have bought for himself. On the back of the picture, she'd written: "Tell me more!"

He thought the hammock was a good sign.

He bought a stamp and mailed the second letter.

And over each ten-day rotation, he wrote another one.

Slowly, he began to tell her about his time in the Marines. Officer Candidate School, the challenge of making Recon. His first platoon, most of them as green as he was, hungry to get into the fight, few of them with any idea what they were getting into. The sergeants who'd taught him all the things he hadn't learned in OCS, which was almost everything.

He told her about Afghanistan and Iraq. The sounds and smells, the stifling heat of summer, the bitter cold of the winter nights.

He told her about Big Jimmy and Manny Martinez, about Spook and Tony and Cho, Bad Bob and Jamal and Smitty and the rest. The ones who lived, the ones who died.

He told her about their interpreter, Asif, who wanted to be called Andy, who loved Simon & Garfunkel, who knew all the words to the song "America." He'd sing it if you asked, and also if you didn't. "Let us be lovers and marry our fortunes together . . ."

Asif had been a pediatrician in Baghdad until his clinic was destroyed by a suicide bomber. He'd asked Peter to write him a letter of recommendation so he could get to the States after the war. He had family in Indiana. Instead he got killed in an ambush in the tall corn along the Euphrates.

Peter tried to tell these stories lightly. He didn't want to put his burden on her.

Over time, he told her everything.

Almost everything.

He hoped, maybe, she'd understand him better, knowing.

He was afraid that she might understand him too well.

He was a trained killer. There was no way around it.

His time in the Marines had changed him profoundly, had turned him into himself. He'd been like red-hot steel in those years, with the war as the hammer and the Corps as the anvil. He couldn't unlive those years, nor did he want to.

Most days, he was proud of what he'd done.

Most days.

He and his platoon had done their job, done it well. Gotten some bad guys, looked out for each other. He could have done better, he knew.

He didn't like to think about the dead, but he did it anyway. Not that he had any choice. It was part of his duty, to carry them with him. Part of his mission. These honored dead.

He didn't know if he could explain that to June.

But he was trying.

It was a strange conversation, because of the gaps in time. He'd mail a letter he spent two weeks writing, get her response to a letter he'd written two weeks before, and start a new letter to send two weeks later.

But somehow it was easier, too, because he could write it down without having someone else there, without having to see the response in her face. He wrote this to her, told her that she didn't even have to read the letters, that maybe what was important was for him to write them.

Her response made him laugh out loud. "Don't be such an asshole," she wrote. "Of course I'm reading your fucking letters."

June's language was as bad as the carpenters Peter had spent summers working with. Worse than some Marines.

She didn't try to tell him she understood his experience. She couldn't, not really. She hadn't been there. But she said the letters helped her understand *him* better, knowing more about his war.

She wrote that she rode her bike the length of the teardrop-shaped valley every day, all the way down to the mailbox on the state highway, hoping there was another letter.

She wrote that she liked the slow pace of their correspondence.

She wrote that it was like living in the Old West, their letters wrapped in oilskin and carried in strangers' saddlebags across the high passes. Like an old-fashioned courtship, although she hadn't put it in quite those terms.

The idea had occurred to Peter, too. He'd started tucking a wildflower into his letters, pressed flat from days between the pages of whatever book he had on the trail.

He'd learned that tactic from the Marines. Use the terrain to your advantage.

It wasn't a war, nothing like it. But definitely a kind of campaign.

And his heart was captured, hopelessly, irrevocably.

Had been since the first time he'd seen her.

Her eyes so bright, so full of humor and ferocity.

Those arms strong enough to carry him home.

He didn't know what their correspondence might lead to. But he knew his campaign was making progress when June's letters began to weave him into her life in the valley.

"You could help in the orchard at picking time," she wrote at the end of July. "If you're interested."

In mid-August, she wrote: "The guest cottages could use some repairs, when you're back this way."

Most promising of all was her last letter at the end of August. Several pages were taken up by rough pencil sketches of a modest farmhouse, with a wide porch off the back bedroom. She'd drawn an arrow to it, marked *Sleeping Porch* in her messy scrawl.

"Maybe a fall project," she'd written. "See you late September?"

So that was the plan.

Until their last day, coming down from the mountain. Cell service was better there, and Henry stepped away to check his messages.

When he came back, his face was grave.

His daughter had called.

Her husband had gone missing, along with a senior employee and a shipment of client cash.

"I could really use your help," Henry told Peter. "Maybe a week, two at the most. Just until I get things squared away."

Peter didn't have to think before he answered.

"No problem." He'd send June a postcard. Maybe leave out a few details. He didn't want to worry her. "Sign me up."

Later, he'd wish he'd answered differently.

He'd have plenty of reasons.

But he knew he'd have answered exactly the same way.

4

enry's pickup was nose-down in the ditch, and Peter's head was killing him.

He remembered the red wrecker smashing hard into the passenger side, knocking the big truck off the road.

He reached for the door handle but couldn't get a grip, something wrong with his coordination.

Then his door opened. A man reached inside, hooked his fingers inside the neck of Peter's body armor, and pulled him out and down, headfirst, banging his shoulder against the ground.

Releasing Peter's armor, the man twisted Peter's rifle from his useless grip while his legs were still up in the truck, then took another grip on the armor and hauled him bodily to the embankment.

The man switched the rifle from safe to fire, chambered a round, and pointed it at Peter with his finger on the trigger, all without having to look at the weapon. He wore combat boots and greasy blue mechanic's pants with black body armor over a black long-sleeved

T-shirt. A black ski mask covered his face and neck. With his black combat gloves, not a single square inch of skin was exposed. He had a matte-black sidearm in a black nylon leg holster.

"Hands behind your head, fingers laced together," he said. "Do it now or I'll blow your knee apart."

Peter still wasn't moving right, he could feel it. His head hurt. He wouldn't have a chance to get to the pistol on his own belt.

He didn't like it, but he did as he was told.

All this while a second man with a shotgun, identically dressed, was pulling Deacon out of the driver's seat. Protected by the air bag, Deacon had managed to keep hold of his own rifle and tried to bring it to bear, but the second man just cracked him on the head with the butt of his shotgun, a very businesslike maneuver that put Deacon on the ground without his rifle.

Peter looked for the ambulance but couldn't see it from his position in the ditch. The red wrecker was parked on the near shoulder past Henry's truck, red lights flashing. Hiding the armed men from the view of any oncoming traffic, but looking like they were there to help.

The hijackers had put some thought into this. It wasn't their first rodeo.

Deacon crawled onto the embankment beside Peter, his dark face shining with sweat, blood matting in his hair. He put his trembling hands behind his head. Peter couldn't tell if the shaking was from fear or rage or the adrenaline burning like gasoline in his veins.

The second man covered them both with the shotgun, a black combat model with what looked like a five-round tube and almost certainly one in the chamber.

"One move, I blow your legs off," he said. "Don't even think about reaching for your pistols. Got me?"

The first man put Deacon's rifle on safe, pitched it out of reach under Henry's truck, and did the same with Peter's weapon. Then without ceremony, he put his knee on the rear driver's-side seat, reached in, and dragged Banjo across the wide bench and out of the truck by the neck-hole of his vest, spilling his rifle to the ground.

Banjo's face was bloody and his arm hung wrong and he was barely moving. Not resisting. Hit hard by the wrecker.

The first man lugged Banjo down the ditch to the embankment and dropped him beside Peter. He landed on his hurt arm and let out a yelp like a kicked dog.

The hijacker quickly turned to the driver's seat and climbed in to get to the passenger side. It occurred late to Peter that the passenger-side doors wouldn't open because of the impact with the wrecker. He still wasn't thinking quite right. He heard the first man grunting as he hauled Henry over the center console and out of the truck to the ground.

Henry wasn't moving at all.

He'd taken the brunt of the side impact. His body was limp and his face and head were covered with blood. But his hands were still clamped onto that rifle. Henry was a big man. The hijacker had to pry his hands free, finger by finger. Henry showed no other sign of resistance. Peter looked for the rise and fall of his chest, but he couldn't see that, either.

Don't be dead, Henry. Please don't be dead.

The attackers were fast and efficient. Peter figured maybe ninety seconds had passed, certainly no more than two minutes.

This was no ordinary carjacking. This was a two-man assault on four armed, trained men.

The hijackers had hit them in motion as a force multiplier. The surprise impact had knocked Banjo and Henry out of commission completely, and banged up Peter and Deacon enough to disorient them, make them take longer to react. Which gave the hijackers a distinct advantage.

Like a roadside bomb, only mobile.

Peter was familiar with the tactics.

He just hadn't expected them in the mountains of Colorado.

The second man stood guard with the shotgun while the first man looked at Peter, Deacon, and Banjo in turn, his eyes dark and empty in the holes of the black ski mask.

The sun was gone behind the mountains, but there was still light enough to see.

"I'm taking your pistols now," said the first man. "Hands stay behind your heads, fingers stay laced. If one of you resists, he'll kill all of you. If you cooperate, you'll live until tomorrow. Understand?" He pointed at Peter. "I'm starting with you."

Peter didn't like it, but he didn't see that he had a choice.

Still, it was the first mistake he'd seen. The shotgun wasn't a precision weapon. If Peter made a move and the second man fired his shotgun, he might kill Peter, but he might also hit his partner.

Peter would bide his time. His head still hurt, but he was improving.

And he didn't need the pistol, anyway. He had a good folding knife in his pocket and a hidden blade built into his belt buckle, something he'd bought after losing his backpack to a big bear that spring. He thought of it as a survival tool, not a weapon, but it would do for both.

Still, he felt the nakedness as the first man stripped the weapon from the holster with practiced speed. Peter watched as the man dropped the magazine into his waiting palm, racked the slide to eject a possible chambered round, then tossed everything into the back seat of Henry's pickup.

He did the same to Deacon, then Banjo, then Henry. Then he retrieved their AR-15s from under Henry's truck and emptied them the same way before laying them in the back seat with the pistols.

31

The blip of a siren pulled Peter's eyes to the road. A police car was rolling up the slope behind them. It was an unmarked black Dodge Charger, but red and blue lights flashed in the front grille and on the dash. A cluster of antennae rose from the trunk.

A state trooper, probably, which was good. Better than the county cops, anyway.

He hoped it wasn't a single trooper, because the man wouldn't last thirty seconds against this crew. He probably wouldn't even get a hand on his weapon. But not many cops traveled two to a car anymore. Budget cuts. So unless the trooper hit the gas and drove on like he'd seen nothing at all, the man was dead already.

But driving on wasn't in the typical state trooper mentality, Peter knew. Often operating on their own, many miles from backup, troopers tended to function more like the Lone Ranger. He was probably already on his radio, calling it in. Calling for more cars on this remote stretch of road, calling for an ambulance. Peter and Henry's crew still had a chance.

The trooper slowed his car and pulled onto the far shoulder. Peter glanced at Deacon, who gave him a tiny nod. He was locked on and pissed off, Peter could see now, although he was bleeding nicely from the head where he'd been slammed with the shotgun.

Deacon's last job in the Army had been as a hand-to-hand combat instructor. He'd be formidable.

Banjo's eyes were closed. He wouldn't be much help.

Henry was unconscious or dead.

Peter looked at the man with the shotgun. He was half turned toward the police car, the muzzle rising away from Deacon.

Peter carefully unlaced his fingers and flexed his legs, trying to get the blood moving. He'd have to move fast. He caught Deacon's eyes again, then pointed his eyeballs at the man with the shotgun, then back to Deacon. Deacon gave another tiny nod. He was closer, he'd take the man with the shotgun. That would be the quickest way to get a weapon. Peter would take the first man, who only had a sidearm.

Maybe the trooper wouldn't have to die.

Peter just hoped he and Deacon wouldn't get themselves shot, either.

Then the first man, still in his ski mask, turned and raised a hand to the trooper.

The trooper raised a hand back and rolled in a slow U-turn, coming up to park on the shoulder ahead of the smashed pickup.

Lights still flashing.

Blocking the view of other drivers, just like the ambulance on the far side, sending the same message to anyone driving by.

No need to stop, no need to call the police. Everything's under control. Keep driving, good citizens, and safe journey to you all.

Fuck me, thought Peter. These guys are good.

He caught Deacon's eye and shook his head. Not yet.

Maybe three minutes gone, now.

He no longer thought he might live.

But he wanted to. More than anything.

Once the trooper's Charger was parked, the first man patted Henry's pants pocket for the key to the big orange toolbox in the pickup bed.

Peter watched Henry for some sign of movement. Nothing.

The toolbox was made of heavy steel, the size of a small refrigerator laid on its back, bolted through its bottom into the bed of the pickup. The specialized padlock sat in a protected cavity, shielded from bolt cutters. The box was basically a big safe for power tools, designed to sit unattended on a truck or at a construction site and guard its contents until they were needed.

With the key, though, it was easy to open.

The first man opened the lock, raised the lid, and removed a single cardboard box, seemingly at random, turning it to look at the label.

Peter had carried some of the boxes. The labels had numbers and location codes, but otherwise carried no indication of their contents. Peter had seen the boxes opened at other drops. Bundles of wrinkled bills, usually twenties and fifties, wrapped with a rubber band that also held a slip of paper with an amount written on it.

Dope money.

Legal dope money, because this was Colorado, but still.

It wasn't worth dying for. Money never was.

Your friends, though. That was another story.

Henry was his friend. Deacon and Banjo, he'd only known them a few days. But they were friends, too.

They'd shared meals together. He'd met Deacon's girlfriend. They were connected by the job, this one and the one they'd done before.

The hijacker raised a hand toward the police car. A thumbs-up. Peter saw the shadowed form of the trooper, inside his car, tilting his head to peek at his rearview mirror.

The trooper, if he was a trooper, still hadn't gotten out of the car.

Maybe he was a real trooper. Peter had caught a glimpse of the plate number, not something he'd forget. If he managed to get out of this, he'd have something to start with.

"Listen," he called out to the first hijacker. "How does this end?"

"Shut up," said the man with the shotgun.

Then the ambulance came back.

Peter had lost track of it in the crash, but now he saw it backing down the road. An older Ford Econoline cab with a rectangular box on the back, red lights flashing but no siren. Smaller than most modern ambulances, and showing its age.

The police car pulled forward to let it in. The trooper, fake or not, got out of his cruiser and lit a half dozen road flares and tossed them down.

He wasn't wearing a mask, but he never turned his face toward the captives. Because he was the one who would have to talk to anyone else who stopped.

Although Peter hadn't seen any other cars yet.

Four minutes since the crash now, maybe five.

The ambulance driver and another man got out of the cab and walked around to the back. They wore blue-and-white paramedic uniforms, blue baseball hats with white logo patches, and blue nitrile medical gloves. They opened the back doors, but the interior didn't look like the inside of an ambulance. It looked like an empty white box with narrow benches over the wheel wells and an ancient gurney taking up the space down the middle.

Peter felt the white static flare at the sight of the empty box. The only windows were small portholes in the rear doors.

He didn't want to know what the ambulance was for.

The fake paramedics pulled out the gurney, dropped the wheels, and rolled it down into the ditch. Their faces looked oddly shiny, stretched somehow. As they got closer, Peter realized they were wearing thin masks made of hard, clear plastic, compressing their features.

The masks gave him hope again. If they didn't want him to see their faces, it was still possible this didn't end with a bullet in the head.

Or maybe it was just because they would be working close to the highway and were worried about being seen by oncoming traffic.

Maybe they were just disciplined.

Maybe Peter would never know.

He didn't have a move just yet.

5

Peter could feel the wind blowing cold off the bony peaks of the Rockies. It was late September, but they were over ten thousand feet. When the sun had begun to drop, the temperature had begun to fall.

It would get colder still before this was over.

The fake paramedics got Henry loaded onto the stretcher with a minimum of fuss. They strapped him down tight for the awkward roll up the side of the ditch. The stretcher was old, low-tech, some kind of surplus item, like the ambulance.

Henry had some size on him. Peter had to give them credit, the two fake paramedics hauled Henry out with no trouble at all.

They didn't need any help from the man with the shotgun, or the first hijacker, who held Peter's rifle.

The armed men stood guard, and the trooper watched the road.

When the fake paramedics had the antique stretcher rolled inside the fake ambulance, they came back for Banjo.

His face was creased with pain, but he was alert now. When the ambulance driver pulled a pair of yellow plastic handcuffs out of a cargo pocket, Banjo kicked out to keep the driver at bay. "Y'all not putting those goddamn things on me."

He was thickset and strong, but he was banged up with only one good arm. When the man with the shotgun stepped over and tapped the barrel against his bad shoulder, Banjo's face broke into agony and he gave up. "Man, y'all can just go fuck y'all," he said bitterly as the plasticuffs tightened down.

Peter watched Deacon twitch slightly beside him on the embankment. A visible urge to move, quickly damped down.

Now Peter knew why Deacon had been shaking before. Rage and adrenaline both.

The paramedics in their clear plastic masks plucked Banjo off the ground like so much empty luggage. One man held Banjo's hurt arm, for control, while the other patted him down. They took his wallet, phone, keys, and a bone-handled folding knife that was a gift, Peter knew, from Banjo's father.

As the paramedics walked Banjo out of the ditch toward the ambulance, the man with the shotgun turned his head to track them and Deacon launched himself out of the ditch.

Peter leaped to his feet behind Deacon, but the man with the shotgun was quick and competent. Standing on the road shoulder, he'd had his shotgun at low ready and barely needed to aim, just raised the barrel and fired.

Deacon was only six feet away, and the tight cluster of heavy buckshot tore down through the top of his vest right below the neck, making a fist-sized hole where his heart used to be.

Deacon fell at his killer's feet, his body dead before his mind got the message.

"Stop right there," said the first hijacker, his voice loud from ten feet away, his pistol aimed at Peter's face. The second man had already racked the shotgun and pointed it at Peter.

Peter was breathing hard, amped up. One man in front of him, another man to his right. Neither man was likely to miss at that range, even if Peter could get to one of them before he fired. The embankment and ditch limited his flight, locking him in like a shooting gallery.

He raised his hands back up behind his head.

Fight or flight. Neither one was working.

Without Deacon, the math had changed for the worse.

These people were very good.

The man with the shotgun stared hard at Peter through the holes in his face mask. "Just so you know," he said, "I don't care how you get up in that ambulance. You can go on your own, or we can hurt you, or we put you down for good like your friend over there. It's up to you. But if you don't piss us off, you got a better chance of walking away from this."

It was the kind of thing you said to keep a prisoner calm. Give hope for his salvation.

Peter didn't believe a word of it.

Banjo was hurt. Henry was hurt badly, maybe dead. Now Deacon was dead.

But he just stood there while the fake paramedics hauled Deacon up the side of the ditch by his arms and lifted him into the back of the ambulance.

Held himself still and calm under the unwavering eye of the shotgun, fingers laced behind his head while the paramedic patted him down, took his wallet, keys, and the good folding knife clipped into Peter's front left pocket.

But he missed the small knife hidden in Peter's belt buckle.

"No phone?"

"It broke," Peter said. "Haven't had time to replace it."

Peter allowed the man to wrap the plasticuffs around his wrists and snug them tight.

Then the paramedics flanked him, each man with a strong hand on one of his arms as Peter walked up the side of the ditch toward the ambulance.

At the sight of the windowless van interior, the white static sparked up his brainstem like Frankenstein's nightmare. Amplified by the cuffs, lightning flashed in his head with each step. His heart hammered in his chest, and the muscles in his shoulders tightened like they were being wrapped in steel bands.

His fight-or-flight mechanism was in overdrive. Not appropriate in a crowded grocery store, or at the DMV. But appropriate as hell right now, one or the other.

He pushed it down. Breathe in, he told himself. Breathe out.

He wasn't ready yet.

For fuck's sake, keep breathing.

He put one foot on the rear bumper and climbed into the back of the ambulance, while the crackling static silently built into a storm.

He distracted his mind by focusing on his prison.

The interior of the ambulance was a white box, maybe seven feet wide and ten long, the surfaces durable and designed to be wiped clean. It smelled faintly of bleach. Narrow boxed-in benches lined each side where the wheel wells bumped in, leaving a wide center aisle. D-rings were let into the walls and floor and benches every few feet, Peter assumed part of the original ambulance equipment deemed not valuable enough to salvage. Or maybe valuable enough to keep.

There was little room to maneuver. Henry lay still and pale on the stretcher, taking up most of the center aisle. His face and neck and

T-shirt were wet with his blood, soaked down to the ballistic vest that had done him no good at all.

They'd loaded Deacon onto the bench behind the driver. They'd laid him on his side, leaning against the wall, to fit him on the narrow bench, the hole in his upper chest ragged and red. They'd strapped him in place with utility webbing clipped to the D-rings.

These people were nothing if not organized.

Banjo sat on the passenger-side bench, hands in front, cuffs attached to a D-ring between his knees with an industrial zip-tie. He was hunched and staring at Deacon, muttering something under his breath.

One of the paramedics pointed at the bench beside Banjo. Covered by the clear plastic mask, his face was distorted and strange. "Sit."

The paramedic was only a few feet away. Peter could do whatever he wanted to the man, but the hijacker with the shotgun would never let him out of the box alive.

Peter sat.

He watched Henry's face. Had he seen some movement there? He looked at the big man's chest and saw it move. Yes. Henry was still alive.

The paramedic fastened Peter's cuffs to a D-ring on the bench with another zip-tie, just like Banjo, then snugged everything tight. Peter still had some play from the movement of the D-ring and the space between the cuffs. He sat up straight, with his back flat against the side of the box. This pulled his wrists down, away from his lap.

His hands were about twelve inches from his belt buckle.

As the paramedic backed out of the box, Peter found himself hoping that the hijackers would simply just lock them in, monitor the prisoners through the steel grate separating the box from the driver's compartment.

Then the man with the shotgun shouldered his way in and looked around, and Peter knew they wouldn't get that lucky.

Peter could see him thinking that there wasn't a good place for him to sit. Peter and Banjo on one bench, Deacon's body on the other, Henry on the stretcher in the middle.

There was room in one corner next to Peter, but it was close quarters and a prisoner in handcuffs was still dangerous, if he could get himself untethered.

Peter was careful not to smile.

The paramedics had strapped Deacon down toward the front of the box, so there was no place to sit by his head, even if you were inclined to sit at the head of a dead man you yourself had killed. But there was a small space to park at Deacon's feet, if you weren't too dainty and didn't mind being wedged between a dead man's boots and the wall of a decommissioned ambulance.

The man with the shotgun didn't seem to mind. Without taking his eyes off Peter, he put one knee against Deacon's boots, braced his hip against the back of the box, and pushed. Deacon was strapped in enough to keep him on the bench, but not so tightly that he didn't slide forward ten or twelve inches until the crown of his head hit the front of the ambulance box with a distinct *clop*.

It reminded Peter of the sound of the lid closing on a well-made tool chest.

Or a coffin.

Breathe in, breathe out.

Under his ski mask, the man with the shotgun moved his mouth in what might have been a smile, and sat himself down at Deacon's feet, the shotgun held with its butt at his shoulder and the muzzle down. He had good coverage of the prisoners, although the long gun would be hard to maneuver in the small space.

41

A pistol would have been a better choice, thought Peter.

Another mistake.

He looked out the open rear door. He saw the paramedic lying on his back under the tail end of Henry's pickup, fishing around in the undercarriage. He scooted back out holding a small plastic box, and Peter knew how they'd figured out Henry's route. They'd put a locator on the truck, some kind of satellite GPS tracker.

He remembered that when the first car had disappeared, they'd lost track of it on the GPS. So maybe there was also some kind of signal jammer for Heavy Metal's own GPS tracker.

Had Henry even thought to look for something like that? Peter certainly hadn't.

Then he heard the rattle of a big diesel and saw the red wrecker backing toward the smashed front of Henry's pickup. The first hijacker got out and began extending the tow bar.

Now Peter saw the plan in its entirety.

An ambush with exact knowledge of the target's location. An unmarked police car and a man in a state trooper's uniform to control the scene. A decommissioned ambulance to haul away the dead and injured prisoners. And a wrecker to remove the evidence. Maybe ten minutes gone so far. By the time they were done, fifteen minutes start to finish.

Everything would disappear.

Which meant that Henry's crew would have to disappear, too.

The paramedic tucked the locator into his pocket and walked to the rear of the ambulance. "You good?"

The man with the shotgun nodded. "Roger that."

The paramedic closed and latched the door, and Peter was locked inside that small white box with the static raging like a thunderstorm in his head.

6

eter heard the police siren blip. Through the grate blocking the driver's compartment, he saw the flashing blue and red lights of the unmarked car pulling slowly forward. The ambulance lurched into motion behind it, laboring up the verge and back onto the highway. Henry on his stretcher bumped forward to the front of the box. The man with the shotgun had his feet braced and didn't move.

Using the shoulder, the police car made a U-turn to head back up the mountain. The ambulance followed, its tired springs rocking. Henry's stretcher now rolled to the back of the box, hitting the doors with a thump. The man with the shotgun might have frowned behind his mask.

They hadn't locked the wheels, Peter thought. Or maybe the wheels just didn't lock on that antique stretcher. Maybe that's what the D-rings were for, to strap it in place. Maybe they'd run out of straps, what with blowing a hole in Deacon and having to secure him.

He began to take deep breaths, thinking of the things the hijackers had done wrong. Breathe in. Breathe out. His head still hurt, but it helped him focus.

"Listen, just tell me the truth," he said. The taste of copper filled his mouth. "We're going to die, aren't we?"

"Y'all shut the fuck up." Banjo's eyes were closed. "All right? Just shut the fuck up."

The man with the shotgun was staring at Peter. "Do as you're told and nobody else has to die. We didn't set out to kill anyone. The guy on the stretcher, he hit his head wrong, that's all. Your friend here?" He patted Deacon's boots. "Tried to get fancy and it cost him. So don't get fancy and you'll be fine."

"Oh, man," Peter said, beginning to hyperventilate now. Oxygenating his blood. Letting the static rise up in him, building its charge. "I don't want to die, I really don't."

He glanced down at Henry, strapped onto the gurney, and saw the big man's eyes open. Saw them slide sideways to look at Peter, then at the man with the shotgun.

Peter slumped down in his seat, the picture of despair as his belt buckle slid within reach of his hands. "I don't want to die, not like this." He pounded his feet on the floor like a child having a tantrum, rocking wildly in his seat, using the frantic motion to distract from his hands straining upward against the restraints to catch and release the two-inch blade from the sheath built into the buckle.

"Hey," said the man with the shotgun, leaning forward on the seat, looking Peter in the eye. "Listen, settle yourself. Nobody's gonna die, okay? Not if you behave yourself."

The paramedic in the passenger seat half turned to speak through the steel grate. "Fucking relax, okay? Be a man. Jesus, what a pussy."

The plasticuffs were designed to be tough and resistant to damage, but the little belt knife was honed like a razor. It sliced through Peter's right cuff at his wrist with a single determined swipe.

The man with the shotgun looked down at Peter's hands. His eyes got wide. The shotgun barrel began to pivot.

A single sharp jerk freed the cuffs from the zip-tie holding them to the D-ring, and Peter leaped across Henry, pushing aside the barrel of the shotgun with his long right arm.

Boom! The shotgun went off, loud as hell in that enclosed space, but Peter didn't turn to see the damage. He slammed the knife into the man's unarmored side, the blade skating sideways off the ribs until Peter turned his wrist to punch the steel between them fast and hard, again and again.

The other man fought back like he didn't know he was perforated, and maybe he didn't. The blade was short and the man was thick with muscle. Peter was hoping to puncture a lung or damage something else vital, but from that close position with a short blade against an armored vest there was no guarantee.

The stretcher rocked forward as the ambulance driver hit the brakes. Peter's weight shifted slightly, and the shotgunner bucked in place trying to throw Peter off.

But his left hand was caught up with the long gun, his right arm constrained by the corner he'd tucked himself into, and Peter's strong legs held him there, one boot wedged into the frame of Henry's stretcher and the other gripping the floor. The white static was now an advantage, supercharging Peter's muscles like a Detroit hot rod.

He lifted himself up and raised his own left arm, shrugging off the man's short chopping punches, then slashed the blade sidearm across the man's neck, feeling the blade tugging through flesh. A hot jet flooded Peter's face, blood in his eye that Peter wiped away with the back of his hand as the man's heart pumped him dry. Peter's knife had found the carotid artery.

The shotgun clattered to the floor. The passenger-side paramedic was shouting through the security grate as he twisted around in his seat. He had a pistol in his hand.

Peter pushed himself off the dead man and turned to look at Banjo, but the buckshot had found him first. The tightly grouped pellets, each the size of a .38 slug, had slammed into the area where his neck met his collarbone. Banjo sat pale and upright, eyes wide in shock and disbelief, his mouth opening and closing soundlessly as his blood saturated his black shirt.

The passenger-side paramedic raised his pistol to shoot through the grate. The driver hit the brakes again, throwing the panicked passenger forward as he pulled the trigger as fast as he could, like a child playing a video game. The same lurch pushed Peter forward and down atop Henry's gurney, and the pistol rounds went through the back door or the ceiling, everywhere but into Peter, although he felt one whisper past his ear.

Peter put one red hand on Henry's leg and reached down for the shotgun with the other. He got a knee on the floor and racked the slide with that beautiful sound and fired through the grate at the passenger.

It would have been difficult to miss with that weapon from that distance.

The steel mesh flowered outward and the passenger crumpled against the dash. The right side of the windshield turned to red spiderweb. The ambulance was slowing fast on the twisting mountain road, Henry's gurney bumping back and forth as the driver pumped the brakes, shouting, "Don't shoot, don't shoot."

"Stop right now," Peter called as he racked the slide again, four shells gone and two remaining. He needed another weapon. Through the fractured windshield, he could see taillights on the long uphill curve ahead of them, their unmarked police escort maybe not yet noticing the noise from the ambulance, or maybe having decided it was better not to notice. Whichever it was, there were no brake lights, not yet.

The ambulance continued to slow.

He could see the face of the mountain through the windshield.

Now was as good a time as any.

Peter raised the shotgun to the grate and blew the driver's heart out through the front of his chest.

He'd thought the ambulance would continue to slow, miss the long curve, and end up in the ditch, coming to a relatively soft stop against the mountainside. Instead some rogue neuron fired in the driver's head and his leg stabbed out, slipping off the brake and onto the gas.

The ambulance surged up the road with a diesel rattle. The gurney slammed back against the double doors at the rear of the ambulance.

Peter dropped himself full-length onto the gurney and grabbed the rails in a push-up position, holding himself above Henry. He didn't know what would happen to the ambulance without a living driver at the wheel.

Peter looked down at himself, the blood on his hand, his face, his clothes. The grim fucking reaper. A faint black border fluttered at the edges of his vision. Adrenaline overload. When he came down, he was going to crash hard.

Then Henry blinked up at him.

"Hey, kid." The big man's hoarse whisper somehow carried over the engine noise. "Why don't you get us the fuck out of here?"

Peter licked his lips. "Yeah," said Peter. "Sure."

He took a deep breath and looked over his shoulder at the ambulance doors. They were punctured by the paramedic's wild shots, the lock hardware shattered on one side. He shifted backward in his push-up position and cocked his left leg, strong from years of powering up mountains with a heavy pack. The ambulance kept rocketing forward.

"Hold on, this isn't going to be fun," he said, and kicked the doors open.

The gurney fell backward through the doorway and out onto the road with a double thump, Henry strapped in and Peter riding shotgun. Peter felt the clack of his teeth and a stab of pain behind his eyes, his head still not recovered from smacking against the window. Henry huffed out a kind of grunt as breath was forced from his lungs.

The gurney had some forward momentum, but less than the ambulance, which was still accelerating, the last act of the dead driver. Peter watched as the ambulance did exactly as he'd expected it to do, but faster. It missed the curve and shot forward into the ditch, then bounced up the sharp embankment and into the mountain with a crunch.

The headlights went out, probably broken by the impact. The gurney spent the last of its forward momentum on the uphill highway, its front wheels swiveling sideways as the ambulance's big diesel sputtered and coughed, then died.

"There goes our ride," said Peter.

He climbed off the gurney, leaving the shotgun lying beside Henry. It had gotten much darker. The wind was cool and strong and blowing clear through him. It smelled like pine resin and rock dust. To the west, the sky had turned a blue so deep it was almost purple, and to the east, it was nearly black. The shadowed peaks rose up around them like ramparts, granite tips still shining in the last rays of the sun. Peter felt his chest expand to the horizon as the static began to fade.

Breathe in. Breathe out.

Then he looked up the road and saw the brake lights of the trooper, now stopped a half mile ahead on the switchback. No reverse lights. No dome light, either, so the trooper was probably still in his car, trying to decide what to do.

He needed a weapon. The paramedic had a pistol, and maybe more ammunition. He began to jog up the road toward the wreck.

Henry called out to him. "Hey. Peter. Hey!" His hoarse voice was loud in the sudden quiet.

Peter stopped and looked over his shoulder. The gurney had turned on its swiveling front wheels, and Henry was beginning to roll downhill. Headfirst, still strapped in.

Peter hadn't put on the brakes, if that antique even had brakes. It was so old the legs hadn't automatically extended when it dropped off the ambulance. A metal trolley a foot off the ground, it resembled nothing more than some adrenaline freak's new way to hospitalize himself, the rider strapped down with no way to steer.

"Shit, hang on." He ran after Henry.

Peter bent and grabbed the rear of the frame, planted his boots, and almost got yanked off his feet. The gurney wasn't going fast, but the road was steep and Henry was a big guy. It wasn't easy to counter all that momentum.

"No," said Henry. "Keep going. Let's get out of here."

Peter looked over his shoulder. The trooper still hadn't moved. Maybe he was on the radio, trying to raise the paramedics. Maybe he was calling for backup.

Peter still wanted another weapon. But how long would it take him to get it? He'd still have to take on the trooper, who would probably have a shotgun in the cruiser, or an automatic rifle, or both.

Maybe Henry was right. Soon it would be full dark. Getting some distance was a good idea.

He didn't want to have to kill anyone else.

He tugged sideways on the gurney, confirming that the downhill wheels were on swivels and the uphill wheels were fixed. Like a shopping cart, he thought. It was possible.

He glanced back at the police car.

Now the reverse lights were on, and the red and blue flashers were lit up.

Henry said, "I thought you were a goddamned Marine."

Peter didn't want to think about the carnage in the ambulance, the man he'd killed with a knife, although he knew it would come back to him later whether he liked it or not. He made a decision.

"Your call, old man." Peter hopped onto the back of the gurney, pushing off hard. "Just don't blame me when your 'chute doesn't open."

He looked down at his friend, injured and bloody, rolling headfirst down a twisting mountain road, picking up speed.

Henry was smiling. His hoarse voice got a little louder.

"Just wondering, exactly how you planning to steer this fucking sled?"

Peter felt the cold mountain wind in his hair, the gathering dark, the steady accumulation of speed.

He was smiling, too.

"What," he said aloud. "You want to live forever?"

7

The road tilted with the curves, and the relentless slope pulled them downhill, faster and faster.

Steering the gurney wasn't easy.

Steering and trying to slow their acceleration at the same time was even more difficult.

Peter had let the antique gurney pick up speed to get some distance from the police cruiser. Now that they were rolling quite a bit faster than Peter could run, he wasn't sure how to stop.

He rode with his left knee set between Henry's feet and the sole of his right boot pressed to the asphalt, acting as a brake and a kind of rudder. His stomach muscles were tight and the bottom of his foot was getting hot from the friction. Henry was still strapped in head-first, eyes rolled back trying to see what was coming.

The county road ran downhill most of the way to the state highway. Most of the way to Denver, actually. Peter remembered the signs he'd seen on the way up. STEEP GRADE.

He figured the sole of his boot was wearing away. At least they were new boots, good boots he'd bought for the job.

The night was dark. The stars were coming out.

"So what's the plan, kid?" Henry's hoarse voice rose above the sound of the wheels, rattling and thumping on the bumpy road. "Not complaining. Just wondering."

They'd been rolling for a few minutes, no longer. Not long enough.

"Putting some highway between us and that state trooper," Peter said. "Maybe gain a few minutes if he decides to come after us."

"There's a state trooper?" asked Henry.

Peter remembered that Henry had been knocked out in the crash. "Helping the hijackers," he said. He glanced over his shoulder. They'd gone around the flank of the mountain and he could no longer see the trooper's lights. "Maybe he's a trooper, maybe not. He had a pretty convincing car."

The heat on the bottom of his right foot was too much. He pulled it back in and changed to his left. By the time he'd gotten set again, they'd picked up more speed, and the gurney had veered toward the outside of the curve.

The blacktop was patched and lumpy and pocked with divots from rockfalls. It was a remote county highway, deep in the national forest. There were no guardrails. The road flew beneath their wheels. Peter couldn't see the bottom of the drop-off.

It wasn't easy to get the rocketing gurney back to the yellow line.

Trying not to show the strain, Peter said, "The farther we get, the more territory he has to search to find us. If I can find a place to get off the road, maybe I can park you somewhere hidden and go for help."

"I might be beyond that," said the big man. "Maybe the best thing would be for you to just find a nice high drop, light me a cigar, and give me a push."

"Fuck you, Henry," Peter said kindly. Now his left foot was getting hot. "I thought you were a tough guy."

Henry looked up at the night sky. "Something happened in the accident," he said. "I can't feel my legs. Or much of anything below my armpits."

The truck had gotten hit hard. "Shit, Henry. I'm sorry."

"Not your fault," said Henry. "You weren't the asshole driving that tow truck. Besides, there's worse ways to die. I always wanted to ride a longboard down a mountain."

"What, you're quitting? I thought you didn't believe in that."

"I don't think of it as quitting." A smile flickered across Henry's face. "More like starting something new."

"Fuck that." Peter's feet were heating up faster as the soles of his boots ground thinner against the asphalt. He switched to his right foot again. They picked up still more speed. The gurney clattered hard over the rough road. The rocky flank of the mountain beside them was a shadowy blur. The front wheels had begun to rattle unpleasantly.

"How much farther you figure," said Henry. "We're really moving."

"Just a few more minutes," Peter said. It was what his mother had always said on long drives when Peter was a kid, when he wanted to know if they were there yet. He wondered if it would work on Henry.

It didn't.

"Ah," said the big man. "You can't stop this fucking thing, can you?"

"Sure," said Peter. "I can stop whenever I want."

"Famous last words," said Henry. His eyes were on the stars overhead. "I'm telling you, just pick the right place and let go. Send me off to meet my maker in style."

Peter smiled. "No fucking way, Henry."

The steering on the lumpy blacktop became harder the faster they went. Small adjustments, that was the trick. Oversteer too much and the gurney would slide sideways and roll. That would end a lot of their problems. Probably cause a few more.

Peter could always let go, of course. He'd curl himself up into a ball, protecting his head with his arms, and try not to come to an abrupt stop against the mountain, or roll right off the edge of it.

Henry would end up airborne, wishing for wings.

So no, that wasn't going to happen.

"You see any of those slow-vehicle pull-offs coming up?" Henry asked. "I remember we passed a few on the way up. Should be one in the next few miles."

"I'll keep my eyes peeled," said Peter. A few miles was a long way when your feet were on fire. "Hey, what's left on your bucket list? I know you've got one."

"Find the sonofabitch behind this stickup," Henry said. "Kick his balls so hard they come out his ears."

Peter smiled. "Roger that."

He tried not to think about June. If Peter had a bucket list, June was on it. Hell, she was the whole list. At least she was safe at home. When they'd met, she was being chased by men with guns.

"I knew Deacon for almost six years," Henry said. "Banjo for two at least. Those boys were friends of mine."

"Me too." Peter had only known Henry four months, but felt like he'd known the man his whole life.

Some friends were like that.

His foot was getting hot again. He could flex his new boots more easily now, almost as if wearing his old running shoes. He wondered how much sole was left. Eventually he was going to run out of boots.

He changed feet again, and as the gurney went faster, it began to vibrate.

It wasn't just the front wheels rattling now. Peter could feel it in his hands, a hum on the side rails that built to a buzz traveling through the whole aluminum frame, getting more violent by the minute. Peter figured the wheel bearings were starting to go on this antique. Eventually they would seize. And the gurney would roll.

On the other hand, if they hit a major pothole, they'd go ass over teakettle, a full-on cartwheel, and end up looking like jellyfish. If they didn't just fly right over the edge.

It was a kind of race, Peter figured. Between the bad bearings, the inevitable pothole, Peter's thinning boots, and finding a place to pull off the road.

Sometimes Peter wished he was religious.

The old asphalt was bleached pale by the Colorado sun pounding down through air thinned by altitude. Although the night had fallen almost completely, the road remained lighter than the darkening world around it. A gray ribbon laid out before them, twisting and turning its way down the mountain.

Peter changed feet again and the gurney picked up still more speed. The buzz got louder still. He had to look down to get his knee set again between Henry's feet. When he got his eyes forward, he saw the road appear to come to an abrupt end. Which couldn't be, because they'd come this way in the ambulance, hadn't they?

Then he realized the road took a hard left, vanishing around the flank of the mountain. He leaned and put more pressure on the rudder of his trailing foot and the shuddering gurney reluctantly followed the road around the bend. To their right was a deep valley that seemed bottomless in the darkening evening. Ahead of them the road was visible again, the gray ribbon curling along the contour of the land.

A pair of pale headlights floated up the ribbon below. An odd, elongated vehicle.

Rotating yellow lights on the roof of the vehicle, brightening up the night.

The red wrecker, towing Henry's truck.

The last hijacker. Coming directly toward them.

Peter said, "You still have that shotgun?" He'd tucked the weapon under the gurney's straps in the first moments of their reckless ride downhill from the ambulance.

The wrecker was getting closer by the second. Over the buzzing vibration of the gurney, Peter could hear the sound of its powerful diesel engine echoing off the granite.

Henry's eyes rolled up in his head as he tried to peer down the road. "Tell me that ain't what I think it is."

"Oh, it is." Peter didn't know how he would do this. He shifted his weight and felt his toe brush the asphalt. He jerked his foot back, knowing the thin leather would wear away quickly, but not before hearing the scrape of metal.

Steel toes. He'd forgotten. His boots had steel toes.

He had another wear surface. Maybe they would last longer than the soles. Or maybe they wouldn't have as much friction as the good Vibram rubber. Only one way to find out.

He perched on both knees between Henry's big feet. Then dropped his own feet down until his toes made contact with the blacktop, and slowly increased the pressure.

Once the leather wore off, the metal made an ugly grinding sound. His balance was precarious, so he kept one hand on the side rail. By varying the pressure from foot to foot, he could even steer a little, although not as well as he had before. But now one hand was free.

The red wrecker came closer still. Peter could see the shape of it now in ghostly flashes under the rotating yellow hazard lights. The heavy steel grille at the front. The big black pickup truck reared up on the tow bar behind.

Henry had worked his good arm free of the gurney's straps and was extracting the shotgun, his face a dim mask of pain.

"Hold on, Henry, I can get it." Part of Peter was afraid the man would drop it, injured as he was.

Henry's breathing was labored. "I ain't dead yet," he said. "Might as well be useful."

"Little late for that, old man." Peter slid the gun the rest of the way free. "Why start now?"

"Was you always such a wiseass?"

The pale ribbon of the road was getting darker now, and harder to see. The big red tow truck was a few bends away, pulling its heavy load uphill. Not exactly flying, but going plenty fast.

Peter let go of the rail and managed to ride hands-free for a long moment, just long enough to rack the slide of the shotgun. The empty shell flew away into the night, and the last remaining shell popped up into the chamber. He fell forward again and grabbed the rail with his right hand and laid the shotgun down with his left.

"Tell me you got a plan," Henry said.

"Send in the Marines," Peter said. "Isn't that always the plan?"

He wanted the gurney closer to the mountain. He wanted to be in the opposite lane. Unexpected, and harder to see. It wouldn't be an instinctive reaction for the driver, to pull into the oncoming lane. Any advantage might be decisive.

The steel of his boots ground away against the asphalt as he maneuvered. The gurney bucked and shimmied, the movement more violent now. He wasn't getting any slower. If anything, he was speeding up.

Peter told himself that would help when the time came.

He laughed softly.

Yeah. Go ahead and tell yourself that.

Glancing down, he saw a trail of sparks from each steel toe where it met the road. The gurney was really shaking. He didn't have much steering left. It wouldn't be long, either way.

He'd lived an interesting life, hadn't he?

June. He wanted to see June. He wanted to kiss her freckles one last time. He wanted to tell her he loved her. Had he ever told her that? God, he hoped he had.

The wrecker was broadside-on now, coming around the last bend. Its headlights lit up the mountainside and the pale ribbon of the road. As it made the turn, he saw a flash of brightness against the rock, an open space there. Maybe a stream coming down the rocks, which would be no help at all. But maybe a few parking spaces for a trailhead, or a slow-vehicle pullout.

Then the wrecker completed its arc and the road ran straight between them.

Headlights bright in Peter's eyes, the gurney vibrating like a failing chain saw, Henry's strong hands gripping the straps.

Peter let go of the rail and straightened up, riding no-handed, barely balanced.

Alive, alive. I am fucking alive.

The gap closed, the road smooth for just a moment. Peter could just see over the top of the wrecker's heavy grille, a broad rectangle of steel slats, edge-on to the world with a wide rubber push bar at the bottom.

Closer now, and the outline of the hijacker's head and neck were just visible over the open half-round of the steering wheel.

Closer still, Peter could see that the man had removed his mask. The pale skin of his face glowed faintly green in the light from the dash.

Peter raised the shotgun and seated it against his shoulder. The weight of it was reassuring, although he did wish it was a little heavier. He was down to a single shell.

Time, ticking.

He fit his finger inside the trigger guard. His stomach muscles flexed, keeping his balance. The gun barrel wove a circular pattern with the erratic movement of the gurney.

He waited for some kind of equilibrium. The shot pattern would get wider over distance, but that wasn't a bad thing. Peter wasn't in a stable firing position, and his target wasn't large. If he hit the man with only one round of buckshot, that was a plus. If Peter could hit with three or four, he could cross the man off his list of troubles.

The hijacker's eyes widened now in some kind of recognition of the apparition on the highway. An EMT's version of the Flying Dutchman.

Peter took up the pressure on the trigger.

The hijacker turned the wheel, veering into Peter's lane.

The sights aligned. The barrel steadied.

Peter pressed the trigger.

The red wrecker's windshield turned to splintered shards in a ragged circle on the driver's side as the kick of the shotgun pushed Peter backward on his tenuous perch.

The gurney lurched. He felt his balance slip.

He put more pressure against the asphalt with his toes, but the gurney was going too fast. The bare steel toes were frictionless, a ballet dancer on bad ice.

He couldn't catch himself.

He fell backward, flailing.

Until Henry's big hand came up, wrapped tight around the barrel of the shotgun, and reeled him in.

"I got you." That raspy voice now barely audible over the sound of the big diesel bearing down on them.

Peter fell forward onto Henry's legs, dropped the shotgun, grabbed the rails with both hands, and set his boot soles down hard on the asphalt.

When the friction hit, it nearly hauled him off his feet, but he managed to drop his ass and keep both boots down and turn the gurney just enough to find the fine-graveled shoulder of the road as the wrecker roared past.

"Hang on," he called out, and looked ahead to see what might be coming.

"Don't roll this sled, I forgot my helmet." Henry's grin was ear to ear.

The shoulder flattened out and Peter's boots slid across the small stones like so many spilled marbles. The road wound downhill to the left, but ahead of them was a narrow flat area, a lumpy gravel pullout. Henry gave a hard grunt as the gurney bucked like something alive, the rutted rocks bouncing them around, eating up their momentum, slowing them finally to a halt.

Peter took a deep breath, then patted Henry on the shin, looking back over his own shoulder the way they'd come. "Sit tight," he said. "I'll be right back."

The red wrecker was slowing in the middle of the highway, red roof lights flashing. But no brake lights. Maybe he'd hit the hijacker. Maybe the hijacker was reloading, figuring how to come at him.

Peter wanted that wrecker. It was their way off this mountain. Maybe their weapons were still in the back of Henry's truck. Their phones.

He looked past the wrecker, but there was no sign of the trooper.

He might still be with the ambulance.

Or just around the curve of the mountain, heading their way.

Peter unkinked his legs and picked up the shotgun and ran, pumping his arms, half-shredded boots strange underfoot. He was out of shells but it would work as a club.

This is what we've come to, he thought.

Angry monkeys killing each other with sticks.

Over scraps of green paper.

The wrecker eased to a stop ahead of him. Still no brake lights, just the engine grumbling slow. He saw the rear window broken and splashed with something dark behind its steel-mesh grate. He ducked his head to peek into the side mirror. No movement in the cab, just a low slumped form aglow in the dashboard light.

He jerked open the driver's door with one hand, the other ready to jab with the shotgun.

The hijacker didn't move. One eye was a red ruin. His cheek was smashed bloody. The hollow of his throat held a soft wet hole.

Peter looked up the road. Still no trooper.

There was plenty of time for the trooper to have reached the wrecker, if he'd wanted to.

If he had stopped to check the ambulance, thought Peter, the carnage inside might have helped him make up his mind. Might have overcome his desire for the money.

Peter doubted it.

With one eye watching for the trooper, Peter reached in and threw the transmission into park.

Hauled the driver down to the highway and into the ditch.

Wiped the blood and broken glass from the seat with the hijacker's mask.

Then he ran that wrecker and its tow load in reverse, three-quarters of a mile down the crooked highway to the gravel pull-off.

Once you learn to back a trailer, you never forget.

8

enry." Peter looked down at his friend, alarmed.

He was different from the big man Peter had worked with in the forest, the man who had swung the double-bladed ax with such skill, who had turned long logs into bridges with a block and tackle.

Something had changed. Henry's grin was gone, and his face was oddly pale.

Maybe it was just the starlight. But he looked a lot worse than he had before the heavy jolts of the truck ramp. Peter thought of Henry's spine.

Peter knelt beside his friend. "We'll stay here awhile. I'll call an ambulance." He held up Henry's phone, already found in the back of the pickup. He'd known the passcode since Memorial Day.

"Faster if you drive." Henry's hoarse voice was smoothed down to a soft rasp. He put his hand on Peter's bicep. "Just haul me up on the back. Tie me down like any other load. Swedish Hospital is closest. And call my daughter. She needs to know."

The big man's eyes never left Peter's face as he wrestled man and gurney up to the bed of the truck. The only way they would fit was with the tailgate down and Henry half-hanging off the back. Peter tucked a spare jacket around his friend for warmth, and checked the straps one last time.

"You good, Henry? We're ready to go."

Henry looked Peter in the eye. "Sorry about this." The rasp of his voice down to a thin trickle of sand. "You were just being a friend. A good friend."

"You'd have done the same for me." Peter put his hand on Henry's chest. "Just hang on, okay?"

But Henry had already turned his gaze to the cold glittering stars overhead.

Climbing into the wrecker, Peter caught sight of himself in the rearview. A diagonal smear of dried blood like war paint across his face.

He put it in drive, pointed downhill, and stepped on the gas.

By the time he pulled up at the Swedish Medical Center ER in Englewood, Henry was dead.

9

Peter had only met Elle Hansen once, three days before, when he went to the office to fill out the paperwork.

It was clearly a shoestring operation, the tiny second-floor office above a taco shop, barely big enough for three desks, faded paint, and stained carpet. Henry had told Peter that his daughter had three little kids and that the company had only been in business for eighteen months.

As Elle explained how things worked, it was evident that every decision was made with careful deliberation. The space was small and cheap because most of the employees never came into the office. The guys got their assignments on a secure website and used their personal vehicles instead of company cars, the best way to keep the protection profile inconspicuous, the overhead low, and her people happy and well paid.

Sitting at her computer, printing an application and permission for a background check, Elle had told Peter that she'd started Heavy

Metal Protection with her husband, who was now nowhere to be found.

"It's hard," she'd said. She sat straight in her chair, her fingers fast on the keyboard, but her eyes were sunken with fatigue. "Randy is gone, along with Leonard Wallis, our head of operations. We need them, and we need that missing money. We don't have deep pockets. The insurance company is being difficult about reimbursement."

She took a deep breath and let it out, then gave Peter a brittle smile. "The police are investigating. My lawyer is talking to the insurance company. I've already done everything I can do. So I might as well get on to my next task. I have clients to protect and a business to run. Thirty men and their families are depending on me."

Peter had never met her husband. Randy and Elle might have started the business together, but Peter figured Elle was the engine of the company, even though she still looked young enough to be cramming for finals at some college library.

Actually, she looked a lot like Henry, the same square head and strong chin, although not in a bad way. Barefoot in casual khakis and a feminine button-down shirt, she was built like her dad, too, tall and big-boned, oversized in the small room, but healthy, like a college athlete. When she'd turned to hand Peter the papers, she'd knocked a picture of her kids off her desk. She didn't blush or apologize or comment in any way. She just shook her head and scooped up the plastic frame and set it someplace else.

Peter didn't think she was clumsy. Just someone who'd outgrown her own skin, not to mention this tiny office.

That was three days ago, when her husband might just have been missing.

Now, standing in the tilted bed of Henry's truck, watching her follow the gurney into the hospital—with the knowledge that her husband was not just missing but almost certainly dead—Peter thought she looked like someone who was holding on to herself for dear life.

Peter didn't go with her. He couldn't even speak to her, not right then.

Her father was dead.

What could Peter possibly say or do to make it better?

He was climbing down from the bed of Henry's truck when his hands started to shake.

It was a chemical reaction, he'd been through it before. After the punishing rush of the day's events and the harrowing drive back down the mountain in the wrecker, the adrenaline was only now starting to bleed from his system. He was crashing.

He felt empty, drained of all color and life. He knew the feeling would fade, but sometimes it was hard to convince himself.

He wanted to wash his face, to find a shower and some clean clothes, but that was a bad idea. His clothing was part of a crime scene. And somehow, Peter didn't feel like he deserved to get clean.

Henry was still dead. With Deacon and Banjo.

He laid himself down on the bench outside the ER doors, closed his eyes, and waited for the police.

In the darkness, he saw again, as he knew he would, the man with the shotgun close up against him. He smelled the stink of the man's sweat and fear. The long muscles of his arm twitched involuntarily as he felt the sweep and catch of his knife in the other man's skin. The blood hot and viscous on his face, the slick feel of wiping it from his eye with a bloody hand.

It was him or me, Peter told himself.

As he had told himself before, more times than he cared to remember. Him or me.

He'd tried to save his friends, but he couldn't.

He'd only managed to save himself.

He'd saved June last spring, though. He'd definitely done that.

Maybe she'd save him, too. He didn't know just yet, but he was hoping.

He needed to call her. He was going to be late getting up to see her.

He had something to do first.

A few things, actually.

He heard the cars roll into the ambulance area, big engines thrumming, tires crunching on the pavement. Two heavy doors slammed shut, then footsteps and the creak and clink of equipment on heavy belts.

He opened his eyes and pushed himself to a sitting position. Two Denver cops approached in summer uniforms, one young and brown with the lean, lazy muscle of a trail runner, the other sun-pink and beefy, late thirties, sergeant's stripes on his sleeve. They had the same cool, watchful eyes that took in everything around them, and stopped at the same careful distance.

Peter had asked the hospital security man to call the police.

The older cop peered at Peter's face. "Sir, are you all right?" He spoke to the younger cop without looking away from Peter. "Go get someone to look at this guy."

"I'm fine," Peter said. "It's not my blood."

The older cop raised his eyebrows. "Sir, are you carrying a weapon?"

"No," Peter said. "They're in the back seat of the pickup."

The younger cop surveyed Peter from top to bottom, until his eyes stuck on Peter's boots. The steel toes ground down showing ragged holes, the soles worn thin from the friction on the asphalt.

"Look at his boots," he said.

The older cop never looked away from Peter's face. "Check the trucks," he said.

While the younger cop walked over to Henry's pickup, still on the red wrecker's tow bar, the older cop took out his notepad and flipped to a new page without looking. "You want to tell me about it?"

The younger cop opened the rear driver's-side door with a single gloved finger, and peered inside. "Sarge?"

Something in his voice made the older cop glance over. "What?"

Peter had left the weapons jumbled in the back seat, rifles and handguns. He hadn't been neat about it. It was a serious pile of hardware.

The younger cop moved quickly to the cab of the tow truck. He saw the windshield blown in and the back of the cab painted with the driver's blood and brains. "Jesus."

The older cop turned back to Peter without expression. "Why don't you tell me what happened."

Peter pointed his thumb at the pickup. "That big steel box in the back? It's full of money. I work for Heavy Metal Protection." He gave them his name and his Social Security number so they could look him up in their system.

"Wait," said the younger cop. "This is dope money?"

"Yes," said Peter. "Strictly legal. We were moving it for a client, there were four of us, and we were attacked. In or near the Arapaho National Forest. Five men, three vehicles. Very well planned. I got lucky. The hijackers killed everyone on the crew but me."

"What about the hijackers?" the younger cop asked.

"They're dead, too," Peter said. "All but one of them."

The older cop had his head down toward his pad, but his eyes were up, glued to Peter's face. He'd seen something there. "Did you happen to shoot anybody yourself?"

Peter sighed. "Are the detectives coming?"

The older cop nodded calmly. "Already on the way."

Peter said, "I'll tell it to them."

The younger cop didn't like that much, Peter could tell.

The older cop told him, "Grab some GSR bags from the car." To Peter, he said, "Just regular paper bags, like for packing your lunch. We'll put those over your hands to preserve any gunshot residue for the evidence techs."

He glanced at Peter's face. "You over in the sandbox?"

"A few years back," Peter said. "How'd you know?"

"You have the look." The cop gave him a thin smile. "Plus a civilian would have lost his shit. We'd be peeling you off the ceiling." He looked back at the wrecker with its red smear. "I was in the reserves," he said. "Called up twice, protecting convoys in the Sunni Triangle. I'm lucky I made it home."

"Were you a cop before, too?" Peter was curious.

That thin smile again. "Protect and serve."

Peter didn't say anything more. He hadn't mentioned that the fifth man was dressed as a state trooper, driving an unmarked car with state plates. He was still wondering whether the trooper was the real thing or an impostor, and how he might determine which.

He'd talked to the police before. He had more practice with it than he wanted.

He hadn't decided how to play this yet.

Two more patrol cars rolled up to protect the scene, but the first detective took another twenty minutes to arrive.

In his late forties or early fifties, he had a slight hunch and a comfortable paunch, colorless hair clipped close to hide the expansion of his bald spot, a bushy brown mustache that drooped down past the corners of his mouth, and a baggy brown suit with his badge clipped to one side of his belt and a pistol clipped to the other. He stopped to talk to the uniformed officers for a few minutes, went inside the hospital, then came back out for a look at the wrecker and Henry's pickup before he approached Peter.

"I'm Detective Steinburger." He put a business card on the bench but didn't offer to shake hands. "I'm going to take your picture now." He took a half dozen photos with his phone, then sat on the other end of the bench, with a few careful feet between them.

"I'm sorry about your friend," he said.

"Yeah," said Peter. "So am I."

"The crime scene techs will be here soon," Detective Steinburger said. "The mobile crime lab will be here eventually. They'll take more pictures, take samples of the blood on your skin. We'll need to take your clothing into evidence." He glanced at Peter's road-wrecked boots. "You got anyone coming? Anyone to bring you something to wear?"

After Peter had used Henry's phone to call Elle Hansen from the highway, he'd sent a text to his friend Lewis in Milwaukee, telling Lewis he'd killed four men in self-defense and that he needed a good lawyer to meet him at Swedish Medical Center in Denver.

Lewis had texted back almost immediately. *On it. Sit tight.*

But there was no lawyer in sight. And no clean clothes, either.

Now, answering the detective, Peter shook his head. "I don't live here. I was just doing a favor for Henry."

"We'll figure something out," Steinburger said. "Once the techs get here, you can clean yourself up. I'll send a patrolman to your hotel for some clothes. We'll go downtown and you can make a formal statement. But right now you need to talk to me, tell me what happened."

70

Peter shook his head. "We can talk all you want, but I'm not going anywhere. I need to talk to Henry's daughter, when she's done inside."

"I'm not asking," Steinburger said mildly. "People are dead. You want the cuffs, we can do the cuffs. I've got four cops with Tasers. We'll put you in the car, then put you in a cell. You can talk to us from there, if you'd rather."

Funny, there was a time when Peter thought spending the night in jail would cure him of his claustrophobia. It was a dumb idea, and the last thing he wanted now. Except maybe to talk about it with a stranger, but that was unavoidable now.

"I can't go inside," he said. "I have claustrophobia. I'll have a panic attack. It's a post-traumatic stress thing."

He felt the heat of embarrassment again. Even after months of therapy, part of him still felt like it was his fault, something personally wrong with him. Not just his brain chemistry altered by eight years of war, locked into that fight-or-flight zone.

Although they were still useful, those wartime reflexes. He'd proven that today.

"Huh," the detective said. "You got any paperwork for that?"

A red BMW sedan, gleaming under the sodium lights, rolled up and double-parked in the ambulance zone, the nose of the car pushing up against the yellow perimeter tape set up by the cops.

Peter heard the door slam.

"Excuse me." A bright, brassy voice cut through the purr of the idling cruisers' engines. "Are you Peter Ash?"

A woman strode toward them across the asphalt. Her hair was blond and kinky and down to the shoulders of the midnight-blue suit stretched tight across her chest and thighs. Four-inch heels, horn-rimmed glasses, the whole package looked expensive as hell to Peter, although admittedly, he wasn't the best judge.

"That's me," Peter said. Wondering who the hell this woman was, hoping that Lewis had come through again.

The younger cop stepped quickly to intercept her, but she held up a palm and stopped, still a dozen feet from where Peter sat.

She looked Peter up and down. "You look like shit," she said, then spun to face the younger cop. She moved like a dancer, comfortable on her toes.

"I'm Miranda Howe, Mr. Ash's attorney." She produced a crisp business card out of nowhere and held it up to the cop, who looked at Steinburger.

The detective nodded and Miranda Howe stepped forward and presented her card to Steinburger.

"Why isn't my client getting medical care? Why hasn't my client been allowed to clean himself off? He's the victim of a brutal crime, and it's only through his own history as a veteran and war hero that he was lucky enough to survive."

She talked quickly and in complete paragraphs, and the detective couldn't squeeze a word between the sentences that kept coming. Peter was going to object to her description of him as a war hero, but he didn't have time, either.

She said, "Surely you're not charging him with anything. You certainly haven't detained him in any way, so I'm assuming he's free to go. We'll make an appointment for a statement downtown. Tomorrow."

She spun back to Peter and reached down for his elbow to help him off the bench, giving him a very nice view down the front of her cream-colored blouse.

He noticed that she wore a red brassiere, although it didn't appear to cover much.

"We'll go inside and find you the necessary medical attention that the local police have clearly neglected to provide. When that's done, I have a change of clothes for you in the car."

Standing up, Steinburger found his voice. "Ms. Howe, wait a moment." His back was straighter, and his suit somehow seemed to fit him better. He no longer looked like a tired, overworked civil servant, a pose Peter realized Steinburger probably used a lot, in order to seem less threatening to victims and suspects alike. Now, with Miranda Howe breathing down his neck, he looked like a pretty capable cop.

"Mr. Ash, is this woman your attorney?"

"I believe so," Peter said.

Steinburger took a deep breath. "Ms. Howe, several people are dead. I still don't know what your client saw or did, and I have a lot of questions about what happened. As for how he looks, the scene techs need to take samples before he can get himself cleaned up, and the techs are on their way. The first officer on the scene offered medical care, and your client declined. In short, he is sitting here at my discretion, Counselor, so unless you'd like Mr. Ash cuffed and put in a car and hauled down to the pokey, I strongly suggest you take it down a notch."

"Hmm," she said, looking at Steinburger a bit differently. "Fair enough. I'd like to speak with my client in private, please."

"I'll give you until the crime scene techs get here," he said. "But then we start asking questions. The state police are on their way. It's likely that they have jurisdiction here."

She nodded and Steinburger stepped away, waving the uniformed officers back before putting his phone to his ear. They moved out of earshot, but still effectively blocked any pathway Peter might have taken to get out of there.

Miranda Howe, Peter's apparent attorney, stared at him. Her makeup was expertly applied, rendering the faint pockmarks of her acne scars almost invisible. He could feel some vast engine of calculation whirring away behind her eyes, though he did wonder why she wasn't completely freaked out by her new client, who was covered with other men's blood.

"Did anyone read you your rights?"

"No."

"Okay, that's good." She sat beside him on the bench. Her perfume was a floral riot, like a hothouse garden in full bloom. He was having trouble getting past that glimpse down her blouse. He was fairly certain she'd done that deliberately, as part of some strategy he didn't yet understand. He didn't mind. It was a nice view.

He really needed to get back to June.

"Tell me what happened," she said. "The short version, but don't leave out anything important. I'm your attorney, so this entire conversation is privileged. That means I can't tell anyone else what you tell me without your permission. You can trust me."

Peter smiled. At the moment, with two hijackings in a week, he wasn't going to trust anyone. Especially someone who told him to trust her. "Maybe first you'd better explain how it is that you're my attorney."

"Mr. Lewis called my office," she said. "He has a relationship with the firm. He said to tell you Dinah sends her love. And that better be good enough for right now, because I left a friend at Guard and Grace to come here, and I only got one lousy appetizer, so I'm pretty goddamn hungry."

Peter's connection to Lewis wasn't something she could have discovered quickly, and Dinah was the reason Peter and Lewis had become friends to begin with. "Good enough," he said.

He told her about the disappearance of the first car, the heavy crew's protection run, the ambulance blocking them on the narrow mountain road, the wrecker slamming into Henry's truck from the side.

He told her about the car that came up behind them, but didn't mention that it was set up to look like a police car, driven by a man in a state police uniform. Peter still had the license plate number. It was the only thing he had to hang on to, the only detail that might lead him back to the remaining hijacker.

He told her how Deacon and Banjo had died, the man with the shotgun, the paramedics. The semi-controlled gurney ride down the mountain with Henry, the death of the hijacker driving the wrecker. Loading Henry onto the back of the pickup.

Miranda looked at him.

"You're shitting me, right? This is the story you're planning to tell?"

He shrugged. "It's the truth."

Mostly.

Aside from the fact that he was leaving out details about the fifth hijacker, the truth was that he didn't want to talk to the cops at all.

But avoiding the cops would be worse. It would limit his movements. It would make him a suspect, which would make it even harder to do what he wanted to do.

Which was to talk with Henry's daughter about why and how somebody might hit her guys. Grill that grower to see if he was part of it. Track down that state trooper, real or fake, and make sure there was nobody else involved in the murder of his friends.

Then maybe beat that trooper to death.

It probably wasn't what Don, his therapist in Eugene, would recommend. Not the best way to get the war out of his system.

But here he sat, with Henry dead, and other men's blood drying on his clothes.

Something had broken loose in him on that mountain. He could feel it, that restless urge toward the fight, like some clattering windup mechanism whose coiled spring never unwound.

It's just who he was, that need to do something. To be of use.

Sometimes, to cause some fucking trouble.

He just hoped he could pack it all away again, when the time came to see June.

"Anyway," he told Miranda, "no matter what I tell the cops, there's a long trail of evidence." He gestured to his clothes, his face. "Whose blood do you think this is? Not much of it is mine. They're going to figure it out anyway. Better to be up front."

"No," she said. "Better for you to shut up right now and let me do the talking." She shook her head. "Your boss warned me that you were a loose cannon, but he didn't say you were fucking crazy."

"Wait. My boss?"

"Yes, Mr. Lewis, the CEO of your company. Unfortunately, I never got his first name."

Peter laughed. Lewis was full of surprises.

She kept talking. "Apparently Mr. Lewis places a high value on your continued availability. I asked what your position was with the company, and he wouldn't say." She looked at him sideways. "Perhaps we'll talk more about that later. However, because your company does a great deal of business with my firm, and pays a substantial retainer for our services, I am under strict instructions to provide any and all possible assistance."

Peter said, "What exactly is your legal specialty?"

She shook her kinky blond hair out of her face. "My official title is senior counsel," she said. "Unofficially, I solve client problems using whatever means necessary." She showed her teeth, which were bright white and far too even to be natural. "In other words, I'm a fixer."

"Huh," said Peter. "That's kind of what I do, too."

10

A black SUV arrived and a man and a woman climbed out and spoke to the older uniformed officer, who pointed them at Steinburger, who pointed them at Peter and at the wrecker with Henry's pickup on the tow bar. They were dressed in black work pants and beige polo shirts with some kind of logo on the breast.

The man carried a big plastic toolbox over to the trucks. The woman carried her own big plastic toolbox over to Peter. She was older than Peter, with her dark hair in a no-nonsense bob, basic makeup, and her only jewelry was modest gold studs in her ears. "I'm going to take some pictures of you now," she said. "Then I'll take samples from your skin and clothes."

Under the watchful eyes of Miranda Howe and Detective Steinburger, the woman removed an enormous camera with flash from her toolbox and captured Peter from every possible angle. Then she pulled on thin blue nitrile gloves, set out a variety of plastic collection bags and containers and tools, removed the paper bags from his hands, and swabbed and scraped his face and ears and neck and hands and clothes. With a pair of heavy-duty scissors, she cut samples from his hair and shirt and pants and the webbing of his ballistic vest and tucked them into individual plastic envelopes.

She looked like a busy, efficient suburban mom, but here she was collecting the remains of the dead from Peter's living body.

Then she turned to Steinburger. "I'm going to need the rest of his clothes now," she said.

Miranda nodded. "I'll get something for you to change into," she said. "Don't say anything until I get back."

She strode to her red BMW, clipping along in her four-inch heels. Both Peter and Steinburger watched her go. "Some lawyer," said Steinburger.

"No comment," said Peter.

"How does a glorified security guard rate Miranda fucking Howe?"

"I have no idea," Peter said. "But I think I'm in good hands, don't you?"

Steinburger made a face like he'd licked a lemon. "Yeah."

Miranda returned with a soft leather duffel, pointing one long-nailed finger at Peter. "What did I just tell you? Not one fucking word."

"No harm done, Counselor," Steinburger said mildly. "Just making conversation. Let's try not to make this adversarial, shall we? Mr. Ash is not under arrest. I'm just trying to determine what's happened."

"Just to be clear, he's cooperating voluntarily."

"Absolutely, and we appreciate his help," Steinburger said. "We're going to have to go inside." The detective waved a hand toward the hospital entrance. "I can't let you get naked out here. And I'm going to ask you some questions."

"I know," Peter said. "But if we take too long, you're going to see my claustrophobia up close and personal."

"Wait," Miranda said. "You're claustrophobic?"

"It's not as bad as it used to be," Peter said. "But I can only be inside for so long. After a while I start to sweat, then hyperventilate. It's basically a panic attack."

"Sounds like my second wedding," Steinburger said. "My third wedding, too, actually."

"Was that you having the panic attack?" Miranda asked. "Or your bride?"

"Play nice, Counselor," Steinburger said, then led them inside. The ER was nearly empty.

After all, it was only eight o'clock.

The night was still young.

A ponytailed nurse in blue scrubs escorted them through the fluorescent flicker of the triage area while Peter's war reflexes looked for lines of fire and escape routes. His clothes were stiff with dried blood, he felt it flaking off with every step.

Breathe in, he told himself. Slow and steady. Breathe out.

With Don, his therapist, Peter had done almost six months of mental exercises. In order to get better at being inside, he'd learned to consciously calm himself, to control his breathing, to keep his mind focused on the present moment, rather than allowing himself to slip into the old mental pathways, into warrior mode. Fight or flight, with emphasis on the fight.

He'd come to enjoy the exercises, had gotten pretty good at them. That's part of what the yoga was about. Focus, discipline. Also strength and flexibility.

Peter worried, sometimes, about getting too good at calming himself. He definitely wanted to be able to live a normal life, a life he could share with June. But he didn't want to lose the ability to react like a warrior when he needed to.

He still did the exercises.

The idea of a life with June Cassidy was a pretty powerful incentive.

Of course, those exercises didn't take into account that Peter might be covered with blood. That he might have just killed four men who were trying to kill him, and lost a good friend in the process. It would be hard to practice that kind of scenario.

Sometimes the static just filled his head, no matter what he did.

The exam room was twelve feet square, a clutter of wall cabinets, medical equipment, an exam table, and three windowless walls. The fourth wall was aluminum-framed glass with a glass door and a view of the nurses' station.

The nurse, whose name tag read SUSIE, began to open cabinets and remove little wrapped packets of medical supplies. She was efficient, still under thirty, maybe five years younger than Peter. Steinburger leaned against the counter with his arms folded against his chest. Miranda Howe walked in last, carrying the leather duffel, and closed the door behind her.

"Uh, little privacy?" said Peter.

"Sorry," Steinburger said apologetically. "Chain of custody. Your clothes may be evidence in a trial. I need to ensure that they haven't been tampered with. The nurse is here to check you for injuries, per protocol and the request of your attorney."

"Miranda?"

"He's correct. And your attorney should be present at times like this, when you're in close contact with a member of law enforcement." She set the duffel on the exam table and removed a short pile of neatly folded clothes. "Don't worry, I'll avert my eyes."

Peter wasn't going to wait. He could feel the static foaming up his brainstem. Slow, deep breaths.

The nurse pulled the curtain across the glass wall while Peter undid the Velcro straps of the black armored vest and slid it over his head. Flakes of dried blood fell like snow. He handed the vest to Steinburger, who slid it into a clear plastic bag taken from the side pocket of his suit. Peter's shirt came next, a once-white super-wicking technical T-shirt that helped keep him cool under the hot vest. Into another of Steinburger's plastic bags. The muscles in his neck were getting tight.

He stood stripped to the waist in his ruined Carhartts while Nurse Susie took a series of alcohol-soaked pads and cleaned the skin on his face and neck and anywhere else the crimson crust had formed under his clothes. Her gloved hands were cool and firm and professional on his body, but she wouldn't look him in the eye.

Peter figured it was because he'd come in covered with other men's blood like some kind of desperado, and she was a nice, normal, well-adjusted young woman.

"Are you in any pain?" she asked. "I'm really not finding anything but scrapes and bruises."

"Just my head," he said, pointing to his skull above his left ear. "Kind of a throb."

She took another pad and began to clean the blood from his hair. He winced as she pressed harder, trying to soak out the blood. "That's a nice goose egg," she said. "Did you ever lose consciousness?"

Peter had been hit harder before. Much harder. "No," he said. "It just kind of rung my bell, you know?"

"You must have a hard head," she said, glancing shyly at him now. Maybe she wasn't so normal. Peter was very aware that he was half naked getting what amounted to a sponge bath by a pretty young nurse. And soon he'd be taking off his pants. Under the watchful eye of Miranda Howe and Detective Steinburger.

He was starting to sweat, the static turning to sparks.

Goddamn he was tired of this.

Breathe in, breathe out.

Nurse Susie looked at him a little more closely. "You sure you're all right?"

"Yeah," he said. "I just don't do well in enclosed spaces. I can finish cleaning up later, okay?"

She nodded. "Okay." She smacked a soft plastic pack on the edge of the countertop and held it out. "Put this cold pack on your goose egg," she said, "it will help with the swelling." It was already cooling in his hand. She pressed a paper packet of ibuprofen into his palm. "Take these now."

She turned away and clicked a few buttons on the laptop perched on a mobile stand. "Pick up your care instructions at the nursing station on your way out. And here's my card, if you have any further questions or concerns."

She gave him an innocent look, handing it over, but the smile tugging at the corner of her mouth was anything but. "I put my cell on the back, in case your headache gets worse, or you have any other sort of emergency." He turned the card over. Her handwriting was wild but the message was clear.

She turned and let herself out, closing the door behind her.

Steinburger had his pad out and a small digital recorder. "While you get changed," he said, "I'm going to ask you some questions."

"Not until he's dressed," said Miranda, who was eyeballing Peter like she wanted to eat him for dinner. "Although I'm assuming you want the pants, too."

He'd been in that crowded room under the flickering fluorescents for twenty minutes and the static was starting to throw lightning bolts. His chest felt like it was wrapped in steel bands, and it was getting harder to breathe.

He said, "Both of you, get the fuck out. Detective, if you want my pants, I'll hand them through that door. Unless you're planning to arrest me right this minute."

Steinburger's eyebrows went up in mild surprise, but his face betrayed nothing else.

"I'll be right outside," he said. "And yes, I need your pants." He glanced down. "And your boots."

Miranda lingered in the doorway. "I don't know if anything will fit," she said. "There's more in the bag. I just grabbed some things from my closet."

Peter didn't care where the clothes had come from. He put his hand on her shoulder and removed her from the room, closed the opaque glass door behind him. He bent to untie and kick off his ruined boots, then shed the stiff, blood-crusted pants onto the floor. He'd taken to wearing miracle boxers that wicked sweat, could get rinsed clean in a creek every night and would be dry by the morning, but the blood had soaked all the way through the pants and into his goddamn underwear.

He leaned on the exam table. He pressed his palms to his eyes and remembered again the man with the shotgun right up against him in the back of the ambulance. The rough wool of the ski mask, the way his eyes changed as his blood pumped out of him. The smell of his sweat and fear.

"Peter?" Miranda's voice through the door. "Are you all right?"

No.

"Yeah," he said. "Hang on."

He sorted quickly through the clothes Miranda had brought, a motley collection in a variety of sizes. There were no socks or shoes. The underwear was all weird, banana-hammock Speedo-looking shit, so he stepped directly into a pair of another man's pre-distressed jeans made of some kind of stretch fabric. The size was his, but they felt too tight on his skin. Like the whole room. Electricity filled his head.

Faster now, the floor cold under his bare feet, he pulled on someone else's Oskar Blues T-shirt and Telluride sweatshirt, shoved the rest of Miranda's oddball clothes back in the duffel, and opened the door.

Steinburger held out another clear plastic evidence bag. Peter pushed past him, the detective solid and more nimble than he looked, pivoting to put a strong hand on Peter's wrist, trying for a come-along hold. "Hang on."

Peter rotated his arm and slipped the grip without breaking stride. "Outside," he said over his shoulder.

In the high-altitude night, the cool mountain wind blew through him like something approaching grace.

He looked around for Henry's daughter, but her car with the Heavy Metal Protection door decal was gone.

Lightning flashed in the west.

He automatically counted the seconds before the crack and grumble of thunder.

At a picnic table on a grassy area past the parking lot, Steinburger asked Peter to tell him what had happened.

Pacing barefoot while Miranda listened, Peter held the ice pack to his head as he told the story from start to finish, beginning with how he'd met Henry Nygaard in the Willamette National Forest, how he'd ended up working at Heavy Metal Protection, the hijacking, his counterattack, and the final drive with Henry down to the hospital. Again he neglected to mention the state trooper's uniform, or that the car was dressed up like an unmarked cruiser.

Steinburger listened without expression, as if the litany of carnage was nothing to him after twenty years as a cop.

While Peter was talking, a black guy walked up with a cardboard tray holding four paper coffee cups. Eyes recording everything, from Peter's bare feet to the clothes that didn't fit.

He was medium height and whip-thin in a dark sport coat and a red plaid Western-style shirt over black jeans and low-heeled cowboy boots. He leaned against the end of the table and listened without comment.

Steinburger was fixated on the fact that Peter didn't have a local address. He waved Peter's driver's license in the air. "This is your parents' place in Wisconsin?"

"I move around a lot," Peter said. "I've only been in town for three days, remember? I'm staying at Henry's until I find a place." He was sleeping on Henry's open back porch. He could fit almost everything he owned in the back of his truck. He told himself it was a lifestyle choice.

Although maybe that could change.

Steinburger backed up further, asked Peter about his background, the company he worked for, what he did for a living. Peter said he was a silent partner in an investment company, which had some resemblance to the truth. Lewis had put Peter's name on the paperwork, anyway. Peter didn't mention where the money had come from. Lewis had laundered it so completely that it might have come from the moon.

Steinburger pointed a thumb at the black guy and said, "This is Paul Sykes, an investigator with the Colorado State Police."

Sykes put out his hand to shake. He was older than Peter by a few years, probably not yet forty. He had a brief smile and bags under his eyes like he hadn't slept for a month.

"Call me Paul, please. I brought coffee. Lattes, actually," he said a little apologetically, handing out cups. "Still a quad skinny mocha for you, Miranda?"

Miranda gave the black investigator a high-wattage smile. Gorgeous, sexy, the kind of controlled radiation that would burn skin in ten minutes. "Thanks, but I've lost my taste for chocolate. How's the wife?"

"We have a little boy now," he said. "And another one on the way."

"That's nice." She turned to Steinburger. "Gentlemen, my client has had a long and difficult day. It's time I got him home. We can come to your office tomorrow, say about noon?"

Sykes nodded agreeably. "I'm very sorry for what you've been through," he said, taking a small notebook from the pocket of his sport coat. "But I have a few more questions."

In fact, Investigator Sykes had a lot more questions, and so did Detective Steinburger.

Peter had been through this kind of questioning before, so he knew he was in for a long night. He was glad he'd managed to recover the money. It was probably the only thing keeping him out of jail.

Sykes wanted to hear the whole story again. He and Steinburger walked Peter through it a half dozen more times, backward and forward. Why had he attacked the man with the shotgun? Why hadn't he gotten the stretcher off the road to hide from the man in the wrecker? Why kill the man driving the ambulance?

Whenever Miranda complained about the questions or the length of the conversation, Peter said it was fine and kept talking. He told the entire truth about what had happened, except for the unmarked car, its uniformed driver, and its plate number.

With Sykes there, who was after all with the state police, Peter was even less willing to talk about the possible trooper.

Sykes could tell Peter was holding something back. He asked a lot of questions about the missing car and driver. What was the make and model? What kind of clothes was he wearing? Peter just repeated that it was a big black American sedan, newer, maybe a Dodge, and the guy wore blue pants and a blue shirt and a wide-brimmed hat.

Sykes wouldn't let it go. Kept coming back to it. Finally Miranda said, "Sykes, enough. He's answered your questions."

Then Sykes stepped away to take a phone call from his partner up on the mountain, who had some questions of his own.

It seemed the hijackers' bodies were gone.

11

don't know what to tell you," said Peter. "They were there when I left. Maybe the guy in the sedan did it. Maybe that's why he didn't come after me and Henry."

"Any idea why?" Sykes asked.

"To hide something, of course," Peter said. "But I don't know *how* he'd do it. Loading four dead bodies in a sedan by yourself? Those guys weren't small. And it would have been really messy. They didn't exactly die in their sleep."

"Unless he had help," Miranda said quietly.

They all sat on that for a minute. It added a new dimension.

"Let me ask you something," Peter said finally. "You know Randy Hansen went missing last week, right? With three hundred grand. That's twice now, with the same security company. So who else are you talking to? Who else has gotten hit? How long has this been going on?"

"I can't comment on an ongoing investigation," said Sykes.

"On that thing last week," Steinburger said, scratching his stubble. "Their GPS tracker cut out just inside the Denver city limits, so for the moment, Denver PD owns it. And I'm the lead. So I'll tell you that we were looking hardest at Hansen and the guy he was with. What happened today probably changes that. But I've never heard of anything like the hijacking you described." He looked at Sykes. "State Police has the highways, Paul. You ever see anything like this?"

Sykes shook his head. "Look, it's no secret the cannabis industry, an all-cash business, has created some new crime. But it's mostly smash-and-grab. Nothing this scale. Nothing this professional."

"Well," said Peter. "There's a lot of money involved. It would have been over a half million dollars if they'd gotten this one. Maybe someone's decided to get serious."

"And it doesn't matter that they got the bodies," Steinburger said. "We've still got the ambulance."

"They all wore gloves and hats and masks," Peter said.

Steinburger shook his head. "This isn't a movie. It doesn't matter how careful they were. There might be fingerprints on magazines and shell casings, and plenty of DNA in the spatter. If these guys are in the system, if they've ever been arrested or been in prison, we'll have prints on file. If they're active or former military? We'll also have their DNA."

Sykes shook his head. "Whoever it was, he—or they—wanted to get rid of everything. Stuck a rag in the ambulance's gas tank, set it on fire."

Steinburger made a sound, a formless groan of anger and pain. "What?"

Sykes smiled. "The fire was just getting started when the first trooper showed up. Trooper was dumb enough to try to put it out with the extinguisher in his unit. He got burned a little, but he managed to preserve a lot of evidence. He'll probably get a commendation."

Steinburger said, "So he just missed them."

"Yeah," said Sykes. "But here's the weird thing. Whoever it was, he put the bodies of your friends on the side of the road, far enough from the ambulance that they wouldn't get burned when it went up. And not all jumbled up in a pile, either, but laid out straight, arms at their sides, like at a funeral."

Or like casualties after a battle, thought Peter.

He didn't like the way this was going.

Nobody said the thing that they all were thinking.

What if there were more than just the five hijackers?

Finally Miranda said, "Detectives, this is fascinating, but we've been here five hours, and my client has had a very distressing day. Unless you'd like to charge Mr. Ash with something, we're leaving."

"Actually," Peter said, "I have some questions of my own. I want to know what you've learned about Hansen and the guy he was with. Also, whose money was taken, last week and today? And what's the name on the registration of that wrecker and ambulance?"

Sykes's brown face, mobile and friendly and endlessly interested in the previous conversation, turned to wood.

Steinburger sighed. "I can tell already that you're going to be a pain in my ass," he said. He stood up and put out his hand to shake. "We'll see you at noon at the Puzzle Palace."

Peter looked at Miranda. "The Puzzle Palace?"

"What some people call police headquarters," she said. "Downtown."

"It looks a little like it's made out of Legos," Steinburger explained.

So reassuring, thought Peter.

12

eter sat in the passenger seat of Miranda's little red BMW, shoeless in a stranger's clothes, holding on for dear life.

The car was nearly new, with black leather interior and varnished wood trim. The front was spotless, but the floor in the back was piled high with empty Starbucks cups. Miranda had slipped off her four-inch heels when she climbed into her seat, no panty hose, working the pedals barefoot, which Peter had to admit he'd always enjoyed himself.

But she drove like she was having an argument with the road, she was enjoying the fight, and she was determined to win. She ran the engine up into the red, punched the clutch, and jammed the shifter into the next gear, then popped the clutch to do it again. As she zigged and zagged through town, she blew past stop signs and flew through yellow lights as they turned red.

"Are we in a hurry?" Peter asked, watching the buildings fly by.

"I'm always in a hurry," she said.

It was long after midnight and traffic was light. Peter was tired. His eyes felt like they had sand in their sockets. He yawned.

She shot a sideways glance at him. "Might be weird going back to your friend's house," she said. "I can put you up at my place if you need to." She looked back to the road. "If you want."

"I'd really rather not be inside," he said. Also, if he was honest with himself, Miranda Howe scared the shit out of him. "Whose clothes am I wearing?"

"I don't really keep track," she said. "Does it matter?"

She flashed him that same high-wattage smile she'd given Detective Sykes, full of promise and pleasure to come. It made Peter understand how a moth might feel about a local floodlight. But he didn't want to sizzle against the hot surface.

And June. Don't forget June.

"No," he said. "I have a change of clothes in my truck. And I'd like some shoes, too. Would you please slow down? I've used up all my adrenaline for the day."

She eased up on the gas. "Peter, you should see yourself," she said. "You really need to get cleaned up. My condo has a giant window in the shower with a great view of the city. Sixth floor. I have a nice big balcony, there's a couch you can sleep on out there." She took her hands off the wheel, still going over sixty on Broadway. "I won't take advantage of you, I promise, no matter how much you beg. We need to talk about our meeting at the precinct. About what your plans are for tomorrow."

"I'm going to find the last asshole in that crew who killed my friend," Peter said.

"How do you propose to do that?" she asked. "Is there something you haven't told me? Or the police?"

"Do you think those five guys brainstormed that plan over bong hits and Cheetos? That plan was meticulous and well executed.

They were pros. And your friend Sykes was all over me about that third car."

"What does that have to do with anything?"

"Better you don't know," he said. "Something else is going on here. I don't want to drag you into it."

They went under an overpass and Miranda veered right as Broadway split into two one-way roads.

"You need to be careful," she said. "Steinburger may look like a middle-school math teacher, but he's a smart and capable cop. He got his rep when he stepped into some kind of battle between two meth crews, bikers. He was the only one to walk away. And Sykes may be even better. You start stepping on toes, they'll lock you up, and I won't be able to get you out."

Peter closed his eyes in the lurching car. The man with the shotgun was there again. The long muscles of Peter's left arm twitched with the memory of the knife in his hand, the slide and catch of the blade in skin. It was him or me, he told himself again. Him or me. He opened his eyes.

"Sometimes you don't have a choice," he said. "Henry was my friend."

A flash in the small side mirror caught Peter's attention.

Peter leaned toward Miranda to catch the angle. Headlights bouncing as the car behind them bucked on the uneven pavement.

Some kind of big sedan was behind them, a newer model, dark, half hidden in its own glare, barely visible on the dim, nearly empty four-lane road.

Miranda was in the left lane, going at least fifty.

"How long has that guy been back there?"

She glanced in the rearview. "I don't know."

They were midway down a long block. The stoplight ahead turned red.

Peter turned in his seat, digging his bare toes into the BMW's carpet. The headlights shifted as the other driver pulled into the lane beside Peter and edged up to pass.

Peter wasn't good at newer cars, but he remembered this one. Big and black, no markings, with a spotlight on the driver's side above the mirror. Antennae coming off the trunk.

The window was slightly tinted, and with the night and the fractured glow of the corner streetlights, Peter couldn't see inside.

If only Peter were driving. Better yet, if he had Lewis's big 10-gauge shotgun.

On a more basic level, if only he had some goddamn shoes. Boots would be better.

The other driver's window slid down. The driver stared straight ahead, his features dim in the dashboard glow. Peter couldn't see enough to recognize the man, but then, he wouldn't. He'd never had the chance to see his face, up on the mountain.

Both cars were approaching the intersection, with nobody in front of them. Miranda slowed for the red.

"Hit the gas," Peter said. "Right now."

"What?" Cars trickled through on the cross street.

"Punch it," he said. "Run the light. Do it now."

Miranda kept her bare foot on the brake. "Slow down, speed up. You don't know what you want, do you?" She flashed that high-wattage grin again. "I bet you have like ten safe words."

They closed on the intersection, bracketed with streetlights. Peter peered out at the other car.

A geometric gleam emerged through the open window.

"Gun," he said. "Fucking *gun*, just *go*, Miranda, *step on it*."

She glanced to the side. Her eyes widened and her mouth opened slightly.

Peter was sure he was going to die right there, trapped between this gorgeous predatory lunatic attorney's high-octane personality and her vestigial remaining respect for the laws of traffic.

Then she faced front and popped the clutch and hit the gas. The little car rocketed forward, threading the needle between a giant green garbage truck and a ladder-loaded painter's van. Peter twisted sideways in his seat, looked back and saw the big sedan maneuver through the intersection, red and blue lights flashing now, and surge after them.

"What the fuck, Peter? Is that the police?"

"Did you see the gun?"

"I didn't see anything," she said. "What the fuck is going on?"

"That thing I didn't tell you?" She flew past a Prius like it was standing still, but stayed in her lane. "Up in the mountains, that third car, the sedan your friend Sykes was so interested in?" He pointed his thumb over his shoulder. "That's the car."

She was going seventy, focused on the road. Cars were pulling over ahead of them. The big black sedan was only a couple of car lengths behind her. "An unmarked police car? With the lights?"

"Yes."

"With a policeman directing traffic for the hijackers? That's a serious allegation. Are you absolutely certain?"

"Or else it was some guy dressed like a policeman, yes. He had a blue uniform and a flat-brimmed trooper's hat, like Smokey the Bear. Either way it did the job." He didn't mention the state plates on the car, or that he knew the plate number. They could certainly have been stolen.

She eased off on the gas, not much, but enough for him to notice.

"Did you really see a gun, just now?"

"You don't believe me."

Another intersection flashed past, then another. They were lucky the lights were green.

He needed to get off this one-way. Downtown was coming up fast, and there were too many residential buildings around. He needed more space. He thought about the map of Denver he was building in his head. "Take this left."

She slowed a little more for the turn onto Bayaud. The black sedan followed, staying the same distance back.

She slowed a little more. The area was more industrial. He'd had a dispensary pickup near here his first day, so he had an idea of the layout. He scanned the side streets, looking for something. He hoped he'd know it when he saw it.

"You're sure you're not just jumpy? You had a long day, Peter. Your friends died," she said. "You also killed four people. I'm guessing that was pretty stressful, right?"

The war fucked you up, she didn't say, although Peter heard her loud and clear.

She wasn't wrong.

Otherwise what the hell was he doing here, in this car?

They bumped over the railroad tracks that ran at an oblique angle to the road. "Take this right," he said.

She turned onto Santa Fe, a three-lane one-way road, and the black sedan followed, keeping its station behind them. The blocks were longer here, the buildings big commercial boxes, not houses, and mostly empty this late at night, so nobody else was likely to get hurt. Beside them to their right, the railroad tracks rose into the air.

"Maybe you're not thinking clearly right now." Her voice was carefully modulated. Calm, thoughtful, persuasive. "After all, I ran a red light. Now he's chasing me."

She was managing Peter now, the same way she'd managed the detectives, how she'd manage any other client or situation. She was good at her job.

The little red BMW flashed through another intersection, toward the railroad overpass. Ahead of them, all lanes were clear.

"Maybe you're right," Peter said, peeking in the rearview.

She eased off the gas even more, down below fifty. "Maybe we should talk to them."

"Maybe," he said. "Tell you what. Put one foot on the clutch and get ready to brake. But don't touch the brake pedal yet."

She moved her feet. The car coasted, slowing. Peter looked over his right shoulder again. The black sedan drifted to the inside lane and pulled forward to come even with them. Lights flashing in its grille, but no siren.

The gun muzzle peeked out of the driver's window. The round black eye turning to look right at him.

"*Stop,*" Peter shouted, knowing she'd respond to the tone more than the word itself.

Miranda hit the brake from sheer reflex as the gunman pulled the trigger.

Peter pressed himself back in his seat, bare toes gripping the floor mat again, willing the rounds to miss him. Three short disciplined bursts raked across the front of the little red car, some kind of semi-auto, maybe a modified AR-15, maybe something else.

The other driver braked hard, too, but a half second later. The BMW was a much lighter car with better tires and stopped more quickly. The shooter tracked them from the open window, his face still mostly in shadow, but now they were a stationary target.

"Pull a U-turn, fast, now now now." It finally occurred to him to take out Henry's phone and pull up a map.

"It's one-way," she shouted, but cranked the car around anyway, the centrifugal force slinging Peter hard against the door. Nice turning radius. They could use that.

He heard two more bursts and the sound of glass breaking, the back window turned to spiderweb. Miranda got to third in a hurry, then chirped the tires in fourth gear, carving lean curves around the few cars coming at them. "You knew that would happen," she said. She was breathing hard.

"Do you have a gun in this car?" he asked. The big black sedan had to do a three-point turn to come after them and was now almost two blocks back. The BMW could accelerate faster, too.

"Not anymore." Her color was high, a pink sheen on her cheeks and forehead. A near-death experience could do that to a person. Make you feel alive.

Some people became addicted to it.

He tasted copper in his mouth, and despite himself felt the smile spread wide across his own face. "Fun, isn't it?"

"You're fucking crazy," she shouted. The wind from her open window blew her kinky blond hair back from her face.

"Yeah, yeah," he said. "Take this right, then the next."

She slowed only slightly for the corner, gunned it again on the straightaway, and powered through the next turn, rubber straining against the asphalt, so they were headed back the way they'd come. "Now what?"

He wanted to take the fight to the other car, but he couldn't. He was unarmed, in a smaller, lighter vehicle. So he'd call this a tactical retreat. Live to fight another day.

Their pursuers would be looking for light and motion in the night. He looked behind him and didn't see the black sedan. At mid-block he said, "Right again. But kill your lights. Foot off the brake. If you want to drop your speed, downshift."

She opened her mouth, then shut it again, turned off her lights and made the turn, pumping the clutch to downshift and again to accelerate. Now they'd come three-quarters of a circle to cross the road they'd been on when the shooter had fired. As they hit the intersection, Peter peered right and didn't see the police car. It had already followed them around the first corner and would be on the other side of the block. Every unobserved turn made the red BMW harder to follow.

"Now the next left," he said, and she slung them around the next corner so they were heading back the way they'd come on a parallel road, what Peter figured was the least likely path of pursuit.

Unless the other driver had followed the same line of reasoning.

Miranda was back up to seventy now, running dark and ignoring all traffic lights and signs at the edge of the grid of multiuse buildings. Looking ahead, Peter saw some kind of trucking depot, a construction yard. Then a modest narrow building with a long row of off-street parking, a dozen or more cars already there.

"Up here, turn here," he said, pointing across her body with one hand while looking back. Nobody behind them.

Miranda took a hard left, slowed fast enough for the anti-lock to kick in, then cranked the wheel all the way right and tucked them neatly into the farthest slot, sheltered behind a big purple SUV and hidden from the road on four sides. The little red car chirped to a stop, then rocked back on its springs. She was gulping air, her face flushed, her eyes dilated like an addict whose fix has just kicked in.

Turning to him, she ran the pink tip of her tongue across her lips and said, "Listen, I think we should have sex." She knelt on her seat and shouldered out of her jacket and began to unbutton her blouse. Her red brassiere still didn't cover much. "I mean, *right* now. I think that would be excellent, don't you?"

13

Before Peter could decide how to react, Miranda reached across his body and tripped the lever that dropped his seat back, putting Peter in a horizontal position.

She slid her skirt, clearly made of some miracle stretch fabric, up to her hips and threw a leg over him. Her blouse was wide open.

She had a lovely plush round little body, and God knows he'd never minded a little crazy in a woman. And Peter was having the exact same reaction, that adrenalized urge toward life and the pleasures of the flesh.

But he kept seeing June's face, and imagined explaining the next series of events to her.

How his actions would change what had happened between them. What might yet come to be.

So he put his right hand under Miranda's left thigh and his left hand under her right butt cheek and picked her up and set her back down half naked in her own seat.

"I'm so sorry," he said, meaning every word. "You're gorgeous and sexy as all hell and I can't believe I'm saying no, but I'm kind of with someone right now."

Or hoping to be, he thought. Or something.

She turned that crackling, high-energy smile on him like some kind of futuristic sex ray and climbed back to her knees. "I don't mind," she said, shucking her blouse. Tan lines, a pink nipple peeking out of her brassiere. Jesus. He was pretty sure she was wearing a thong. She put her left knee on the seat between his legs and leaned in. She smelled like wet flowers. "You don't have to tell her a goddamn thing."

"That's the problem," he said, closing his eyes. Maybe if he made the sign of the cross? Wore a necklace of garlic? He opened his eyes again, looked directly at her. "Because I would have to tell her. It's that kind of thing."

She stared back at him for a long moment, her body all but bare to him. Then closed her eyes, gave a kind of full-body shiver, and dropped back into her own seat. "Get the fuck out of my car."

Peter got out.

Still barefoot. Wearing another man's clothes.

What the hell was he doing?

He walked the narrow length of pavement between the parked cars and the building, stray stones sharp under his bare feet, taking deep breaths. Committing that moment to memory, the sight of Miranda in all her glory, because it was one for the vault, no matter what happened with June. He was still human, right?

When he approached the edge of the parking lot, he stepped between a Hummer and some bland beige compact sedan and peeked out to the street. A few sporadic cars, no lights or sirens or any other evidence of shots fired on a September night between the railroad tracks and the river.

There were advantages to driving a police car—or pretending to be driving a police car.

When you behaved badly, nobody called the cops.

Maybe Peter should think about that strategy.

But first he needed his own wheels. He wasn't sure his libido would survive another close encounter with Miranda Howe.

His truck was parked on Henry's block. They'd taken Henry's pickup that morning for the day's rounds. Fourteen hours ago, but it seemed like a week.

Henry's house in Cap Hill was too far to walk barefoot.

He pulled out Henry's phone and looked for a shoe store, figuring he'd break in, steal some sneakers, leave some money.

Found nothing but women's shoe stores.

They probably wouldn't stock men's twelves, extra wide.

He looked back. Miranda's car hadn't moved. He'd give her a few minutes to cool down.

Unless she was sufficiently pissed to simply leave. At least then he wouldn't have to worry about her safety. He was pretty sure he was the bullet magnet, not Miranda.

He pulled up the text app, moved his thumbs. *Pls call when free.*

Ten seconds later Henry's phone vibrated in his hand.

"Jarhead." Lewis stretched the word out. His voice was like motor oil, slippery and dark, latent with combustion. Peter could hear his friend's tilted smile in that single word. "How was the cavity search?"

"Close call," Peter said, smiling himself. "Thanks for finding me a lawyer. She's really something."

Lewis still thought he owed Peter for something that had happened in Milwaukee a few years back. As far as Peter was concerned, the debt went the other way.

"So catch me up," Lewis said. "You some kinda gunslinger now?"

Briefly, Peter told him about the hijacking. About the dead. About the maybe-police car that had found them on the streets of Denver ten minutes ago.

Lewis said, "Did some work in Denver a few years back. Might still know some people out there." Peter heard the clicking of a keyboard. "Be there first flight out."

"You're not coming out," Peter said. "You're getting married in a few months. You have those boys to raise."

"You got it backward." Lewis was a career criminal and one of the most dangerous men Peter had ever met. "Dinah getting ready to kill *me*, I don't get outta her hair. She told me, 'You just show up on the day. Other than that, you'd best stay out of my way.'"

Peter could hear her saying it, too. Both because he knew Dinah, and because Lewis had caught the cadence of her voice just right.

Lewis kept talking. "You'd be doing me a favor, Jarhead. 'Sides, I already bought the ticket. Nonrefundable. I know you're the cheapest living white man. Think of it like my bachelor party."

"Well," Peter said, "you're the CEO."

He heard a long, deep chuckle before the connection went silent.

He took Henry's phone down from his ear and pulled June's number from his memory. They'd written pages of letters, but he hadn't actually spoken to her since the end of March. She deserved a real-time update. And he really wanted to hear her voice.

"Who was that?"

Peter turned, the phone still in his hand. Miranda stood tall on her heels, clothing immaculate, hair brushed and fluffed, makeup perfect.

"I wasn't sure you'd still be here when I got off the phone," he said.

She looked at him, her face neutral, composed. Peter had no idea what was going on behind that implacable mask. She didn't answer him.

Then he noticed that she'd left an extra button undone on her blouse. He was certain it was not an accident. She saw his eyes drop down and back up. It was involuntary. He was a man, she was a woman. A flicker of triumph crossed her face for the briefest moment. Then she was back to her calm, professional self.

"My client is at risk," she said. "Someone shot up my car. We need a strategy. And I'm your attorney, so you need to tell me everything. Starting with who you were just talking to."

Peter shook his head. "Better for you to have limited knowledge," he said. "You want some level of deniability."

"Deniability of what?" she demanded.

He wanted to get to his truck, to get into his own clothes. To get some boots on his damn feet.

He looked at her with more calm than he felt. "Of what's coming."

14

aniel Clay Dixon stood at the window of his darkened hotel room and stared out across the naked rooftops and parking lots of Denver. The television was on with the sound off, a reporter standing on the side of a rural highway with a microphone, red and blue flashing lights in the background.

It was after midnight and Dixon badly wanted a drink. Tequila, straight from the neck of the bottle. It was the sin he allowed himself from time to time, strong liquor providing a kind of anesthesia against his other, more profound sins, the finely ground wreckage he'd made of his life. But he wouldn't allow himself anything stronger than coffee until this was over.

Dixon carried a secure smartphone in the pocket of his crisp tan summer-weight suit, registered to a company he didn't really own, and two disposable phones laid out on the desk, registered to nobody at all.

Beside the phones stood a half-empty paper cup holding the special kind of bad coffee that only cheap hotel-room machines produced.

One of the burner phones was for incoming, the other for outgoing.

He replaced them at irregular intervals.

His whole life was irregular.

It always had been, despite all his efforts to the contrary.

Daniel Clay Dixon was waiting for a call from a man who didn't exist, about a series of events that had never occurred.

He had a lot riding on this.

The man who didn't employ him had made that quite clear.

The coffee was gone and Dixon was still thinking about tequila when his incoming phone buzzed with a text. A solicitation for a time-share in Florida, with an 800 number.

Not what Dixon was waiting for, but important enough.

A night message from this person was unusual, but these were unusual circumstances.

On his outgoing phone, he touched in the number, but changed to a Maryland area code, with 2 added to each of the first two digits of the last four numbers. It was the twenty-second of the month. Best to keep these things simple.

"Yes," Dixon said.

"You know that name on your watch list?"

The man on the other end of the line was an Army major who worked in personnel at the Pentagon. Part vacuum cleaner, part town pump. Part of the team, for a price. A price that kept climbing.

Dixon didn't much like the major, how he kept massaging the price upward. No integrity. Dixon didn't mind the money, it wasn't his anyway. It was the principle of the thing, a matter of honor.

Not that Dixon had much honor left himself.

But what he had, he was holding on to hard.

The Army major said, "We got another request, this time from the Denver PD. Your guy's definitely surfaced."

"Context?"

"This was through regular channels, so they just asked for the file. But I asked for details, told them it would facilitate cooperation. They said it was in connection with an attempted hijacking and multiple homicides."

Which would be that mess in the mountains, thought Dixon. Bad news.

The major said, "What do you want me to do?"

"Keep stalling," Dixon said. "They're used to it." The federal government had a long history of poor cooperation with local government.

"What if they come back with a higher authority?" the major said. "Not the chief or the mayor, but like a senator or governor? Or somebody here?" Meaning the Pentagon.

"Cross that bridge when we get there," Dixon said. "Keep in touch."

He figured the police wouldn't care so much if the guy ended up dead.

At least, that was the plan.

Plans didn't always work out.

Dixon had known Peter Ash as a lieutenant in Iraq. He'd followed the lieutenant's work, seen him get shit done. The guy was the real deal. Persistent, talented, and once he got his teeth into something, pretty much impossible to discourage. Dixon had been looking for the man, hoping to hire him, but he'd gone underground.

If he'd surfaced now, and had staked a claim to the wrong side of this particular problem, things were serious.

They had to take him out of the picture, and fast.

His incoming phone buzzed again, another text.

who dis.

The call Dixon had been waiting for.

This one from the operator who called himself Big Dog.

A textbook sociopath, according to the psychological testing, but extremely talented in the field.

Dixon pulled the operator's number from his fractured memory and plugged it into the outgoing phone.

"You ain't gonna like this." Big Dog's voice had a Western twang that always made Dixon think of cowboys. But not in a good way.

"I already don't like it," Dixon said. "You lost four men. What now?"

"I tried again, but it didn't take. You know, with that bad apple? Turned out to be a really bad apple."

Dixon missed being a Marine colonel, where you could talk about killing people right out in the open. It was the whole job, when you boiled it down. When all else fails, call in an air strike, make some craters. Simpler days.

But he'd learned to speak obliquely a long time ago. About a great many things.

"Keep after it," he said. "One bad apple can spoil a whole barrel."

"How far you want me to go?"

"I thought you were a precision instrument," said Dixon. "Get rid of the apple. Keep the barrel."

"Yeah, that might be harder than you think."

Dixon knew how hard it would be.

But not impossible.

Big Dog was no slouch, either.

Dixon said, "I don't mind a few extra apples. Just make sure you get it done. But be discreet, understand? We don't need any more attention. There's already too much as it is."

"Roger that."

———

Daniel Clay Dixon had spent almost twenty-five years as a United States Marine. A veteran of two wars, he'd been awarded the Bronze Star for Combat Valor in Gulf I. As a young infantry lieutenant, he and his fire team had captured an Iraqi tank. He was a lieutenant colonel by the end, if only for a few weeks.

He was proud of that.

But he'd lost it all because of his own weakness, his own sinful and degenerate nature. Lost his wife and daughters and everyone else he loved. Lost his rank and command and pension. Lost his own self-respect, too, although that had happened long before.

Dixon considered himself a Southerner, a devout Christian, a life-long patriot, and an irredeemable homosexual. Not "gay," definitely not that, because to be gay implied a lightness of heart that Dixon had never felt, not since the summer he turned fourteen, when he spent those summer afternoons in Brad Spangler's rec room, damning his immortal soul to the flames of hell.

He'd not told anyone, of course. Not his friends on the football team or at his church. Not his pastor, who swayed at the rough pulpit, eyes rolled back in his head while God's tangled words spoke with his tongue. And definitely not Dixon's family.

His father might well have beaten him to death. If Dixon survived the beating, his mother would have banished him from her house. If the news got out, he'd have had to leave his school, his church, the town where he was born and raised. Abandon his whole life like a sinking ship. To be someone he despised? No.

To Dixon's surprise, God somehow remained a presence in his life, although Dixon only felt Him occasionally, peering over Dixon's shoulder from a great distance, rather than standing by Dixon's side each day. Dixon never heard His voice again, not after that summer.

Dixon knew he would surely be punished in the end.

He had done his best to redeem his sinful soul, to resist the temptations of the flesh. He became a warrior, joined the Marines, tested himself in combat, found a wife. He did his duty in the marital bed and tried not to drink himself to death, for the sake of his family.

He'd never accepted his hidden self, only burned with shame when his doomed homosexual soul forced itself to the surface for a few secret hours or days or, once, for two weeks in South Carolina ten years before, when he'd gone for a conference and a handsome bartender had winked at him on the second night.

The conference was a week of secret sinful bliss, but the bartender, whose name was Billy, invited Dixon to a little rented house on the ocean for the following week. Dixon, unable to resist, had called his wife and lied. It hadn't seemed like much, one more lie after so many.

He'd thought it would be like Billy's little apartment, just the two of them. But Billy had failed to mention that he'd also invited dozens of his friends. All men.

That first night's party had made Dixon supremely uncomfortable.

Until someone offered Dixon some white powder on a tiny silver spoon.

Dixon knew what it was, and what would happen, and he did it anyway.

They were so kind.

His soul was on vacation, too, he told himself. Just for this week. He was free.

And the world was changing, wasn't it? It was no longer illegal, to be what he was. In the eyes of his church, Dixon was still a sinner, destined for hell. But could it really be wrong in the eyes of God to feel this good? To feel like himself? He wondered, maybe, if he was strong enough to face himself, to become someone new.

When he went back to work at Camp Pendleton, he received a letter. Not from Billy the bartender, from someone else, someone he'd never met.

With photographs. Dixon with the silver spoon. Dixon naked with men. And a demand for payment.

That was how Dixon discovered that he wasn't strong after all.

He was the worst kind of sinner.

The kind that covered his sins with more sins.

He'd paid. And paid. And paid.

When he realized he could no longer spend his own money without his wife's knowledge, he arranged for the sale of a shrapnel-damaged Humvee to a collector. Then several cases of used M16s.

After that, they owned him.

Dixon learned it was possible to be in hell while still on earth.

After that, he got caught.

He narrowly escaped federal prison through some legal sleight of hand from his expensive private attorneys that seemed somehow shameful. But his debts were enormous beyond reckoning.

The legal fees had taken everything Dixon owned and would ever own for some time to come, it seemed. Early on, he'd told the attorneys there was no money left to pay them, but they'd kept working, racking up the billable hours. They told him there would be a colossal civil suit, he would pay them out of the proceeds. But the settlement that kept him out of prison also disallowed any civil action on his part. In the end, his own attorneys sued him for nonpayment.

He'd protected his wife from the debt through the divorce, but her losing his government medical benefits was far worse. She had a chronic immune disorder and couldn't work. Some days she couldn't get out of bed. Her treatments were frequent, painful, and expensive. Not to mention Dixon's youngest daughter applying to private colleges, his middle daughter at Notre Dame, and his eldest planning an elaborate wedding.

He owed his attorneys, but he owed his family more.

Daniel Clay Dixon was a man who paid his debts. He would do his duty.

Regardless of his many other failings before God, his family, and his country, Dixon could at least do that.

He'd only been an ex-Marine for two months when the call came.

Dixon had jumped at the opportunity.

He'd done far worse in the name of his country.

How could he not do this for his family?

15

The little red BMW was definitely the worse for wear, with a shattered rear windshield and two parallel creases across the hood where the rounds had made contact but not punched through.

Miranda took pictures with her phone. "For the insurance company," she said.

"You're going to need a police report, too."

"Paul Sykes will do it," she said. "He owes me."

Peter could only imagine.

He directed Miranda on an indirect route to his truck, which was parked down the block from Henry's place in Cap Hill. Miranda drove only slightly slower than she had before the shooting, barefoot again, her skirt hiked up to mid-thigh. But she kept checking her mirrors.

"How did they find us before?"

"Two possibilities," Peter said. "Either someone gave them a description of your car and told them when we left the hospital. Or they followed me down the mountain to the ER, waited in the parking lot, and tracked us from there."

"If it's the first, they might be real police."

"Yes," he said. "They took a big risk tonight. I didn't know anything. All I had was the back of the guy's head and a license plate. Which they didn't even know I had, and which might not even mean anything. To come after us like that, on the street? Willing to make such a public mess?" He shook his head. "Somebody fucked up," he said. "Fucked up big-time. And it looks like they'll do pretty much anything to make it go away."

"What you said before," she said. "About finding them. How will you do it?"

"How well do you know Steinburger and Sykes?"

She glanced at him. "I used to be a defense attorney, before I took this position with my current firm. So I know a lot of cops. I only had one case involving Steinburger, and he was very good at his job. A smart cop. That thing with the biker crew I told you about, that's how he made detective, and he's moved up the food chain pretty fast. But I can look into him a little more, make some calls."

She turned off Colfax by Voodoo Doughnut. Peter hadn't been inside. Maybe tomorrow, he thought. A heathy breakfast is the foundation of a productive day.

Although tomorrow was actually today. He yawned. What he really needed was a good night's sleep.

"And Sykes?"

She kept her eyes on the road. "Paul is more complicated. He doesn't mind bending the rules."

"And you have some history."

She gave a short, humorless laugh. "Yeah," she said. "You could say that."

"Tell me about it."

"No," she said. "It's not relevant."

"Okay," said Peter. "But maybe you'd look a little deeper into him, too. Past your personal knowledge. See what you can find out."

"What are you looking for?"

Peter had a bad experience with a detective, once upon a time.

"I want to know if I can trust them."

Cap Hill was an old city neighborhood working its way toward hipster respectability after decades of abuse and neglect. Its narrow streets lined with parked cars had a mix of ratty apartments, single-family row houses, and formerly grand homes near Cheesman Park now becoming grand again. The central location made it an easy bike or bus ride to LoDo, RiNo, Five Points, and other trendy neighborhoods.

Henry told Peter he'd bought the house because it was on a double lot with a driveway, rare in a city of alleys. Twenty years ago, he'd said, the neighborhood was still rough and cheap. He'd complained that Cap Hill was now only rough enough to get your car broken into, or your bicycle stolen off your porch. When Whole Foods moved in a few blocks away, Henry had considered total gentrification to be inevitable.

Peter and Miranda arrived at Henry's block.

Peter thought about asking her to circle while he looked for watchers, but didn't think the bad guys knew enough about him to know where he was staying, or what he was driving. Traffic had thinned out, and he hadn't seen anyone on their trail. If someone was following them now, it could only be by satellite or some kind of fucking drone, and he wasn't prepared to take steps to evade those.

Besides, he was too fucking tired. Between the city noise and the armed protection job with Heavy Metal, he hadn't had a decent night's sleep since getting to Denver. He just wanted to shower off his bloody day and crawl into the sack.

Although maybe he'd see if June was still awake first.

He pointed at his truck, parked on the street. "That's me."

She pulled up and peered out at the green 1968 Chevy pickup with the custom mahogany cargo box on the back. It hadn't been washed for a few months. "Jesus, really? You can pay my rates but you can't afford a new truck?"

He wasn't going to explain it to her. Finding it in a barn in central California, restoring it between deployments. The deep rumble of the engine followed the gearshift into the palm of his hand. The funky dog smell he couldn't quite get out of the heating system. It was the closest thing he had to a home.

He opened the door of the BMW and swung a leg out. "I'll call you in the morning," he said. "Dig into Steinburger and Sykes first thing. Or tonight, if you can't sleep."

She gave him a look with something else in it.

"Thanks again," he said, then got out of there.

He was way too tired to resist that futuristic sex-ray smile twice in one night.

16

enry's house was tall and square and more than a century old. It had an elaborate stone façade with a broad bow-front window and a small, ornate entry porch. Brick on the sides and back, parapet walls hiding the low tar-and-gravel roof, and a wide wood porch facing the deep rear yard.

After Henry had shown Peter the kitchen and bathroom and the beer fridge and the liquor cabinet, he'd said the only house rule was not to park in the narrow driveway because he hated to shuffle cars. Then amended the rule, and said when he was dead, Peter was welcome to park wherever he wanted.

It was funny at the time, when Peter had thought Henry would probably outlive the world.

Peter staying there was Henry's idea. He said he could use the company, and Peter believed him. Even if he hadn't, the big man wouldn't hear of Peter staying anywhere else, had given Peter a key, told him if he wasn't going to sleep indoors the least he could do was put the damn key on his ring like a civilized human being.

Peter had slung the hammock on the back porch.

He wasn't exactly sleeping well, though. Even when Henry was alive.

At first he told himself it was the noise of the city, the new environment. He'd spent so much time in the mountains that he'd become almost allergic to civilization. That was true, as far as it went. But he knew it was also the work, too much like the war. Spending his days wearing a ballistic vest and a pistol strapped to his hip, the AR-15 so familiar in his hand. The rough jangle of sleep deprivation just added another layer of muscle memory from his years of deployment.

He hadn't slept more than five hours a night since he'd come to Denver.

With the kind of day he'd had, he wasn't sure how well he'd sleep tonight, either.

He parked in the driveway, took an old waxed canvas duffel with his spare clothes from the mahogany cargo box, and let himself through the gate to the backyard. His plan was to take a long, hot shower to get the blood off, then send a text to June. Maybe she was still awake. She was on Pacific time, after all, and also a night owl.

But at the back porch, Henry's door stood open.

All the lights were off.

Peter sighed.

It was after midnight now. Too goddamn late for this shit, whatever the time.

And whoever was inside already knew Peter was there, from the rumble of his truck. It wasn't exactly a stealth vehicle.

In Fallujah they'd cleared buildings one by one, in platoons and squads and fire teams, the whole fucking city, the point man first through the door with the rest of the team filling in behind to check cover and adjoining rooms for gunmen and booby traps. The point man was the most likely to get shot or blown up. Peter had taken his turn at point with the rest of them, Lieutenant Ash leading from the front. High as a kite on adrenaline and fear for himself and the men at his back.

Don, the therapist he'd been talking to in Eugene, thought Peter's claustrophobia came from those long days and weeks, his body and mind highly tuned to that hazardous indoor environment.

Now the white static sparked its electric agreement.

The pistol Henry had loaned him for work was now in police custody. Peter had wanted to believe he was done with firearms since the war. But somehow he still found himself, time and again, with a gun in his hand.

He wished he had one now.

The moon was a sharp sliver. The neighbors' security lights were dimmed by the big black maple trees in Henry's backyard.

Peter set his bag gently on the driveway and walked barefoot through the shadow past Henry's boxy old travel trailer to the rebuilt garage, where a box of scrap lumber sheltered under the eaves, kindling for the fireplace.

Henry had originally bought the house as a rental because he moved around so much for work. When he retired, he'd moved in and started renovating. Henry was the first to admit that he always needed a project, something to keep him busy.

Peter understood perfectly.

It only took a few seconds to find an old railing baluster, a spindle about thirty inches long, tapered in a smooth elegant curve from three-quarters of an inch at one end to an inch and a quarter at the other. Longer than a baton, but more mobile than a baseball bat. The hard oak gave it a nice weight.

It wouldn't be the cops, sitting there in the dark. Steinburger and Sykes would turn on all the lights, sit at the table, move right in. If they had to wait long enough, they'd make a pot of coffee and raid the fridge. Henry was dead, after all.

Maybe the trooper had found the house, or there was another player Peter didn't know about, someone less professional. Leaving the back door standing open wasn't something a pro would do. Either way, Peter would get to work off some of the extra aggression from his day.

Peter twirled the baluster as he walked toward the house.

For the third time that day, he tasted copper in his mouth. The fatigue fell away. The adrenaline rose and propelled him forward, floating frictionless and barefoot through the darkness. Risk and reward. Alive, alive.

Who wouldn't love this feeling?

Up three silent steps, a pause to listen, then through the open back door to the connected kitchen and dining room, the big farmhouse table wiped down and dishes put away, Henry a man of meticulous habits.

Nobody there. Peter's heart thumped, blood thrummed through his veins.

Off the dining area was a dark hall to the living room, the winding stairs to the second floor and basement, and the spare bedroom Henry used as an office, its door ajar. Peter stepped through the open doorway, baluster raised and ready to strike.

The office was empty. The papers sat neatly squared on the heavy desk, the computer screen unlit. Curtains blocked most of the streetlight. Peter stalked the perimeter of the room where the old floor was less likely to squeak. The closet was empty. The attached bathroom was empty, the glass shower doors concealing nothing.

He peeked through the next door to the living room. The thin blinds were down but pale from municipal glow.

Someone was slouched on Henry's oversized couch, feet up on the coffee table.

Henry's daughter, Elle Hansen, staring right at him.

17

The adrenaline drained out of Peter like his throat had been cut.

"The kids are at my sister-in-law's," she said. Quietly, as if Henry were asleep upstairs instead of on a slab at the morgue. She wore old jeans with torn knees and a Colorado School of Mines hoodie, her hands tucked into the kangaroo pocket. "They have no idea what's going on. What's happened to their father, now their grandfather. And I don't, either. The police were no help."

Peter lowered the baluster, heart slowing in his chest, surprised at how badly he'd wanted some kind of fight. He needed to go for a long run, or find a heavy bag to pound out this fury and aggression.

Or maybe just get some sleep.

"I'm sorry," he said. "Your dad was a good friend."

"That's not why I'm here."

She produced a small chrome pistol from the pocket of her sweatshirt. She didn't point it at him, not exactly, but she held it comfortably, finger outside the trigger guard, so Peter knew she'd had some training. Her face was calm but set. Her father's daughter.

"Who the hell are you, Peter Ash?"

He didn't know what conversation he was expecting, but this wasn't it. He told himself her anger was standing in for grief. She'd lost her husband and her father, he was going to cut her all the slack she needed. But it was late, and he was tired.

He bent carefully and leaned the baluster against the windowsill. He hadn't been this tired since Iraq. He didn't think he had any adrenaline left.

"You ran a background check," he said. "You know all about me."

"I know your driver's license is expired and your credit is good and you have no criminal record," she said. "I also know an Army major who works in personnel at the Pentagon. He pulled your file. There's nothing there but postings and commendations, the rest redacted or removed. You're a ghost."

He smiled politely. "You remember I brought that money back, right?"

"I do remember, and I'm grateful, believe me. But I want to know how you ended up here."

"You already know. Your dad and I worked together. He told you about me. He asked for my help."

"How did you get a lawyer so fast?"

"On the way down from that mountain, after I called you, I texted a friend. Asked him to find me a lawyer. She showed up, I never met her before."

"I need more than that," she said.

"That's all I've got," he said, turning back toward Henry's office. "Shoot me later, okay?"

"I'm not going to shoot you," she said, putting the gun away. "We need to talk."

"I'm getting in the shower. We'll talk tomorrow."

Peter had been using the office bathroom. He was working to adjust to the small space, training himself to resist his own reflexes, to breathe through the static, but he still didn't like to close the door.

Leaving the lights off, he turned the water to full hot and began to strip out of the secondhand clothes Miranda had brought for him.

"We need to have a conversation." Elle stood behind him. It was easy to forget the size of her, slouched on the couch. Standing in the doorway, she filled it, almost as tall as Peter, with broad shoulders under that hoodie. A formidable woman.

Peter was leaning against the counter, trying to peel the weird elastic jeans from his oversized hiker's calves. He still wore no underwear. If she wanted to shoot him, now was the time. "Do you mind?"

"Are you kidding?" She looked him full in the face. "I've got three boys under the age of six. I see way too many penises in the course of my day already. Believe me, yours is nothing special."

Peter was a guy, so he'd always felt his penis was something special. But he didn't say anything. The room was dark and the shower partition was already steamed up. He awkwardly finished extracting himself from the jeans, opened the opaque glass door, and stepped inside for some privacy.

Henry had replaced all the plumbing in the house and drilled out the little flow-reducing disks in the showerheads. The water pressure was enough to peel the skin off his body, which was pretty much what Peter was looking for. To be out of his skin.

"I met Randy at a bar the day after he finished basic training," she said, her voice carrying over the sound of the shower. "I was an eighteen-year-old good-time girl, and Randy was a *very* good time. Then he got deployed and I found out I was pregnant. I dropped out of college and we got married over Skype. Every time he came home on leave, I got pregnant again. My friends called me Fertile Myrtle. I had to grow up in a hurry. Before I knew it, I had three little kids and any hope of college was long gone. Randy came and went, redeployed, reassigned. I stayed in Denver. My mom helped out some until she got lung cancer at forty-five. Then it was just me and the kids."

Peter soaped up as she talked, then scrubbed his face and neck with a washcloth. Harder than he needed to, maybe. He was glad it was too dark to see the color of the water.

"When Randy came home for good, he carried a headful of memories he was trying hard to forget. He spent his time out partying with his buddies or alone in the basement playing video games. Doing anything but face the next war, the war called 'grow up and change some diapers and get a goddamn job.' And I didn't blame him," she said. "I really didn't. I knew it would take time before he could get his shit together. But while he was trying to outrun his memories, I was walking the floor with a crying baby at two a.m., watching the money run out, trying to figure out how we were going to survive."

Peter knew this story. A lot of guys had trouble figuring out how they fit back into their old life, or imagining the new one. Peter was one of them. He was still trying to figure it out. Maybe he'd always be trying. The static didn't help. It was there now, even in the darkened shower, that dissonant discomfort just past the edge of hearing. It made him more alert, that tension. Part of him liked it.

"Then a friend of my mom's, who ran a little medical grow, got held up at gunpoint. He called me to ask if Randy might come along on his next cash run, offered two hundred dollars for an hour's work with a pistol on his belt. They had just voted to legalize recreational, and I saw how things could be. All those new businesses, all that cash, banks unwilling to touch the money, people getting robbed, it was like seeing the future. I called my dad, and he pitched in pretty well for an old guy who barely knew he had a daughter. He was the one who helped me figure out who to hire and how to get the job done. He loaned us the money for day care, so Randy could work protection and I could drive around finding clients."

He could see her shadow through the glass, oversized in the small room.

Now Peter understood what she was doing there.

"It's not Randy's business," Peter said over the top of the glass. "It's yours."

"You're goddamn right it's mine," she said, her voice echoing off the hard tile. "I built it working eighteen-hour days with my kids at the sitter's or on my lap or in the backyard. This was our lifeline, the only chance we were going to get. My husband had the operational skills and the résumé, but I made it happen."

She was pacing now, back and forth.

"And it brought Randy back to life, you know? The work felt important and immediate. It gave him a clear mission, a reason to get out of bed. My idea was working. After eighteen months, we had thirty employees. I hired Leonard as our new operations manager, everybody was making money. I could see it laid out, the three-year plan, the five-year plan, the ten-year plan. Diversification, real estate, investment."

"Until Randy disappeared," Peter said. "Then you called your dad, who came to the rescue again. Now he's dead, too."

She didn't say anything.

Peter kept talking.

"He's only been gone, what, six hours? So why are you here, talking to me, in the middle of the night?"

But he already knew the answer.

"My lawyer tells me you're dangerous," she said. "I should put you on unpaid leave until things get straightened out. After that, he says I should fire you. But I don't want to do either of those things. My husband is gone. I've lost Leonard, I've lost my dad. I need somebody to head up operations, to keep us doing the job we're hired to do, protecting our clients. And you've proven yourself extremely effective at that."

Peter turned off the water. He'd soaped and scrubbed three times. His head was still sore from the wreck, and his lungs were tight from the static. He cracked the shower door and reached for a towel. "You don't have any other guys?"

"Not the right ones," she said. "After Leonard vanished, my best guys were Deacon and Banjo and my dad. That's why they were on that big run with you. I need a leader of men."

She was sweating in the steam, strands of hair plastered to her neck and forehead. Looking right at him.

"What about my empty file, at the Pentagon? You're not worried about that anymore?"

"Recon Marine with a Silver Star? Who protected the client's profits with his heroic recent actions on the mountain?" She looked at him now, tall and lean and ropy, the towel wrapped around his waist. He felt like a horse getting his teeth checked at auction. Elle seemed older than her twenty-five years. "You'll do just fine," she said. "There'll be a pay raise, of course."

"Of course." Peter stepped past her, out of the bathroom, leaving wet footprints through the office and the kitchen to the back porch, where his skin steamed in the cool, dry night air. His old canvas duffel still sat in shadow on the driveway. He felt his lungs open up again, and the tension in his shoulders began to ease. The damp towel began to cool around his waist.

She came through the door behind him. "We can discuss the

money," she said. "For now, can we agree that you're coming to work in the morning? There's a lot to do."

"I have to meet the police," he said. "I don't know how long that will take."

"My phone is filled with voice mails from reporters," she said. "Coverage could be very good for the company, depending on how it's presented. Are you comfortable talking to the press?"

Peter wasn't going to talk to anyone but that trooper, real or fake.

"How will you spin my empty Pentagon file?"

She shrugged. "It's classified," she said. "You can't talk about it. From a public relations standpoint, it's actually a plus."

He thought of what Henry might have been like at her age, especially if he hadn't been carrying the burden of his war. Smart, capable, driven. She couldn't do anything about her missing husband or her dead father, so she was moving forward in the best way she knew.

He thought about what she'd said when she'd hired him. Three kids to feed and thirty men relying on her for a paycheck.

He doubted she needed him, but she thought she did.

He'd help if he could.

For Henry.

As long as it didn't get in the way of his main project.

She touched him on his bare shoulder, her fingers warm on his rapidly cooling skin.

"We'll talk about it," she said. "I'll call you tomorrow."

She walked past him toward the back gate, trailing a hand behind her. He felt the softest tug at the fabric wrapped at his waist. He heard the click of the latch on the closing gate at the exact moment his towel dropped to the ground.

Shit, he was definitely awake now.

18

The lightweight hammock June had sent him was one of the best gifts he'd ever received. It was so light he never felt it in his pack, and she'd included a rain fly to hang over it on wet nights, although he hadn't needed it much so far. It was his new favorite way to sleep alone.

Sleeping with June was his favorite way to sleep. Although in those few nights together, he had to admit there hadn't been much actual sleep.

Five nights, he thought. That's what they'd had, back in March.

Now, in late September, he hoped those five nights were enough to build something solid on.

He dug a T-shirt and some boxers out of his old canvas duffel, then slung the hammock between Henry's porch posts as he'd done the last three nights. He pushed back through the static long enough to raid the liquor cabinet and pour four fingers of Henry's good Bulleit bourbon into a heavy glass tumbler.

He took a burning gulp of liquid courage before he picked up Henry's phone. Suck it up, Marine. He'd written more than a half dozen letters to her, each more than a half dozen pages, but he hadn't spoken with her in person since spring.

He chickened out with a text.

This is Peter with a borrowed phone. Are you awake?

He'd always tried to keep his texts more or less grammatically correct, but he tried even harder with June, because she'd been an investigative reporter for almost ten years. She was also a night owl who kept odd hours, and it was an hour earlier in Washington State. So she could still be awake.

Before he could get properly settled into the hammock, Henry's phone rang, loud in the late-night quiet. Peter very nearly spilled his drink, scrambling to answer. "Hey."

"Is this a booty call?" she asked. "If it is, I might need to change out of these sweatpants."

In his mind, he could see clearly the smirk on her face, the spray of freckles across the tops of her cheeks. In his mind, she wasn't wearing sweatpants. She was either wearing her battered old mountain pants and hiking boots, or nothing at all.

"No," he said. "I called to tell you I was propositioned twice today."

"Gosh, you must be tired."

He smiled. "You have no idea."

He pictured her wide, generous mouth, the long, narrow nose. The bright heat of intelligence in her eyes.

"I'm guessing this isn't really a booty call," she said.

He took another bite of bourbon. Might as well get to it.

"Listen, did you get my postcard?"

"Actually, it came today," she said. Her tone was different. "But it didn't say much. Do you think you'll be able to make it up here?"

She was being careful now. They both were.

They'd made no promises to each other. They hadn't spent enough time together, before. Now it was all too theoretical. Their letters crossing paths in the night.

He knew there was something between them, something real.

But it felt fragile.

"I really want to see you," he said. "I mean that. This was just supposed to be a quick detour. Favor for a friend. But something's happened."

She heard it in his voice. "Tell me."

He let out his breath. "Remember Henry? From the trail crew?"

"Your friend," she said. "The bridge builder. Vietnam vet."

"Right," Peter said. "Henry's daughter runs a little security company in Denver. Her husband and another guy went missing with a pile of money, and Henry asked me to come help out for a little while, just a week or so." He took a slow breath and let it out. "Today, some people tried to hijack a cash delivery. And Henry got killed, along with two other guys I know."

The phone went silent for a moment, the way they did when nobody was talking. He hated that eerie digital silence. Sometimes it sounded like the other person had hung up.

"That's not all of it," she said. "Tell me the rest."

"Well," he said. Cleared his throat, swirled the liquor in the glass.

"What, you were there?" He heard the scrape of a chair on the floor, then her fingers clicking on a keyboard. A simple web search would be enough. He heard the sharp intake of her breath. "Holy shit."

"Yeah," he said. "I was there."

"Jesus, these pictures," she said. "Are you okay? Did you get hurt?"

"I'm fine," he said. "Just talking to you, I'm fine."

There was a pause. Then, "The *Post* says four hijackers were killed."

"Yeah." He felt the tug in the long muscles of his left arm. The hot spray in his face.

"Listen, Peter," she said. "No bullshit here. I know who you are, okay? What you can do. What you were trained to do. I've seen it up close. Are you really going to make me ask?"

He'd forgotten how strong she was.

"No." The glass was heavy in his hand, but he didn't take a drink. No excuses. "I killed all of them. Four bad guys. One with a knife." He felt it welling up.

"Oh, Peter," she said.

"I couldn't save Henry," he said. "I tried, but I couldn't save him."

"Sometimes you can't," she said. "It's not your fault, Peter. You can't save them all."

Something in her voice.

Not pity. Never pity, not from June Cassidy. And not fear, or disgust, which were what he'd worried about the most.

Something else. Maybe some kind of understanding. Some kind of grace.

He felt the weight begin to lift off his chest.

"Was it bad?" she asked quietly.

"Yes."

"You were protecting your friends?"

"Yes."

"Did you have a choice?"

"No."

"It was you or them?"

"Yes."

Her voice was gentle. "You get to choose you, Peter. It's okay to choose you."

"Yeah," he said. "I know."

And he did. Right then, he did.

————

"**So what are you going** to do?" she finally asked.

"What I did for you," he said. "Find out who's responsible. Solve the problem."

"Isn't that what the police are for?"

"There's a possibility some police are involved."

"Fuck," she said.

"Yeah. And the police have limits," he said. "Things they can't do. I have more, ah, freedom of movement. And I'm good at this. Remember?"

She sighed. "You are such a fucking cowboy jarhead *asshole*."

"That's not how I think about it," he said. "You know who I am, remember? Since the day we met."

"Can't you just come here?" she asked, her voice thickening. It was catching up to her now, what had happened. The pictures she'd seen online.

"You don't mean that," he said. "Do you?"

"Yes, I do," she said. "I really fucking do."

"Henry was my friend," he said. "I have to help. Besides, you're the one who sent me away."

"Yeah," she said. "To get better. To learn to sleep inside. Not get yourself fucking killed."

"That wasn't exactly clear at the time," he said.

"That's because you're fucking stupid."

"Yes," he agreed. "I'm definitely stupid."

She sighed. He heard the thump as she set the phone down, then a wet honk as she blew her nose.

He loved her. That was the thing. It hadn't even taken the five days. He'd known after a few hours, watching her drive full-tilt in her old Subaru down that winding gravel road in California. Or maybe earlier. Sometimes you just know.

What he didn't know was more complicated.

Could she love him back?

"**All right, Marine**," June said, coming back on the line. "Tell me how to help."

She was definitely tough. He said, "I was hoping you could put on your investigative journalist hat."

"I *knew* this wasn't a booty call. What do you need?"

"This was a very specific style of attack," he said. "I want to know about any other marijuana-related robberies in Colorado. Actually, make it the Mountain West and West Coast. Whether it's outright legal or just medicinal. If there are any missing persons, any mention of a tow truck or ambulance involved in the robbery. I have a license plate for the police car, a Dodge Charger." He told her the number. "I'd love to know where that comes from. And some deeper background on the people involved, the company owners and my friends. Maybe this was a personal thing." He gave her the names.

"Okay," she said. "Two things from me. One, have you talked to Lewis?"

"He's coming in the morning, early flight."

"Good," she said. "I'm coming, too."

"No," he said. "Definitely not." He wasn't going to tell her they'd already tried to kill him a second time.

"You might need a getaway driver," she said. "Besides, it's not your call. You've obviously forgotten that I'm the boss."

She'd hired him to protect her, back in March. His fee had been ten dollars a week.

"I never got paid for the last time."

"Oh, you got paid, Marine."

He smiled. "I was hoping I could be the boss this time," he said.

She snorted. "Oh, hell no. It takes a woman to run these things."
He heard the wicked smile in her voice. "Plus you know I like to be
on top."

"I do seem to recall," he said. "Is that two things?"

"That was one thing," she said. "It was kind of a long thing."

"Are you talking dirty now?"

"Not yet," she said. "Trust me, you'll know. But here's the second
thing. Did you really get propositioned twice today?"

"Why, yes," he said. "I'm a very attractive man, you know."

"Were they both women?" she asked.

He grinned. "In fact, they were. One is my attorney. The other was
a nurse dressing my wounds."

"Well, you stay away from those bitches, you hear me?"

"Yes, ma'am," Peter said. "You're the boss."

"Thaaat's what I like to hear."

It was well after two when they got off the phone.

Peter left the bourbon unfinished on the porch railing.

Steinburger and Sykes woke him before first light.

19

From his fancy hammock, Peter blinked up at the pair of policemen.

Sykes carried two very tall cardboard cups of coffee. He bent gracefully and set one on the porch floor beside Peter. He wore fresh clothes, jeans, and a black Rockies T-shirt under a black synthetic shell, but he looked, if anything, even more tired. "Time to go," he said, and nudged the hammock with the toe of his running shoe. "Get dressed."

It was still dark out.

Steinburger wore the same brown suit from the night before, or maybe it was a different but identical suit. He picked up the squat, heavy glass from the porch rail and took a sniff of the inch of liquor that remained.

"Bourbon?"

Peter nodded. He was still zipped inside his sleeping bag, although he was waking up fast. Steinburger swirled the glass, took a sip, raised his eyebrows. "Not bad."

Sykes looked at him. "For real?"

Steinburger shrugged. "Shit, Paul, it's too early to count as morning. The sun isn't even up yet."

Sykes shook his head, but he popped the top off his coffee and poured some bourbon into the cup.

"Good to see you guys are committed to top performance," Peter said. Three hours' sleep, he figured. All he was going to get. The birds were already making a racket.

Steinburger pulled a folding knife out of his right pants pocket and opened it with the thumb stud. It had a matte-black handle and a black-finish serrated blade, and Peter'd had one almost exactly like it, until the hijacker took it from him.

"Rise and shine," Steinburger said, holding the knife to the hammock's sling strap. "Or I'm cutting you down."

"What is this, the Royal Navy?" Peter unzipped his bag and swung his bare legs down to the cool porch floor. "Should I be calling my lawyer?"

"Absolutely," said Sykes. He took Henry's phone from the railing, unplugged its charger, and handed the phone to Peter. "Knock yourself out. But this isn't that kind of visit."

Steinburger tossed back the remains of the bourbon, wiped his mustache with the heel of his hand, and set the glass down with a thump. "We'd like to show you something," he said. "Come on, move your ass." He pointed the knife at the coffee cup Sykes had set on the porch floor. "That's yours. Get dressed."

Peter made sure to put on comfortable clothes, including his old combat boots.

The dark was beginning to fade when they put him in the back seat of a big unmarked Ford Crown Vic. There was a time not long ago when being in the back seat would have set off the static. It still wasn't comfortable, particularly not in a police car.

But there was no grate or partition blocking off the front, so Peter sat forward with his arms folded on the seatback, drinking his coffee, shaking off yet another short night's sleep, watching the light come up on the wide city streets through the big windshield.

Steinburger drove with expert speed, lights but no siren, and thin early traffic moved out of his way. They were headed to a part of town Peter hadn't seen before. Denver was a city on the Plains, but his eye kept finding the Front Range rising up to the west like a rampart against the barbarians.

They came over the freeway and railroad tracks into the northeast corner of the city. New tilt-up concrete slab buildings with fresh paint, older brick warehouses with offices tacked on like afterthoughts. Signs for wholesale roofing and sheet metal, a corporate distribution center, cannabis cultivation supplies, multiple trucking depots. Wide streets designed for semis, with aggressive drainage for the heavy storms that came down from the Rockies.

Sykes handed back a stained paper bag. "Bagel and cream cheese," he said. "To go with the coffee. Although you might want to wait until after."

"After what?" asked Peter.

Steinburger turned onto a side street of smaller buildings from an earlier time. He came to a stop at a deep, narrow lot, vacant but for tall brown grass and a rutted gravel track curling behind a rusting metal prefab shed the size of a two-car garage. The gravel track was partially blocked by a Denver Police SUV. Some development site awaiting financing, or the arrival of the first local Starbucks.

Steinburger rolled his window down to raise his hand to the officer standing guard, who nodded and waved him past.

Peter could smell it already.

Steinburger eased the cruiser down the dirt drive and behind the shed, where a pair of Tyvek-suited techs stood waiting beside their van.

Sykes opened Peter's door. "Out," he said. "Take a good look."

Peter stepped carefully across the gravel to the big American sedan with a familiar profile. It was a blackened shell, paint crackled off the sheet-metal skin, the frame warped from the heat. The glass had melted. It would have been difficult to identify the burnt item sitting upright in the back seat as actual human remains, except for the grinning skull atop the dark column of spine.

The smell was unmistakable, deeply lodged in Peter's memory from his years at war. Burned plastic and something like roasted pork, made worse because you knew it was human flesh. It stuck in the nose and back of the throat like a physical thing. Not like the corruption smell of a two-week-old corpse, but somehow not that different, either.

The brain knew what it knew.

Death was death.

Peter looked closer and saw that the seat buckles were connected, the diagonal remains of the strap melted, sagging but still visible. The man had been belted in. Something about that was especially disturbing.

The trunk yawned open. Peter stepped around and saw the remains of three more bodies tucked into the trunk. They lay on their sides, their contours aligned, their limbs entwined like lovers.

The man in the trooper's uniform had come down the mountain with his dead. He'd driven them around the city. Had probably stopped for dinner while Peter went fifteen rounds with the cops. Then chased Peter and Miranda with the corpses of his comrades in his car.

Steinburger loomed behind him. "These crispy critters ring any bells for you?"

They were different now, Steinburger and Sykes. Last night they'd been professional, exacting, thorough. Good cops on good behavior with an attorney present, still sorting through what might have happened, with only the red wrecker and Henry's truck and Peter's story to guide them.

Now they were less controlled, though still not sloppy. They were tired and angry, powered by caffeine and a deep desire to know what had happened, their human selves peering through their official masks.

The burned car had changed something.

Peter wondered if that meant the car was a real police car, the state trooper a real trooper.

"I don't know what to say," Peter said. "Tell me what happened here."

"Us tell you?" Steinburger asked, rounding on Peter, the remains of his placid civil-servant façade now entirely fallen away. "That's not how this works, fuckhead." He stepped in close and tapped Peter hard on the sternum with one thick finger. Peter could smell the bourbon and coffee on his breath. "We don't tell you. You tell us. So what the fuck happened up there? Was this the car up on that mountain?"

"How do I know if this was the car?" asked Peter. "It's all burned up. I don't even know what color it used to be."

But he knew.

Sykes was watching him. Sykes knew, too.

"Let's try this," Sykes said. "A citizen called in a report of a red BMW sedan being chased by a police car, with shots fired. The police car is reported as unmarked, no light bar on the roof but flashers on the grille and back window." Sykes's eyes gleamed amid the planes of his dark face. "Detective Steinburger and I happened to see you drive off in a red fucking BMW. And this burned-up car here, this has every appearance of being a fucking police car. Unmarked, no light bar. Flashers in the grille and rear window."

"So this is a police car?" asked Peter. "Do you have any reported stolen, or otherwise unaccounted for?"

Steinburger took a deep breath, then let it out. He smoothed his mustache with his hand. "I think there are a few details you've neglected to share with us. That's the impression I'm getting here. In fact," he said, "I think you're a regular shit magnet. Wouldn't you agree, Investigator Sykes?"

"Yes, Detective Steinburger. I agree completely."

"In fact, I think the shit magnet should come downtown with us for some more conversation. Best case, he's handcuffed to a chair by my desk for a few hours while we work this out."

"Or cooling his heels in an interview room," said Sykes. "That'd be the next step. Locked door, cuffed to a ring bolt on the table. More secure, really."

"He's a dangerous character," said Steinburger. "By his own admission. He killed four people less than twelve hours ago."

"Those rooms are pretty small," said Sykes. "No windows. Ceiling kinda low."

"After that, of course, the next step is a holding cell. Bigger room, but filled with some not-so-nice people."

"He can take care of himself," said Sykes. "Tough guy like that? He's not scared of the Mexican Mafia."

Steinburger nodded. "But maybe he's tired, what with killing all those people last night. So that interview room is probably best. Small, safe, secure. Waiting while we call his lawyer."

"Although sometimes that can take a while. Maybe she gets sent to a district station by mistake."

"Or the desk sergeant can't find the paperwork. It happens."

Just listening to the conversation, Peter could feel the static crawling up his brainstem.

He said, "You guys practice this routine, or improvise as you go?"

They just looked at him, utterly without mirth. Pale, looming Steinburger in his baggy brown suit, beside lean, dark Sykes in his fitted black shell jacket, both of them cops to the bone.

Peter was stalling. They knew it.

It was only a matter of time.

If they went to look at Miranda's car—hell, if all they did was call his lawyer and she drove up to the precinct—they'd see the creases in the hood, the bullet hole in the rear window.

If she showed up in a rental, they'd ask about it.

And she'd tell the truth. She was an officer of the court. She wasn't about to lie to the police, not for him. Not with four dead bodies in a burned-up car.

For all she knew, he'd done it.

And Peter's path to find the people who'd killed Henry was gone with this burned-up car, and these dead bodies.

Which was maybe why they'd done it. Whoever they were.

"Okay," he said. "The car on the mountain was dressed up like an unmarked car. No light bar, but it had flashers like this one. State plates." He gave them the number from memory. Sykes wrote them in his notebook. "The fifth man, the one who got away?" He looked at Sykes now. "Wore a state police uniform. Pale blue shirt, darker blue pants, that Smokey the Bear hat with the flat brim. He was directing traffic around what they worked hard to make look like an accident, the ambulance and tow truck already on the scene."

Sykes's face was serene and composed. "And you chose not to share that information," he said. "Why?"

Peter shrugged. "I've had mixed experiences with law enforcement," he said. "I wasn't sure I trusted either of you. The guy looked like a state trooper. And I don't know how he found us again last night, unless he had help."

"I don't like your tone," Steinburger said.

Sykes patted at the air with both hands, an attempt at keeping things calm. "We know it's not a patrol car," he said. "We'll know for sure when we pull the VIN off the engine block, but it doesn't have any of the gear that a state police vehicle would have. No dashboard camera, no computer stand or shotgun rack, no puke-proof back seat, no sergeant in the trunk."

At Peter's curious look, Sykes explained, "A 'sergeant in the trunk' is what we call the location hardware, so the supervisors know where the car is at all times. But it's not a police cruiser. Anyone can buy those lights. The security guard at the mall has those lights."

"What about the license plate," said Peter. "Is the plate real?"

"Probably from a different state-owned vehicle," said Sykes. "The DNR or something. We'll know soon enough."

Steinburger pushed his breath out, shaking his head. "Okay, hot-shot. What the fuck else haven't you told us?"

"Well," Peter said, "I was thinking. The payday for both robberies would have been just over a half million dollars, right?"

Sykes cocked his head. "What about it?"

Peter shrugged. "It doesn't seem like enough money," he said. "This is a big operation, well planned and ruthless. Three vehicles and five people. They disappeared Randy and Leonard on the first run, and were going to do the same to the four of us yesterday."

"What's your point?" Steinburger was clearly annoyed but interested despite himself.

"For both robberies, five men, that's about a hundred grand each. For six murders? That's a lot of risk, and not much reward."

"Are you kidding?" Steinburger said. "You go to the state prison in Cañon City, you can buy a hit for an ice cream sandwich."

Peter shook his head. "These were professionals," he said. "Something else is going on here."

Steinburger and Sykes looked at each other for a long moment. Some unspoken communication between them.

Then Steinburger nodded and Sykes stepped away and pulled out his phone. Steinburger waved a meaty hand in the air and a uniformed officer hustled over.

Steinburger said, "Get this man out of my crime scene. Mr. Ash, try not to kill anyone for the rest of the morning. I'll see you downtown at noon."

That was when Peter understood they meant to use him as bait.

He didn't mind.

Peter had plans of his own.

20

The uniformed officer escorted him away from the clinging stink of the four burned-up bodies in the burned-up car.

They walked up the winding dirt track through the tall grass of the vacant lot to the street, where Peter stood a few feet from the police SUV guarding the scene, looking up and down the road, acutely aware that Steinburger and Sykes were dangling him like a worm on a hook.

Henry's phone buzzed in his pocket.

A text from June. *Got a minute?*

She answered after a single ring.

"You're some kind of trouble magnet, you know that?"

He smiled, just hearing her voice. "So I've been told. How'd you sleep?"

"I didn't, much," she said. "I did some digging instead." Because of her association with Public Investigations, a deep-dive journalism nonprofit run by and for refugees from the slow death of newspapers, June had access to a number of subscription-only databases.

He heard her yawn. "Heavy Metal Protection has never been hit before last week. Their financials seem pretty robust for a new business, although these hijackings will certainly change that. And there have been no other major marijuana-related armed robberies reported west of the Mississippi."

"Nothing?" He couldn't quite believe it. Almost the entire cannabis economy operated in cash.

"Oh, there's plenty of small stuff," she said. "Stickups and smash-and-grabs, spread out all over the West. A few people have been killed, thieves and employees both, although it looks pretty rare. Most of the journalists covering this stuff seem to think there's probably a lot more crime that doesn't get reported, because the cops are bad for business, legal weed or not. But I can't find anything with the size and scope of this one."

"So you're telling me there's no vast crime ring of professional dope money thieves."

Hearing only Peter's side of the conversation, the uniformed officer gave him a look.

Peter stepped away from the patrol car as June said, "Dope money is the best kind of money to steal, because criminals can't call the cops. Cannabis legalization is supposed to help solve that, but until they get the feds on board, that cash will always be a temptation. But it doesn't look like that's what's happening here. Lewis heard back from his contact at the Department of Defense about the guys you worked with. He forwarded me their official files."

"Lewis has a contact at the DoD?"

"Lewis has contacts everywhere," June said. "Anyway, Randall Hansen, a minority owner of Heavy Metal Protection Inc., has no criminal record other than a single DUI two years ago. His Army file shows an honorable discharge as a PFC, a few commendations, nothing outstanding, nothing horrible. His commanding officer's comments were lukewarm."

"How many deployments?"

"Two."

And he didn't even make corporal?

Most guys, when they signed up for war and landed in the infantry, had no idea what they were getting into. Most took a step forward and worked hard to learn the job and do it well, take out some bad guys, and protect their friends.

Others just tried really hard not to get killed.

Randy seemed like a guy trying not to get killed.

Shows how well that approach worked out.

Although Peter wasn't one to talk. He'd started out a lieutenant, and had remained a lieutenant for eight years. Albeit for very different reasons.

"What about his wife, Eleanor Hansen?"

"She owns fifty-one percent of the company, to her husband's forty-nine. She's got a single drunk and disorderly, back before she got married, and something like two hundred parking tickets, mostly since the business took off. Other than that, she's clean."

"What about the other guys?"

"Your friend Henry did two tours in Vietnam, no police record, not even a speeding ticket. Parents deceased, three ex-wives, a sister in Minneapolis, Eleanor his only child. He owned his house free and clear, and had enough in the bank for a modest retirement."

"That sounds about right," Peter said.

"Deacon Jones, thirty-four years old, was a highly decorated soldier, including a pair of Purple Hearts. Also maybe an anger management problem. There were discipline issues noted in his file but by all reports he was an excellent sergeant. His father was a minister, his mother a housewife. His wife divorced him after his second deployment. He has no criminal record and died with money in the bank."

Peter thought of Deacon looking at Peter out of the corner of his eye, readying himself to jump the hijackers. Deacon who had switched to nonalcoholic beer. Deacon who had a new girlfriend, and had just bought a house in Aurora.

"And Banjo?"

"David Fleck, lieutenant, twenty-seven. Genuine war hero, multiple commendations including a Bronze Star and a Purple Heart. An English major at Kentucky. Came from a prominent family in Lexington, could have chosen to do a lot of things with his life. Apparently he told the recruiter he wanted to join the Army to pay it forward."

That sounded like Banjo. Peter had imagined him ending up running an organic farm or some damn thing. Hands in the dirt, feeding people.

"Leonard Wallis, now, he's a different story," said June. "The other guys, their lives are open books. They're all over social media, even your friend Henry, who kept up with his ex-wives on Facebook. Paper trails a mile long, military records go back forever. A sharpshooter badge in basic training, dysentery in Ramadi. This guy Wallis, he has what looks like a relatively normal financial history, given that he was in the Army for twenty years. A couple of credit cards, a loan on a Dodge Durango. But his Army record is basically empty."

"What does that mean?"

"It means, aside from his photo and basic details of his units and postings, there's nothing there. Cleaned and sanitized. No fingerprint card, and according to Lewis's source, the DNA sample is gone."

Like Peter's own file, he thought. Because of a Marine Corps major in Iraq who had removed some items from Peter's record. A kind of reward, Peter supposed. For doing something ugly that needed to be done.

What had Leonard Wallis done to earn that reward?

And for whom?

"So listen," June said. "My plane should get in around twelve-thirty."

"Hang on. This is a bad idea. Can you at least wait a day or two?"

"Peter Ash," she said, "if you think I'm going to wait around and watch CNN to see if you've been shot or killed, you obviously don't know me very fucking well. So if you'll excuse me, my flight leaves in three hours and I still have to pack and drive to Portland."

Then she hung up.

Well, hell.

Peter didn't like it.

But there wasn't anything he could do about it, either.

He looked down the dirt track toward the metal shed. The crime scene techs were poking through the burned-out car, and Steinburger and Sykes were both on their phones.

He walked south toward Forty-fifth Avenue. Not a lot of traffic yet. It was just after seven in the morning. Lewis's plane should already be on the ground.

Time to put the bait on the hook.

He made another quick phone call, then checked the map on his phone. He was about fourteen miles from Henry's house. He wore broken-in combat boots, clean dry socks, comfortable mountain pants, and a green Deschutes Brewery T-shirt.

He looked both ways, clocking the cars parked on the street, then started to run.

21

He'd tried out a lot of names since he'd got started with his little hobby, but those were onetime names, only put on for a few hours. When the Colonel had hired him, it was for the name his daddy gave him, all that true history. He hadn't wanted to, but it was special circumstances, opportunity come knocking. A chance to use up that old name and get rid of it for good.

He'd never liked his daddy, and he'd never liked that name, neither.

In his mind, he thought of himself as Big Dog.

No collar, no license, no fence. Big Dog goes where he wants. Does what he wants. Takes what he wants.

Big Dog was free.

The Colonel had hired him because he had a connection, a way in, and it made him extra valuable. He could get inside deeper than anyone else, and do it faster, too. He'd even negotiated a bonus.

The work required playing nice, fitting in, getting the trust of strangers. The Dog could do the job, hell, he'd been fooling every-body his whole damn life. He could play nice for a little while longer.

But it was tiring, having to wear that friendly mask all the time.

He was looking forward to being himself for real. Unleashed.

Normally, Big Dog would have been all over a tasty young piece like Elle Hansen. He knew from years of experience that Elle was the kind of girl who would do absolutely anything in the sack. At least with the right kind of discipline.

He could see it in the way she'd stood in the doorway in her thin robe that one time, sash coming undone, the filmy fabric practically falling off her big, lush body, nothing underneath but skin. Hell, she was asking for it.

The Dog had wanted to bend her over the porch rail, right then and there. Throw up her robe and take her from behind in front of God and everyone. Not even tie her up. Sometimes that was part of the fun, just being spontaneous, following his urges. Although the Dog was trying to be more careful about that.

He sure as hell hadn't stopped because of her idiot husband. The Dog had served with the man in the Army, had in fact saved the man's ass on several occasions, but the husband never was much of a soldier, and wasn't much of a man afterward, either, always chewing those pot cookies. Big Dog wouldn't even let the man carry a loaded weapon. Although the Dog had more than one reason for that.

Anyway, this deal with the Colonel was work, not pleasure. The Dog couldn't jump on Elle Hansen because she knew his real name, and she was connected to this whole thing, it was her damn company. Better to keep things clean.

When the police asked their questions, the Dog wanted the cops to think he was no different from the husband. Just another sad-sack Army vet missing and presumed dead. That was how it was supposed to look.

Maybe he'd circle back for Elle, when it was all over.

When Big Dog had taken himself out of the world for good.

He'd spent twenty years living under the harsh regimentation of the United States Army. Without the Army's discipline, the Dog knew he'd have ended his days as a shiftless goat-humper living in some abandoned West Texas cabin, dead before his time. The Army had organized his shiftless young life in a productive manner, had given him rank and responsibility, had made him a man.

Most importantly, the Army had taught him the discipline necessary to be more than a hungry hound, chewing up every piece of tasty pussy he could find. He'd learned to focus, to control his appetites, to be the Big Dog.

He still woke up early for PT every day, his belly as taut as it was when he was twenty, his body harder and stronger and faster than the younger men he'd worked with.

The Dog hadn't loved the Army or the war, but it had sure as shit showed him what he was capable of, and in that way he missed it. A certain kind of freedom.

It's why Big Dog had jumped on board with the Colonel. The Colonel was a tight-ass, but he knew his business and the work was fun. There was money in the game, too, real money, and the Dog liked money. Money was freedom. Freedom to slip his leash.

He wasn't going to work for the Colonel forever.

Until that time came, the Dog had work to do.

Like kill this here sonofabitch, who'd singlehandedly taken out Big Dog's entire team, not to mention interfering with their second informal bonus.

The Colonel had said the guy was too tenacious to let live.

Big Dog was up for that. He wanted the money, sure.

But he would have done it anyway.

Dog's gotta hunt, right?

———

The sonofabitch in question was running down East Forty-fifth like a goddamn jackrabbit in combat boots. No, not like a jackrabbit, thought Big Dog, because jackrabbits were sprinters. This guy ran like a goddamn coyote, smooth and easy and faster than he looked, like he meant to cover some ground.

He ran with his phone in one hand, checking it from time to time. Big Dog figured he was using it for wayfinding in the big city, but he didn't otherwise appear to be packing any kind of heat.

The Dog was supposed to be dead and gone, so his Durango had vanished into a chop shop in Greeley. He had a backup vehicle registered under another name, an older but serviceable shit-brown Dodge that looked like any other workingman's pickup, including an empty gun rack across the back window of the cab.

His ideal plan was to roll up alongside the guy and empty a magazine into him, make it look like a gang hit, but that was out of the question now. The guy had an unmarked law enforcement unit tailing him a block back, trying to be subtle and not doing a great job of it.

The Dog didn't mind killing a cop if he had to, but knew it would bring down too much heat. The Colonel would shit a brick, and it was a bad play anyway with Big Dog's team of pros gone to the happy hunting ground.

So the Dog idled along in the parking lane for a while, a half block behind the unmarked, waiting for an opportunity. He watched with grudging appreciation as the runner angled left through a parking lot, crossed the road to a self-storage outfit, then went up and over the chain link like it wasn't even there, leaving the unmarked idling at the curb.

Big Dog passed the frustrated cop and turned right on Havana.

Even in his jacked-up Durango, the Dog knew he could never have

153

followed the runner over the berms and through the plantings that divided each little section of that industrial-park maze of dead-end streets and parking lots. He'd spent three months driving all over town for Heavy Metal Protection, and taken the time to scout the bike paths that wove around that corner where Northeast turned to Northfield. There was a decent-sized grow operation tucked between the shipping companies and office buildings, and he'd once thought that a small off-road motorcycle would be a great way to hit it, because you could take the bike paths across the freeway in a couple of places, then disappear into the city. Although he'd never gotten around to cleaning out the grow, he figured the bike paths would be a good way for a man on foot to try to lose a tail.

Still in view of the cop, Big Dog took it easy up to Forty-seventh, swung left, then put the pedal down as Forty-seventh became Northfield, cutting around the maze, turning left again on Central Park Boulevard, which in this neighborhood was nothing like it sounded. He throttled back here, coasting along with the windows down in the still-cool morning, comfortably anonymous in the old brown truck, watching the parking lots to his left.

The runner popped out of the scrub ahead of him, veered left, and hit the bike trail that paralleled the road. Big Dog gunned the motor to catch up, but saw a problem.

The bike trail crossed the freeway on the same bridge as the cars, but the Dog would have to fire the machine pistol across two lanes of oncoming commuter traffic. Shooting from the driver's seat, the MAC-10 wouldn't be accurate past twenty feet, even without all the damn cars. It'd be like trying to hit the guy from the moon.

Big Dog thought he knew the route the guy was taking. So he goosed the truck along, weaving through traffic across the train tracks to Thirty-sixth, where he pulled a quick U-turn, grinning at the upright finger from a pissed-off lady in pearls, to come up toward the runner in the right lane, where he got ready to fire out the passenger window from ten feet away.

Then the guy dropped off the bike path down toward the river, where dirt paths wandered under the railroad bridges along the Sand Creek Greenway. There were no real roads down there, only footpaths, and the Dog didn't know the territory. So he put his flashers on, grabbed the little laptop, and pulled up the sat map, trying to figure where this guy was going.

When he saw the chain of parks curling down the screen, he threw the truck into drive and pulled another U-turn and hauled ass down to Thirty-fifth, where he turned toward the greenway and stopped a half block short. He was in the middle of Stapleton, a new neighborhood on the site of the old Denver airport. Sidewalks, small landscaped lots with big fancy houses and townhomes, all surrounded by wild, prairie-looking parks. No place the Dog could ever live.

He pulled the little Nikon binoculars from the glove box and waited until he spotted the runner on the bike path.

Moving fast, the guy was harder to recognize now. He'd peeled his shirt off, carried it balled up in one hand and what looked like his phone still in the other. But the Dog would know that forward stance and that loose, easy stride even without the binoculars.

Then the runner turned his head to glance down Thirty-fifth, just for a moment, and Big Dog knew.

The runner wasn't some scrawny little coyote.

He was a goddamn wolf.

And now the wolf was hunting the hunter.

Big Dog smiled right then, felt it all the way down to his happy place.

He surely did enjoy a challenge.

155

———

Piloting the Dodge purely on instinct, he spotted the runner cutting through Central Park by the Pavilion, then flying across the oval at Twenty-ninth past that weird-ass sculpture, and twice more along the greenway headed west before diverting into what the sat map called Fred Thomas Park. Big Dog never caught the runner looking directly at him, and it wasn't clear he'd been spotted each time.

But the Dog was sure the runner knew he was there.

The sonofabitch was up to something.

What the hell was it?

The Dog had his police scanner tucked between his legs, and hadn't picked up any unusual chatter. He hadn't seen any other cars paralleling him, either, so he wasn't worried about the police. According to the cop quoted in the story in the *Post* that morning, the runner had just moved to Denver from Oregon and was brand new to Heavy Metal, so he probably didn't have any buddies around for backup. The Dog was thinking the guy was trying to lead him somewhere, maybe back to where he was staying, maybe where he had a weapon stashed, which would be just fine.

Big Dog had never met this guy personally and didn't know jack shit about him, but he was starting to get a feel. He was one of those sneaky fucks. But the Dog wasn't about to back off. He was having too much fun to stop now.

West of Fred Thomas Park was an oddball grid of streets, mismatched older homes with alleys running between the lots, but the runner moved west in a relatively straight line, on East Twenty-sixth for a while, diverting north to Twenty-eighth for a few blocks, maybe to avoid the school, another sign that he knew the Dog was behind him. Then stepping back south a block for every few blocks west, ending up on Twenty-third and headed for the slot between the golf course and the Denver Zoo.

Big Dog had grown up hunting whitetail in West Texas with his no-account daddy, and as a grown man had learned to love tracking big predators in the rugged mountains of Idaho and Montana. He'd grown very good at hunting men with a squad of soldiers, and lately with his smaller team for the Colonel, but this single-o deal was different, something he could get a taste for.

Pick a man and kill him, a man who knew he was being hunted. Sure made a body feel alive, didn't it?

It's true, the Dog already had a serious hobby, a special pleasure he'd been chasing for many years. That's why he was getting off the radar, so he could take his hobby full-time.

But there wasn't no law against having more than one hobby, was there?

The Dog was a block back as the runner crossed Colorado, sticking to the bike lane on the westbound side of Twenty-third, the golf course on his right, the ball fields' parking lot and the zoo coming up on the left. Big Dog figured he'd catch up, put a few rounds into the man through the passenger window, then pull over, get out, and park a final round in back of the man's skull. Do it right.

But the Dog got stuck behind a Prius at the light on Colorado, the runner getting smaller but still clearly visible on the roadside bike path. The wait gave Big Dog a minute to think.

Why was the guy still running along the road?

He'd always headed toward green space before, so why hadn't he diverted to the shadier bike path along the baseball diamonds? Or a nicer trail through the golf course, or around the zoo or the lake?

Now the runner had slowed to a stop, half bent, hands on his knees, sideways on. Maybe looking back the way he'd come. Why would he stop here? The guy had run for an hour without slowing down at all.

Then Big Dog saw, across the road to his left, the black nose of an SUV poking out from behind a tree, ready to leave the parking lot by the baseball diamonds.

There was something wrong about it. The Dog scratched his chin. What was wrong about it?

The light turned green. The Prius in front of him was slow to move out. Normally the Dog would have hit the horn, a special dislike for slowpokes in general and Prius drivers in particular, but now he watched the SUV.

No turn signal, although you couldn't hold that against him. Big Dog didn't use his own signal half the time. That wouldn't have caught his hunter's eye.

What stuck out was the fact that the driver was still there. He'd had a half dozen chances to pull out into traffic, but never did.

Maybe the driver was just on his phone, checking his email. People stopped to stare at their phones in all kinds of stupid places. Regardless, it put Big Dog on his guard.

The Prius finally got rolling and the Dog stepped on the gas. The runner still hadn't moved. The SUV hadn't moved, either, and when Big Dog finally came up even with it, he saw some damn jigaboo in a bright white shirt and sunglasses standing by the driver's door, staring right at him. Even at speed, Big Dog could see the man's balance, his readiness.

Then the jig raised some kind of long gun to his shoulder and dropped his eye to the sight in a single smooth motion. Without conscious thought, the Dog cranked the wheel hard to the right, across the verge and onto the golf course.

He heard the *BOOM* of a large-bore gun going off at the same moment as the sound of breaking glass behind him. *BOOM* again and the clanks of what must be shotgun pellets against the sheet metal of the Dodge. The Dog hoped like hell he didn't lose a tire as he tried to manage the terrain and find the black SUV in the rearview at the same time.

He saw the runner sprinting toward the SUV. The MAC-10 lay on the floor out of reach. The Dog swore and stomped down on the gas, scattering an early-morning foursome like so many chickens before he was out of the line of sight and away into the scrub.

Man, that runner? And his pal with the shotgun?

Before this was over, the Dog was going to track them down and eat them for lunch.

22

By the time Peter had sprinted fifty yards to the Jeep Grand Cherokee, Lewis was back in the driver's seat with his seat belt on and the windows down, hollering, "Can't you run any faster?"

He wore a tilted grin and a starched white button-down shirt, the sleeves rolled back in two crisp turns, the fine cotton bright against his dark skin. His sunglasses had probably cost more than Peter's truck.

If Lewis hadn't been thumbing fresh shells into the shotgun, Peter thought, he might have been headed for a business breakfast, or an elegant picnic in the park.

Peter slid slick and sweaty into the passenger seat as Lewis handed him the weapon, then punched the accelerator before Peter even got his door closed.

But instead of following the brown pickup into the golf course, Lewis turned right, back onto Twenty-third.

"I know you're the driver," Peter said, "but why aren't we following him?"

"Faster this way," Lewis said, eyes on the road as he took a tight left onto the wrong side of Colorado Boulevard. The big Jeep surged forward, Lewis weaving effortlessly through the oncoming cars. "He'll be looking for the nearest exit, which oughta be cutting this corner. Plus the golfers won't take our picture with their phones."

Peter had one hand on the shotgun, the other holding hard to the oh-shit handle. "I thought that's why you outlaws wore bandannas over your faces."

"Who, me?" Lewis put some street into his voice. "I ain't no outlaw. I'm jes' a bidnessman."

"Going seventy the wrong way down a one-way street." Peter didn't have a free hand to get his seat belt buckled. He'd developed an appreciation for their functionality. "And heavily armed."

"Reminds me," Lewis said. "Watch your feet."

Peter set the shotgun butt-down in the footwell, the barrel back against the center console, so he could buckle up. He saw a cloth bundle on the floor, the wrap starting to come apart with the bumpy ride. The gap gleamed with the dark shine of walnut grips and oiled steel.

"Pair of revolvers down there, and a rifle under that blanket on the back seat. You know I like to be prepared."

"Always the Boy Scout," said Peter.

Lewis snorted and looked left toward the golf course. "There he is." The brown Dodge pickup came out of the trees on the far side of the fairway, now running parallel to the road maybe eighty yards away. "You crazy motherfucker. Where you going?"

"Not crazy," Peter said. "Smart."

"Smart enough to spot our setup," said Lewis. "I don't like that."

"He got lucky," Peter said. "Stuck at the light with time to think."

"Never underestimate," said Lewis.

"I was trying to make you feel better about being spotted," Peter said, angled in his seat to track the pickup. "I know you're sensitive."

Lewis scratched his nose with his middle finger as he slid into the bike lane to dodge a bus, chasing a string of two-wheeled commuters up the curb. "Lotta cyclists in this town," he said. "Love these bike paths."

Then the Dodge veered away into the dried-out scrub, heading toward the center of the course, trailing a rising plume of dust behind.

Lewis looked at Peter.

Who said, "What're you looking at me for? Go get him."

Lewis grinned and spun the wheel.

The Jeep bounced up the high curb in mid-turn, and for a moment Peter was afraid they'd snap an axle, or worse yet, roll the damn thing. But Lewis twitched the wheel and the Jeep landed on all four tires like a big black motorized cat, then leaped ahead.

The white-lettered tailgate of the brown Dodge was visible for just a moment before it disappeared in its own dust cloud.

Lewis moved his hand and the Jeep's windows went up as they followed the pickup into the swirling haze.

They could see forty yards ahead, then twenty, Lewis slowing to avoid killing a stray golfer. "If he was really smart," Peter said, "he'd hop onto one of those cart paths and sneak out through the dust."

"How I'd do it." Lewis angled right, then left, looking for fresh tire tracks in the dry ground already marked up by a thousand golf carts over a long dry summer. They slid through a pair of surprise sand traps, leaped back into the dusty rough, then bounced out of the cloud onto a putting green between a pair of middle-aged hipsters in straw fedoras and salmon-colored shorts. Golfing ironically.

"There," Peter said, pointing. The brown Dodge flew away from them on the cart path, farther ahead now. Lewis launched the Jeep forward, leaving behind a four-wheel divot.

They roared down the narrow asphalt, past trees and bushes and too-green grass, gaining ground while golfers shook their fists. The pickup veered left and disappeared behind a screen of trees, where there must have been more dry ground, because another dust cloud rose up higher than the treetops.

Lewis didn't slow, just kept the pedal down. "I got your tracks now, motherfucker." The dust rose higher and thicker, and then they were in it.

The tracks were clear in the scrub, twin trails where the tires had run. Straight ahead, then curving hard left, the tracks getting wide and sloppy where the Dodge had circled in the dust to raise a thicker cloud. Lewis followed behind.

Was the guy waiting somewhere? Had he gotten behind them? Peter thought of the little submachine gun from the night before. Imagined the guy crouched now behind the cover of his engine block, taking aim, while he and Lewis still had their windows up to keep the dust out of the Jeep.

He hit the button and the glass slid down. Everything got much louder, the engine and the noise of the tires scraping at the ground. Peter set the shotgun butt to his shoulder, the barrel out the window as the roiling dust filled the car.

This was all a bad idea.

"Get us out of here," he called.

Eyes slitted against the airborne dirt, Lewis brought the wheel around and the Jeep straightened. He hit the gas and they shot forward across a cart path, slid between two trees, and came to a rocking halt on a tee mown within an inch of its life. The cloud behind them rose like a thunderhead in the still morning air.

Lewis dropped his own window and killed the engine. They listened.

To the left, in the middle distance, a big engine revved high.

From behind a small building, bathrooms or something, where cart paths came together.

Lewis cranked the engine and threw it into drive. He headed left around the back of the building, hustling past four elderly women in white visors and bright prints who scooted toward the safety of the structure while Peter scanned ahead.

"There he is." Peter pointed down a long narrow path, the brown tailgate with DODGE in dusty white letters far out ahead of them, following the curve behind a row of trees.

Lewis put the pedal down, wiping the grit from his eyes. The acceleration pushed Peter back in his seat.

They rocketed forward and around the curve. The path continued down a long lane of trees, but there was no brown pickup in sight.

A soft haze hung thin in the air. "Stop," Peter called.

Lewis stood on the brakes.

Peter craned his neck out the window and saw faint tire tracks leaving the path on the right, headed back toward Twenty-third. A narrow passage between two trees. They'd come almost full circle. "That way."

"I see it," said Lewis, already palming the wheel.

They bounced out over the grass to a bus stop, sign mown flat by a passing vehicle, their heads on a swivel, searching for the brown tailgate with the white letters. Left or right?

"Straight ahead," Peter said. "The parking lot."

Lewis punched it and roared through traffic into the parking area for the Denver Zoo. He cruised the long curves, almost empty at this time of day, while Peter looked at the map on his phone and tried to game it.

The Dodge driver could have circled right and headed back through the lot to Twenty-third. He could have gone to the end of the lot and turned right, toward the museum, or left to circle between the zoo and the lake and into City Park. He could have done anything. And he was too far ahead of them.

Lewis stopped at the end of the lot, looked around, and made a face. "Too many exits."

Peter popped the door and climbed up to stand with one boot on the leather seat and the other on the armrest, shotgun in his hand, breathing deeply, scanning for something, anything, that might be their guy.

Nothing.

"Well, hell," he said.

Behind them, the rising song of sirens.

"Time to go, Jarhead," Lewis called. "Get that shotgun out of sight."

Peter climbed back in the Jeep and Lewis drove calmly off into the park.

23

Peter and Lewis sat outside an upscale coffee shop in Cap Hill. The sun was bright, the day starting to heat up, and Peter was glad their table was still in the shade on the west side of the building. But in the distance he could see dark clouds gathering over the Front Range, angled tendrils of falling rain visible through the thin, clear air. The weather could change fast at the edge of the mountains.

After the adrenaline rush of a ten-mile run and a high-speed drive through the golf course, Peter was starting to come down, and it wasn't pretty. The events of the last eighteen hours, not to mention his short-age of sleep for the last few nights, were starting to catch up to him.

He'd already wolfed down a pair of breakfast burritos from a taco truck in the park, which helped with the growl in his stomach. Now he sipped his coffee and felt himself coming back to life.

Lewis slurped loudly at a triple mocha with extra whip. It had given him a little whipped-cream mustache, but it didn't begin to hide his nature. He watched Peter thoughtfully across the table. As always, the force of his gaze was substantial, like a hot desert wind.

"What?" said Peter.

"Maybe you better fill me in," Lewis said. "About who's trying to kill you. And why."

Peter shook his head. "I wish to hell I knew," he said. "I got nothing to grab on to here. Everybody's dead but me."

"There it is," Lewis said, nodding once. "Why you're so damn exercised about this."

"What are you talking about?" Peter asked.

As if he didn't know.

"You lost a lot of guys over there, more than most," Lewis said. "It's burned into you. That need to take care of your people. Even if they were just randomly assigned to your damn platoon. They still your people."

Peter sighed. "Henry was my friend. You'd do the same thing." He looked at Lewis. "You already have," he said. "It's why you're here."

"Man, don't embarrass me." Lewis made a show of glancing around as if someone might overhear. "That sentimental shit bad for my reputation."

Lewis the career criminal with the mercenary soul, who'd refused to take his full share of their unexpected Milwaukee windfall because their little adventure had reconnected him with Dinah, his first love. Lewis was raising her two boys as his own. Plus there was a lot more money than any of them had expected.

"Sorry," Peter said. "I forgot. You're a heartless bastard."

Lewis lifted his mocha in a salute. "Likewise, motherfucker." He took a sip, then patted his lips with a napkin. "Any word from June?"

Now it was Peter's turn to look down the street.

"I think she's a little pissed," he said. "I'm supposed to be learning how to sleep inside, not getting shot at, or chasing assholes around the city with you."

Lewis smiled his tilted smile.

"You remember that time in Milwaukee, when I asked if you really thought you could go back to being a citizen? Get a job, swing a hammer all day?"

Lewis smiled wider. "That was right after you sent my two guys to the ER. You had that same damn look on your face this morning, sprinting your ass up to the Jeep. Alive for real. 'Cause the sun never shines brighter than when somebody shooting at you."

He sat forward in his chair, effortlessly balanced, eternally ready, his mocha cradled gently in one big hand. Watching Peter with that implacable stare.

"You think June doesn't know who you really are?"

Peter thought about the letters he'd written her over the summer.

"She says she does." He swiped his hand across his face. He was still tired. Coffee did only so much. "But I don't know how that'll go when she sees it up close."

"She's already seen it," Lewis said. "Up close and personal. And she's still talking to you. Doesn't that tell you something?"

"Her life was on the line," Peter said. "She might feel differently when I'm doing it for a stranger."

Lewis looked at him. "Give the girl some credit. You're not just some asshole looking for a fight. If that's all you were, she wouldn't be interested. But you stand for something. For somebody. That's what makes you worth talking to."

"What about Dinah?" Peter asked. "What's her take on all this shit?"

"Hey, I start to get itchy, Dinah tells me to go find you." He put on a screechy voice that sounded nothing like the proud, regal woman

Peter knew. "'Where that jarhead Peter Ash? Go find that mother-fucker and get yourself into some righteous trouble. Go save lives, baby.'"

Peter said, "Dinah Johnson never said 'motherfucker' in her whole entire life."

"You know," Lewis said thoughtfully, "I don't b'lieve she has."

"She doesn't want to know, is that it?"

Lewis shrugged. "What she knows is I'd go apeshit if all I did was make lunches for the boys, walk that damn dog, and babysit the money. I got to stretch it out sometime, use those old muscles. And she'd rather I roll with you, 'cause she trusts you to keep me on the right side of things." He flashed the tilted smile. "She did give me a little lecture this morning. 'Don't end up in the hospital, don't get on the news, and don't touch another woman or I'll cut it clean off.'"

Peter snorted. "I *know* she didn't say that."

The tilted smile got wider. "She got access to nice sharp scalpels in the hospital, but she told me she'd use a spork." The shrug got more elaborate. "She seemed pretty serious about it."

"Anyway," said Peter, "I actually did talk to June this morning. She did some digging into the guys I used to work with."

"Told you," Lewis said. "That girl sweet on you."

"Shut up." Peter told Lewis what he'd learned about the men he'd worked with, Deacon and Banjo. "This Leonard Wallis character is a little interesting, though. Maybe he was some kind of special forces or something. June said his service record is all blank. Wiped clean."

"Anyone involved who has the juice to do something like that?"

"Nobody I've found yet. I'm still trying to figure out who benefits."

"This got to be about the money," Lewis said. "We know whose money got stolen?"

"That would be a place to start," Peter said. "I'll call Elle in a minute."

"But why they still after you? The cops have the money now, right? Seems like a lot of work for no profit."

"That's what I can't figure out," Peter said. "I can't even identify the last remaining guy. I never saw his face. And as far as he knows, I've already told the cops everything, so where's the percentage in chasing me down? Unless it's retaliation, like a gang thing."

"Maybe that part is personal," Lewis said. "That last guy, you killed his partners. Messed up his game."

"It's the only way it makes sense," Peter said. "Sure as hell is personal for me. But here's the other thing. These guys were total pros. Maybe ex-military, definitely experienced, this was not their first rodeo. The planning and execution were excellent."

"Except for you," Lewis said. "The walking monkey wrench."

"My point," Peter said, "is for people like this, I don't think there's enough money to justify the risk. Would you hijack a car and kill two guys for three hundred grand split five ways?"

"Not split no five ways," Lewis said. "Sixty apiece less expenses?"

"Fifty apiece on the second one," Peter said. "If you live to collect."

Lewis shook his head. "That thing with the tow truck and ambulance, that's a great idea. Money and evidence all vanish, right? But you can't hide the disappearance, the fact of it. So how many of these can you really do? Once the cops and the protection companies see a pattern, it only gets harder."

"And once you make the news," Peter said, "citizens get scared. This isn't like robbing a bank. This is robbing a bank and killing all the tellers. You do five or six, the police response is going to be huge."

Lewis nodded. "And you do it in more than one state, you got the feds on your ass. That's no kind of business model."

"Not like your business model," said Peter. "Back in the day."

"Never robbed nobody who could call the cops, never hurt nobody who didn't deserve it."

"You're never going to tell me, are you? How you used to make your living?"

"Don't want to lead you into temptation," Lewis said. "Nice young man like you? I fear for your immortal soul."

He considered his coffee cup, turning it in his hand. Still perfectly balanced in his chair, effortlessly ready.

"So the hijackings aren't personal," he said. "And the money's not worth the risk. So it's about something else. Something worth more money. Or worth more than money."

He looked up at Peter.

"What's worth more than money?"

24

First, they needed to know whose money it was.

Peter called Elle Hansen and asked her. She didn't even have to think about it.

"Zig McSweeney," she said. "One of our first big customers. He runs two grow facilities. It was his money in both shipments."

"Did you tell the police?"

"Of course," she said. "I told them after Randy and Leonard disappeared, and again last night. Why do you want to know?"

"Do you happen to have his cell number?"

"It's in Henry's phone," she said. "Which I'm going to need back, by the way, it's a company phone. But I already talked to Zig last night. It's complicated. Don't go muddying the waters."

Peter said, "If I'm going to be your new head of operations, I should be looking into what went wrong."

"Just come to the office. We have things to discuss."

"I'll call you after I meet with the police."

They found Zig McSweeney leaning against the hood of a curvy new green Volvo wagon. He was parked outside the gate of the same concrete-block building where the Heavy Metal team had gotten behind schedule the day before, the grow facility with the employees napping in the sun.

When the breeze picked up, Peter could smell the heady, distinctive funk of healthy cannabis plants. To the west, the clouds were moving in from the Front Range and getting darker.

McSweeney was a wiry guy in his mid- to late-thirties. He had a clean shave and a crisp, blond, chamber-of-commerce haircut, but he was dressed like a Colorado slacker in a green athletic hoodie, minimalist cargo shorts in some new synthetic fabric, and trail runners. Lean and sleek as a greyhound.

"Would you guys care for something to smoke?" McSweeney asked after shaking hands with Peter and Lewis. "Fresh sticky bud? Or maybe one of our gift samplers, to help you relax after work."

His grip was strong but not obnoxious, and his sun-browned face held an expression of perpetual amusement. Like he was having fun just standing there.

It was hard not to like the man.

"No, thanks," Peter said. "We're working. As I said on the phone, we're looking into the hijackings. You lost quite a bit of money."

"Yeah." McSweeney sighed, the amusement falling away for a moment. "But it's only money, and you recovered part of it. I'm more sorry about your people."

It was the right thing to say, and Peter was glad he said it. "Why would someone want to rob you?"

"For the money," McSweeney said. "Isn't that why people do things?"

"Sometimes," Peter said. "What do the police think?"

"They think it's about the money," McSweeney said. The amusement had crept back onto his face.

"Do you find it strange that both these robberies hit your business? What do you make of that?"

"Actually, they hit your business," McSweeney said pleasantly. "It just happened to be my money. Like a bank robbery. The police don't investigate the customers, they investigate the robbers."

"Unless the bank has only one customer," Peter said. "And the bank is insured. I wonder if the police have thought about that idea? Or maybe you'd rather not talk to the police again."

McSweeney looked at Peter.

At Lewis, standing dark and silent beside him.

Then he glanced up at the broad sky, which had been blue a half hour before.

The heavy weather over the Front Range was moving down toward the Plains, leaching the color from the land. Bright flashes lit up the foothills to the west, and gray streaks hung from the clouds like thin penciled lines.

"Three hundred days of sunshine my ass," McSweeney said, watching the rain to the west. "We didn't have to worry about lightning storms in California." He shook his head. "You wouldn't believe what it cost to have this building grounded." He turned back to Peter. "Why don't you come inside? I'll give you the tour."

He pulled out his phone and hit a few buttons and climbed into his car. A moment later the chain-link gate rolled open. Peter and Lewis got in the Jeep and followed the green Volvo inside the fence.

The building was concrete block painted white with a high flat roof. The big windows and front loading dock had been filled in with bricks, although a section of the back wall, inside the fence, had been replaced with a heavy steel rollup big enough for a box truck. McSweeney led them to a set of steel double doors with a single knob. A camera perched in a metal cage far above. McSweeney waved at the camera. There was a buzzing sound as the lock released. McSweeney turned the knob and pushed the door open.

They walked into a small white-painted concrete-block room, with another double door at the far end and a thick window set into the concrete sidewall. Peter felt the static begin to spark. He stopped himself from reaching for a pistol he didn't have.

"Bulletproof window," Lewis said. "Doors, too, I'd guess. A sally port, right? One set of doors won't open until the other set closes."

"Yes," McSweeney said. "What we grow is worth a lot of money. And there's a big market, legal or not." He raised a hand to the brown-skinned man behind the glass, neatly dressed in a blue polo shirt with the Heavy Metal logo on the breast. "Morning, Tonio. How are you this morning?"

"Not so good," said the man behind the glass, his solemn voice filtered through the speaker. "I heard about the hijacking last night. Ms. Hansen sent out an email. Those guys were my friends."

"Yeah, I'm really sorry about that," McSweeney said. "The police will probably come by again to talk to you. Just tell them what you know, okay? We want to do everything we can to help."

"Yessir." Tonio did something with his hand and the far door buzzed. McSweeney stepped forward, opened the door, and walked through.

They were in a small white changing room, brightly lit, with benches and white metal lockers and a white-tiled floor with a drain in the middle. Peter's static flared higher. He kept breathing, in and out.

McSweeney opened a locker with his name on it, dropped his trail runners inside and stepped into a pair of Crocs. "We do our best to keep out contaminants," he said. "Mites, molds, whatever, we don't want them in the grow. We seed the area outside with ladybugs to help control pests. Should be some spare shoes in that cabinet behind you."

A tall open cabinet held bins of spotless Crocs and stacks of folded white garments wrapped in plastic, organized by size. McSweeney unwrapped what turned out to be a lab coat and pulled it on. His amused look was firmly back in place.

Peter glanced at Lewis, who nodded. They changed their shoes and put on lab coats, then followed McSweeney's example by putting on hairnets and sterile blue nitrile gloves.

They went through the next door into another world.

It was impossible to tell that they were in a large warehouse in Denver.

It looked like a garden on the moon.

The space was subdivided into orderly rooms with white plastic paneling on the walls and ceilings. Bright lights and silver cooling ducts overhead, long metal tables connected to nutrient irrigation systems, circulation fans everywhere. Rooms with "mother" plants, sexed and used to produce cuttings for propagation of new plants. Rooms with those cuttings taking root, rooms with rooted plants growing to the flowering stage, rooms with mature flowering plants where bud growth was forced by changing the light cycle. Rooms with harvested plants hanging upside down for curing. The heady smell of the green growing plants was everywhere, but strongest in the flowering rooms. A few workers in scrubs, face masks, hairnets, and gloves walked the aisles, tending to the plants and the elaborate systems that kept them growing, including a young woman who had peeled off one glove and stepped slowly between the rows, touching each plant individually with a gentle caress.

"Nice, isn't it?" McSweeney said, speaking a little louder than normal over the sound of the air circulation. "Right now, we're about seventy-five degrees, fifty percent humidity. The plant likes what we like. Regulating the climate is a hugely important part of cultivation. Electricity for lighting and cooling is our single largest expense."

Peter's static was starting to crackle nicely, crawling up his brainstem. Lewis glanced at him. Peter nodded, kept breathing, and kept following McSweeney, who was explaining as they walked.

"Everything you see can be washed and sanitized between cycles," McSweeney said. "We grow organic product in a hydroponic medium, no dirt, no pesticides, so air and water filtration is also very important. We have six unique strains here, with grow cycles running from eight to twelve weeks depending on the strain, and we're breeding new stuff in the experimental rooms. That's a big profit source for us, our unique strains. As the market gets more mature, retail pricing is going down. We have to grow product that is in high demand and that sells for higher prices."

They stepped out of the clean rooms and into a small area that looked more like a working warehouse. Pumps and pipes and nutrient vats, packing stations for the finished product. Peter felt the openness of the twenty-foot ceiling as a kind of relief, although not the kind that walking outside would bring.

"I'm impressed," Lewis said. "I don't know what you're using for nutrients, but you're running double bulbs and a five-by-five grid to get the most from your lights. You're using trellises in the flowering room, which help keep the plants vertically compact but get that extra side growth, grow more buds."

Peter looked at his friend, surprised again. As far as Peter was concerned, Lewis might as well have been speaking Martian. But that was Lewis.

"Do you still think those hijackings are an insurance scam?" Mc-

Sweeney asked. "Steal my own money and the insurance company pays the claim?"

"Been done before," Lewis said. "But that's not you."

McSweeney gave him a challenging stare. "Yeah? Who am I, exactly?"

Lewis smiled his widest smile.

"Homeboy, you were in the life," he said. "Had to guess, I'd say you were working some shitty minimum-wage job, twenty years old and trying to save up for community college. But a couple of your friends were growing dope in their basement or backyard shed or maybe on public land. Pretty easy money for ditch weed, tax free, and it was barely even illegal if you got medical clients on board. So you said to hell with college, rented a two-car garage, and taught yourself from there."

McSweeney stood listening as Lewis kept talking.

"You're an entrepreneurial guy, got a lot of energy, I'm guessing you did pretty well. Had some fun, too, right? You liked the excitement, doing deals, dodging the cops. 'Fore long you had two garages, then five. Crazy money for some kid from Bakersfield never went to college. But somewhere along the way, you had a setback. Maybe police problems, maybe the other kind. Lost everything, or almost everything, had to leave the state. But here's Colorado, voting to legalize. You land on your feet and hit the ground running. You find a backer, get to work, and now you're a big deal in Denver and it's all legal."

McSweeney looked slightly hypnotized. Like Lewis was reading his tea leaves and seeing the past.

"So no," said Lewis, "I don't think it's an insurance scam, not for a measly half mil. You got too much to lose. What's the economics on weed these days? For an operation like yours, high end, efficient, maybe a dollar a day per square foot? That's net, after expenses, give or take. Stop me if I'm wrong. That old two-car garage made you about a hundred and fifty grand a year. But this place is ten thousand square feet. Which works out to three and a half mil a year. And you got two of them? You're making serious bank, for you and your backer. No, a half million isn't anywhere near enough. You have a much bigger problem."

Zig McSweeney stared at Lewis, then turned to Peter. "How'd he do that?"

Peter smiled. "He's kind of an idiot savant. Without the idiot part."

To Lewis, McSweeney said, "I was actually running a small landscaping business," he said. "Three guys, one truck. Twenty-eight and trying to finish my dissertation in plant genetics at night. I wasn't having any fun and I wasn't making any money and I wasn't spending any time skydiving, which was why I started the whole thing to begin with." He shook his head. "Other than that, you're pretty much right on. I had six garages, then decided to scale up and rented a warehouse in East L.A. But that was a dirt grow, no air scrubbers, you could smell it a mile away. The cops never knew my real name, but they backtraced everything they could find. My house, my cars, all the money buried in the backyard. I got out with my laptop and my seeds and the clothes on my back."

"What about the bigger problem?" Peter said. "How'd he do on that one?"

McSweeney looked at Peter. "What's your interest, here? Do you actually work for Heavy Metal Protection?"

"For about four days," Peter said. "I was in the truck yesterday. I knew the men that died. I want to know why. And who killed them."

McSweeney shook his head. "I can't help you with that," he said. "It wasn't my fault."

"It was your money," Peter said. "What's going on?"

McSweeney sighed. "This was all so much easier before things got legal."

Lewis gave him a smile of infinite kindness. "Come on," he said. "Tell Uncle Lewis your problems. You'll feel so much better."

McSweeney looked at Peter. "Why should I tell you anything?"

"You have to tell somebody," Peter said. "Because the rising tide of shit that was swirling around your ankles is now up to your chest. Pretty soon it's going to be up to your mouth. And I'm the guy throwing you a shit-proof life preserver."

The muscles clenched in McSweeney's jaw.

He opened his mouth, then closed it again.

Then said, "Someone's trying to take my business."

"I'm listening," Peter said. "Although maybe we could have this conversation outside?"

"When the recreational law first passed, the medical guys had a head start," McSweeney said. "They were already in production, had dispensaries open. They actually had access to banks. But they were also mostly small outfits. Idealists, most of them, not really businesspeople. There was no way they could scale up to meet the new demand. It was like a gold rush. Hell, it still is. Everybody's hustling to stake their claims. I had the skills, I had the seeds, the opportunity was obvious. But I didn't have the capital."

"How much did you need?" Lewis asked.

"Two million dollars to start a commercial-sized grow like this. So I found an investor, a money guy in Boulder. That was two years ago. It took six months for permits and legal. Another six months to get the space built out. All the while I'm bleeding money. Then the first crops come in, my three best strains, and I can't keep up with demand. Customers love it, retailers love it, my product is the first out the door. Clean flavor profiles, highly differentiated effects. Super-

180

tasty smoke. Money coming in like crazy. Retailers are telling me to start another grow. I'd be an idiot not to, right?"

"I think I know where this is going," Peter said.

McSweeney nodded. "I decided to finance the second grow out of the first one. Investing back in the company. Why borrow more than you have to?"

"Plus you liked the risk," Lewis said. "That's half the fun for you."

McSweeney flashed a smile. "Of course. And it was a great idea until we lost a crop to powder mold, and another to spider mites. So cash flow was a problem. I was overleveraged. It was a close thing. The terms with my investor were pretty basic. Double his cash out in two years or he owned everything."

"Everything?" Peter asked. "You agreed to that?"

McSweeney shrugged. "I had the skills and the seeds and nothing else. So I took what I could get. Like I said, it was close, but I was going to make it. I had to clean out every safe, empty my change jar, check under the couch cushions, and stop paying all my bills to put those last two money runs together. A half million dollars, my final payment. And now it's gone."

"What about your investor? Is he pulling the strings on this?"

"That's the thing," McSweeney said. "He's not my investor anymore. He told me he got underwater on a land deal, so he sold my loan to some holding company back East. They sent me a letter a month ago, or their lawyers did, letting me know the last payment was coming due, and reminding me what would happen if I couldn't pay."

"When's it due?"

McSweeney gave a small, pained smile. "Today. Heavy Metal was going to deliver the whole thing to their lawyer's office today."

"So who's your contact at the holding company?"

"I've tried all that. I can't get anyone on the phone. My lawyers can't get their lawyers on the phone. They sent over the transfer paperwork last week."

"Do the cops know about this?"

"I told them. But the cops care about murder in the streets. Armed robbery. They don't care about me losing my business."

"Who's your former investor?"

McSweeney took out his cell. "You're using Henry's phone, right? His name is Jon Jordan, I'll send you the contact. I think he actually met someone from the holding company. But he stopped returning my calls weeks ago."

"What do they get when they take ownership?" Lewis asked. "Cash on hand? Existing inventory? Intellectual property?"

"They get everything," McSweeney said. "The insurance payment when it comes. The money from the evidence locker. My procedures manual, my nutrient formulas, seeds and seedlings for my proprietary strains." He sighed. "My life's work, basically."

McSweeney went back inside. Peter and Lewis walked back to the Jeep. The clouds had gotten closer. Peter could smell the rain in the wind.

"Where'd you learn so much about growing weed?"

"You mean cannabis cultivation?" Lewis kept a perfectly straight face. "We've invested in the industry."

"As in, you and me? We own pot farms?"

"Not the farms," Lewis said. "Equipment and technology. Lights, chillers, hydroponics, software. Although we could invest in farms, too, if you like. I'm told daylight grows are the coming thing. Greenhouses, that kind of thing. Lower start-up and running costs, lower energy bills, smaller carbon footprint, better for the planet. The local soils give the product a uniqueness, a *terroir*, like wine. Although it's harder to get consistent results, if you want to be the McDonald's of weed."

Peter had thought he'd eventually stop being surprised by Lewis. His voracious urge to learn, and his capacity to hold that knowledge in his head. Now he wasn't so sure.

He looked at his friend. "You're still the most dangerous man on the planet."

It was a reminder of Lewis's favorite quote, something Malcolm X had said. Lewis gave Peter his full-on grin. "Black man with a library card."

"So what do you think," Peter said. "About McSweeney."

"You know he's not telling us everything."

"I know," Peter said. "But he's all we've got."

"Let me guess, we not gonna make your meeting with the cops."

"We might be a little late," Peter said. "Depends how fast you can make it to Boulder."

"I guess we gonna find out." Lewis grinned as he pulled out of the parking lot. "Hey, you never saw what I got for ordnance."

Peter lifted the cloth bundle from the floor, a threadbare old bath towel turned gray from gun oil. He unwrapped the folds and saw a pair of antique revolvers.

"Colts," Lewis said. "The Single Action Army, .45 cal. Also called the Peacemaker."

"I know what they are," Peter said, taking one in his hand. The revolver was huge and heavy with a long barrel. He could feel the age in it, could see it in the machining. Definitely not a reproduction. The aggressively curved walnut grip felt more comfortable than he expected. Compared to a modern handgun, the SAA looked like a dinosaur, primitive and atavistic. If it was a dinosaur, though, it was a velociraptor. An ancient but refined killing machine. "The cavalry model, right?"

"That's the one. And take a look in the back."

Peter turned in his seat and lifted the edge of a Mexican blanket laid on the rear seat. Beside the 10-gauge shotgun and three boxes of shells, he saw a Winchester 94 with the lever cock mechanism. The same rifle from every Western movie he'd seen as a kid.

"What happened, you rob a museum?"

"Short notice, motherfucker. My Denver contact stopped selling hardware, said he makes more money with his YouTube channel on historical firearms. This was the only stuff he'd part with. Told me they were made in the fifties, quality stuff, came from a retired rancher who used 'em on rattlesnakes and coyotes. But he promised they'd shoot straight."

Beside the Winchester was a black metal combat tomahawk, elegant and deadly. He'd known a few special ops guys who'd used tomahawks instead of knives. Effective, and more than a little scary.

"My guy threw that in with the guns," Lewis said. "I think it embarrassed him."

Peter turned to Lewis, a big Colt in each hand. "So who are we supposed to be, Wild Bill Hickok and Billy the Kid?"

"Well, we can't both be named Bill," Lewis said reasonably. "I figured you'd be Annie Oakley."

Peter wrapped the guns in the towel, then put on his seat belt as Lewis hit the on-ramp toward Boulder. "You are a piece of fucking work, Lewis."

Lewis grinned and punched the gas. "Takes one to know one, Jarhead."

25

McSweeney's initial investor, Jon Jordan, was a former Wall Street guy who'd gone west to enlarge his fortune. He ran an investment fund in a newer four-story mixed-use block, just off the Pearl Street pedestrian mall, across the street from a coffee-shop-slash-bookstore.

Old Boulder was nice. Tree-lined streets and old houses, a funky business district full of restaurants and head shops. The tang of pot smoke floated through the Jeep's open windows in a kind of ambient hippie potpourri. And to the west, visible on the hills and in gaps between buildings, the vast angular slabs of the Flatirons tilted up toward the Rockies like unused building blocks of the gods.

When they got out of the Jeep, Peter looked down at himself.

The sweat from his long morning run was dried into his wrinkled clothes, which hadn't been particularly stylish to begin with. His shirt was itchy from the salt, and he had to resist the urge to scratch. The side of his head still ached from the impact with the window in the crash. His eye sockets felt scoured from lack of sleep, and the caffeine was definitely starting to leave his system. He could feel his brain grinding to a halt.

"Coffee," he said. "Coffee would be good."

Lewis shook his head in mock sympathy. "You getting old, Jarhead. You only ran, what, ten miles this morning?"

"Something like that." Peter yawned so hard his jaw popped. "And miles to go before I sleep."

"What's that from, a Charles Bronson movie?" Lewis asked, that tilted grin sliding across his face.

Peter gave him a look.

He was pretty sure Lewis had never made it through high school, but the depths of his curiosity and knowledge about the world never stopped surprising Peter. The fact that Lewis might carry a Robert Frost poem around in his head—specifically a poem about the lure of death in the midst of life, one of Peter's mom's favorites—added yet another layer.

Lewis's tilted grin got wider.

Peter just shook his head.

He wasn't going to give Lewis the satisfaction.

"Come on," he said, pulling open the door to the coffee place. "You're buying. Quadruple espresso for me."

"You don't want to wait on the sidewalk?" asked Lewis.

"Of course I do," said Peter. "But I'm trying to spend more time inside. Get myself used to the static."

"Part of your therapy."

"Something like that," Peter said. "I'm trying to grow as a goddamn person, okay?" He yawned again.

They took their coffee to go, and walked across the street and up the stairs.

Jordan's investment fund had most of the third floor, the reception space dominated by giant windows with broad views of the Flatirons and the brown grassy hills leading up to them. The view helped with the static. An expensive carbon-fiber road bike hung from a rack on one wall. Behind the reception desk was a double row of promotional posters from the Fillmore and Red Rocks Amphitheatre, but the desk was covered with brown cardboard banker's boxes, and there was no receptionist.

"Hello," called Peter. "Anyone here?"

A trim, elegant woman with hair dyed a deep maroon, wearing a black sweater over black jeans, came down the hall with an empty box hanging from each hand. Her eyes were sunk deep in their sockets. "Are you with the movers?" she asked.

"No, ma'am," Lewis said. "We have an appointment with Jon Jordan."

She took a deep breath and straightened herself up. She held the boxes closer to her body.

Peter had a bad feeling.

"I'm sorry," she said. "We're closed until further notice. I thought his secretary had canceled all his appointments."

Gently, Peter said, "Does that mean Jon's not in today?"

"No." She cleared her throat. "I'm his wife, Ruth. He was killed three days ago, riding his bike up to Estes Park. A hit-and-run accident."

"How terrible," Peter said. "Do the police have any idea who's responsible?"

She shook her head. "Another cyclist riding a few miles behind Jon, a friend of ours, said that she was passed by a pickup truck. A few miles farther up, she found Jon." Ruth cleared her throat again. "In the ditch on the side of the road. He died on the way to the hospital."

"Did your friend notice what kind of truck? Or the color?"

"She said it was older, and brown. With the word 'Dodge' in white on the tailgate. She told the police, but . . ."

"I'm so sorry for your loss."

"Thank you." She raised a hand and turned back down the hall. "Now if you'll excuse me, I have more packing to do."

Peter wasn't going to ask Jordan's widow why he'd sold his investment in McSweeney's grow operation.

"Our guy has already started cleaning up loose ends," said Peter.

"Doing a pretty good job of it, too," said Lewis.

26

Daniel Clay Dixon was on his way to the airport when he got a text on his incoming phone.

who dis.

The phones were laid out on the passenger seat of the rental. It was a decent enough car, although to Dixon KIA would always stand for Killed In Action.

There was a time when Dixon would always ask for an American car, but with the modern global economy, none of that seemed to matter anymore. Hondas and Toyotas were made in the U.S., and Chevrolets made in Mexico. And the money went wherever it went.

Dixon was just trying to get a tiny little piece of it. He had promises to keep.

Steering with his knee, he found the outgoing phone and called his operative.

"What took you so long?"

"That ol' boy shot up my truck and slipped the noose."

Dixon felt himself tighten up. "Again? That's unacceptable."

"You think I like it? He's not alone, got some spook with a shotgun."

"You sure you're up to this, Leonard?"

"Don't use that goddamn name on the phone. Call me Big Dog. That other man's dead, with all his debts and troubles."

"Well, you got what you wanted," Dixon said. "But you're not giving me what I need."

"I'll take care of business," said Leonard. "But I'm gonna need some leverage."

"I'll try something on my end," Dixon said. "Maybe there's an easier way. Stay ready. We'll have to go kinetic again."

Dixon already had the number memorized. He plugged it into his outgoing phone, pressed Send, and listened to the ring.

He thought it was probably time to change out his burners. He liked to cycle through at least once during a given operation.

He thought about the last time he'd talked to the Marine lieutenant.

He thought about a bartender named Billy. Then he thought about the taste of good tequila as it bubbled down the neck of the upraised bottle. It was what he allowed himself, although not now, not until he was done, but it was a vivid sense memory, down to the feeling of the bubbles against his teeth, the sour heat rising in his stomach, the roar in his skull like a gong being struck.

He pushed the thought from his mind and listened to the ring.

"Hello," said the voice on the other end. The Marine.

"Listen to me closely," Dixon said. "You're involved in something in Denver. You should stay out of it."

"Who is this?"

He didn't sound as young as he once did, Dixon thought. It would have been seven or eight years ago, that last conversation. Back when they both still wore the uniform.

"You know what I'm talking about. You should leave this alone."

Silence from the other end. "Do I know you?"

"You aren't listening to me. You need to leave town. People could get hurt."

"People already got hurt," the Marine said. "Good people. Maybe we should get together and talk about it. Where can we meet?"

Dixon shook his head, remembering why he'd liked the kid. He'd never met anyone with such a deep drive to complete the mission and take care of his people. When the two goals aligned, he was the best platoon leader Dixon had ever seen. Clearly the kid hadn't changed a bit.

But Dixon had seen what could happen when the two goals were not aligned.

He'd been there, seen the consequences.

Creative decision-making. The young Marine excelled at that.

Decision and execution.

But Dixon wasn't going to allow it now. Dixon was running this show.

"Forget about the dead," he said. "Think about the living. Vulnerable people. Women and children. Do you want them on your conscience?"

A short pause. Then, "They wouldn't be on my conscience," said the Marine. "They'd be on yours. If you have one."

"I have no conscience," Dixon said. "I have no soul. I have no qualms about killing everyone involved to get what I want. Do you hear me, Marine?"

"I do know you," said the Marine lieutenant. "But I can't quite place you."

"You don't know me," Dixon said. His voice creeping louder. "But I know everything about you. And you should take your friend with the shotgun and get the hell out of Dodge before I rain so much fire down on your heads this whole goddamned city will burn to the ground."

His hands were shaking when he ended the call.

Rage, absolutely, that clean, righteous rage that gave him such pleasure.

But also fear. For what he might be forced to do.

For what he might do willingly, just to see something burn.

More than anything, Dixon wanted to be someone else. Anyone else.

God, he wanted a drink.

But God was no longer talking to Daniel Clay Dixon. Hadn't for a long, long time.

27

Peter put Henry's phone back down on the center console. The caller ID was blank.

Lewis was going eighty-five on the highway heading back to Denver, tall dry brown grass giving way to sporadic housing developments. "What was that about?"

"A guy telling me to stop causing trouble and get out of town."

Lewis smiled. "Man clearly don't know you very well."

"That's the thing," Peter said. "He sounded familiar."

Lewis glanced at him. "How familiar?"

"I don't know. Maybe if I hear his voice again."

"How'd he know you got Henry's phone?"

"That," Peter said, "is an excellent question."

They drove in silence for another minute.

"Tell me what else," Lewis said.

"He told me to forget about the dead. To think about the living, about women and children."

Lewis kept his eyes on the road. "I don't like that. Not at all."

"Me neither," Peter said.

Lewis increased their speed to ninety. Then ninety-five.

Elle answered her cell on the first ring.

"You're still using my dad's phone," she said. "I need it back. That's a company phone."

"I know," Peter said. "I was just checking in before I meet with the police. Are the kids with you?"

"It's a weekday," she said. "They're at day care, preschool, and kindergarten. When will you be done? We need to firm up a few things."

"You're at the office now?"

"Yes," she said.

Peter pictured the cramped room above the taco shop. Three old steel desks, frayed carpet, walls pockmarked and unpainted for years.

"You have anybody with you?" Peter asked. "Any of the guys? Just curious."

"No," Elle said. "Everyone on shift is working, which is the way it should be. Taking care of customers, making money. Why are you asking all these questions?"

"One more," he said. "Do you still have that pistol with you?"

"Are you kidding? Today I brought the extra magazine. What's going on?"

"Listen," he said, "do me a favor. Lock the office door, then push Randy's old desk up against it."

"Jesus Christ," she said. "You're scaring me. What the hell's going on?"

"I got a phone call," Peter said. "Some asshole told me to butt out or more people are going to get hurt. I don't want one of them to be you."

"What?" Her voice was loud.

"I'm just being careful," he said. "We'll figure something out. Maybe get you a room at a hotel or something."

"Hey, I can't disappear. I'm trying to save my business. I have to pick up my dad's personal effects. I have to meet with clients."

"Don't worry," he said. "Just be careful. I'll come to the office after I meet with the police." He thought for a moment. "Actually, why don't you call the investigating officers and tell them you just got a threatening phone call. Maybe they'll send a couple of uniforms over."

"Really? You think that's necessary?"

"Yes," Peter said firmly. Then he thought of something else. "While I have you," he said. "Can you email me the manifest for our route yesterday?"

"Well," she said, "you've got my dad's phone, so you've got the manifests. That's why I want you to return it. It has sensitive information in there."

"Like what?"

"We're a lean company. People don't come into the office every day, they log on to our website to get their assignments. You've done that, right?"

"Yes." It was a pretty slick system. Saved everyone time and money.

"So, if you're a team leader, you get the day's formal cargo manifest, listing every stop. If you're the head of operations, like my dad was before I hired Leonard, and again after Leonard disappeared, you see every employee's assignments, and the cargo manifests for every team."

"But I don't know Henry's log-in," Peter said.

She sighed. "My dad had a bad habit of allowing his phone to remember his log-ins. He also left the site open on his phone all the time. You're probably logged in right now."

"Thanks," he said. "I'll find it."

"Peter."

"It's okay," he said. "But don't forget to lock your door. And move that desk."

He didn't think the door or the desk would stop the people who'd executed an almost-successful hijacking against four armed, trained men.

But he figured he'd have a few hours before anyone tried anything else.

He was wrong.

28

owntown Denver was a busy grid east of the Platte River, centered on an oblong group of towers. Not Manhattan, but not Milwaukee, either. Scattered black-bottomed clouds loomed over the foothills, dark islands in the blue sky. Thunder rattled in the distance. Peter kept looking for rain.

Miranda Howe was waiting for them in a crowded parking lot south of the DPD headquarters complex. Her shot-up red BMW parked in the narrow shade of a street maple on the south side of the lot, she was clearly visible as a beacon of frizzy blond hair leaning against the hood.

Pissed off, of course.

When Peter climbed out of the Jeep, she launched herself off her car and laid into him.

"How in hell do you expect me to represent you if we don't plan strategy ahead of time?"

"I had to run an errand," Peter said.

"We need to talk," said Miranda. "Figure out what angle we're going to take."

"We're just going to tell the truth," said Peter, who planned to do nothing of the sort.

Miranda was dressed in an open suit jacket over a nearly sheer blouse, with a skirt that appeared even shorter than yesterday's, and five-inch heels. Peter hoped she was just trying to distract the cops.

She glared at him. "Are you a child? Do you not understand what's at stake here? You could go to jail."

"That's not going to happen." Lewis walked around the front of the big black Jeep. "You're not going to allow that to happen, Ms. Howe, because you're very good at your job."

All trace of the street was gone from his voice. He sounded instead like an East Coast WASP, all private school and corner office. Peter was rumpled from his run and covered with dust from the open-windowed drive through the golf course, but Lewis's white shirt and black jeans were somehow still crisp and clean. He held his expensive mirrored sunglasses in one hand.

Despite all of that, he still reminded Peter of a mountain lion, stalking his prey.

Miranda's face was bright. She'd seen it, too. Not everyone did. "And who are you?"

"I'm Lewis," he said. "We spoke on the telephone yesterday."

"Oh," she said, and smiled. "You're not how I pictured you."

Lewis smiled back with every appearance of genuine pleasure. "You'd be surprised at how often I hear that. Now, what's your plan of attack on this meeting?"

Miranda leaned in. "Well," she said, "I don't know how much you know about what happened yesterday."

"I know everything," he said pleasantly. "Peter had to kill some people. It happens."

Peter saw a faint but unmistakable tremor cascade through Miranda's body. Lewis had that effect on people, when he wanted to.

"Let's talk on the way," said Peter. Police headquarters was a long block to the north.

"I'll drop you," Lewis said. "Save Ms. Howe the walk in those shoes." He raised his eyes to the uneven western sky. "It's going to rain before long."

Peter opened the back door for her. She went to climb in, but stopped when she saw the long striped blanket across the seat. "There's something back here." She lifted a corner of the folded fabric and saw the 10-gauge and the Winchester neatly laid out.

She straightened abruptly.

"Who the fuck are you people?" She lifted the angular black combat tomahawk with the tips of two fingers. "And what the hell is this?"

"So sorry," Lewis said over his shoulder, still sounding like the corner office. "Just wrap those in the blanket and put them on that little cargo shelf behind you."

"In you go," Peter said. "We don't want to be late, right?"

"This is why I left the fucking public defender's office," Miranda muttered as she rolled the weapons up in the lumpy Mexican blanket. "Why I quit being a private-practice defense attorney to be senior counsel at a good firm. I got tired of goons with freaky weapons."

"We're not like that," Peter said.

"Speak fo' yo'self," said Lewis, his accent gone from East Coast WASP to L.A. ghetto in a single sentence.

Miranda had arranged for the meeting to take place outside police headquarters, a blocky sand-colored bunker sharing a concrete public plaza with the Denver City Courthouse and the newer glass-and-brick Denver Crime Laboratory.

The plaza was protected by a low concrete wall, the entrance and exit to an underground parking garage, and concrete-and-steel pylons designed to prevent lunatics from blowing up the visible manifestations of municipal law enforcement.

Lewis pulled the Jeep onto the parking strip across the street. Peter and Miranda got out.

Lewis called to Peter through the open window, "Who are you meeting?"

Peter didn't ask why Lewis wasn't coming with them. He figured Lewis had his reasons, including a kind of metabolic incompatibility with law enforcement.

"A state police investigator named Sykes, and a Denver PD detective named Steinburger."

Lewis's face widened in a smile. "Would that be Steve Steinburger?"

Peter blinked at him. "I believe so."

"You go ahead," Lewis said. "I'll be right there."

As Peter and Miranda crossed the street, the Jeep cut smoothly into traffic and around the corner.

They walked between two pylons and into the plaza. The wind whipped through the narrow gaps between buildings, clouds moving fast overhead. People in office clothes hurried through, trying to get where they were going before the weather turned.

By the main entrance to police headquarters, three men stood in a loose triangle in a temporary patch of sun. One of them looked at his watch.

"Sorry we're late," Peter said as he approached. "Tell me what you know about the bad guys."

"Not how this works." Lean, dark Sykes held yet another tall paper cup of coffee. He had a fat three-ring binder, stuffed with paper, tucked neatly under his arm.

"Can we please just lock him up?" Pale, looming Steinburger held a can of Coke in one hand and a cigarette in the other. Neither man looked like he'd caught any shut-eye since the early-morning wake-up call.

"Wow, you guys look like shit," Peter said, pretending he didn't need another gallon of coffee and twelve hours of rack time himself. "Is that why you're so grumpy?"

"Shut up, Peter," Miranda said. She put her hand out to the third man, who'd been watching with dry amusement. "Hello, Andrew."

"Miranda," he said. "I didn't think we'd be doing this again." He was in his late forties and very tall with slightly rounded shoulders, as if he'd long ago had to come to terms with a shorter world.

"Believe me, I've been trying very hard not to," she said. "Peter, this is Andrew Jones, with the attorney general's office."

Jones offered Peter a smile. He wore blue suit pants and a starched white shirt, no tie, and frameless glasses over thoughtful eyes that functioned, Peter imagined, somewhat like camera lenses, capturing everything in view.

"I'm the person who will likely decide whether the state of Colorado will charge you with a crime." Jones had the quiet voice of one accustomed to others listening closely. "Although we may end up with some jurisdictional issues, given the scope of events."

"Pleased to meet you." Peter extended his hand on the theory it might be harder to decide to prosecute a polite person, no matter that he'd killed four men in the last twenty hours.

Jones looked down at Peter's hand for a short moment, likely with Peter's recent history very much in mind. Peter got the impression the attorney didn't do anything without thinking it through first. When they shook, Jones's hand was large and warm and dry, and also more calloused than Peter had expected.

"Part of the problem, Mr. Ash, is that we haven't gotten your service records from the Pentagon yet. They're not known for cooperating with local authorities."

Miranda spoke. "I'm not sure that's relevant, Andrew. My client and his coworkers were attacked by armed men, and he acted both in self-defense and within the parameters of his employment."

"Mmm," said Jones. "I've read the statements of the investigators. I'd like to hear it directly from Mr. Ash."

So Peter told it again to the man from the attorney general's office, who leaned in with gentle questions ruthlessly designed to catch any flaws in the story. This time Peter included details about the man in the state police uniform, and the black sedan set up to look like an unmarked police cruiser, and the cruiser's midnight chase of Miranda's red BMW.

While Peter talked, Lewis ambled through a narrow space between the buildings and leaned on the wall a dozen feet away. He wore a baseball hat pulled low over his sunglasses, and appeared to take a stand-up nap in the fleeting sun like any other bureaucrat on his lunch break. Peter saw Sykes note Lewis, then disregard him. Steinburger looked at Lewis, looked away, then looked back.

When Jones was done with his questions, Miranda said, "Do you plan to charge my client?"

Jones took off his glasses and cleaned them with a cloth taken from his pocket. "Not at this time."

"That's good," Peter said. "I really do want to know what you've learned. The company I work for has other shipments out there, and other employees. The owner has lost her husband and her father and is alone with her three children. And my friends are dead."

Jones gave a small smile as he put his glasses back on. "Your concern has been noted, and also your interest. Frankly, it's your interest that is problematic. You don't appear to be a person willing to, ah, sit on the sidelines. I am concerned about interference in the investigation, which might hamper prosecution, and also with preventing future violence."

"What about catching the bad guys?" said Peter. "You have any interest in that?" His tone was sharper than he'd intended.

"I have every interest in that," replied Jones, enunciating clearly. "Don't mistake me for a nice man, Mr. Ash. I won't have any Wild West bullshit in my town. If I catch you misbehaving, I will come down on you like a fucking landslide. Am I clear?"

Peter smiled, liking the man and not doubting him a bit. "Crystal."

"Good." Jones checked his watch. "Now. That said, I believe Mr. Ash has earned some credibility." He looked at Sykes and Steinburger. "Are you willing to share anything?"

Sykes looked at Steinburger, but Steinburger was still staring at Lewis. "Steve."

Steinburger waved a hand. "Sure, tell him."

Sykes said, "No usable fingerprints in the ambulance or the tow truck. The sedan, as you'll recall, was burned to a crisp. We're waiting on the DNA, that will be a while."

"What about the cars?"

Sykes tossed his coffee cup in a trash can, opened the fat three-ring binder and flipped through the pages. The wind rattled the paper.

"According to the VINs, the ambulance was sold almost four weeks ago out of an auction lot in Pueblo. Cash sale, the buyer's ID was from Arizona, but Arizona never heard of him. Multiple security cameras on the lot, but the resolution is crap. All they caught was ten grainy minutes of a cowboy hat."

He flipped another page as if reading, although Peter was certain Sykes had it down cold already.

"The wrecker was stolen three days ago from a service station in North Platte, no video, no leads from the locals. The sedan was so burned up the garage techs had to pull the VIN off the engine block. It was a Dodge Charger, registered to the Colorado Department of Military and Veterans Affairs in Centennial. It's a pool car, and it was never reported stolen. Someone there told me, off the record, they thought it had been 'misplaced.' The last known use was six days ago. And the plate on the car was taken from a different car in the same lot."

"So the Charger and the wrecker were taken *after* the first shipment disappeared a week ago? Along with Leonard Wallis and Randy Hansen?"

Sykes raised his eyes from the binder. "Gold star to the new guy."

"So either a different method on the first one, or different vehicles?"

Sykes nodded. "The Charger and the wrecker were stolen, so we're thinking they just picked up what they needed for the job. They probably had to buy the decommissioned ambulance because real ones are harder to steal, and they have tracking systems, LoJack or something like it."

"What about the electronics they pulled out from under Henry's truck?"

Sykes made a face and turned the page. "Two separate pieces there. Our guy tells me one was a GPS tracker, probably to get the location of the truck, and the other was a multi-signal jammer, for blocking cell signals and Heavy Metal's own GPS tracker when the bad guys got close enough for a visual. The tracker is fairly cheap. Companies use them on delivery vehicles, helicopter parents buy them to track their teenage drivers. But that signal jammer is for the serious paranoid and/or criminal. The one they were using cost a couple thousand dollars, you can pick and choose which frequencies to jam, and blocks everything within a hundred and fifty meters."

"Serial numbers?"

Sykes nodded. "We're backtracking the sales right now, but with what we've seen with our bad guys so far, I wouldn't hold your breath. Our electronics guy tells me most of these devices are sold online, and there are any number of ways to buy anonymously these days. The most common way is to log on at a hotel lobby computer or Internet cafe. Use a pre-paid credit card, which you can load with cash at any Target or Walmart or a thousand other places. Then have your stuff delivered to one of those mailbox stores. We'll do all the legwork, in case someone got sloppy, but they haven't been sloppy yet."

Peter sighed. "The weapons?"

Sykes flipped through more pages. "Four pistols in the burned car with the bodies. Our techs managed to get a serial number off one of them. It was originally registered to a man in Cheyenne who says he sold that gun in a lot of five, a month and a half ago. Private sale, cash, no background check, perfectly legal. The guy sells fifteen guns a week over the Internet. He met this particular buyer in person but can't seem to remember anything about him. He's faxing us his paperwork, but Wyoming doesn't require shit on a private sale so the paper won't tell us anything."

"And the shotgun?"

"From Western Arms in Cheyenne. Legit sale from a legit store, but again, it's fucking Wyoming. They don't require checks for long guns. The store video is overwritten after two weeks, so that's useless. Store records say the sale was the same day as the pistols, six weeks ago."

"That's it? That's all you've got?"

Sykes snapped the binder shut and closed his eyes. "Give us time.

It's been less than twenty-four hours. These people are planners, and they are very good."

"Yes," said Peter. "They are. What about an inside man? Are you looking at Randy Hansen and Leonard Wallis?"

Sykes looked at him. "We have done this before, you know."

"You've had a week since Wallis and Hansen disappeared. You must have found out something."

"Hansen was a pothead and a functional alcoholic. According to his VA caseworker, he was probably clinically depressed, and according to his coworkers he never did more than the absolute minimum. No evidence of the kind of motivation required to commit a crime of this scale and make himself disappear. His wife was the one with the ambition, but the disappearance has hurt the business, so she's not on our list of suspects."

Peter thought of Elle's ambition, recruiting him to be her new operations manager before her father was in the ground. The cool way her eyes had appraised him, as if he were some kind of equipment she was considering acquiring. For the moment, he'd keep that to himself.

"And Wallis?"

Sykes sighed. "Wallis is a weird one. Still waiting on military paperwork from Uncle Sam, of course, so we don't know much. Financial history is pretty basic. We know he moved to the area from Henderson three months ago, right before he started his job. The owner, Elle Hansen, says he served in the Army with her husband, that's why they hired him. She says he's very bright, very good at the job. No wife, no girlfriend that we know of. He rents a little shitbox in Arvada that's got almost no furniture in it. Just an air mattress on the floor, a folding chair, a television with no cable connection, and a very nice set of free weights. Not even a computer, although his financial records show that he bought a laptop. We're assuming he had it with him."

LIGHT IT UP

They didn't know much more than Peter had learned from June.
But they had something.

"You talk about him like he's still alive."

Sykes shrugged. "We just haven't found his body."

"But."

"Well, like I said, Wallis is a little weird. His coworkers said he
was a great guy, funny and good company, but none of them spent any
time with the man after work. Nobody had been to his house. Nobody knew anything about his family. Nobody could tell us anything
truly personal about him."

That was odd, in Peter's mind. He'd spent three days with Deacon
and Banjo and got their whole life stories. You had a lot of time for
conversation, working protection. Hurry up and wait.

"Apparently," Sykes said, "Wallis has three favorite topics. He talks
about the Army, which makes sense because he had twenty years in.
He talks about firearms, which isn't unusual in a career infantryman,
or here in the great state of Colorado, for that matter. And apparently
he talks a lot about women." Sykes glanced at Miranda, then back to
Peter. "Kind of a poon hound, I guess. He told his coworkers that he
could pick a woman out of a crowded bar and have her buck naked
and doggy-style inside of thirty minutes."

"Yuck," Miranda, making a face.

"Yeah," said Sykes. "Put it all together, you have an intelligent,
charming loner who loves guns and uses women. Classic shithead
personality."

"And by shithead," Miranda said, "you mean psychopath."

"You think Wallis is involved in this?" Peter asked.

"Let's just say I'd like to find him," Sykes said. "Alive or dead."

"Maybe we can help with that," Lewis said, walking over.

He gave Steinburger a tilted smile. The Denver detective just
stared at him.

"Who the fuck are you?" Sykes asked.

"This is Lewis," Peter said. "A friend of mine."

"Is that a first name or last?" Sykes asked.

Lewis gave one of his elaborate shrugs to accompany the tilted smile. "Just the one."

"Like Madonna?" Sykes said. "Or Cher?"

"Or Björk," Lewis said. "Or Liberace."

"What would it say on your driver's license?"

"Can't remember," Lewis said thoughtfully. "Lost it a few weeks ago. Still waiting for the replacement."

"How about fingerprints," Sykes said. "Is there a name on those?"

Steinburger finally broke into the conversation. "What are you doing here, Lewis?"

"Catching up with old friends," Lewis said. "How you been, Steve-o?"

Sykes looked at Steinburger. "You two know each other?"

"Years ago," Steinburger said. "Bad penny kind of thing."

Jones, the man from the attorney general's office, had been quiet through the conversation. "Is there something I should know?"

Lewis looked at Steinburger. "I'm not sure," he said. "What do you think, Steve-o?"

Steinburger looked away. "Ancient history."

Peter saw the opening. To Sykes, he said, "You mind if I take a look in your book, there?"

"Yes, I fucking mind," said Sykes, tucking the book back under his arm. "This is an active investigation."

"I'm only interested in one thing," Peter said.

Jones said, "Something tells me I don't want to be around for this conversation. So I'm going back to the office before the weather hits." He caught Peter with his eyes. "Right now you're off the hook," he said. "If you act like an asshole, that can always change. Agreed?"

"Agreed," Peter said. "It's been a pleasure." He extended his hand again.

Jones took it. "Four armed men," he said. "By yourself. Jesus Christ." Then he turned and walked away.

When he was gone, Lewis smiled brightly at Steinburger. "How's your mom doing, Steve?"

Steinburger filled his chest with air, then let it out. "I always thought you might come back."

"I'm not here for myself," Lewis said evenly. "I promised you that, and I'm keeping that promise. All we need is a little help. After that, I'm gone forever."

"Steve," Sykes said, "what the fuck is going on?"

"Show them the book," Steinburger said.

"Steve, how long have I known you? We were in the same god-damn class at the academy. We worked together for ten years before I left for the state police."

"Paul." Steinburger ran a big hand down his face. "Just show them the fucking book, okay?"

Sykes stared at Steinburger for a minute, then turned to Peter. "What's your play here?"

"I told you. Those were my friends who got killed."

"But why the fuck am I letting you in? Why are we talking to you at all?"

"Because Lewis has Steinburger's nuts in a vise. And because we can do things you can't."

"Like what?" Sykes said.

Lewis tipped his chin at Steinburger. "Ask Steve. He knows."

Steinburger shook his head. "Don't ask. Some things you don't want to know."

Sykes sighed. "All right. What do you want to see?"

"I want to see a copy of McSweeney's shipping manifest. What the grower claims was in Henry's truck when we got hit."

Sykes flipped through the book and came up with a printout. The list of items headed for their final destination, Zig McSweeney's cabin in the mountains.

To Peter and the other guys, the cargo was a series of numbered cardboard boxes sealed with tamper-resistant tape. On the manifest, they were packages listed with their contents, place of origin, and destination.

There was nothing unusual on the list. Peter pulled out Henry's phone. He used Henry's passcode to unlock the phone, then opened the Web browser. As Elle had thought, the Heavy Metal website was open and Henry was still logged in. He found yesterday's manifest for their team.

The Heavy Metal manifest was the same as McSweeney's in Sykes's binder. Nothing different.

"What are you looking for?" Sykes asked.

"I'm not sure," Peter said. "Something that doesn't belong. I'm hoping I'll know it when I see it. Can you show me the list of evidence recovered from Henry's truck?"

Interested despite himself, Sykes flipped through the book and found several lists, one for each vehicle, and one for Peter's clothes.

On the truck list, the shipment boxes were numbered and described. Peter correlated them with the manifest. "We already did that," said Sykes. "Twice. Boxes were opened and inventoried. Nothing was taken from the shipment."

Peter kept reading. A list of the weapons thrown onto the back seat. Henry's big green Thermos. Deacon's coat. Jumper cables, a toolbox, a Pelican case with Henry's mountain survival gear. Nothing Peter couldn't identify after three days' driving around in Henry's truck.

There had to be something, he thought. Something special, to make it worth killing four men.

What would it look like? he wondered. How big would it be?

How in hell had anyone known it was there?

On Henry's phone, Peter touched the text icon. It was how the Heavy Metal crew leaders had kept in touch with the clients and with the office during the day. There was a long string of recent texts from yesterday's stops. *On my way. There in 20 minutes. Leaving now. Stuck in traffic.*

Peter found Zig McSweeney in the phone's contacts, then hit the text button to find the history. He scrolled down. And there it was.

From McSweeney: *I have a favor to ask. Something personal I want you to carry to the cabin tomorrow. Not product, not on the manifest.*

Henry had replied: *Happy to help. If you're not there, leave it with Tonio.*

Peter showed the text to Sykes and Steinburger. "We were carrying something that wasn't on the manifest. You do any digging into Zig McSweeney?"

"The dope grower," Steinburger said. "Yeah, he says he's having money troubles. We got a letter from his lawyer to that effect. He wants his money out of the evidence locker."

"You think he might have arranged the hijacking to salvage some cash out of this?"

Steinburger shook his head. "The hijacking *caused* his money troubles, according to him. Our financial crimes guys are looking into that. But honestly, I don't see him for armed robbery." He looked at Lewis. "That takes somebody who's either crazy, stupid, or a true outlaw."

Peter said, "You dig into McSweeney's investor?"

"What, that holding company? They're not returning phone calls. Our financial guys are working on it."

"No, the original investor," Peter said. "The one who loaned him the money to start with."

"Yeah," Sykes said, and flipped through his binder. "Jon Jordan. Boulder money guy, a Wall Street refugee looking for that Rocky Mountain high. I talked to him the day after the first shipment went missing. Seemed nice enough on the phone, told me he'd sold his loan to that holding company a month ago."

"You know he's dead?"

"What?"

"He was riding his bike. Got run off the road three days ago. Dead on arrival."

Sykes and Steinburger looked at each other.

But something else was nagging at Peter.

The manifest hadn't shown McSweeney's personal delivery. The bad guys might have hacked Heavy Metal's system, but they wouldn't have learned about it that way.

McSweeney had made the request via text.

Which meant either McSweeney was calling the shots, or the bad guys had an inside man, or someone had access to Henry's texts.

Peter didn't like the last possibility.

He felt it deep in the pit of his stomach.

"Lewis," he said. "Can someone read your texts without having your phone?"

"Sure," Lewis said. "I do it all the time. When you send me a text, it comes to my phone, but also to my laptop. You can set it up that way on your main account preferences."

"Could someone do that without your knowledge?"

Lewis gave Peter a tilted grin. "Not *my* knowledge," he said. "But if you had the account log-in and password, you could change a lot of shit. Is that a company phone?"

"Elle says it is. She keeps telling me she wants it back."

"So somebody with Heavy Metal has access to that account infor-mation. Could be the owner, could be someone else in the company." Lewis looked at Steinburger and Sykes. "Like Leonard Wallis. The operations manager."

But Peter didn't care about any of that anymore.

The pit in his stomach got deeper.

"Listen," he said. "How hard would it be to find out someone's identity from their phone number?"

"Not hard," Sykes said. "Not hard at all."

Peter took out Henry's phone and pulled up the texts again.

Scrolled down through June's messages. Found the one with her flight number and arrival time.

She'd landed about an hour ago.

Then he saw a text he'd missed, probably while he was on the phone with Elle. A selfie of June, a wide smile on her face, standing before a new blue Mustang convertible with the top down. *See you soon, sucka!*

The pit in his stomach felt bottomless.

Like he was in free fall.

This was all his fault.

He found her number and pressed call.

The phone rang and rang.

29

The offer had come out of nowhere, less than a month after Dixon's dishonorable discharge.

He was woken in his crappy second-floor studio apartment by a ringing phone. He didn't recognize the ring. It wasn't his phone. But it wouldn't stop ringing.

It took Dixon several painful minutes to locate the damned thing inside a padded FedEx envelope he'd found in his mailbox the night before. He hadn't opened it because the return address was a law firm in New York. Dixon wasn't eager to view any mail from lawyers, even his own.

It took him another shameful minute to slice through the layers of tape with his pocketknife. His hands were shaking.

The phone was the only thing in the package. It was still ringing.

Dixon hit the green button. "Who is this?"

"Good morning, Mr. Dixon," said the voice on the other end of the connection. A male voice, mid-Atlantic accent, pink and hearty and sure of itself. "I have a business opportunity I'd like to discuss with you."

Dixon looked at the cheap futon couch that folded out into a bed, at the unwashed glass standing by the sink, at the empty fifth of tequila atop the fridge. Evidence of his sins. It was early. His head throbbed. He swallowed the rising bile.

"Sure," he said. "Fire away."

"How'd you like to start your own consulting business? An attorney will help you set up the entity. You'll be reimbursed, of course."

The voice named a dollar amount, Dixon's monthly stipend. Half again more than he'd been making as a lieutenant colonel. "Plus expenses and bonuses. You'll be paid by multiple business entities. Your instructions will come through me."

"And you are?"

"An attorney," said the voice. "I'll introduce myself in person once you've actually retained me. At that time, our conversations will be protected by attorney-client privilege."

"What's the work?"

"The kind you'll be familiar with. A series of discreet interventions."

"Interventions?" Dixon asked. "Intel or hands-on?"

"Discreet," said the man. "Operations will vary. This is sensitive work, vitally important but completely off-book. Deniability is crucial."

Deniability for whom? Dixon wondered. But he didn't say it.

The attorney said, "After you're set up as a corporate entity, you'll form a team. Freelancers, combat veterans, experience is a must. A particular psychological type. I'll arrange for testing. Start by looking for people who miss the war. They'll be having trouble adapting back. Few social ties. The pay will be good. They'll be grateful."

Dixon recognized the strategy.

It was what the lawyer was doing with him, after all.

Dixon didn't like it, but he didn't have to.

Between his personal obligations and the money the lawyer was offering, he would do whatever was necessary.

There was honor in that, he told himself.

Dixon found freelancer candidates online and flew the best out to a rented hunting camp for assessment. Expense money was wired directly into his business account. Dixon tried to be frugal. The lawyer never complained about costs.

The freelancers were a strange bunch. The testing had winnowed the candidates down to a small cadre of true mercenaries. Which, Dixon supposed, now described himself, too.

He'd told them the work was critical to national security. Work they could feel good about.

They didn't believe it, either. Nor did they care.

Dixon hired four men. The mission was to destroy a large office building in Jakarta. The lawyer told Dixon that the building was owned by a front company for Jemaah Islamiyah, an Indonesian terrorist group. Three months to plan and execute. A truck bomb detonated at midnight local time, minimal casualties. Bonus on completion.

They got their bonus.

Dixon added four more men. The second mission was very different.

According to the lawyer, the goal was to take down the finance arm of a multinational African insurgent network. Targeted assassinations, in the end more than a dozen, spread out over as many months. Some were explicit murders, others had to appear random or accidental. Long-range sniper shots. A sharp knife in a public market. A restaurant robbery gone bad. A nightclub bombing. An armed attack on a fortified compound by what appeared to be members of a local militia.

The work was difficult, the environment brutal. Half the time they were operating in the middle of a civil war. Every time Dixon thought it couldn't get worse, it did.

Of the eight men on the team, only three survived. Dixon prayed for their souls.

He had plenty of time to figure out who he was really working for.

He didn't want to know, not exactly, but the degraded remains of his professional self required it. He needed to make sure he wasn't working for the Russians, or worse.

In the end, it wasn't difficult.

All he had to do was follow the money.

The owner of the building in Jakarta was not a terrorist front, but an overleveraged and underinsured family-owned company. The bombing forced the company to liquidate several of its other properties to survive, including a large undeveloped oceanfront parcel on the island of Bali. That parcel was sold to a local holding company, then resold to a flamboyant American investor who sold it yet again to a British hotel chain for more than three hundred million dollars, three times what he'd paid.

The targets of the African assassinations were all members of the continent's economic elite. Dixon discovered that each of the dead had professional or family connections to a large mining operation in the Democratic Republic of the Congo, and each death changed the ownership structure of the mine. A week after the death of the youngest adult son of the man with sole remaining controlling interest, the mines were sold to a French national acting as a confidential representative for the same American investor, who turned around and sold it to a Chinese consortium for twice what he had paid, almost a billion dollars.

Dixon's so-called consulting business, his discreet interventions, were part of a billionaire's negotiation strategy.

Dixon kept the knowledge to himself. He found he didn't mind as long as the money kept coming in and he had a bottle of tequila to help him sleep.

After all, his daughters still needed college tuition. Their weddings would come soon after. His wife's expensive medical care would be necessary for the rest of her life.

Dixon was already going to burn in hell for who he was, for the things he'd done.

What did it matter that he was a few steps closer to the devil?

After Africa, the lawyer scheduled a meeting at a charter flight service located just outside the Richmond airport, two hours south of D.C. The charter company had two big hangars, an office, a terminal building, and a service center for fuel and provisioning trucks, all flanking a broad asphalt apron with various Cessnas and Citations and Lears parked along the perimeter.

Dixon's texted instructions were to drive to the far side of the apron, closest to the taxiway, where a big white jet loomed over the smaller aircraft like a hawk among sparrows.

Marked only with its tail numbers, it was a shortened, corporate version of the Airbus A320, with the same up-curved wingtips and sleek profile. A set of stairs had been rolled to the cabin door. The air smelled of spilled fuel and hot exhaust and the burned-tar stink of recently coated tarmac.

As Dixon got out of his car, the jet's door opened. A woman's head peeked out, and a pale, slender arm beckoned him inside.

She wore a long fitted skirt and a snug white blouse with a string of pearls against the fabric. Even Dixon could admire her lush figure and the soft beauty of her face, framed by thick dark hair held up off her neck with a heavy silver clasp.

"I'm so sorry, he's on the phone right now." She carried herself like a beauty queen, projecting a warm Southern charm that concealed a glint of something beneath, something wicked and slightly desperate. She gestured at the elegant little galley kitchen. "May I pour you coffee or a cold drink while you wait?"

Dixon accepted a glass of cucumber water and stood waiting in the main cabin.

Instead of tight rows of narrow seats like a commercial airplane, the jet had the fine furnishings of a luxury yacht, with dark, gleaming wood and buttery leather seats. A powerful voice boomed through the closed partition door. It rose and fell like a fine musical instrument, alternately cajoling and berating the unheard person on the other end of the conversation.

Dixon was pretty sure that he wasn't meeting the lawyer.

Then the partition door banged open and Russell Palmer strode out, wearing his trademark red double-breasted blazer over a white silk shirt and designer blue jeans. It was his favorite color scheme, well advertised by the investor's many appearances in public and on the business pages.

Now Dixon knew why he'd been summoned. Palmer wanted to see what his money was buying. He wanted to meet the new head of his personal special ops team, his private team of killers. Palmer would want specifics. He'd want to hear stories. He'd want firsthand confirmation of his own wealth and power, the fact that he could order the deaths of other human beings without consequence.

Palmer looked Dixon up and down with that plump pink smile spread across his jowls. "I just had to meet you in person," he said. "You know why you're here, right?"

Then Palmer frowned. "Did Sandra wand you? Goddamn it, girl, what are you thinking? I'm doing sensitive business here."

Sandra hurried to produce a black box smaller than a deck of cards with two stubby antennae on the top. With careful grace, she passed it over Dixon's arms, legs, chest, groin, back, and shoes. When she nodded at Palmer, his plump smile returned.

"No unauthorized listening devices, that's the only way to do business. Listen, you've done such good work, I had to meet you. My lawyer said no, I should keep things separate, but screw him, right?" He gave a dismissive wave of the back of his hand. "Lawyers."

Dixon opened his mouth to respond, but Palmer just kept talking. It wasn't a conversation, it was a monologue, delivered as if Palmer already knew the answers to any question Dixon might ask.

"Hey, I understand your wife isn't well. You know there's a doctor in Switzerland who specializes in her particular illness. You don't? He runs a private clinic, he's developed some promising experimental therapies, had some real successes. It's expensive as hell, you can only imagine." Palmer raised his eyebrows. "You'd need to earn a lot more than I'm paying you now."

Dixon felt a numbness spreading through him.

Of course Palmer would know about his wife. Palmer would know everything. Dixon felt the weight of his shame, his lifetime of sin, along with the pull of Palmer's wealth and access. As Palmer surely intended him to.

"Anyway, as a special favor to me, this doctor has agreed to review your wife's medical records. Maybe there's something he can do. Meanwhile, I have another project, a bigger one. But I'll need more out of you. If you want to step up, there's a pile of money to be made. You ever work in Venezuela?"

Just like that, Palmer pulled Dixon further in.

No, Dixon thought. Palmer didn't have to pull. Dixon went willingly.

That's how the devil worked.

You had to actively choose to sell the next piece of your soul.

To step down into the next circle of hell.

With each new operation, Dixon saw more of Palmer's organization. Now this latest oddball project in Colorado.

Dixon didn't like the idea of working anywhere domestically, had in fact advised Palmer against it, even if the project seemed small enough. But it required a specific kind of hire. A personal connection. Dixon had consulted with the Army major to find a recently discharged sergeant.

The sergeant's psychological testing results were somewhat disturbing. In person, however, he was an excellent operator. Talented, experienced, physically fit, charismatic enough to lead the field team, a true predator.

More importantly, the sergeant had a direct inside line to the next target.

His price was to have his military jacket wiped clean, which Dixon could get done through the Army major.

In the planning stages, the Colorado thing had seemed like a cakewalk.

The first phase went like clockwork.

The second phase was a disaster.

Now Dixon was summoned to Palmer's jet again, this time at Jeffco Airport between Denver and Boulder. As always, Sandra met him at the cabin door with the bug detector. As she wanded him, she gave him the same complicated smile. Palmer had told Dixon that she'd been Miss Georgia twenty-three years ago. Palmer had a fondness for former beauty queens.

Dixon and Sandra hadn't become friends, exactly, but each recognized in the other a fellow degenerate. A fellow servant and plaything.

He accepted another glass of cucumber water and sat at the elegant conference table, listening to Palmer in his office shouting into the telephone. Dixon would have preferred to have this conversation on the phone, but Palmer liked to do this delicate business in person.

Dixon didn't mind the chain of command. From his father to the church to the Marine Corps, there had always been a structure to his life that Dixon found reassuring. But that structure had also always told him, either silently or out loud, that there was something deeply wrong about him, that he would never fit into that world.

Maybe it was just Dixon's own inner voice, telling him.

At least here, in this flying island of luxury, Dixon did not want to fit. Grace and honor and integrity, the things he valued most and had most fully lost, had no place here.

"Status report," Palmer barked as he strode from his private office. Today he wore a blue blazer over a white shirt and red pants, a variation on his usual outfit. He didn't offer to shake hands. As if Dixon's many sins and failures might be catching.

"As you know, the first operation was successful," Dixon said. "My lead operator got it done as planned. The second operation was also well planned and well executed, but there was a wild card. The fourth man."

"Yes, I saw something on the news," Palmer said. He dipped a hand into his jacket pocket, pulled out a pair of individually wrapped candies, shucked them from their wrappers, and popped them in his mouth. "Unfortunate. I trust you got what you were after?"

"No," Dixon said. "My people didn't get the money or the special package. We don't even know where the hell it is. We lost the whole team except my lead operator. We've made two more attempts on that wild card, just to clear a path for the next steps, but we've been unsuccessful."

Palmer's face was unreadable. "So you're utterly incompetent, is that it?"

"No, sir. This wild card is extremely resourceful. He's already brought in another man who almost took out my remaining operator. The Denver Police and the state police now have teams investigating. The state attorney general's office is involved. I have to tell you, this isn't going to get any easier. We need to rethink our strategy."

"The strategy is simple," Palmer said. "I only buy distressed assets. That's where the value is. If it's not distressed, it's not a deal." He gave his famous smile, the cat who swallowed the canary. "Sometimes, in order to get the deal, you have to distress the assets yourself."

"I know you believe there's a great deal of upside here," Dixon said, "but there's more risk, too. And more people are going to die."

"You dumbfuck," Palmer said, hard candies rattling against his teeth. "You can't begin to imagine the upside. The risk is irrelevant. Be a professional. Get it done."

He didn't complain about killing people, Dixon noted. That wasn't a risk Palmer was considering. The only risks he concerned himself with were strategic. Financial. Legal.

"I need more resources," Dixon said. "I need to rebuild my team. We have time. The insurance company won't pay off on the first operation, and the police are holding everything from the second operation as evidence. The financial effect is the same. The company is yours."

"You're forgetting the package," Palmer said. "And if it goes to court? American judges are so hard to buy, with their goddamned balanced scales, and when you do, they're *expensive*. That grower is in clear breach of contract, but he might be able to argue *force majeure* and use the unpaid insurance claim and the money in police evidence to gain time. In fact, he's likely to get his money before the case ever goes to court, so my position is screwed."

"You can use your influence to keep things bottled up," Dixon said. "Have your lawyers reach out to the insurance company. Also to the police. These things can drag out a long time. Years, if you want them to. All while the legal expense builds, and the stress takes its toll."

"But we still won't have the *package*," Palmer said. "You need to stop making excuses and execute." He let out a hard sigh. "Tell me more about the troublemaker, the one who stopped the second operation. What do we know about him?"

"He's a Marine," Dixon said. "Combat veteran, highly decorated, elite unit. Years of service. I haven't been able to find out anything about the new man he brought in."

Palmer smirked. "Are they nancy boys like you?"

Dixon felt the self-loathing rise like bile in his throat. Palmer liked to remind Dixon of his sins. This humiliation was punishment for his failure. But he pushed his feelings down.

"No," he said. "There's also a woman. She's flying in today."

"Then it's easy," Palmer said, waving a hand. "Carrot and stick. Take the woman, put her someplace he can't reach. Send him a few photos. Voilà, the troublemaker is working for us."

Dixon shook his head. "Sir, that's a bad idea. This man was a lieutenant in my battalion. He and his platoon got more done than the rest of the company combined."

Palmer looked at Dixon. "It's all about leverage," he said. "Just get it done. Or are you completely useless?"

For a moment, Dixon didn't know what to say. It was one thing to threaten women and children in the heat of anger, as he himself had done earlier. It was another entirely to target a noncombatant in cold blood. It went against every idea of honor and integrity he'd ever had.

The next circle of hell.

He still needed the money. For his daughters. For his wife.

"I'll get it done," he said.

30

June Cassidy grabbed her carry-on from the overhead, threw her faded old backpack over one shoulder, and walked down the aisle after the other passengers. Her stomach felt kind of fluttery, but she didn't know if it was a good feeling or a bad feeling. Or both.

It could have been a good feeling because she was going to see Peter again, something June, an independent goddamn woman, had been thinking about far too often since he left. She didn't like that, having him on her mind.

After he was gone—after she'd told him to leave, she reminded herself, it was her own decision—she kept telling herself that she'd worked too hard for too long to banish the ghosts of her horrible ex-boyfriends, a long list of assholes and control freaks and serial philanderers.

She told herself again and again that there was no way she was going to dive into anything serious, not for a while, and definitely not with Peter Ash, a messed-up unemployed ex-military dharma fucking bum, no matter how he made her feel.

But oh, how he made her feel.

Not just in bed, although that was a factor, his exquisite attention, shall we say, to detail. Now she was blushing in the aisle of the goddamn airplane, and June did not blush.

And was that a little tingle, down below?

Christ, he could get her motor running long distance, just thinking about him.

Some kind of fucking sexual telepathy is what it was.

No, it wasn't that at all.

It was the way he looked at her.

The way he *listened* to her.

How he liked that she was smart and bossy and *herself.*

How funny he could be, and how serious, and how kind. How unafraid he seemed of anything, especially her. And how safe she felt when she was with him.

Despite the violence that lived inside him.

Not that she needed Peter to make her fucking life *complete* or anything. She had her work and her friends, and she was making up for lost time with her dad, too. Her life was going great. Her attraction to Peter was just a reaction to the circumstances, what they'd been through together. That was what she'd told herself.

Then he started sending those letters.

Such a dirty trick.

Letters? Fucking *letters?*

With pressed wildflowers inside?

That sonofabitch. Not fair at *all.*

Reading those letters was like staying up all night with him on a long car drive, hearing the calm murmur of his voice from the seat beside her. Like they were the only two people in the world, the rolling road lit by their headlights, the darkened landscape passing by as if in a dream.

He wrote at first about the Oregon backcountry, fixing trails and bridges, the people he worked with. He'd written a lot about Henry, a Vietnam vet, a real friend. Then he told her about Don, the therapist he was seeing on his days off, and the assignments Don gave him—go ride an elevator, go sit in the laundromat—to make progress with his claustrophobia. Eventually he began to tell her, in fits and starts, about his war. Not so much the horrible parts of it, although she knew those were there, lurking. He told her about his regrets. The mistakes he'd made. The friends he'd lost.

She'd wipe her eyes and blow her nose and read the letter again, to make herself learn. How it had been for him, for all of them. She wanted to take him in her arms and hold him, to help him feel better.

She wanted to take him to bed.

Although, come to think of it, they'd never really been *in bed*, because of that goddamn claustrophobia. They'd never really been inside together at all, not for more than a few minutes at a time.

And that was the question, wasn't it?

How would it be, her and Peter, in normal life?

What would normal life even look like?

Because that was the other reason for the fluttering in her stomach.

It wasn't just what he called the white static.

Someone was trying to kill him. Again.

And here she was, for no logical reason that she could claim, getting off this plane. Showing up to do whatever she could to help.

He'd done the same for her, hadn't he?

She'd talked to Lewis about this once, about the strange pull she felt, being around Peter. Like he had his own peculiar gravity.

Lewis had smiled at her. "Why you think all those men followed him into combat?" he asked. "Going door to door in Fallujah? His men went willingly. Not for God and country, not really. They went for each other, and for him."

"Is that why you're here?" she'd asked.

"No." Lewis's voice had been gentle. "I came because he's my friend. He did something for me I could never have done for myself. And he needed me."

As if Lewis didn't know those were the very same reasons.

She'd upgraded herself to business class and watched out the window as the plane climbed into the air, waiting for the Wi-Fi to go live. She'd done more research for Peter in the Portland airport, and wanted to keep at it.

One of the benefits of her work with Public Investigations, a group of independent investigative journalists, was access to excellent subscription databases. Although they weren't anywhere near as powerful as a certain invasive algorithm her mother had developed, June could still find out a lot about a person. Lewis's source in the Department of Defense had helped, too.

Take Leonard Wallis, for example. His Army record was stripped bare, not even a photograph after twenty years. June ran a deep credit check and learned that he'd worked for Heavy Metal Protection for three months after he got out of the Army. She also found records of payments from a company called Fidelis International Risk.

So June ran Fidelis International Risk through her databases. She found an oddball little company based in Delaware, which was one of the easiest and cheapest places in the U.S. to incorporate, and also one of the best if you wanted to keep your corporate information private. Something like half of all U.S. corporations were registered in the state of Delaware.

She started looking into Fidelis.

But she could find no public presence. No company website, nothing on the business networking or employment sites. Not even mentions in online newspapers or blogs.

Which was odd for a company doing business in the modern era.

In fact, the only public mention of Fidelis was on the Delaware state website—God, she loved the Internet—where she found the basic corporate listing. But the owner of record was hidden.

The papers had been filed by a registered agent with a physical Delaware address, as was required by the state. June paid the fee for the extended report. Delaware took Visa, MasterCard, and Discover.

With the long-form report in hand, she dug around in her private databases and found credit reports for Fidelis. Bank accounts with large balances. Corporate credit cards with big borrowing limits. That didn't just happen. There had to be a lot of money running through this invisible company. Fidelis was only a few years old.

She took a longer look at the registered agent. Most registered agents were business entities set up for the sole purpose of registering corporations, with large, well-designed websites offering a wide array of services. Most of these entities registered hundreds, if not thousands, of corporations each year. Agents could also serve as the sole point of contact, which was handy if you wanted to conceal ownership or just make it difficult to obtain information.

But Fidelis's registered agent wasn't one of those companies.

There was no website offering to incorporate your business for $295 or register your yacht in tax-friendly Delaware. Just a company name and an address.

The address was in Bethany Beach, on the ocean. Prime real estate.

The owner of the house was an attorney, a partner in a small white-shoe New York firm.

Not a very nice man, apparently.

He was featured in a prominent article in the *New York Times*, noting that he'd been linked to several Justice Department lawsuits aimed at one Russell Palmer.

June already knew who Russell Palmer was.

An unabashedly aggressive investor often described in the financial papers as having a magic touch, Palmer had an uncanny knack for buying underpriced assets at exactly the right time, often reselling only a few months later at an enormous profit.

A proud capitalist, a larger-than-life figure, a showman.

Palmer tended to dress in combinations of red, white, and blue.

For most of a decade, he'd been a regular on the Sunday-morning talk shows, and there'd been speculation about Palmer's running for office until a string of scandals, lawsuits, and legal settlements had taken the wind from those sails.

Despite that taint, Palmer was still considered a brilliant investor. He'd just flipped some African mining operation for nine hundred and seventy million dollars.

She didn't know why Palmer would be involved with a guy like Leonard Wallis.

She certainly couldn't prove Wallis's connection to Palmer, not on a two-hour flight.

But now she knew where to dig.

There was a common flaw, she'd found, with a certain kind of person.

After years of bad behavior without ever really getting caught, they began to feel untouchable.

Sometimes they got lazy.

By the time the flight attendant asked her to close her laptop, June was rubbing her hands together with glee.

———

Once off the plane, June put her arm through the other strap of her backpack and pulled her wheeled carry-on through the airport.

After giving far too much thought to what she might take to Denver, she'd just thrown some shit in her suitcase, brushed her teeth, freshened up her deodorant, and driven to Portland wearing what she'd put on that morning, what she often wore in the little pocket valley where she lived and worked. Her favorite hiking pants, a T-shirt that fit her curves from the excellent Counterbalance Brewing Company in Seattle, and well-worn trail shoes.

She might have spiced up the underwear a little, although she'd never admit it.

She'd made sure to add a heavy fleece and a rain shell in her pack. Travel with Peter could be unpredictable. Who knew where she'd be by the end of the day?

She'd be lying if she said that wasn't part of the appeal.

There was a little subway that took passengers from the gates to the main terminal. The layout funneled people toward the baggage claim area. At the bottom of the funnel, by a sign pointing the way toward a lightning shelter, she saw a middle-aged man with weather-beaten skin, cropped hair, and excellent posture standing by the wall, talking on his phone, a crisp black business backpack at his feet.

June had been a journalist for almost ten years, and she was always looking for the telling detail. The man wore a tan suit with a pale blue button-down shirt and no tie. The very picture of a modern man of business.

But his shoes were wrong.

They should have been sleek and polished with thin leather soles.

Instead they were thick and solid with heavy lug soles.

And he wasn't staring vacantly at the floor or into space as he focused on his phone conversation, as most people did.

Instead he watched the funnel as passengers spilled through, looking for their luggage or their relatives.

His eyes flicked to June's face for a long moment, then away.

June had taken self-defense classes after a bad experience in college. She'd learned that the easiest part of self-defense was simply staying away from potentially dangerous situations. The most obvious of those was somebody paying more attention to her than he should.

After what had happened last spring, when she first met Peter, she'd begun paying a little more attention herself.

She'd also started carrying what looked like a pink lipstick. But under the cap, instead of lipstick, was the trigger for ten pressurized blasts of capsicum pepper spray. In her back pocket she kept a nice steel ballpoint pen that also happened to conceal a two-and-a-half-inch blade where the ink refill would normally be. It wasn't a fantastic pen, but it was great for opening the mail.

June often felt like she was being more than a little paranoid.

But most days she also felt a little safer.

She always carried the fake lipstick in her backpack, which basically served as a large purse. Putting the pen in her back pocket had become a habit, just like her phone. And she hadn't gotten on a commercial flight in years. So she'd forgotten to disarm herself for the trip through airport security.

But the nice TSA people in Portland had been thoroughly distracted by a large man who appeared to be hallucinating, seeing dragons instead of the luggage conveyors. She just dumped the pen in the plastic tray with her phone and her belt and her backpack and hadn't realized she'd broken several laws until she went to the bathroom and found the fake lipstick in the pocket with her hairbrush.

Now, walking past the trim middle-aged man in the tan suit, she felt better knowing she still had them, and tucked her hand into her pack and found the comforting shape of the pepper spray.

Instead of heading out to the rental car shuttles, she turned toward the baggage claim. Not the first carousel, with her flight number on the monitor, but the third, where luggage from Phoenix was just starting to emerge.

She found a place to stand and watch.

When the man in the tan suit came around the corner and walked toward her, she felt herself tense up.

She was safe at the airport, she told herself. Cameras, police. He would do nothing here. And she had her lipstick pepper spray ready in her hand.

Without even a sideways glance in her direction, the man in the tan suit stepped toward the Phoenix carousel, plucked a basic black rolling suitcase from the moving track, and walked away.

June let out the breath she hadn't quite known she was holding.

This was almost always what happened, she told herself.

She noticed something, changed her behavior a little, and it turned out to be nothing.

Which was good. It meant that she was paying attention, and that the world wasn't as dangerous as she sometimes feared.

She walked to the other end of baggage claim and back, killing a little time just in case, then went outside across the series of medians toward the shuttle buses, feeling smart and safe as she tucked the lipstick tube back in its place.

She hadn't reserved a car when she'd booked her flight because she hoped Peter would offer to pick her up at the airport. Then she decided she didn't want to be a distraction, given that he'd asked her not to come anyway. And maybe he was more involved than he'd let on with that woman lawyer, or the woman who owned the protection company. Anyway, June was her own goddamned woman who wanted her own goddamned wheels, so she texted him that she was renting a car and would meet him at her hotel, which would let him know that he shouldn't count on getting laid.

Then she realized she was being a little crazy, and she should just fucking relax already and see how things went. Right?

She climbed on the first shuttle she found, put her crap on the shelf, and found a seat. There were two other people on the bus already, a large white woman in a floral blouse and a beanpole college-age kid wearing a Bob Marley T-shirt, grinning like an idiot. She figured the kid was here for the Colorado cannabis experience. Then wondered if she was making a judgment because of his T-shirt. Maybe he was a naturally cheerful person, and the woman in the floral blouse was the total stoner.

Then the man in the tan suit came up the steps.

He had his backpack slung from his rolling bag and his phone in his hand. He took a seat far from the rest of the passengers and devoted his attention to his phone, holding it sideways and typing with both thumbs like a teenager.

Before she could decide what to do, the shuttle driver climbed into his seat and closed the doors and hit the gas.

The shuttle served two different rental car companies. June figured she'd wait to see where the man in the suit was going, and pick the other company. Better safe than sorry. Worst case, she'd stay on the bus, ride back to the terminal, and pick yet another company. They were all on the same road.

She put her hand in her pack again, found the fake lipstick.

She was being paranoid, now, she was sure.

But it was also kinda fun. Like a game.

His suit was a little old-fashioned, she decided at the first stop, watching as he collected his things with practiced efficiency and moved smoothly down the shuttle steps. Kept his eyes on his phone the whole time. The kid in the Bob Marley T-shirt got off with him.

June got off at the next stop with the woman in the floral shirt.

One of the benefits of her second job, keeping an administrative eye on the tech incubator her dad had started, was a considerably larger paycheck than a freelance journalist was used to. So she splurged on the car and got a sky-blue Mustang convertible, which she'd always wanted to drive.

Plus it was parked right outside the building, so she wouldn't have to wander around in that huge back parking lot all by herself. Safety first, that was June's motto.

She texted Peter a picture of the car to yank his chain. *See you soon, sucka!*

There were two people ahead of her and the rental paperwork took forever, like always, but climbing into the Mustang was her reward. Man, that engine sounded nice.

She put on her sunglasses, then punched the gas leaving the parking lot, just to see what the car would do. She left some rubber behind, so she knew she was going to have to behave herself. The car really wanted to go fast. It didn't even seem to see the yellow light at the end of the long access road.

But there was another car waiting ahead of her, a white sedan, so she hit the brake and slowed to a stop.

Then an old brown Dodge pickup, coated with dust, rolled up behind her and bumped the Mustang good and hard.

The impact rolled her forward a few feet, so she was jammed right up against the car in front of her. She felt her heart pounding in her chest. The truck bumped her again, more lightly this time, closing the gap. Both cars were tight against her. She took a deep breath and touched the gas, felt the engine rev, but the car didn't move.

The pickup driver had hopped out and was striding up to her car. She half expected him to be the man in the tan suit, but he was someone else. A man of maybe forty with a big round head, small ears, and a nub of a nose, wearing an orange Western plaid shirt and tight Wranglers with a big belt buckle. He looked like a rodeo rider, or at least her idea of a rodeo rider. All balls, no brain.

Man, she was pissed.

"Dang it, lady, where'd you learn how to drive?"

She pushed her door open hard and whacked him in the knee. She heard him bark with pain. She slammed her door shut and punched the gas with her front wheels turned, hoping to push the Kia out of the way.

The tires screamed and the Mustang lurched, the back end skating sideways a little but not enough to do anything. Was it possible the sedan was pushing back in reverse? She tried to reverse herself but got nowhere against the mass of the truck. She couldn't get enough momentum to push her way free. She was boxed in.

"Come on, lady, I'm tryna help you out, here. Don't make this any harder than it has to be."

He spoke loud over the sound of her car. He had heavy shoulders and a narrow waist, close-cropped black hair, and an impatient frown on his face. She hit the door locks and reached for the pepper spray in her pack but the top was still down so he just reached in and grabbed one of her upper arms in each hand and pulled.

June was strong and fit, but the beefed-up rodeo rider wasn't going to have any trouble lifting her weight. Plus she was confined in the cockpit of the car, and with his superior position above and behind her, she wasn't going to make any progress by staying in the seat. So she let go of the steering wheel and straightened her legs and let him lift her up.

Wishing all the while that she'd just asked Peter to pick her up at the goddamned airport.

The rodeo rider rested her weight briefly on top of the door, moved one hand around her waist to improve his leverage, then plucked her out of the car with a surprising amount of grace.

To anyone passing by, he might look like a good Samaritan.

June knew better.

If the first part of self-defense was keeping yourself out of dangerous situations, the second part was defending yourself when you had no choice. Self-defense techniques only got you so far, so she'd added some judo and kickboxing over the years. It made her feel capable and independent. She knew the right places to hit somebody, and she wasn't afraid to do it. The training had also given her some practice getting hit herself, which was important, so the pain and fear didn't make her freeze or submit without a fight.

She waited until the rodeo clown relaxed his grip, then turned in close and raised her right knee into his crotch as fast and hard as she could, pivoting from the hip and raising herself up on her toes for maximum force. She felt the soft contact in those tight jeans and knew it was a good shot when she heard his breath *woof* out and he began to curl into himself.

"Ohhh," he said. She could hear the pain in his voice.

She twisted away and turned to run, thinking she had the shoes for it and could outrun this tight-pantsed broken-balled muscled-up sack of meat any day of the week. The rental place was less than a mile down the road. She'd be there before he could stand up straight.

But he still held her T-shirt bunched up in one big hand.

Her legs were the strongest part of her, so she planted her left foot and rotated her hip socket to knee him in the stomach with her right leg. She didn't want to be that close to him, and she didn't have the leverage or momentum to hit him as hard as she'd like, but she wanted him hurting, distracted, so she could tear herself free or slip out of the T-shirt altogether.

His stomach felt too solid, all those muscles already contracted with the curl. She didn't think she'd made a dent. But he let go of her shirt. She felt that freedom and dropped her right foot back to the asphalt, pivoting to run.

Then felt a silvery explosion in her head as a heavy fist hit the back of her skull.

She stumbled through pale fireworks, her legs not quite obeying orders.

He hit her again, this time with the back of his hand across her face, red pain spinning her like a wobbling top. This was bad, very bad. No sparring helmet, no gloves.

Ahead of her, the white Kia's door opened and the man in the tan suit got out, moving fast, full of purpose. His thick black shoes gripping the gritty road.

"That's enough," he said, his voice commanding.

Maybe he would help, she thought. Although she couldn't count on him, he was older, slimmer, she didn't know if he could stop the rodeo rider.

But the bigger man turned to look. June leaned into her wobbling spin and bent her arm and used the momentum to slam the back of her raised elbow into the side of the rodeo rider's head as hard as she possibly could.

"Agh," he said. "Fuck." Stumbling back from her, his face bright red, his body still crimped around his sore testicles.

She'd hurt him twice, she thought, the pain in her face and head bringing a kind of clarity of purpose. She had a chance.

Maybe the man in the tan suit would do something.

"Call the police," she called to him, and tried to ready herself.

The man in the tan suit reached into his jacket pocket.

"Don't hurt her," he said, still striding forward.

"Too late for that." The rodeo rider turned back and stepped toward her in a fighting shuffle, hands open and ready, his face a mask of rage. "I'm gonna fuck you up."

He feinted in. June danced back, her own hands up, legs imperfect but getting better.

"How are those balls?" She showed him her teeth. "Nice and sore?" Her kickboxing instructor had been a big fan of trash talk. He'd taught her some dirty moves, encouraged her to use them. June had rung his bell a few times, too, and not because he'd let her.

"We need her intact, Leonard," the man in the tan suit said. "Just hold her for a minute."

And brought out a thin cylinder, red on one end.

A syringe. The red was the cap.

He took off the cap and slipped it into his pocket.

He was not here to help.

Taking advantage of her distraction, the rodeo rider came in fast and hooked her ankle with his foot as she shuffled back. She fell in a hard tangle, banging her hip and elbow, and before she knew what'd happened, he'd pinned her to the asphalt.

Then the man in the tan suit stepped in, stuck the needle through her shorts into her butt cheek, and pushed the plunger.

Color drained from the world. Her limbs were made of concrete, too heavy to move.

The rodeo rider caught her eye and smiled. "Now I own your ass," he whispered.

He walked back to his truck, came back with a small duffel and dropped it with a clank into the back seat of her car. Guns, she thought.

Then he scooped her up in his arms like a newlywed bride. As he turned back toward the Mustang, she caught a better look at his truck. The broken rear window, pockmarked sheet metal.

He laid her gently down in the Mustang's passenger side, reclined the back, and climbed behind the wheel. The last thing she heard before the engine revved up high was the rodeo rider's voice.

"Man, I like this car."

The Kia pulled forward and the Mustang followed.

The bright afternoon turned to black.

31

Big Dog heard an unfamiliar phone ring somewhere. He looked over at the girl still slumped in the passenger seat. The phone would be in her pocket or backpack.

He remembered the folded square of aluminum foil in his shirt pocket. Traffic was thick on I-70, and he wasn't about to pull over. So he reached over and patted her down, found the phone in her back pocket, then steered with his knees long enough to wrap the phone in the big sheet of tinfoil, making it invisible.

He sure liked the Mustang, even if it was a little banged up now.

Just like the girl. He was gonna bang her up some more before he was done with her.

He'd wait until she was awake. More fun that way.

But where to put her?

Man, his balls ached something fierce.

He was following Colonel Dixon in his white sedan, the plan being to stash the girl and get what they needed to accomplish the mission, but the Dog was real tempted to just keep driving. Find some little abandoned house out in the middle of nowhere, take his time with the bitch. But there was real money to be had in here somewhere. The Dog had a good nose, he could smell it.

Girls, they were disposable. Dime a dozen.

But money was time.

Money was freedom.

Now that Leonard was dead, Big Dog was ready to roam.

The Dog hadn't minded being Leonard Wallis. He'd learned a lot from Leonard's time in the Army. Discipline, and hard skills. Plus Leonard knew how to have a good time.

But Leonard was restricted. Leonard had a past. Leonard's face and fingerprints were on file, and his DNA, too. There were certain things Leonard just couldn't do until he'd gotten the Colonel to agree to his terms. That was the whole reason the Dog had taken the job.

The promise of becoming his true self.

He'd met guys like the Colonel before. The man was an empty shell, all hollowed out by his own personal ruin. That shell was the only thing holding him together. But the shell was stronger than it looked. Maybe because it was the only thing the man had left.

With the Colonel, the Dog figured a goodly part of that shell was his word. Whatever fractured remnant that remained of his personal integrity. His honor, as a Marine.

When the Big Dog had recognized that, he'd known this was his time.

The Colonel had the connections to erase Leonard from the Army's records.

The Colonel would keep his word.

Not that the Dog was going to trust the Colonel's word. He didn't trust man or beast. But twenty years in the Army had given Leonard a long reach. Contacts of his own. Ways of finding out. He just hadn't had a way to erase himself before now.

And it had worked. The Dog's check on his own records had turned up almost nothing. No prints on file, DNA swab gone missing.

Man, he was gone. Practically a ghost.

But he had a few chores left to do.

Kill that interfering Marine, for one thing. He was looking forward to that. It would surely be a challenge, something worthy of the Big Dog's skills. And not from a distance, either. Close up.

Then bite off a piece of that money, wherever it was.

After that, bite off a piece of that prickly bitch all drugged up in the seat beside him.

He was tempted to start with the girl. But that was like eating dessert first, wasn't it? Plus his ol' huevos were too damn sore to do much of anything, so he'd be a good boy and eat his vegetables.

When he was done in Denver, it would be all dessert, all the time.

Ahead of him, the Colonel in that white car turned on his signal and pulled off the highway, coasted left through the light, then pulled onto a frontage road and into the parking lot of a cheap-ass chain motel.

The Dog was right behind him.

The Colonel parked at the edge of the lot and stayed in his car, but the Dog drove directly to the office, with the girl clearly visible in the passenger seat.

The motel was long and low, pale stucco two stories tall with exterior stairs and walkways linking the rooms. They would be visible coming and going, but the Dog didn't think there was much risk of anyone paying attention, either the management or the other guests. It wasn't that kind of motel.

He checked in using his operational ID and credit card. The clerk was young and scrawny in a wrinkled blue button-down shirt, but he didn't need much muscle to do this job. His name tag read DAVID. The Dog peeked over the desk divider and saw a stack of old books by the motel's computer, and another book held open by a weird-looking pen lying across blank pages. One of the pages was partly filled by messy blue handwriting.

"Hey," said the Dog. He made a point to look through the big plate-glass window at the Mustang outside, then back to the clerk. "Do you mind if I ask you a personal question?"

The clerk blinked at him. Maybe looking at the mark on his temple where the bitch had hit him with her elbow. "Uh, sure, I guess."

"My girlfriend, she's in the car?" said the Dog. "We're from out of town, here on vacation? And I think she ate too many of those cookies, you know, with the pot in them? She's pretty sleepy. Should I be worried?"

This was why he was the Dog, not the Wolf. The Dog could smile and be friendly to people he might otherwise chew the ass out of, could wag his goddamn tail and pretend to be domesticated to get the job done.

"You need to be pretty careful with those," the clerk said. "The dosages are all over the place with edibles. Was she freaking out, before? Paranoid?"

The Dog nodded. "Yeah. She smacked me one right here." He touched the side of his head. "Pretty hard. Then she tried to run away and fell over. Now she's just really sleepy. I kept shaking her on the way here, to keep her awake, but she's probably passed out in the car by now."

"But she's breathing okay? Like, full, deep breaths?"

"Oh, sure. When I got on the freeway she started snoring." He gave a short laugh. "So I guess she's okay?"

"Well, I'm only an English major," the clerk said. "But she's probably fine. Just let her sleep and keep an eye on her."

"Thanks, man. That makes me feel a lot better. Listen, do you have a room on the first floor? I don't want to have to carry her up a flight of stairs. And maybe around back, so the afternoon sun won't come in the window?"

32

From across the lot, Daniel Clay Dixon watched as Leonard drove the banged-up Mustang around the building.

Dixon went in the opposite direction, arriving as Leonard backed into a parking spot. He watched as Leonard made a show of trying to wake the woman, then hopped out of the car, propped open the motel room door with a chair, picked her up gently in his arms, and carried her into the room.

Dixon got out on the far end of the row of rooms, walked down the sidewalk under the balcony overhang like he belonged there, and followed them in.

Two double beds, a combination desk and TV stand, light-blocking drapes over the big front window, industrial carpet. It would do.

He shoved the cheap chair back to the desk, freeing the door to slam shut behind him. "Nice work."

With the girl drugged up and in clear view of the desk clerk, Dixon had been afraid Leonard lacked the soft skills to make it work, but the man was disturbingly capable. It made Dixon wonder what else Leonard might do.

"Secret is, you do everything out in the open," Leonard said. "Daylight like this? In a damn electric-blue convertible? What can I possibly be hiding at two o'clock in the afternoon?"

He stood with the girl in his arms as if deciding which bed to lay her out on. Then bent his head and took a deep sniff at the angle where her neck met her shoulder. He showed his teeth in a grin. "Man, she smells good enough to eat."

"Put her down," Dixon said. "And keep your hands off. You want a girlfriend, find one the normal way, once the mission's over."

"You got it, boss." Leonard grinned again, and Dixon suppressed a shudder.

Leonard was turning out to be more than he'd bargained for.

Dixon looked at his watch. They had most of an hour before the sedative would begin to wear off. He had some decisions to make. And a phone call.

Leonard laid the girl down on the bed farthest from the door, then straightened out her limbs. It was an excuse to touch her, Dixon thought.

Time to clarify some things. He took a pistol out from under his jacket. It was a Beretta M9, the same model sidearm he'd carried for almost thirty years. He held it down at his side.

"Leonard, step away," he said. "She's not part of this. Off-limits. Do you understand me?"

Leonard looked at him. Amusement coming through despite his utter lack of reaction. "You threatening me?"

Here it comes, thought Dixon. "I'm just reminding you who's running this show," he said. "You think I don't have leverage on you? You think I don't know who you are? You should see your psych workup.

I don't know how you made it into the Army, or how you lasted twenty years."

Now Leonard's eyes narrowed, but he turned from the bed and took a step toward Dixon.

Dixon lifted the Beretta in his right hand, his index finger inside the trigger guard.

"Leonard, you work for me," he said. "If you're not clear on that, I can find a hundred more like you. Happy just to get paid and willing to follow orders."

Leonard's sidearm was in his bag in the back of the Mustang.

He took another step forward. It wasn't a big room. His voice was soft. The man truly was a predator. "What if I don't want to follow orders?"

Dixon stood with his back to the closed door. He raised his left hand and cupped the butt of the Beretta in a textbook two-handed shooter's stance. He'd fired more than a hundred thousand rounds from weapons just like this one, mostly at the range, but also in combat. He knew the amount of recoil deep in his muscle memory. He didn't need to count the rounds fired. His hands would tell him all of it.

"Then you can die in this motel room," he said. "Your choice. Are you going to follow orders, do the job you signed up for, get paid, and walk away? Or end up gutshot, bleeding out in a motel bathtub?"

"What did you mean, you have leverage on me?" Leonard said. He didn't take another step, but he leaned forward just slightly.

Dixon could see the tension. It made him think of a cable pulled taut, vibrating imperceptibly.

"Your service record," Dixon said. "The one you wanted cleaned up? I have a complete copy, with full prints and DNA sample, waiting in a PO box. And a letter with an attorney, directing him to take certain actions if I'm not in contact at specified intervals."

249

Leonard didn't appear to move, but something changed. Some deliberate release. He straightened up and shook his head.

"Man, that is one world-class pussy move," he said. "A letter with a goddamn lawyer? Shit, I thought you were a goddamn Marine."

Dixon shifted his aim slightly and pulled the trigger. The flat crack of the Beretta was loud in the hotel room. A small hole appeared where the ceiling met the wall, directly past Leonard's head.

Leonard didn't flinch, but he lifted his open hands out from his body at shoulder height. It was a casual gesture, but still, a surrender. His smile was tight, showing no teeth.

"All right," he said with a nod. "You're the boss."

Good enough for now, thought Dixon.

"Do your job," he said. "You can have her when we're done."

He tried to sound like he meant it.

Then he took out his outgoing phone.

33

Standing in the cement plaza outside police headquarters, Peter already had Henry's phone in his hand when it buzzed.

It was an incoming text from an unknown number.

No words. A video.

The Play arrow overlaid a dim, prone form.

Peter took a deep breath, bringing in as much oxygen as he could. He was going to need it. He touched the arrow.

June lay completely dressed on a large, fully made bed, arms down at her sides, legs straight. Eyes closed.

She looked wrong.

Normally, June had a lot of energy. Even working at her laptop, when her fingers weren't flying across the keys, they were dancing above them, conjuring words out of the air. The only time he'd ever seen her truly stop moving was when she was asleep, and that was always in a tomboy tangle of limbs, like she'd fallen from the jungle gym directly into bed. He liked to watch her sleep. He could see what she'd looked like as a girl.

But he'd never seen her like this, like she was laid out in a coffin. So vulnerable. She couldn't be dead, he told himself. He could see the slight rise and fall of her chest with each shallow breath.

But someone else had been in the room with her, taking the video.

He clenched the phone so tight he was afraid he'd crush it in his hand.

The bed had a white blanket or comforter on it, the wall behind painted a garish red. A hotel, and not a nice one. The camera zoomed in on her chest, to make sure Peter saw that she was breathing. Then it panned up to her face. He saw a red mark high on her cheek, the beginnings of a bruise.

"What?" Lewis leaned over to look at the screen. "Oh shit."

"What?" said Sykes. But the video had ended.

Peter held the phone out so Steinburger and Sykes could see and played the video again.

"Her name's June Cassidy," he said. "She flew in today. Was supposed to arrive an hour ago. Some asshole sent me this."

"Let's think about this," Steinburger said.

Peter had already pressed Call. Put it on speaker so everyone could hear.

The man on the other end didn't ask who was calling. "You got my message."

"What do you want?" Peter asked.

"I want the seeds."

"What seeds? I don't know what you're talking about."

"There was a special package with the money. Seeds, from the grower. You want your girl, you get me those seeds."

Now Peter knew what McSweeney hadn't told him, what hadn't been on the manifest. But he was focused on the voice, the same familiar voice as the earlier call. Peter heard the faint remains of a Southern upbringing despite the clipped syllables.

"What did you do to her?"

"Just a sedative," the voice said calmly. "A few bruises. No lasting harm. Not yet, anyway."

Peter felt the adrenaline surge, the taste of copper in his mouth, fight or flight rising up in him again. There was no question which he'd choose. But he wanted the voice to keep talking.

"Was that you who took out my friends on the highway? Who chased me across town?"

"No," said the voice. "That was my subordinate. He's a dangerous man. You got lucky twice. You don't want to see him again. You *really* don't want him to get too close to your girl."

By now Peter thought he knew who was on the other end of the line.

It had been years since they'd talked, but that conversation had stuck in Peter's mind.

It had made the difference between the needle at Leavenworth and four more years at the tip of the spear, taking care of his guys.

"If anything happens to her—"

"Follow orders, Marine. Get me those seeds." The voice was sharp. If Peter'd had any doubts, they were gone now.

"I can't," he said. "I don't have any seeds. I don't even know what your seed package looks like. They're probably in the police evidence locker."

"You're a resourceful guy. Make it happen. You have two hours. Keep that phone on you, I'll be in touch."

Then the line went dead.

———

Peter closed his eyes a moment. When he opened them again, he looked at Steinburger and Sykes.

"Either of you see any package of seeds?"

Both men shook their heads. "The evidence techs might've found it," Steinburger said.

"I don't suppose either of you have the authority to deputize a civilian."

Sykes shook his head. "Those days are long gone," he said. "You two shitheads need to back off and let us handle this."

Lewis looked at Steinburger. "Oh, really? Go through channels? Chain of command?"

Steinburger looked away.

"I'm just going to lay this out," Peter said. "I'm in it with or without you."

"We could always put you in a cell," Sykes said. "You and Beyoncé here."

"You have no basis for that," said Miranda.

"Protective custody," said Sykes.

Lewis looked at Steinburger. He didn't say anything. He didn't have to.

"Paul," said Steinburger.

Sykes pinched the bridge of his nose. "I don't like this, Steve. We were partners, yeah, but that was ten years ago."

Steinburger leaned toward him. "Don't go all tight-ass state police on me here. You stood up at my weddings. All three times. And I stood up at yours."

"Steve."

"You remember that domestic, back before Cap Hill went upscale? The guy with the meat cleaver? You remember how that turned out?"

"I can't believe you're bringing that up," Sykes said.

"All I'm saying," Steinburger said carefully, "is we've been through some shit together. It's a dirty fucking job. You and I both know that nobody gets out clean."

"I don't even know what he's got on you."

"It doesn't matter," Peter said, louder than he intended, panic climbing his spine. "June's the only one who matters now. When this is over, I'll turn myself in, okay? Waive my right to an attorney. You can lay everything on my head. I just need to get her out of this."

Sykes looked at him like he'd just declared the world was flat. "I'm just supposed to believe you? You lied to us about the car dressed up like a police cruiser, and the guy in the uniform. You lied about getting chased all over town, getting shot at. Hell, you killed four men."

"He didn't lie about that," Lewis said. "He turned himself in. With the money. His word is good."

"That's fucking rich," Steinburger said, "coming from you."

Lewis turned to Steinburger again, with that stare like a hot desert wind. "Tell me," he said. That dark explosive force latent in his voice. "How did it go, when we knew each other? Did I do what I said I'd do? Did you get what you needed? How is your mom, by the way? Still in remission?"

Steinburger closed his eyes. "Yeah," he said. "Okay." Then turned to Sykes. "Come on, Paul. What's it gonna take?"

"Give me a better reason," Sykes said.

Peter looked at him. "You want to catch the bad guys, right? That's the whole thing."

Sykes let out his breath and bowed his head. "I cannot fucking believe I'm gonna do this." Then looked up at Steinburger, then Peter. "But okay. I'm in."

"Good," Peter said. "Now I need a couple of favors."

"**Can you track June's phone?**"

"Not without a court order," Steinburger said. "And I'd have to talk to the commander first. So no."

"It can take a while, too," Sykes shook his head. "Since Snowden, this has gotten a lot more complicated."

"What about this car she rented?" Peter pulled up June's texts again, found the photo of the late-model Mustang convertible. There was a time stamp on the text. "Companies track their cars, right? LoJack or something?"

"Depends on the company," Steinburger said. "And the car."

"Let me see that." Lewis took the phone, zoomed in on the picture, scrolled up and over. "There." He'd found the bottom corner of a multicolored sign in the background. It was badly out of focus.

He handed Henry's phone back to Peter. "Better not search on that one," he said, taking out his own. "Don't know what they can see." He pulled up his browser and found a collection of rental company logos. "Got it," he said. "See that orange triangle?"

Sykes nodded. "I'm on it," he said, took out his own phone, and stepped away.

Peter looked at Steinburger. "Does Denver PD still have the evidence from yesterday?"

"Yeah," Steinburger said. "The case'll probably end up with the state police because of where it happened, but you showed up in the city, so everything's still in our locker." He jerked a thumb at the blocky police administration building behind him. Then frowned. "There's no way I'm taking anything out of there."

"But can you get access to it?" Peter asked.

"Sure, I'm the lead on the case, at least for now. But I don't know what I'm looking for."

"Not yet," Peter said. He took Lewis's phone and dialed Elle Hansen.

"Heavy Metal Protection."

"Hi, Elle. It's Peter. The doorman at Zig McSweeney's grow, his name is Tonio, right?"

"Yes," she said cautiously. "Whose phone are you calling from? What's going on? When are you coming over?"

"In a while," he said. "I'm still with the police. Do you have Tonio's cell number?"

"Peter," she said, "we really need to talk. About the future."

"We will," he said. "I promise. What's Tonio's cell?"

"You still have Henry's phone, right?" she said. "Antonio Marron, his info's in there. And I need that damn phone back."

"You'll get it," Peter said. "I'll be in touch."

He found Marron in Henry's contacts and called him from Lewis's phone.

It rang and rang, then went to voice mail.

"Shit," Peter said. Then realized Marron was on guard duty. He wasn't supposed to be answering a call on his company phone from a number he didn't recognize.

Peter called back from Henry's phone, now on speaker, and Marron answered right away.

"Who is this?" Suspicious. A little worried. Steinburger leaned in to listen.

"Hey, Tonio, my name's Peter Ash. I'm with Heavy Metal. You saw me at the grow this morning, I came in with McSweeney."

"Yeah, I remember. Why do you have Henry's phone?"

"I was in the truck with him last night." Peter paused to let that sink in a minute. "Listen, McSweeney gave you something for Henry yesterday. Remember?"

"Yeah. Uh, I better get hold of Mr. McSweeney."

257

"Henry's dead." Peter used the sharp tone of command. Maybe sharper than he intended. "I'm your supervisor now." He softened his voice. "You're not in trouble. You didn't do anything wrong. Just tell me what it looked like, that package you gave Henry."

Peter could practically hear Marron making up his mind.

"It was small, a black case like, I don't know, something you'd put your sunglasses in. Maybe a little smaller. I couldn't see it real well because it was in one of those semi-clear plastic bags they pack product in, only without all the air sucked out of it."

"Did it have a shipping label?"

Bulk cannabis, usually pounds and half pounds vacu-packed in plastic, each had a sticker noting the type of product, the licensed facility where it was produced, the licensed facility where it was going, and a unique number for tracking purposes. Part of the state requirements.

"A blank one, like tape holding the bag closed. Someone had written on it in black marker. The letters 'K,' 'G,' and 'For Henry.'"

Peter raised his eyebrows at Steinburger, who nodded that he'd heard.

"Thanks, Tonio, you've been a big help. Better not tell McSweeney about this—we're still trying to recover that package."

"Roger that."

Steinburger was already walking into the department headquarters.

Peter jogged over to Sykes, who was pacing on the plaza while talking into his phone with the forced calm of a man attempting to reason with a deranged kindergartner.

"No, I'm not going to fax you a police report. This is an emergency. I'm an investigator with the Colorado State Police." He recited his badge number. "No, I can't wait forty-eight hours for your response team. We believe this car is being used for a crime in progress. Wait,

I thought I was already talking to a supervisor?" He sighed and rolled his eyes at Peter. "Fine, move me up the food chain as far as you can."

"Call me when you get a location," Peter said.

Sykes covered the phone with his hand. "Where the hell are you going?"

"To find out what's so damn important about those seeds."

34

Peter called McSweeney on the way to the Jeep.

"I think I found something that belongs to you. A kind of oblong black case in a plastic bag with a label that says 'KG For Henry'? I'll bring it. Where are you now?"

He hung up and Lewis cranked the engine. "Location?"

"The second grow facility. Near the Sand Creek Landfill. You know where that is?"

"Yep." Lewis glanced at the side mirror and pulled out into traffic to a chorus of horns. "We going hard?"

"Oh hell yes."

The downtown streets were clogged before them. Peter mapped the slowdowns on his phone and Lewis pulled into oncoming traffic to get around stacked delivery trucks. The chorus turned into a symphony. "Those big revolvers on the floor behind you. Shotguns and ammo back on the rear seat under the blanket."

Peter felt it welling up again, the rising panic that came when he thought of June laid out on that bed. Like the static had a whole new reason to be. "Listen." He cleared his throat. "Lewis."

"Don't say it." Lewis kept his eyes on the road, the pedal down, his face a mask of concentration. "She's strong. She'll be fine, Jarhead. You hear me?"

Breathe in, Peter told himself. Breathe out.

He closed his eyes and felt the Jeep shuddering around him. Heard the engine revved up high, the tires straining against the asphalt on the turns. He took another slow, deep breath. He pictured June in her old apartment, beer forgotten in her hand, head thrown back with laughter as he made mango salsa for fish tacos. He remembered the smell of sunshine on her bare legs. The dirty grin on her face as she parted the shower curtain and climbed in with him, slick and sweaty from her morning run.

He held all that in his mind.

Then turned in his seat to reach the weapons.

Lewis slowed as they entered the area around the Sand Creek Landfill. On the map it was a triangular section bordered by three freeways, with a freight railyard running down the middle. On the street it was another mixed commercial area of broad streets and long, low structures with wide parking aprons. Trucking depots and repair shops and parts wholesalers and retail strips with oddball shops.

The sky was darker now, the clouds crowding in from the west to fill the sky.

McSweeney's second grow was in a dirty brick building, segmented like a caterpillar. Six rectangular sections, each stepped back from the one before it, following the angle of the railroad tracks behind. Once, each section would have held a small business, Peter thought. A couple of brothers or friends who made tools or furniture or machine parts, back before most of the small manufacturers went out of business. Now the space was used for growing a product that went up in smoke.

New economy, my ass.

The loading docks at the front had been bricked up just like those at McSweeney's warehouse facility. To the north was a truck leasing company with a wide dirt lot full of semitrucks and trailers. To the south, between McSweeney's facility and a company that apparently made disposable packaging for the fast-food industry, was a high chain-link fence with green plastic strips woven through the mesh and the gate standing open. McSweeney's green Volvo sat inside on the lumpy gravel yard.

Lewis pulled the Jeep in a circle and parked directly under the security camera, facing out toward the gate. Peter had noticed this habit before, Lewis always parking so he could leave quickly if he needed to. Peter had the same habit.

Peter handed Lewis a pistol and opened his door.

He was glad enough that Lewis had managed to find them sidearms on such short notice, but he wasn't crazy about the old Army Colts. He would have liked a weapon he knew better, something more modern, and a little smaller. Like the Sig Sauer .40 Henry had loaned him, or a sidearm he'd used in the Marines, the Beretta M9 or one of the 1911 variations. Certainly something with more than five rounds. A spare magazine, for example. And a holster.

He wasn't going to touch the combat tomahawk.

But as he got out of the Jeep, he felt the weight of the big Colt Peacemaker hanging at the end of his arm.

It would do just fine for what he had in mind.

———

He walked across the gravel, awash in adrenaline, Lewis striding beside him. Lewis had the second Colt tucked into his belt at the small of his back, the 10-gauge held down along the side of his leg.

If it weren't for June, Peter might have been smiling. Instead he bared his teeth.

Rounding the corner, he saw McSweeney leaning against the building, looking across the fenced-off railyard at the black clouds boiling across the sky. He still wore his sleek green sweatshirt, and he had a tall paper coffee cup in his hand.

"Hey," McSweeney said, smiling. "Thanks for finding that package, I really appreciate it."

Peter walked up to him, raised the big Colt and jammed the tip of the barrel right up against McSweeney's nostrils.

"I lied," Peter said. "I don't have your shit. Some kind of special seeds, right?"

"Hey," McSweeney's eyes were wide, his head bumping against the dirty brick. "Wait. What?" His face had lost its expression of perpetual amusement. He dropped his cup and the lid popped off, splashing his retro sneakers with coffee.

Peter felt his heart thumping in his chest. He was out on the ragged edge. He liked the feel of the big Colt in his hand. Part of him just wanted to pull the trigger. "What are those seeds? Why are they so important?"

"That's my best strain." McSweeney's head was tilted against the wall, voice distorted by the blued steel compressing his nose. "I was pretty sure I was losing my business. That leaf mold I told you about, the one that ruined a whole crop at the other grow? I also had to destroy my entire experimental stock. Those seeds, the ones I gave Henry, those are all I have left to start over."

"That's why they're valuable to *you*," Peter said. Pushing the Colt harder into the other man's face, he thumbed the hammer back with a satisfying click. "Why would somebody else think they were valuable enough to kill four people? What aren't you telling me?"

To Peter's left, he heard the thunk of a steel security door opening. In his peripheral vision he saw Lewis raise the shotgun in a single smooth motion.

"Drop the gun. Hands where I can see them."

"Oh, shit. Okay. Okay." Whoever it was, he sounded scared. Peter heard the soft clank of metal on gravel.

Peter glanced sideways and saw a beefy young guard with his hair growing out of a buzz cut, arms up and hands held at shoulder level. He wore a shirt with the Heavy Metal logo on the breast, and an empty holster on his hip. His gun lay by his foot. "I, uh, just came out to, uh."

"It's all right, Brandon," McSweeney said, hands making a vague patting motion. "They're not here to rob us. We're just having a conversation. Right, Peter?"

"Sure," said Peter. "You were going to tell us why those seeds are worth killing for."

"I didn't kill anyone," said McSweeney. "I told you that. It's not my fault."

Peter wasn't going to mention June Cassidy, drugged and helpless in a cheap motel. It would only make him want to blow McSweeney's head off. Which wouldn't help Peter find her.

"Tell me," Peter said, "about the fucking seeds. Let's start with what you wrote on the label. KG. What's that?"

"KG stands for Klondike Gold, that's what I call the strain. You know how some of the best dope has purple hairs in the buds? Klondike Gold has these little gold-colored crystals."

"Tell me about that."

"Those gold crystals, they're magic. Crazy powerful. We did consumer tests, focus groups. People really love this product." McSweeney was beginning to relax into his favorite subject.

"That's not enough," Peter said. "This whole state is sky-high on all kinds of superpowered weed. What makes your Klondike Gold worth killing for?"

"I'm sorry, do you mind? It's hard to focus like this." McSweeney carefully reached up and pointed a finger at the tip of the Colt's barrel.

McSweeney didn't seem to have much trouble talking, but Peter figured he'd give the grower a little room. He backed the long barrel an inch off McSweeney's nose.

"So much better," McSweeney said with a casual smile. "Now, in the old days, at the bottom of a big bag of really good dope, you'd find this fine golden dust. You smoke that, you have a conversation with God. It's fantastic shit. So I started experimenting. I never finished my dissertation, but I do have a PhD-level understanding of plant genetics."

Lewis looked interested. "Wait, this is genetically modified cannabis?"

"Definitely not." McSweeney sounded like his pride had been hurt. "I've been cultivating cannabis for twenty years. This isn't frankenweed, there are no gene splices here. Just what Gregor Mendel did with his pea plants a hundred and fifty years ago. Selective breeding toward a desirable trait."

"So it's good pot," Peter said. "Why does someone want it badly enough to kill for it?"

"It's not just good," McSweeney said. "It's *religious experience* good. And there's something else." He looked at Peter. "How much do you know about the medical applications of cannabis?"

"Not much," said Peter.

This wasn't true. Peter knew that people used weed for all kinds of medical problems, from chronic pain to epilepsy, even post-traumatic stress. The feds had made cannabis research absurdly difficult, so most of the medical evidence was anecdotal, but Peter figured mostly that people liked to get high, and if it made them feel better and didn't do any harm, good for them. You could make an argument that booze and cigarettes were almost certainly worse for society, all things considered, so who was Peter to judge? As long as they were all consenting adults, it was none of his business.

"Well, aside from the recreational effects, members of the focus groups reported that using Klondike Gold still made them feel good after the high wore off. Several reported a change in their feelings of depression. We could make an extract, put it in pill form. You know how much that would be worth?"

Peter blinked.

Lewis said, "The market for anti-anxiety and depression drugs is something like ten billion dollars in the U.S. Nearly twice that worldwide."

McSweeney nodded. "And there's one other thing." A smile played across McSweeney's face. He couldn't keep himself from bragging. "It might be slightly addictive."

Peter raised his eyebrows. "Might be? Slightly?"

"Maybe more than slightly." McSweeney shrugged. "It could be the *Nicotiana rustica* crossbreeding I did a few years back. That's a kind of wild tobacco, particularly potent in nicotine."

"So you're a mad scientist," Peter said. "With the perfect product for the age of anxiety."

"I'm a businessman," McSweeney said defensively. "Trying to help people."

Peter took a deep breath, stepped back to move the giant Colt Peacemaker away from McSweeney's face, and eased the hammer off cock.

"Okay," he said. "Time to help. Make another packet of seeds, just like the one you gave Henry."

"Absolutely, you bet. I have another black cigar case, that's what I put them in. I have seeds, too, but they won't be Klondike Gold."

"Can anyone tell them apart but you?"

McSweeney shook his head. "The only way to tell them apart is to germinate them into plants, then look at the mature buds. Which will take about eight weeks."

"These assholes won't live that long."

McSweeney went inside the grow to put together another seed packet. Peter asked Lewis for his phone to call Steinburger at the police evidence locker.

"Any luck on finding the seeds?"

"There's a lot of stuff here," the big detective said. "Including a bunch of guns and a giant pile of cash. But I haven't seen any small black case wrapped in plastic like your security man described."

Peter wasn't going to ask him to grab Henry's Sig Sauer .40. That was never going to happen. He'd have to stick with the Army Colt for now.

"Have you heard from Sykes on the location of June's rental car?"

"I texted him a few minutes ago. He says he's still on hold with someone corporate."

"Okay," Peter said. "Keep me posted."

"Wait," said Steinburger. "What are those seeds for?"

"Some kind of super-weed," Peter said. "Probably addictive, possibly with medical applications. Worth a hell of a lot more money than you're looking at right now."

"I miss the old days," said Steinburger. "You could smoke a little grass and not end up paralyzed or crazy. Spend your free time in some mountain meadow, not working nights and weekends cleaning up after rabid shitheads."

"Wait," Peter said. "You're a hippie cop?"

"I'm a cop who married a tie-dyed retro-hippie chick twenty years ago," Steinburger said. He sighed. "We had a lot of fun while it lasted."

"You're a goddamn romantic," Peter said.

"Not anymore," said Steinburger. "Sykes'll call when he knows something."

Peter hung up and looked around McSweeney's parking lot. "Think we can bring them here?"

"Good a place as any," Lewis said. "I was thinking we might need another set of wheels."

Peter nodded. But he didn't want to lose twenty minutes driving back to Henry's for his pickup.

He ran a search on Lewis's phone, then made another call, this time to Denver Towing.

"How long would you need to pick up my truck at a friend's house and drop it off across town?"

35

Dixon sat in the blue Mustang with his laptop open on the center console. Through the windshield, he could see the motel bed past the open motel room door. The girl was still laid out on the bedspread, dead to the world.

Leonard sat in a chair with his feet up on the bed, watching her. Like she was a new kitten he was forbidden to play with until it woke up. Dixon thought he could see Leonard's long fingers twitching. He hoped it was his imagination.

He looked back to the computer and the scene frozen on the screen, the consumer test video that had started this whole thing. He'd watched it at least a dozen times.

He knew why Palmer wanted the seed package as much as the business itself. The business was a glorified farm. The seeds were something different.

Palmer had an instinct for weakness, Dixon had to admit. His business model was impeccable, if you didn't consider the sheer immorality of it. But Palmer had no more morals than a shark, swimming in search of the scent of blood in the water.

To the business world, Russell Palmer was a brilliant investor with a spectacular record of being in the right place at the right time. He purchased distressed assets at rock-bottom prices and later sold them, sometimes whole, sometimes in pieces, but always at enormous profit.

Palmer's secret was the source of the assets' distress. It was always, obliquely and at a discreet, deniable distance, Russell Palmer himself.

Using Dixon and his freelancers as his tools.

Dixon had learned that Palmer usually found his projects by flipping through the reports of the many corporate intelligence firms he had on retainer. Some reports focused on global economics, others on national security, still others on world politics. Palmer had a freakish ability to put that information into the blender that was his brain, see the faint potential weaknesses invisible to so many others, then exploit those weaknesses using his own particularly effective methods.

Palmer would have been a good black-ops intelligence officer, Dixon thought. He had the same kind of fertile, twisted mind. The Africa operation in particular was a chess game played on a continent-wide board. Palmer's advantage was that the other side didn't know they were playing, or not at the beginning. Just that they were dying.

If Dixon had thought his soul was doomed before, now he knew for certain that he'd never be clean. No preacher's river dip could give him new life, not anymore.

The Colorado project had seemed simple enough at the beginning. The owner had actually reached out to one of Palmer's corporate surrogates, ostensibly a venture capital firm, seeking investment into his business.

A little like lowering a bleeding limb into a shark pool and hoping you wouldn't get pulled into the water. Although Dixon figured it wasn't the owner's fault. He'd thought the pool was filled with goldfish.

He'd sent a note of introduction with an investment proposal and twelve minutes of video. The same video now set to go on Dixon's laptop.

Dixon had to admit, the video painted a pretty compelling picture.

He was starting to think about trying some of that Klondike Gold himself. It might be better than drinking most of a bottle of tequila every night.

Dixon was well aware of his own hypocrisy. It was part of why he needed the tequila.

He glanced back through the windshield at the motel room. Leonard remained in his chair. The girl lay still on the bed.

Dixon pressed Play.

The video quality wasn't bad, given the hidden cameras. A half dozen people sprawled on plush couches and comfortable chairs in some kind of grubby retail space, a few with hand-rolled joints, another with a bong, the rest with a kind of electric pipe, what Dixon later learned was called a vaporizer. They had odd little smiles on their faces, trying to sound coherent while talking to a sleek man with a computer pad about what he called "Sample Eight." He was asking the smokers about possible names for the product. They seemed to like Green Zombie and Smile Factory.

The first time Palmer had showed Dixon these few minutes of footage, Dixon had shaken his head. America was already a nation of couch potatoes, high on Cheetos and reality TV. Legal marijuana would only make things worse. He definitely hadn't understood Palmer's enthusiasm.

Dixon wasn't stupid. He knew the legal market was just getting under way, and the growth potential was huge. Nobody ever lost money by underestimating the moral fortitude of the average American. But the state regulations were too different, and the federal government was keeping its foot on the brake with the bank laws. There was no national policy plan in sight. All the big players were staying out. Dixon couldn't imagine Palmer's exit strategy.

He couldn't be planning to run an actual business, especially one that was basically farming and retail. Palmer didn't have the attention span for that. Palmer lived to buy low, sell high, and move on to the next kill.

When he'd said "I don't get it" and reached to turn off the video, Palmer had told him to keep watching. Then the video jumped forward in time.

It showed the same room, with the same people on the same furniture around the same oval coffee table, but wearing different clothes. The light was different, too. Earlier in the day, Dixon thought. Maybe lunchtime. The table held a lacquered tray with four clear display jars of cannabis and a variety of smoking paraphernalia. The boxes were numbered nine through twelve.

A big bearded man in a paint-spattered sweatshirt sat forward on a worn leather armchair. "Where's that Sample Eight?" he asked. "I'd love some more of that. I've been having the best dreams."

"With the little gold flecks in it?" asked a middle-aged woman wearing a pink cardigan sweater and a wide pink ribbon in her well-brushed hair. "I dreamed I could fly. Oh, it was wonderful. I'd like more, too."

"Definitely Sample Eight," said a third man with sculpted hair, a bright orange T-shirt, and distressed jeans. "I haven't had a cigarette since smoking that good shit, like, a week ago? So I'm here for that."

"I'm sorry, but we don't have that variety today," said the man with the computer pad, sleek as a seal in his snug green hoodie, looking generally pleased with himself. "I do have some new varieties for you to try today, with extra to take home and share with your friends."

"Yeah, I don't want anything else," the big bearded man said. "I want that Sample Eight. Can I get more? Can I just buy some today?"

"Me, too." The woman in the pink cardigan stood from her chair, took her pink wallet from her purse, and walked right up to the sleek man. "I want Sample Eight. I have had the best week, maybe of my whole life. So whatever you're charging, I'll pay."

A man in kitchen whites stood next. "What she said. Sign me up."

"Absolutely," said a woman in a gray designer suit with her hair pulled tight in a bun. She stood and began to hunt through the gray leather purse hanging in the crook of her arm. "Please tell me you take credit cards."

"Hang on," the man with the computer pad said. "I'm offering you four other varieties, all of it excellent stuff. You're telling me you don't want free cannabis?"

"We want that Sample Eight." The big bearded man climbed painfully to his feet. He towered over the sleek man with the computer pad, but his voice was plaintive. "You gotta have some around somewheres, right? Please?"

Now they were all standing, trying to get closer to the sleek man with the computer pad, bumping the coffee table with their legs. The lacquered tray with the smoking paraphernalia and the clear display jars of inferior product were jostled to one side, then fell ignored to the floor. The talk got loud enough that the microphone couldn't pick out individual voices from the clamor.

The sleek man tucked his computer pad under his arm, pulled a slim silver cigarette case from his pocket, and began handing out machine-rolled joints.

As the others scrambled for the disposable lighters scattered on the floor, the sleek man turned toward the camera with a broad smile on his face.

Then the video ended.

One of the reasons Palmer had pulled Dixon deeper into his organization was his experience as the executive officer of his Marine battalion. Along with his leadership and strategic and tactical abilities, he had the administrative skills required to oversee battalion operations. He was as familiar with complex budgets and balance sheets as any top-level corporate vice president.

The grower's proposal was far simpler.

It called for an investment of fifty million dollars in exchange for a ten percent nonvoting ownership stake. A half million square feet under cultivation within a year of signing. Detailed cost and revenue breakdowns were included. The grower's initial investor would be bought out with current cash flow, leaving the business unencumbered.

The indoor farm would be set a few miles off the interstate in Colorado farm country in a building twice the size of the biggest Walmarts. Although it would take a year to get up and running, expected net revenue for good-quality hydroponic cannabis in year two was two hundred million dollars.

If that was as far as things went, the return on investment was forty percent in the second year, and every year after that. Better than the best hedge funds, better than most private equity firms.

After seeing the video, Dixon thought things would go quite a bit further than that.

Klondike Gold would create its own market, and the grower could charge a premium for his product. The proposal laid out plans to double cultivation with a second farm in year three, and double again with two more farms in year four. ROI in year four alone was a hundred and sixty percent, eighty million dollars. Over time, more states were sure to sign on to the cannabis tax revenue juggernaut. There was too much money to pass up. Demand would only increase. It was possible the operation could double in size each year for a decade.

The grow facilities needed a lot of manual labor, but that was also a plus. Jobs would make the farms attractive to rural communities that might otherwise not want a pot farm nearby, and it was clean work compared to slaughterhouses or private prisons.

Palmer had already unleashed his lawyers to confirm the numbers and the product itself. If anything, the lawyers reported the grower was too conservative. Costs would likely be lower than estimated, and revenue higher. It was an attractive proposal, even without Palmer's special methodologies.

But it wasn't enough for the deal to pencil out as proposed. That wasn't how Palmer operated.

For Palmer to win, someone else had to lose.

Dixon's job was to exploit the weaknesses.

Palmer told his lawyers to look into the grower's early investor, a small fish in Boulder. A Seattle corporate security firm got hold of a copy of the investment agreement. The terms were generous, which indicated how desperate the grower must have been to get started. If the grower defaulted, the early investor owned everything.

So Dixon had his fulcrum.

For the lever, it was a simple matter of finding the investor's weakness. He had a few. Colorado was booming, and most of the investor's money was tied up in a land development deal outside of Denver. His deadlines were coming up fast, and he was overleveraged, just like banks before the last crash.

Palmer's lawyers arranged for quiet payments to a few members of the local board of supervisors. Questions came up regarding the water rights, and the development's permits were denied pending a new and expensive environmental impact evaluation. The investor's development partner had a weakness, too—a second wife in Utah. Rather than get two divorces and a prison term for bigamy, he agreed to sue, and the investor was forced to sell his position in the grower's operation.

At the same time, Dixon plugged Leonard into the grower's security firm. Soon enough, the grower was in trouble, couldn't make his last payment. The legal wheels were in motion, and the grower's business was all but gone.

The grower, though, wasn't stupid. He'd felt the invisible hand of Palmer's manipulations. Maybe it was Leonard running Jordan, the investor, off the road. Dixon had thought it was a bad idea. Leonard had needed to speak to Jordan personally, to convince him to sell. The man was on the verge of arranging new financing. In the end, Leonard had threatened the man's wife and he caved. Palmer had gone to Leonard directly to tie up the loose end.

The grower hadn't figured out who was behind his problems, though. Palmer's lawyers were too devious for that. But the grower knew what his new strain was worth. He'd arranged to get the seeds to a safe place.

Dixon had arranged to take them away.

The Marine had changed the equation.

Dixon was changing it again. But he didn't like it.

He looked through the windshield at Leonard. Had he gotten closer to the girl?

This was going to go bad. He could feel it. The heat of hell on the back of his neck. His immortal soul starting to burn.

Dixon wondered exactly how far he was willing to go.

His incoming phone rang.

"Status report." It was Palmer.

Dixon sighed. The man was a walking irritant. Human itching powder. Every conversation made Dixon want to take a shower.

"We have the girl," he said. "We're working on the seeds."

"Work faster. I have a dinner meeting in Singapore tomorrow." Palmer's voice got a little whiny when he got impatient. The man had the attention span of a fruit fly, but he wasn't wrong about the timing. Unlike the third world, where bribing the cops was as easy as calling up the local police chief and negotiating terms, it was hard to buy large-scale police corruption in the States. Two armed hijackings had gotten everybody's attention. The clock was definitely ticking.

"It might get ugly," Dixon said. "These people are no joke."

"If you'd done your job, we'd be gone by now. Get me what I need. I don't care if there's blood in the fucking streets. You read me?"

"Loud and clear," Dixon said. "I'll be in touch."

He heard another voice in the background.

"Do it soon," Palmer said. "My pilot tells me the storm is getting closer, and the tower is predicting lightning. I don't want to get grounded."

"It's your plane," Dixon said, goading the man, just a little. "Don't you get to take off when you want?"

"I should," Palmer said. "You're right. It is my goddamn plane. Why can't we take off?"

Dixon heard the pilot murmur again.

"Some shit about highly variable winds in a storm," Palmer said.

"But we're fueled up and ready to go. This baby has a seven-thousand-mile range. I'll drop you in San Francisco, isn't that where you people go?" Dixon closed his eyes. It only made the smirk he imagined on the man's fat face more vivid. "As soon as you bring me those goddamned seeds."

In the motel room, Leonard moved again. He put his hand on the girl's leg.

"I have to go," Dixon said. "I'll be in touch."

36

Peter sat in the Jeep with Lewis, trying to keep his breathing deep and even, trying not to think about what June was going through. Light rain speckled the windshield. To the west, the clouds were coming together into a single low dark mass.

When Henry's phone rang, Peter answered before the first ring had finished.

Steinburger said, "Sykes is on the line with their vehicle recovery people now. They just pinged the car. It's in a hotel parking lot near the airport."

Peter put the phone on speaker. "Give me the address."

"A tactical team is gearing up," Steinburger said. "You need to wait."

"We're not waiting. What's the goddamn address?"

"This is a police matter—"

"Steve," Lewis's voice was low and calm and dangerous. "You're in deep now. No way out but through. Tell us where she is."

"You really don't want to get in the way of the tactical team," Steinburger said. "They're not known for their subtlety."

An aggressive team with machine guns and body armor would not be good for June. Peter felt the static flare. His head filled with electricity, his voice like a clap of thunder. "Give me the motherfucking address."

Steinburger made a strangled sound.

Then gave them the address.

Peter found it on the map as Lewis drove.

It wasn't far. Just off the freeway, part of a modern development wasteland designed so you'd only have to get out of your car to use the bathroom. And they were probably working on that, too.

The street number showed a chain hotel in a group of three buildings surrounded by access roads. It stood at the edge of the larger area of warehouses where the fake trooper's car was burned and abandoned.

Lewis cruised the road that curved around the complex at exactly the speed limit, Peter's head on a swivel looking for the car, looking for June, looking for the owner of the voice on the phone. The big Colt Peacemaker heavy in his hand.

He found the bright blue Mustang convertible parked on the far side of a weedy gravel strip, in the back corner of the lot with its top down in the rain.

The back bumper was pushed inward, badly misshapen, the taillights cracked and fallen away. "That's it," he said, and pointed.

Lewis turned to look. "They're not here," he said.

Peter nodded. "I know."

If they were still using the car, they'd have left the ragtop up. And no pro would ever have chosen this four-story fake-Spanish hotel, with its restrictive lobby entrance and long narrow hallways, as an operations base. They'd have found something low, with direct access to the room and parking immediately outside.

"You think they're watching it?" Lewis slowed at the intersection, looking at the Mustang.

"No," Peter said. "They already have June. They'll use her to get us where they want us."

"They had a signal blocker on the Heavy Metal truck," Lewis said. "They could have used another one on the rental if they wanted to. Maybe they're letting us find it."

"Maybe," Peter said. "But I think that's too complicated. How would they know we'd be able to find the car? Anyway, this whole thing doesn't feel like something they planned. They're improvising now."

Lewis nodded and cranked the Jeep around the corner and into the parking lot, where he rolled up to the blue convertible. The front bumper was also banged up, although not as badly.

They left the Jeep's doors open and walked over to the Mustang, Lewis scanning the hotel windows, the road, the traffic. The rain was light but cold through Peter's thin T-shirt.

The car keys lay on the damp driver's-side floor beside a slim rectangle wrapped in tinfoil. Droplets beaded up on the dull metal.

Peter leaned in, picked up the package, and unwrapped the foil. A nearly new smartphone.

Peter touched the button with his fingernail.

The screen lit up with a photo of June's father looking shyly into the camera, half-hidden behind his long white hair.

"Motherfuck," Lewis said.

Peter felt the static rise up hard. The taste of copper in his mouth as he grabbed the Mustang's keys and took three quick steps around to unlock the trunk.

The rush of relief that it was empty.

He sagged against the side of the wet car and ground the heels of his hands into his eye sockets.

He needed more coffee. He needed to find June.

He needed to sleep for a week.

After he found June.

And maybe killed some people.

At this point, what was a few more?

Jesus Christ.

"Hey," Lewis said. "You said the guy who called, the guy who sent you the video of June, sounded familiar. Did you ever figure out who he is?"

"Yeah," Peter said. "I think he was the XO of my old battalion, a major named Daniel Dixon. Most of us thought he'd end up a general."

Peter had some history with Dixon.

In Peter's eight years of active duty and innumerable missions of varying success, a single unauthorized operation stood out as the mission Peter was most ashamed of. It had probably also done the most good for the most Marines.

Dixon had discovered it, then covered it up. For the same reasons.

It meant Peter hadn't ended up sentenced to life in Leavenworth or death by lethal injection, but it also meant he'd stayed a lieutenant, boots on the ground, leading a platoon, watching out for his guys.

Which was just fine with Peter.

He hadn't really wanted to be a captain anyway.

"I don't know why Dixon would be involved in this," he said. "June told me you have a contact at the DoD. Can you make a call?"

Lewis murmured into his phone for a few minutes, listened for a few minutes more, then found a pen and paper in the Jeep's console and scribbled down a few lines. "She'll get back to me on Dixon," he said. "She already pulled the service jacket on Leonard Wallis. It was heavily redacted, almost nothing there but basic service information. But I think I know a guy who used to be in Wallis's unit, now a cop in Atlanta. Maybe he'll remember something. I hope he's still got the same number."

While Lewis talked on the phone, Peter stood and looked at the hotels in their little cluster, thinking.

Lewis ended his call. "My guy definitely remembers Sergeant Wallis," he said. "The man had an early history of sexual assault complaints, but victims and witnesses kept refusing to testify. Some of them actually disappeared. The Army kept moving Wallis around, in part because that's what the Army does, but also because none of his CO's wanted a problem child on their books. Like the Catholic Church and the pedophile priests."

"Jesus," Peter said.

"Yeah," Lewis said. "Eventually the complaints stopped, either because Wallis cleaned up his act or because he got better at covering his tracks. You can imagine which one. They only kept him because they needed all the warm bodies they could get after 9/11. Apparently Wallis turned out to be a pretty good soldier, made it through Ranger school with flying colors. The only reason they didn't take him was because of his tainted record."

"You're not making me feel any better," Peter said. "I think we need to stop chasing him and try to figure out where he's going to be next." He looked at the three other hotels in their little commercial ghetto. "You got a laptop with you?"

"'Course," Lewis said.

"If you were these guys, what kind of hotel would you pick?"

Lewis smiled.

———

Peter climbed into the driver's seat while Lewis focused on the map pulled up on his laptop. "Nothing in this little corner," he said. "Too nice. Business travelers. Suites and conference rooms. You'd want something cheaper for sure. Not 'cause they worried about money, but 'cause of the other people staying there. More likely to mind their own business. Less likely to call the cops."

"That reminds me." Peter called Steinburger. "We found the car. Abandoned, the top down in the rain. I don't think they're there."

"We're still gonna look at it," Steinburger said. "Tac team is en route. Prints and the rest."

"I know," Peter said. "Thanks for the shot."

"She means something to you," Steinburger said. "This woman they abducted."

"Yes," Peter said.

"Well," Steinburger said, "you're going to do what you have to do."

"Yes," Peter said.

"Just try not to hurt any civilians, okay?"

"I'll do my best."

"Got something," Lewis said, fingers flying on the keys.

"What?" Steinburger's voice thinned as Peter pulled the phone away from his face. "What have you got?"

"Gotta go." Peter hung up.

Lewis pointed. "Get out of this parking lot and go west on Peoria, under the freeway."

Peter put the Jeep into gear and hit the gas.

Past the overpass, they found an older commercial strip, a six-lane tangle of access roads and parking lots fronting mom-and-pop businesses and cheap motels. The rain still light but the clouds massing overhead.

"I like this one best," Lewis said, tilting his chin. It was a long two-story off-white chain motel with a long line of first-floor room doors opening onto the broad parking lot, and second-floor doors opening onto a long balconied walkway with multiple sets of stairs down. "This don't pan out, I got two more possibles, one around the way and another across the street."

"They're going to know this Jeep." Peter eyeballed the building as he pulled onto the frontage road. "If it's the guy in the brown Dodge truck, he's seen us before."

Thinking, if it was Dixon, he'd probably remember Peter's face.

"Lot of black SUVs on the road," Lewis said. "He only got one clear look, and I was pointing a shotgun at him. After that he was looking ahead, not in his rearview. And we were lost in the dust."

"Well, first we'll look for that Dodge," Peter said. "We don't find it, we go talk to the desk clerk." He turned into the parking lot, began to circle the building, eyes flicking from car to car.

Not many vehicles, most of them tucked into a parking spot by the rooms.

No shit-brown Dodge pickup.

"We still don't know how many people they have," Lewis said, his own head on a swivel.

"Four fewer than yesterday," Peter said.

Lewis didn't smile. "That's the right direction."

Peter thought about the blue Mustang, crunched in the front and back. "Look for cars that have been in accidents. Front or rear. Even just a fender bender."

Eyes burning, Peter finished the circuit and turned to take another look going the other way. He needed coffee. He was tired enough that he'd almost settle for battlefield coffee, a couple of single-serve packets of instant Folgers dumped dry into his mouth, followed by a swirl of funky sun-warmed water from his CamelBak. God, he could taste it right now, just thinking about it. The flavor was horrible, but the blast of caffeine that followed would be wonderful.

"Anything?"

"Nothing that looks right to me," Lewis said. "Let's go talk to the desk man."

The desk man was a thin kid in a wrinkled blue button-down shirt, slouched in a desk chair scribbling in a blank book with a fountain pen. He looked up when they walked in, set his journal down next to a stack of books on screenwriting. "Help you guys?"

"I hope so," Peter said. "We're looking for a friend of ours, driving a bright blue Mustang convertible, a little banged up? He might have had a woman with him. He turned off his phone and we can't reach him. We're a little worried. They had a rough couple of days, you know?"

The clerk nodded. "Yeah, I remember him. He checked in, like, a few hours ago. His girlfriend never got out of the car. You guys want a room, too?"

"Maybe," Peter said. "We should probably talk to them first. What room are they in?"

"I'm, ah, not really allowed to give out that information."

"But you know the room," Lewis said, smiling pleasantly.

"I do, yeah," the clerk said. "I'm sorry." He looked from Lewis to Peter. He saw something in Peter's face. "That guy, he's not really your friend, is he?"

"No," Peter said.

"And that girl he was with. Passed out in the car. Was she really his girlfriend?"

"No."

"But you guys aren't cops." This time it wasn't a question.

"We're friends of the girl," Lewis explained.

"But what are you? Like, some kind of desperadoes?"

Peter was out of patience. "Yes," he said. He pulled out the big Colt pistol, pointed the long barrel at the young clerk's face, and thumbed back the hammer with that crisp, satisfying double click. "We are fucking desperadoes. Now do you help us or do your brains exit the back of your head?"

The clerk stumbled back a few steps, eyes wide, hands rising involuntarily. "Let me get you a key," he said. "Whatever you want. Whoever you are, we never met, I never saw you, don't shoot me, okay?" He was smiling. No doubt memorizing the moment for his screenplay.

"Something else," Peter said. "You get a credit card when you rent a room?"

The clerk nodded and reached the keyboard. "I can print it out for you. Here it is, room 168, first floor back of the hotel. Leonard Wallis."

The printer hummed as Lewis came around the desk. "That's great, kid. Now give me your belt and your phone. You got a storage closet or something?"

"Uh." The smile faded from the clerk's face. "What?"

"Two options," Lewis said. "Lock you up or blow your head off. You choose."

Lewis drove around to the back of the motel while Peter watched the door numbers.

In front of room 168, three parking spaces stood empty between an ancient Ford station wagon and a dark red Honda sedan. The curtains were pulled tight across the big picture window. Lewis rolled by without stopping.

They left the Jeep around the corner out of sight, got out, and strode back toward the room side by side along the wide concrete walkway under the cantilevered balcony. Peter with the Winchester lever gun in one hand, the room key in the other. Lewis held the 10-gauge down along his leg, extra shells rattling in his coat pocket. Each had a big Colt SAA tucked into the back of his pants.

A holster would have been better, Peter thought, if he had to run. But maybe more obvious than carrying a long gun out into the rain in the middle of the afternoon.

What they really needed were armored vests and helmets.

And June safe at home and Peter on his way to see her.

But that wasn't how things were.

The adrenaline rose up through him yet again, bringing clarity and focus.

Lewis stood on the hinge side of the cheap slab door, shotgun up and ready, protected somewhat by the concrete block wall of the motel. Peter listened at the door and heard nothing. He had a narrower range of protection, only twenty inches between the door and the window.

Room 168. He looked at Lewis. Lewis nodded.

Peter gently inserted the key, tumblers ticking smoothly. Turned the knob and pushed the door open in a single clean motion.

Lewis slammed it back into the wall with his shoulder as he burst through the doorway, the 10-gauge sweeping the room.

Peter angled past him with the lever gun up and the static rising. Stalked quickly along the narrow aisle between the bed and the dresser, nobody on the floor behind the bed, then into the sink alcove by the doorless closet, through the open door to the bathroom, sweeping aside the shower curtain with the Winchester's barrel to see an empty plastic tub, then back to the room to see Lewis on one knee verifying that the bed was on a solid pedestal, with nobody beneath.

Nobody anywhere.

Lewis shook his head and stepped to the door to watch the parking lot.

Peter looked at the bed.

A dimpled outline rumpled the otherwise undisturbed white bedcover. The size and shape of a smaller person.

The same white bedcover from the video Dixon had sent. The same color on the wall.

He felt something catch inside, almost the same sensation as the tug of the knife blade in the long muscles of his arm. Yet another feeling that would stay with him, maybe forever.

Peter went after Lewis, then turned to scan the room from the doorway.

"Look."

Lewis turned.

Peter pointed above the entry to the sink alcove, the corner where the ceiling met the wall. A small black hole in the drywall.

A bullet hole.

Peter felt the breath go out of him.

Lewis put his hand on Peter's bicep. "She's okay. There's no blood, right? Maybe it was a warning shot. And with this place, that hole could be from last year."

"Yeah," Peter said, as the static expanded inexorably into his skull. "Okay."

"We're gonna lock up the room again," Lewis said. "And wait."

37

June Cassidy woke into a lurching, thumping darkness.

She was adrift, floating, disconnected from her body.

Her head hurt like the worst hangover ever.

Her mouth tasted like soured milk.

Then her inventory sharpened. She couldn't open her mouth. She was curled up on her side, with her knees bent and her hands caught behind her. She tried to move her arms and legs and felt a sticky restriction. She moved her jaw and felt the wide adhesion across her lower face.

Her mouth and wrists and ankles were taped.

The thump and lurch was the tires on the expansion joints of the road.

She was in the trunk of a car.

Then she remembered the rodeo rider, and the man in the tan suit.

She was in trouble. Bad fucking trouble. She felt it grip her, the panic.

Unable to change position, barely able to breathe through her nose, the small space closing around her like a coffin sized for a child.

She couldn't catch her breath. Her heart fluttered like something wild trapped in her chest. She pumped her legs and jerked her arms, then lost it entirely. Her muscles erupted uncontrollably into a frenzied, mindless animal attempt to get herself free, pulling and twisting and shaking, for what seemed like time without end.

Until she was slowed by exhaustion. Spent, she lay still again. Bound hand and foot. Her position utterly unchanged.

She thought of Peter.

This was his experience every day. Trapped inside, panicked. Just riding an elevator, or buying groceries, or doing his laundry. What did he do?

She remembered his letters.

She breathed, flaring her nostrils to take in as much air as she could. In, then out.

Breathing, she let her mind slowly calm to the rocking motion of the moving car.

How would she get out of this? What would she do?

She thought of seeing the man in the tan suit in the airport. Something about that nagged at her. The airport. What was it?

Then she remembered.

The steel pen. With the knife blade where the ink refill should go.

Had he taken it? Was it still in her back pocket, where she tucked it every day, by habit?

Her wrists were wrapped but not her hands. Her fingers were free. She reached down and searched for the narrow cylindrical lump in the fabric.

There.

She sighed. There it was. Her pen. Her handy letter opener and weapon of last resort.

Ha! Not so paranoid now, are you, June Cassidy?

Okay. Now, the next thing. Be careful. Her fingers were tingling, but not too numb. Only one thing to remember. Pay attention. Don't drop the knife.

Out it came, the slender steel cylinder. She felt the seam where the two sections came apart. Gripped one end tight in each hand and tugged. Separation. Which end was the blade?

There, she felt it. She turned it carefully in her hand, so that the blade was down toward her little finger. Not quite so sharp now, from opening all that mail. And not really a slicing blade anyway, but a stabbing one.

She'd get to the stabbing later, she thought savagely, wrists bent painfully as she sawed away at the thick layers of tape. She'd put so many holes in that goddamn rodeo rider he'd leak like a sieve. Like a fucking Tom and Jerry cartoon.

The car sped up, slowed, sped up. Was she on the freeway?

Through the noise of the tires on the pavement, she thought she heard voices, but she couldn't tell who they were. Maybe just the radio, for all she knew.

She felt the space between her wrists open slightly. Gripping the knife tightly in one hand, the cap in the other, she tried pulling. The skin stretched, the tape slid. She felt a few reinforcing threads separate, gaining a little more space.

She could roll her wrists now, get better leverage. She sawed at the tape with more force, cutting her skin from time to time, but she didn't care.

Then her wrists were free.

She was still having trouble breathing through her nose. She put the cap back on the blade, put the pen back in her pocket. She didn't want to stab herself in the cheek when she pulled the tape away from her face.

She knew it was going to hurt. But she also knew she only had so much time before the rodeo rider and the man in the tan suit came to get her out of this fucking trunk.

To do whatever they were planning to do with her.

Use her against Peter, somehow.

She felt the sorrow and regret like a yawning pit.

And slammed the goddamned lid on it, turned it into ferocity and determination.

Just like her mother would have done.

June steeled herself. She'd always been one to rip off the Band-Aid, so she did it again with the tape across her mouth. She got her thumbnail under a corner and raised a flap. It didn't feel good.

She got a better grip. Thumb and two fingers. Pulled hard and fast and felt the tape take some skin with it. *Fuuuuuuck*, she screamed silently.

She sucked in painful red mouthfuls of air, remembering how she had rejoiced at seeing the article in the science section of the paper, conclusive research that swearing made things hurt less. It validated what she herself had known for years. Swearing was good for you.

Even if it was only in your mind.

No time to rest, though. She took the pen from her pocket, freed the blade, and went to work on the tape around her ankles. It was painful to contort herself in the small space, she couldn't bring her knees forward far enough to get to the tape from the front. But she could hold her ankle behind her back with one hand and hack at the tape with the other. Her hand slippery now, with the blood from her nicks and cuts. She held the knife tightly.

The car slowed, then hit a bump.

The knife squirted from her grip.

She scrabbled with her hands as the car went around a corner. Panic rising up, she imagined the knife rolling into some far dark corner of the trunk, never to be seen again. She needed that knife, needed some kind of weapon, needed her feet free of that thick-wrapped tape, needed to get out of that fucking trunk.

The car went around another corner and the knife rolled back against her fingers and she snatched it up, holding on to it for dear life.

She got back to work sawing her feet free, still trapped in the small space and not knowing where they were going or when they would stop or what she might do when they did.

She capped the knife and put it back in her pocket and peeled away the cut tape and felt around with her hands again, taking inventory of the trunk, hoping for a tire iron or a crowbar. But it was a newer car and the trunk was sleek and clean and empty of anything useful but some rectangular bulk behind her that kept banging into her on the turns. The car was in city traffic now, maybe.

She reached around, felt a handle and a crimped plastic ID tag. It was her carry-on, her rollaway suitcase, not that she had anything worth a shit in there but clothes and a toothbrush. But maybe, she thought, and reached past the suitcase, hoping beyond hope.

Felt the familiar worn fabric, the shoulder strap of her pack.

She pulled the soft bag over her suitcase and into the cocoon of her cupped torso. Here was the zipper of the main compartment with her laptop and book, here the smaller compartment with her chargers and headphones and notebook, and here, the smallest pocket.

She turned the pack so the top was facing toward the lid of the trunk and gave it a careful shake, settling the contents to the bottom, then unzipped the smallest pocket. Reached past her hairbrush and the slender tube of lip balm—where is it? where the fuck is it?—then, in the bottom corner, under the little pouch of nail clippers and tweezers, she found it.

The rounded shape of the fake pink lipstick, her pepper spray, firmly in her hand.

The knife still safely in her back pocket where she could reach it.

The car slowed again, more than it had before, made a turn. Picked up speed again, but less than before. Getting closer to wherever it was they were going.

She struggled through a rotation so she was on her side facing the rear of the car, armed and ready. Still locked in the trunk of a car but not helpless, *not* fucking helpless. And saw something glowing before her eyes.

Glowing greenish-white. A simple sideways push lever. Glowing in the dark, with a little picture on it. International iconography: the rear of a car, with the trunk lid standing open.

A safety latch, so kids didn't get locked inside by accident.

No good if you were all wrapped up with duct tape. But now?

Okay.

It's time to prepare, June told herself. For what you have to do. For whatever might happen.

Pepper spray in one hand, knife now in the other. The latch right in front of her. Surprise was her only advantage. She'd use it.

She flexed her muscles one by one, getting the blood flowing through her limbs, through her mind. Car-trunk yoga, she thought absurdly.

But she was fucking ready.

The car slowed again, turned sharply, and came to a stop.

38

aniel Clay Dixon was in the back of the Kia, on the passenger side, Beretta held loose in one hand, a clear view of Leonard behind the wheel. Leonard had retrieved his gym bag with his guns and ammunition from the Mustang. The Big Dog was on Dixon's leash, at least for now.

They'd needed to get rid of the girl's Mustang. Normally Dixon would have done it himself, walked a few minutes away, then caught a cab back.

But there was no way Dixon was going to leave Leonard alone with the girl.

Dixon was a lot of things, but he wasn't that.

Plus he was too keyed up to stay in one place. And he didn't trust Leonard out on his own for one fucking minute.

So Leonard had driven the Mustang to that parking lot while Dixon followed in the Kia, and now they were circling the city, killing time instead of each other, giving Lieutenant Ash his few hours to get those seeds.

A few lousy seeds. For what? How would he even know they were the right seeds?

He didn't care. This was all going to shit. Dixon could feel it.

Leonard was talking to Dixon over his shoulder now. "I don't get what you bring to the table, boss. What's your job here, exactly?"

"Just drive, Leonard."

"But how we gonna do this? What's the plan? We gotta work together here."

Dixon was not remotely convinced Leonard was looking to work together. Leonard was looking to slip his leash. To take everything.

"Just follow my lead," Dixon said. "I know this guy, we can work with him."

"Wait," Leonard said. "You know this guy? The guy who fucked all this up? Who killed my people?"

"I didn't know it at the time. He served under me in Iraq. He was a very talented Marine. Don't underestimate him. But I know how he'll react. Seeds for the girl. Follow orders and everything will go smoothly."

"Right." Leonard faced front. "Just like they have so far."

The weight of the Beretta was comforting. Dixon couldn't believe how he'd been fooled by Leonard Wallis. It was only a slight consolation that everyone else had been fooled, too, including the psychologists who administered the tests for Palmer's lawyer. A true, off-the-charts psychopath shouldn't have made it through the filters. But Leonard was smart enough to see through the tests, had tailored his answers to the result he wanted to show.

Dixon had seen three ugly wars and a great deal of human atrocity on all sides. He'd been afraid for his life and the lives of his men many times, had come to terms with that and pushed forward as he pushed forward now.

But Leonard Wallis was one scary fuck.

Dixon had always been able to compartmentalize. It was the only way he had survived the complicated mess of his life as a Christian, a homosexual, a loving husband and father, a Marine Corps warrior, and now a mercenary for hire. He'd built strong, high walls around the separate pieces of himself, walls made of honor and will, and isolated those pieces from each other.

Those walls had doors, though. Usually they were locked tight. Sometimes Dixon peered through the peephole, one part of him getting a glimpse of another.

Sometimes a door swung open, and Dixon could stand in the opening, one foot in each room.

It was hard to be a Christian Warrior, although there was some precedent for that. Not killing the infidels, he'd never bought into that idea, but fighting for what was right, for the ideals in the Gospels. And he could fight for his home, to protect his family. He'd become a mercenary to protect the family he'd lost, the family he still loved.

But after the damage done the last time his homosexual self had opened the door to his prison, Dixon had closed and locked that door for good. Now that part of him could only peer through the peephole.

But sometimes that part of him watched. And wanted.

He had no desire for Leonard Wallis. Far from it. Leonard with his macho swagger was the opposite of the kind of man Dixon was attracted to.

There was no particular physical trait that caught Dixon's attention. Although there was a physical component, obviously, because if it wasn't physical, he wouldn't be damaged. He would be a normal man. Not damned to hell for all eternity.

He loved his wife. Just not in that way.

He wasn't attracted to the men he thought of as queers, effeminate, although in a way Dixon thought maybe that would be better. That would make him still a man, somehow.

No, Dixon was drawn to kindness. Strong men, but kind. Strong enough to show that kindness, to share it. Willing to show you how they feel.

The way Dixon never could.

The car lurched and Dixon pulled himself back from his thoughts to see Leonard's cool eyes watching him in the rearview mirror.

Dixon made a decision.

"Let's swing back to that motel," he said. "Have some coffee, get cleaned up. Then we'll make our plans, set up the exchange."

Dixon knew it was possible he wouldn't succeed. He was willing to take this step precisely because he felt that risk growing.

But alone, with Leonard dead, Dixon might be able to appeal to Ash's honor as a Marine to make this exchange in good faith. It was still possible he could accomplish this mission without killing the girl.

Dixon's part of the bargain would be simple.

Ash could come after him another time. Maybe he would agree to that.

It was probably inevitable, no matter what Dixon wanted. Once Ash knew who he was, if he didn't already.

Dixon had six more months until the terms of his exorbitant life insurance policy would fully apply.

He could survive six months.

Accidental death paid double. His wife was the beneficiary.

It would be enough.

39

Peter had found a corner at the far end of the covered walkway where he could stand out of the rain and watch the door to room 168. He leaned the Winchester on the wall behind him, harder to see, easy to reach.

Lewis had walked into the wet parking lot and disappeared.

Peter didn't need to look for Lewis to know he was there.

He held Henry's phone in his open hand, glancing down at the screen from time to time. What people did now instead of smoking, he figured. The new excuse to stand around and wait.

He almost jumped out of his skin when the phone buzzed in his hand.

It was Lewis.

"My contact called back," he said. "Your friend Daniel Dixon was promoted to lieutenant colonel four years ago. He was being groomed for battalion commander, a big promotion. Then the battalion's new

XO discovered that Dixon had been selling government property off the loading dock. Small scale, not much actually taken. At first he said he was being blackmailed, but when they asked him for more details, he changed his story. He should have gone to jail, but he had good lawyers. He was given a dishonorable discharge and stripped of his pension just shy of his thirty years. Now he owes his lawyers a couple million bucks. It's sad, really."

"So how did Dixon get involved in something like this?"

"Actually, June was pulling this string from the other direction. I just checked my email, she sent me something from the plane."

"Wait. You were checking your email?"

Lewis arched his eyebrows. "Some of us have a life, you know. Anyway, June found a company called Fidelis International Risk this morning, by backtracing Leonard Wallis. He's a Fidelis subcontractor. And Fidelis is owned by your friend Dixon."

"So we know they're connected."

"Yes. But more importantly, it looks like June found a connection between Fidelis and a man named Russell Palmer."

"I know who Palmer is," Peter said. "Kind of a high-profile corporate bandit."

"'Bandit' is too nice a word," Lewis said. "The feds have been after him for twenty years. Interpol, too. He's built a financial empire through intimidation, bribery, blackmail, and assassination. No convictions but multiple settlements totaling half a billion dollars. He's got homes all over the world, but supposedly lives mostly on his yacht and on several private jets held under other corporate entities. The great thing about a private jet is that, if you don't get off your plane, most small airports don't really check passports, even in the U.S. and Europe. So Palmer can go pretty much anywhere. And he has the reputation of a guy who likes to be there for the kill."

"Are you saying he might be in Denver?"

"Probably not at Denver International," Lewis said. "But maybe at Jeffco, where most of the private planes land."

A white Kia sedan rolled into the parking lot and came to a stop outside room 168.

Even through the steadily increasing rain, Peter could see the cracked back bumper, marked with blue scrapes.

He reached behind him for the Winchester.

"This is us," he said, and hung up. The adrenaline rose, crackling.

The lever gun had a long reputation as a reasonably accurate rifle, but Peter hadn't checked the sights, had never even fired the weapon. The Colt SAA was a serviceable hand cannon, but not much use past ten yards, not anywhere off a target range, and carried only five rounds. Both were antiques. Lewis's 10-gauge was new, but as indiscriminate as a Claymore.

So Peter needed to be closer.

He held the lever gun down beside his offside leg and ambled along the walkway, still holding Henry's phone up one-handed as if occupied with the screen.

The back passenger-side door of the car opened and a man in a tan suitcoat climbed out. Peter could only see the back of his bare head. If he felt the rain, he didn't show it.

The driver's door opened and another man got out. Peter only saw him from the back. He had a head like a cannonball, wore an orange plaid Western-style shirt, and held some kind of fat-bodied machine pistol in one hand, maybe a MAC-10.

Four rooms away, off the front of the Kia on the driver's side, Peter slipped the phone into his back pocket, raised the Winchester to his shoulder and cocked the lever in the same motion, bringing his eye down to the sight.

"Hands up," he called. "Where's the girl?"

The man in the plaid Western shirt turned, impossibly fluid, the muzzle of the fat-bodied machine pistol now pressed hard to the trunk of the car. "She's in here," he said, his voice carrying easily. The shoulders of his shirt darkened in the rain. "Don't fuck with me or I'll give her some extra holes."

It was Leonard Wallis. Peter recognized him from the photo Henry had shown him. Broad shoulders, narrow waist, big round head, a wide smile on his face that said, Ain't this fun?

The man in the tan suit didn't even turn to look at Peter. He had his own pistol up in a crisp two-handed shooter's stance, facing the parking lot.

Facing Lewis, who stood on the shining black asphalt not twenty yards away, rain beating down on his head, arms, and shoulders, the shotgun raised and ready.

None of them wearing armor. Not even a raincoat.

"Double-ought loads." Lewis's voice was pleasant. "Lead, not steel. I can cut you in half with one shot."

"But you'd put some holes in the trunk," said the man in the tan suit. Peter knew his voice. It was Dixon. "In the girl. You don't want to do that."

"She's wearing some mighty fancy underwear," Leonard said. His smile got wider. "I mighta peeked a little. Tasty little piece you got there."

Peter stepped closer, still under the shelter of the walkway, angling for a shot, lining up the sights.

"Oh no you don't," Leonard said, sliding around to the rear of the car and ducking down behind its shelter. "Stop right there, bub. I can put one hole in her, or I can put ten. How many is up to you."

Peter felt that tug of the knife in his gut again, sorrow and shame and fear. June curled into a ball in that trunk, alone and afraid, shying away from the muzzle of the unseen gun, not knowing where the bullet might come from.

His fault.

All his fault, like all his men dead, all over again.

"Take me," he said. Then louder. "Take me instead. Please, I'll do whatever you want."

He raised his cheek from the butt of the Winchester and stepped forward.

"Just take me instead."

40

With the car stopped, without the sound of the tires humming on pavement, June could hear again.

Pepper spray in one hand, knife in the other.

Except for the pale glow of the emergency trunk release, it was dark as night in there. She was blind, but ready.

Her other senses perfectly attuned.

She heard rain drumming on sheet metal.

She heard the soft release of the car doors opening.

She felt the springs shift as the men got out, first one, then the other.

Then a loud voice saying, "Hands up."

It was Peter.

A loud, heavy *thunk* on the trunk lid, metal on metal, right over her head. The rodeo rider, threatening to shoot her. His weight on the lid.

She wanted to scream *Peter*, but she didn't.

It would be just a scream. It would change nothing.

Surprise was all she had, her only advantage. The fact that they thought she was silenced and helpless, trussed up like a chicken in a pot.

She reached for the trunk release. Tightened her grip on her little knife, readied her finger on the pepper spray. She'd push her way out, goddamn it.

Then she heard him say it. *Take me*, he said. *Take me instead. Please, I'll do whatever you want.*

It filled her again, a heavy wash of sorrow and regret, like a faucet filling a flawed vessel to overflowing.

She had put him in this position. Of sacrifice. For her.

But she could still do something to save him. To save them both.

Not quite yet.

But soon.

She kept herself ready.

41

eter." Lewis had a warning in his voice. "Don't do this. We don't even know she's in there."

Dixon swiveled his eyeballs to look at Peter, his pistol still pointed unwaveringly at Lewis.

"Lieutenant Ash," he said. "The girl is in the trunk. I promise you that. And she is unharmed."

Lewis stood ten yards into the parking lot with the shotgun in firing position. He couldn't miss at that distance. Leonard crouched against the back of the Kia, the fat-bodied machine pistol barrel-down against the trunk. Peter with the Winchester still raised, but his eye no longer at the sights.

Rain coming steadily down. Thunder rattling the cheap motel windows.

Each of them ready to kill or be killed.

Peter could see Leonard's eyes and the top of his cannonball head and his raised elbow and part of the hand holding the machine pistol with its long, ugly magazine.

If it was the small magazine, it would hold thirty rounds, and empty in a second and a half, a wild spray of rounds.

He wasn't going to risk June's life on a snap shot with the Winchester, a gun he'd never fired.

"Lewis, don't shoot. Dixon, we can work this out."

"I'm not trading you for the girl, Lieutenant," Dixon said. "I want that package of seeds and this girl's my leverage. Where are the seeds?"

"I can take you," Peter said. "Leave June here with Lewis. It's not far. You and I and Leonard can go in our car. It's a black Jeep, right around the corner. I'll give up my weapon. You have my word, if June stays here, I'll give you the package."

"Hell no," Leonard said. "Here's how it's gonna go. I'm gonna take the girl in the car. I can shoot into the trunk just as easily from the driver's seat. You there, boyfriend, you're gonna take the colonel in the Jeep. The jig with the shotgun stays behind in the parking lot."

"Not happening," Lewis said. "No way that ends well."

Peter felt himself at the edge of a bottomless pit. The chasm yawning beneath him.

"There's no way any of this ends well," he said. "The only thing that matters is June. I accept your terms. Lewis stays behind. Leonard takes the lead in the car. I follow with Dixon in the Jeep. I'll drive and give him step-by-step directions to relay to you over the phone as we go."

Dixon nodded. "That works. But no police. This is private."

"Agreed," Peter said. "No police." His only hope was to make this as smooth and clean as possible.

Lewis kept the shotgun locked onto his shoulder, the barrel unmoving, but Peter could see his posture shift just slightly. Resigned, but still ready.

"All right," Lewis called. "How we going to do this without anybody getting killed?"

Peter said, "I'll start toward the parking lot. Leonard, you circle back to keep the car between us. Dixon?"

"You, with the shotgun," Dixon said, "step backward, nice and slow. You'll still have me, I'll shift to the girl. Peter, you start moving toward the Jeep. Leonard will get in the car and cover the girl in the trunk from there. Peter and I will get in the Jeep and pull out after Leonard. Lewis will stay here and do nothing."

"Works for me," Leonard said.

Peter did the choreography in his mind. "Okay," he said. "Lewis?"

"This is a bad idea, Peter. How are you still alive at the end of this? Or June?"

"Dixon guarantees it," Peter said. "If he gets the packet of seeds, June is free and safe. On his honor as a Marine."

Dixon looked at Peter. "I was dishonorably discharged."

"I don't care about that," Peter said. "You give me your word? On your honor?"

Dixon nodded, his face composed. "Yes."

That was when Peter knew Dixon's part of it would work.

"What about Leonard?" he asked.

"Leonard will follow orders," Dixon said. "Won't you, Leonard?"

Peter said, "I want to hear it from him."

"Shit, yeah," Leonard said. "I'll do whatever. I just want to finish this thing and get my ass out of here in one piece."

Which was when Peter knew that Leonard would be a problem.

Maybe in the next few moments. If not soon, definitely later.

"Okay," Peter said. "Let's take it slow. Everybody ready? I'm going to start."

He stepped down to the parking lot beside the Kia and walked toward Lewis. The rain fell cold and hard. His T-shirt was soaked instantly.

Dixon stepped back eight or ten feet to split Lewis's fire and give Leonard room to move. Peter kept the Winchester aimed at the visible part of Leonard's head as he ducked low around the far side of the car, the muzzle of the MAC-10 still trained on the trunk.

Dixon shifted his aim to the trunk while Leonard opened the passenger door and scrambled across, partially obscured now by the water running across the glass.

Lewis stood like a bronze statue turned dark with patina, rain pouring from the folds of his jacket and the hard planes of his face, utterly devoid of emotion.

Leonard cracked a window. Peter could see the dark shape of the machine pistol pointed back between the seats. "Okay," he called, and the car's engine started with a soft chuckle.

If it was going to happen, it would happen now, Peter thought.

Lewis had thought the same thing, because he'd stepped back between two parked cars so Leonard couldn't just reverse right over him.

But the reverse lights didn't come on.

Dixon shifted his aim to Lewis again. "Let's keep moving."

"Listen," Peter said. "The place we're going, it's not far. But it backs up onto the train tracks, and the area is kind of enclosed by the freeways. So there's no direct route. The directions are going to be roundabout, but it's the shortest way I know to get there."

"Roger that," Dixon said. "I think we all have the same motives here."

Peter sidestepped around the Kia, his back to Lewis's position. In the moment when he blocked Dixon's view of Lewis, he heard his friend's voice, soft but clear. "I'll get there."

Then Peter was facing Dixon and the Jeep was twenty yards away, just around the corner of the building. They left Lewis and Leonard behind and walked three paces apart, their weapons now leveled at each other.

Hard for either of them to miss at that range, Peter thought. Then wondered how the antique Winchester would do in the rain. If it would even fire. The Colt pistol in the back of his belt was wet now, too, and just as old.

Had any of them seen the Colt? He'd always kept his back to Dixon and Leonard.

Could he get into the driver's seat with the pistol still there, unseen?

They approached the Jeep from the passenger side. Peter circled ahead, still facing Dixon with the lever gun ready.

Peter couldn't read the man. He'd never really known Dixon personally, despite what had happened in Iraq. Dixon had always seemed to keep himself hidden, a deliberately closed book. But he seemed even more closed now.

Peter said, "I'm assuming you want to be in the back, right?" Dixon nodded. "Then I'll get in the front passenger side and climb over to the driver's seat. I'll leave the rifle on the passenger side where you can reach it."

Dixon nodded. "That works."

"I'm going to move a little faster now," Peter said. "I'm worried about Leonard."

"Roger that," Dixon said. "Go."

Peter backed into the Jeep and shifted himself across the center hump, leaving the Winchester behind with his right hand while his left carefully pulled the big Colt Army pistol from the back of his belt and placed it between the seat and the door.

Dixon opened the rear passenger door and climbed in, his own pistol steady, pulling the rifle muzzle-first through the gap between the seats with his free hand. Peter hit the Start button, found the lights and windshield wipers, cranked the heat up high, and put the Jeep in gear. "I'm driving now. I don't want to lose him."

"Understood," Dixon said. He took a phone from his pocket and hit a speed-dial button. "Leonard," he said. "We're coming. Move out."

Dixon relayed the directions as Peter goosed the big Jeep down the traffic lane, following the Kia, Leonard driving, June in the trunk, toward the access road, headed for the busy street.

Passing Lewis, Peter glanced at the clock on the dash.

Lewis stood in the rain and watched them go.

As soon as they were out of sight, he zipped his wet coat up to his neck and launched himself at a run in the opposite direction, arms pumping hard.

Shotgun in one hand and the big Colt pistol in the other.

42

eonard wants to know where you're taking us." Dixon held his
phone to one ear. "This access road leads nowhere."

Peter had directed them past the correct turn to Peoria Street.
At the next possible turn, they'd only be able to go south onto Peoria,
when really they should have crossed the median to drive north at the
last intersection.

"Sorry, I missed our turn," Peter said. "It's confusing over here."

"You never got confused in your life," Dixon said flatly. "Don't
fuck with me."

Peter was buying time.

But he was thinking now that he might need less of it than he'd
thought. The threatening rain had pulled people out of work early,
and the streets were clogged with traffic, windshield wipers on their
highest speed, the storm gutters rising with bubbling, leaf-thick
water.

He said, "Just tell Leonard to pull through this parking lot ahead, go back the way we came, and take the next right. We want to be going north on Peoria under the freeway."

Dixon relayed the information over the phone. Peter watched as the Kia cut around in front of them and followed behind in its tracks.

"Nothing better happen to her," Peter said.

"Then stay right behind them," Dixon said. "Your best chance of getting that young woman back is to give me what I want."

Peter looked in the rearview mirror. Dixon had the bottom of the phone, including the mouthpiece, resting against his wet suit jacket.

Quietly, Peter said, "Can you control that cowboy asshole?"

"Long enough," said the older man.

They made it to the six-lane and through the left turn at the light. The Kia was right in front of them, moving slowly. Bad weather and freeway on-ramps. The Jeep's heater was cranking now, although Peter was still cold and wet.

"You were a good Marine, Dixon. What happened?"

Dixon looked back coolly. "You're really asking me that question?"

Before the Fallujah incident, First Lieutenant Ash hadn't had much contact with Major Dixon, the battalion's executive officer.

Peter had always figured Dixon for a buttoned-up guy, very by-the-book. Colonel Graham was the battalion commander, well liked by the men. As XO, Dixon was the colonel's second in command, tasked with the thankless job of chief administrator and enforcer. Dixon wasn't liked, but he was respected. He seemed like a hard man, a man who held himself to a rigid standard, but a man who knew his job and didn't miss much.

There were far worse men to serve under in a combat zone than Colonel Graham and buttoned-down, by-the-book Major Dixon.

Like Peter's new captain, Ken Swenkie. An overpromoted politically connected careerist asshole looking to boost his combat résumé by clocking the most dangerous missions for his platoons without adequate planning or safeguards, and winning brownie points with the brass by conserving battalion resources, like decent overwatch or armor backup.

Fallujah was a disaster.

Marines died on the cracked and dusty streets.

They died in the mud-brick and cinder-block buildings, and on the baking rooftops, their blood black in the bright white sun.

Peter's men. Good men, capable men. Men with families.

Peter spoke to Captain Swenkie several times about better planning, more support. Keeping his people safe so they could keep fighting. Win the fucking battle and get some rest. Win the fucking war and go home.

Swenkie's mission orders continued, unchanged.

Peter found five minutes to talk alone with the XO, Major Dixon, who said he'd put in a word.

Captain Swenkie's missions continued.

If anything, they got more dangerous.

Like maybe Swenkie was hoping Peter might not make it back to lodge a formal complaint.

Peter shrugged. "I had no choice," he told Dixon now. "That asshole was getting my guys killed. You know I went through channels. I went to him, I went to you. It got me nowhere. So I did exactly what the Marine Corps taught me to do. I made a moral decision. I improvised in a combat situation. I solved a fucking problem."

Dixon regarded Peter calmly from the back seat. "You murdered your superior officer."

Peter nodded.

Dixon was completely correct.

Peter had left his platoon in the capable care of his sergeants and used a dead man's call sign to locate Captain Swenkie, waiting safely in a cleared area. Peter had made his way alone through the ruined city, climbed up half-collapsed stairs to the crumbled fourth floor of a shelled office building, and put a captured rocket-propelled grenade into the man's Humvee.

Then, knowing Swenkie to be the special kind of cockroach who could survive a stomping and still find a way to devise his revenge, Peter took an extra thirty seconds to reload the tube and put another RPG into the wreckage.

He watched it burn with great satisfaction.

Then went down the rope he'd slung out the far side of the building and made his way back to his platoon.

"What I thought was admirable," Dixon said from the back seat, "was that you didn't try to hide it."

"Hell yes I did," Peter said. "I took all kinds of precautions. I didn't want to get the death penalty for killing a dangerous asshole. You just figured it out."

"I couldn't prove it," Dixon said. "But when I called you in, you didn't deny it."

"No," Peter said. "I did what I did. It was the right thing to do. I'd do it again."

"That's why I let it go," Dixon said. "Why I never called the colonel. Because you were right and we both knew it."

A faint, fleeting smile slipped across Dixon's face, like a butterfly in the rearview mirror.

The smile came and went so quickly Peter wasn't sure he'd actually seen anything. Dixon's face was locked down as tight as ever.

Peter thought of the static forever rising in him, that had taken up some kind of electric permanent residence at the back of his brain since that morning. The rushing frantic fear, the flooding adrenaline joy, the endless immediacy of the pure moment.

He'd thought he wanted to rid himself of the static. To try to be normal.

But maybe he didn't, not if the price was to be locked away inside himself, like Dixon.

It was worth thinking about.

But first, he had to get June free.

After that, nothing else mattered.

The Kia still right in front of him, bumping slowly down the wet, traffic-flooded street.

He glanced at the clock on the dash. The heat was cranked up high, his clothes still cold and wet on his skin.

He said, "Tell Leonard to turn left on Forty-fifth Avenue."

43

Big Dog drove the shitty white sedan through the wide wet streets, rainwater pouring through the deep runoff troughs, watching ahead for traps, checking his mirrors for the Jeep behind.

Dixon kept feeding him directions over the phone.

Left on Forty-fifth. Right on Havana.

He was watching for a telltale dark spray of blood on the Jeep's windows. He wouldn't be surprised if the boyfriend managed to put one into Dixon. The Dog had seen a lot of combat and a lot of shit in training, but he didn't think he'd ever seen a man as focused as the Marine was today.

He'd been plenty focused up on that mountain highway, too.

Just yesterday. It seemed like a long time ago now.

Big Dog knew how things would have gone if he'd been in the back of that decommissioned ambulance himself, instead of driving ahead in that doctored-up state car.

The Dog would have kicked that Marine's ass. Gutted him like a fish.

Shit, it had been a great plan, hadn't it? With the wrecker and the ambulance and the mocked-up cruiser, it had gone like clockwork. Until it didn't.

The problem was the guys Big Dog had brought in to help. They hadn't been strong enough. Ruthless enough. Other people's weakness was always the problem.

It was the Marine's problem, for damn sure. If he didn't give a shit about the girl in the trunk, he and his buddy could have put an end to Big Dog right there at that motel, the Dog and Dixon both.

The Dog had a theory about other people. A helpful theory.

They didn't really exist.

Not the way the Dog did, anyway.

He knew other people were alive. He could read their thoughts, their intentions, through their faces and bodies. He knew the right things to say to motivate them, to make them like him, almost.

He could see right through them. Like ghosts.

But he couldn't *feel* other people, not the way he felt himself. The power of his desires. Other people were like animals to him. Maybe not even that. More like puppets, made of meat.

The Dog liked doing bad things. He always had. Simple as that.

But he didn't want to get captured, put in a box.

Self-preservation came first.

So the Dog had learned to control his desires, at least to a certain extent.

It was so damn tiresome, keeping himself on the leash.

There were so many things he wanted to *do*.

More directions from Dixon. Left on Forty-seventh to Quebec Street. He'd driven part of this before, chasing the Marine that morning. Shit, they could have taken the freeway, it was only three exits.

But the freeway was probably a parking lot. And it didn't matter anyway.

The Dog had a girl in the trunk, all wrapped up like a birthday present.

He hated this little white sedan. It was too small, too low to the ground, and didn't take up anywhere near enough space on the road. With his old Dodge, he could bully the other drivers, move them aside to slide through traffic. The sedan was a pussy car.

But he did like the trunk.

He *really* liked it.

He didn't know why he'd never figured that out before.

The trunk was a great place to keep something hidden and contained until you were ready to use it.

Leonard smiled. He was getting close now.

He was wondering about those seeds, though. About how the hell he'd know if they were the right ones. He figured he'd just take everything he could get, sort it out later.

His phone buzzed on the console. Not Dixon this time. A text message.

It was Dixon's boss again, that Palmer guy. The one who'd told him to take out Jordan on his little bicycle.

He'd texted the Dog earlier in the day, while he was driving the Mustang, wanting to give the Dog a promotion. And a bonus.

How nice.

All the Dog had to do was terminate Dixon's employment. Permanently.

Palmer didn't spell it out. He didn't have to, the Dog knew what he meant.

Hell, he was gonna do it anyway. Dixon was getting on his nerves.

But maybe Palmer could do a little something extra for the Dog.

He'd texted back about Dixon's lawyer with Leonard's Army records. He wanted all copies destroyed. If Palmer could make that happen, the Dog was ready to bite.

And now here he was, texting again.

The guy had attached a video. The Dog's records in close-up, sliding through a big office shredder. Did they have an agreement?

Big Dog sent Palmer the big thumbs-up.

Damn, wasn't technology cool?

It was time to end this thing.

The Dog was hungry.

The girl in the trunk would only last so long.

44

June felt the car speed and slow, speed and slow.

Flexed her strong legs, then her arms, then her core. Trunk yoga, keeping her muscles warm and ready.

Peter wasn't going to trade himself for her.

June Cassidy wasn't going to be anybody's fucking hostage, and she wasn't going to let Peter be, either. She was going to fucking fight, goddamn it.

The question was, did she pop the trunk herself, or let the rodeo rider do it?

Did she want to control the timing, or go for maximum surprise?

She felt like she could decipher the driving patterns now. She could picture the car on the road. A long straight run, then a turn, another long straight run. Slow in places, but the sound of other cars around her. Traffic. They were headed someplace.

The turns came more frequently, with shorter runs between them.

Getting closer. Then the shift of weight that meant a long slow sweeping curve, like circling a parking lot.

The sound of rain on the trunk lid. The tires crunching on loose gravel.

Then a definitive, rocking halt.

The end of the line.

Pepper spray in one hand. Knife in the other. Thumb on the trunk release.

Pop the trunk? Or maximum surprise?

Then she heard another car roll up and come to a stop.

She felt the car shift as the driver got out. Footsteps as he walked around toward the back.

Then she heard Peter's voice.

"Let me see her."

She pulled the release latch.

But the trunk didn't open.

45

Lewis ran.

The rain came down hard and fast, and through it, he ran.

Shotgun in his strong right hand, the hog-leg pistol in his left. Without pause or hesitation, without wiping the water from his face, his nose, his eyes.

He figured it was four miles. He already knew the way.

Down long industrial blocks lined with parked semi-trailers, past distribution warehouses and construction sites and parking lots and gas stations and vacant lot after vacant lot, red clay and brown dirt turning to mud in the heavy rain, he ran.

Lewis had run his whole life, ever since he was ten years old. Before that, as a kid so skinny they'd called him Sticks, his prized possession was a bicycle. It wasn't new. It wasn't even secondhand, it probably had five or six owners before it got to Lewis. A gift from his auntie for his tenth birthday. Five speeds, only one worked. Lewis didn't care. One speed was enough.

Until the Center Street Boys took it from him. He'd only had it a week. They were a scruffy bunch, mostly teenagers dealing crack and weed, nothing as fancy as powder or skag. The smallest of small-time, he knew now.s

But where Lewis lived, the Center Street Boys were the warlords. They wanted the bike, so they took it.

What kind of people would take a fucked-up bike from a ten-year-old boy?

Lewis knew, in the way everybody in the neighborhood knew, that if he put up a fight he'd get beat bad, hurt, maybe killed. It happened. So he picked himself up and stepped away, let go of the bike his auntie had given him. His auntie who had nothing.

He couldn't even steal the bike back, because that would be a challenge to the Center Street Boys. They'd know who'd done it, would catch him and beat him hard for sure. And the next day it didn't matter anyway, because he found his bike all broken up, wheels bent and frame cracked. 'Cause that's how they did, those motherfuckers.

After that, Lewis ran everywhere. Training himself.

In his cheap-ass used-up Goodwill kicks, because his auntie didn't have the money for real sneaks, and she wasn't dumb, either, knowing the Center Street Boys would take good shoes off him, too. But he ran, and even if he was stuck in that desperate neighborhood, he could run to the library and be free in his own mind, which was the only place that mattered.

He watched those Center Street Boys, too. He watched their corner, he watched who held the dope, he watched the runners who picked it up, he watched the runners who took the money, and where the money went. The cash stash in a plastic bag was held down by a cinder block and guarded by a big guy with a baseball bat named Elliot.

And one day—Lewis was thirteen, he remembered like it was

yesterday—he took a gun from one of his auntie's friends while the man was sleeping, put on clothes he'd never worn before, and he ran up to Elliot with a ski mask over his face and the gun in his hand and took the cash stash and ran. Just like he'd planned it. They never saw him coming.

In the plastic bag was three hundred forty dollars in dirty crumpled fives and tens and twenties.

It seemed like all the money in the world.

Lewis ran two neighborhoods over, being careful, and bought his auntie two fat sacks of groceries. When he walked in the door, she looked at him hard, searched his face like she was trying to find something she'd lost.

But she took the groceries and she took the money. She thanked him.

Lewis never looked back.

When he was fifteen, his auntie died. Lewis was on his own.

He left school to make his way. He survived. Jacking that first money bag, he'd found a blueprint that worked. Hell, he'd made something of himself. Something hollow, something lacking, but something real, which was more than a lot of people got. He wasn't hungry. He wasn't hurting. He wasn't worried about the Center Street Boys anymore.

Then Peter had brought Dinah back into his life. Dinah and Charlie and little Miles.

Everything had changed.

Lewis wasn't hollow anymore.

And it wasn't just Dinah and her two boys.

Lewis had known a lot of people, running his old business. Acquaintances, informants, paid help, eventually a pair of semi-partners, Nino and Ray.

But not since Jimmy, his best friend from school, had Lewis had a real friend.

Not like that goddamn jarhead.

Equals.

And he knew for damn sure Peter had never had anyone like June, who'd become a friend to Lewis, too.

Which is why Lewis was running now.

Like his whole world depended on it.

The road ended and he ran into the greenway and along Sand Creek, the water already rushing full and high from the runoff.

Lightning cracked from low clouds and lit the dark and ragged landscape. Rain, unrelenting.

Lewis's breath came hard, his heart like thunder in his chest. This was not some training run with a heavy pack along the Milwaukee River trails back home. He watched his feet on the uneven ground, wishing he had the Winchester lever gun, or a scoped deer rifle. He could have shot out the cowboy's right eye at fifty yards with either weapon. Instead he had this shortened 10-gauge, which was as subtle as a motherfucking hand grenade, and about as accurate.

He sprinted the footbridge in the shadow of the freeway, ran up through the scrub and across that traffic-clogged four-lane with its startled commuters safe and dry looking out at him, then onto the packed gravel of the trash-strewn railyard, looking for the tall fence with green plastic strips woven through the chain link.

Behind the fence would be the stepped sections of a dirty brick building, McSweeney's second grow.

He was going to have to climb a twelve-foot fence with razor wire on top, carrying the shotgun.

He'd done more than that before.

But he wasn't going to throw the shotgun over. They'd hear that for sure.

He looked around him at the ground. A stray length of electrical wire would do for a strap.

His leather coat would get him over the wire.

Ain't no time like right now, his auntie used to say.

He wrapped the wire around the stock and the barrel and took off his soaked coat. He swiped a few handfuls of mud across the front of his bright white shirt to make himself less visible, then tied the arms of the coat loosely around his neck, and began to climb.

46

Peter followed close behind the Kia, gunning the Jeep through the curving streets of this evolving industrial neighborhood once laid out around the diagonal path of the train tracks.

They passed his green 1968 Chevy pickup, left by the towing company in front of the grow facility, and through the open gate to the narrow side lot.

Lewis had been right. The way this was going, he would probably need another set of wheels.

Leonard brought the Kia around in a sweeping arc to come to a stop parallel to the building, the driver's side protected by the solid brick wall, facing out through the gate toward the street. A good spot for a quick getaway, and the building's secure steel entry door was only ten feet behind his trunk.

Peter eased off on the gas to see where the other car was going, then curved around to block the front of the Kia with the nose of the Jeep. Before the big SUV had stopped rocking on its springs, Peter had snatched up the big Colt revolver, slid out of the Jeep into the rain, and stood behind the open door, the gun hidden in his left hand.

"Let me see her," he called.

Thunder rolled, loud and metallic. Raindrops banged on the sheet metal. Wide puddles grew on the gravel. McSweeney's green Volvo wagon was the only other car in the lot, parked ten feet on the far side of the building's entry. Peter figured McSweeney had sent everyone else home for the day.

It wasn't a bad position for Leonard. The brick building protected his rear flank, and the body of the Kia and the open driver's-side door limited what Peter could see. But the thin panels of the car doors wouldn't stop the Colt Army .45.

Barely slow the slugs a little. Maybe make them tumble. Do more damage.

The static raged.

Fueled by adrenaline and sleep deprivation and a cold, hard fury, Peter was ready to do anything.

Leonard slipped out of his seat and stalked toward the back of the Kia, calling out, "Let's get this bitch done."

Peter had no shot. Leonard kept the ugly little machine pistol always pointed toward the trunk, his finger hard on the trigger. At the rear of the car, he leaned on the trunk lid, showing his ownership. The muzzle of his weapon chipping the paint.

"Okay, where's them seeds?"

Peter wiped his face, using the movement to glance toward the back fence, willing Lewis to arrive. The cold rain beating down. The static and adrenaline alive in him and rising like some second vengeful soul newly arrived in his body. He held the big Colt down along his thigh. He still didn't know if it would fire in this weather.

He said, "I'll have to call my guy." Peter tipped his head toward the green Volvo, a cold runnel of rain ran off his chin. "That's his car. He must be inside. Now open that fucking trunk and let her go."

"Everybody stay calm." Dixon was out of the Jeep on the passenger side. "Nobody needs to die today." His voice was crisp and full of command, thirty years a Marine officer, standing erect with the Beretta pistol in one hand and the Winchester lever gun in the other. His tan suit soaked through now but still holding its shape. "Let's take care of this business and get out of here."

The heavy steel entry door of the grow facility opened six inches. "I'm here," said a voice. McSweeney. "I have the seeds."

Dixon was crossing behind the Jeep when Leonard shifted as if to move.

"Stay right where you are, Leonard," Dixon called out, his voice cutting through the rattle of the rain. "Nobody move. I'll take those seeds."

Peter transferred the Colt to his right hand, but Dixon had already known it was there. Coming up behind Peter, Dixon's automatic was pointed at Peter's spine. He held the Winchester almost negligently, his hand high on the stock, lower fingers through the cocking lever, but his index finger was on the trigger.

"Drop that horse pistol, Marine."

This was the calm, capable Dixon that Peter remembered from Iraq. As if he'd made some decision, back in the Jeep. Peter remembered the smile he'd glimpsed for just an instant on Dixon's face in the rearview mirror. Wondered what had gone through Dixon's mind at that moment.

Peter hesitated. Dixon was almost within reach.

"Go on, drop it," Dixon said. "We're going to do this clean and easy. We all want to go home."

Peter dropped the big revolver to the gravel.

"Now kick it away, nice and far. See if you can hit the building."

Peter kicked the Colt. It slid farther across the loose gravel than he'd intended, ending up beneath the Kia. Too far to be of any use to him now.

He was unarmed and unarmored, his naked heart beating out of his chest. Amped on adrenaline, white static rising almost higher than he could bear.

He was helpless, waiting for June.

He would live or die with her.

Dixon walked toward the steel security door, open halfway now.

Leonard still leaned on the lid of the trunk like it was his private possession. That wasn't good. Nor were the steel rectangular tubes in his back pocket. Spare magazines for the machine pistol.

Dixon caught McSweeney in his line of sight. "Show me your hands. Good. Come over here now, and bring that package." He gestured with the Beretta. "Come on. Do your part and you'll be fine."

McSweeney stepped forward, the technical fabric of his sleek green hoodie somehow shedding rain for a few moments before it began to soak in.

McSweeney carried an oblong rectangle, a folded plastic bag with something dark inside, sized to fit in a shirt pocket.

He glanced at Leonard, then back to Dixon, a pair of professional killers. McSweeney's familiar air of amused detachment was gone. The pleasurable excitement of his adventure had become deeply unsettling.

"We could have made a fortune, all of us," McSweeney said, blinking the rain from his eyes. "But your boss decided he wanted everything."

"He does that," Dixon acknowledged with a nod. "He's not an honorable man. We're all doing our best to make this turn out right today. We're all going home."

Peter caught a flash of movement at the back corner of the lot.

A dark figure in a white shirt appeared at the top of the fence, obscured by the silver streaming from the sky. Peter willed himself not to look.

"Okay," he said. "You guys are getting the seeds. So now June goes free."

"I been thinking on that," Leonard said, shifting his balance just slightly. A little less weight on the lid of the trunk, a little more on his feet. "How do we know those are the real seeds?"

"See for yourself." McSweeney held out the package. "It's still labeled from yesterday. Henry never picked them up. They never left the facility."

McSweeney was a pretty good liar, even scared shitless.

Dixon looked at Peter.

Something passed between them, something almost tangible.

Dixon kept his pistol aimed loosely at McSweeney, but raised the Winchester one-handed toward Leonard, his finger on the trigger.

"It's fine," he said. "They're real. We're done here."

"We ain't done," Leonard said. "We don't know if they're real. Seed boy, get over here. I want to see what you got."

Peter didn't look toward the fence. He tried to picture where his Colt had ended up. He eased sideways away from the Jeep, trying to get clear of the open door.

McSweeney took two steps toward Leonard, holding out the package. "They're the real thing," he said, pleading now. "I promise."

"Leonard, that's enough," Dixon said. "Put down your weapon."

"But how we gonna know?" Leonard asked, suddenly the voice of reason. "We need some leverage. I think seed boy oughta come with us. The girl, too. I think we keep 'em all until we know those seeds are the real deal."

McSweeney was desperate now. "Hey, listen, I can give you more than just this. I have a cabin, I have money there. Good product, more seeds, different kinds. They're worth a lot. I'll give you directions. You can take everything."

It was the wrong thing to say.

"Aw," Leonard said. "That's real nice of y'all." A smile stretched across his face. He pushed himself off the trunk lid, the machine pistol now held in a textbook two-handed grip.

Out of the corner of his eye, Peter saw the dark form leap down from the top of the fence. It landed like a cat, but Peter could hear the crunch of combat boots on gravel. Softened by the sound of the rain but still distinct, maybe twelve yards away.

Dixon spun and saw the white-shirted figure silhouetted against the dark fence, arms reaching for something behind his back.

In a hurry, Dixon dropped the Winchester and raised the Beretta, his familiar service weapon, and fired rapidly, a triple-tap.

Lewis staggered as if punched, but he'd already pulled the shotgun around and lifted it to his shoulder. He steadied himself for an instant, taking fluid aim, then fired. Racked the slide, aimed, and fired again.

Four left in the tube, Peter knew without having to think about it. He leaped for the Kia, for the Colt beneath it.

Dixon collapsed in on himself with the first shotgun blast. The second put him down on the ground.

Lewis took a step and his leg gave way beneath him.

"Now it's a party," Leonard called, face splitting wide in a grin.

As he raised the ugly little machine pistol toward Dixon and Lewis and McSweeney, the Kia's trunk lid rose like a ghost behind him.

Peter wasn't moving fast enough. He was cold and wet and slow.

He saw June lift herself from the compartment, her face pale, arm outstretched.

Something in her hand, something small and red.

A mist flew out from it, touched Leonard on the ear.

He shook his head as if trying to dislodge a fly.

"Hey!" June called. "Asshole!"

Leonard half turned toward her and the mist leaped out again and again, catching him full in the face. The wind had shifted and Peter could smell it, the bright caustic burn of capsicum pepper.

"Fuck," Leonard shouted, swiping at his eyes, the machine pistol coming around one-handed.

"June, get down," Peter called, legs pumping, still too far away, "get down and run."

She dropped like a rock over the lip of the trunk and came up off the ground in a rough roll, coughing, running.

Leonard spun like a ballet dancer and the MAC-10 erupted in a manic purr, thirty rounds sprayed wild in a second and a half.

The machine pistol was notoriously inaccurate at any kind of distance and difficult to control on full auto, especially one-handed. But it threw a lot of lead, and at close quarters it could kill everything in a room.

Peter felt a tug at his sleeve, midair in his dive toward the Kia. He scrambled beneath it now, groping for the Colt on his belly, unable to see much of anything.

"Fucking bitch," Leonard shouted. Peter heard the soft clank of a magazine hitting the ground, the hard click of a new magazine slammed home.

Boom. The shotgun went off. Peter felt the shrapnel of brick fragments as buckshot hit the building.

Boom. More brick fragments. *Boom. Boom.*

"Ow, shit, fuck this," said Leonard's voice. Peter found the big Colt submerged in a puddle. He pivoted on his belly, looking for feet.

"You're driving, bitch. Get in the Jeep. Go, you pussy, or I'll blow your fucking head off."

Peter saw two pairs of shoes, close together. Boots and some kind of sleek retro Nikes.

"June," Peter shouted. "June!"

He aimed at the boots and pulled the Colt's hammer back and pressed the trigger.

The hammer dropped but the Colt didn't go off.

The boots shoved the Nikes into the Jeep and climbed into the back seat. The Jeep roared forward and out of the parking lot.

Peter scrambled out from under the Kia, the Colt dripping in his hand, the rain pounding down.

Dixon lay in a twitching heap ten feet away.

Lewis was on his side, pulling himself across the gravel toward June, who stood holding the shotgun at her waist like a street fighter, blind and coughing from her own windblown pepper spray, pulling the trigger on an empty chamber.

"Hey." Peter dropped the Colt and caught the shotgun just as June shifted her grip to swing it like a club. He pulled her, red-eyed and weeping, into his arms. "I got you, I got you."

"Jesus Christ," she said, her whole body shaking. "I did *not* like it in there."

"I know," Peter said, holding her tight. "I know exactly what you mean."

"Save that lovey shit for later," Lewis called. "Some asshole put a hole in me. And that other asshole got away."

47

Peter sat June on the wet gravel next to Lewis. She took Lewis's hand in hers. Lightning crackled overhead. Their clothes were all soaked through.

Peter knelt beside them both and pulled out his phone, which was dripping water but somehow still working, to call 911.

Lewis had a sizable chunk of muscle blown out of the side of his calf, although with the rain and his black jeans, Peter couldn't quite tell how much blood he'd lost. There was an angry red crease along his side where another bullet had skidded along his ribs and torn away some skin.

"Good thing you're so tough," Peter said. "Bet it hurts, though."

"Like a motherfucker," Lewis said. "Gimme the drugs."

Peter got closer to the leg wound. There was quite a bit of blood. He slipped off Lewis's belt and wrapped it above the leg wound as a tourniquet. "Leonard took McSweeney?"

"Yeah."

Peter placed June's hand on the tourniquet to keep it tight and walked over to Dixon, who blinked slowly up at him. Lewis had put two clusters of buckshot into his belly, wrecked most of his internal organs and probably his spine. His heart and lungs still worked, but he was pale and cold. A slow, ugly way to die.

The Beretta was still in Dixon's hand. The Winchester lay on the ground beside him. Peter didn't bother to take them away.

He thought Dixon might want the Beretta, if the pain got too bad.

"You have to go," Dixon said. "After Leonard."

"You're worried about McSweeney?"

"Leonard." Dixon's voice was ragged. Fluid in his lungs. Maybe it wouldn't be so slow. "He'll always be coming. Up behind you. And her."

"The cops will catch him," Peter said. "I'm not going anywhere."

"You don't understand," Dixon said, each breath a labored sigh. "I didn't, either. He's a predator. He'll take his time. Other women. More than a few. Before coming for her."

Not what Peter wanted to hear.

He looked at June.

She was still coughing, but it seemed to be slowing. Her eyes were red and puffy. She raised her face to the sky, maybe hoping the rain would wash out the windblown pepper spray.

Lewis looked at Peter. Even in considerable pain, with a chunk out of his leg, the force of his stare was palpable.

"If you going, Jarhead, you best go now," he said. "Cops be here any minute. Then you ain't going nowhere."

June coughed and spit and cleared her throat. "Hey. Marine."

"Yes?" Peter went to her and bent close. She looped an arm around his neck and crushed her lips against his. A kiss like the spiciest pepper he'd ever tasted.

When she let him go, she said, "I'm coming with you. I owe that fucker."

"You stay here," he said. "I'll be right back."

"No, goddamn it," she said, peering at him through her puffy red eyes. "You're not going alone, for one thing. For another, I'm fucking in love with you, okay?"

"Okay," he said. His heart breaking wide open. "Okay. Got it. Just give me a second."

He scooped up the Winchester and the wet Colt Army revolver and walked to the Kia.

Opened the door and climbed in.

Put it in drive and hit the gas hard.

Through the gate and away.

Tears rolling down his face like rain.

48

Peter had been driving for thirty minutes when the rain turned to snow, just past Idaho Springs.

June had stopped trying to reach him after five unanswered calls.

Peter couldn't talk to her. He wasn't going to tell her he loved her. Not if he wasn't coming back.

Because Peter was responsible for June being trapped in that trunk to begin with, just like he was for the hole in Lewis's leg. For all of them nearly getting killed. Even McSweeney.

War was one thing. But this was supposed to be something like normal life.

Wasn't it?

Maybe Peter was too damaged. Maybe he was just plain broken.

Maybe he'd never manage to live anything like a normal life because he couldn't keep himself from getting into the middle of things.

It's just how he was wired. To be useful. To help.

That was how he thought of it, anyway. Take out the bad guys, do some good in the world.

But it wasn't so good for the people he cared about. Lewis had almost gotten killed. June had almost gotten worse than that.

As Peter saw it, he had two choices.

He could butt out of the world, stop trying to solve problems.

He didn't think he could do that.

Or he could keep doing his jarhead thing, but alone.

Without June, without Lewis.

It occurred to him, as the Kia slid on the first patch of ice, that maybe he was looking to die. As his penance for all those dead Marines under his care, over there.

It wasn't the first time this had occurred to him. But it was the first time he allowed himself to acknowledge the thought. To think it out loud.

The woods are lovely, dark and deep.

But I have promises to keep.

And miles to go before I sleep.

Leonard would be waiting for him at McSweeney's cabin, seventy miles into the Rockies. Peter wasn't sure how he knew that, but he did. And Leonard knew it, too, that Peter was coming behind him. Some kind of fucked-up promise.

A promise Peter was planning to keep.

He made good time in the Kia, which felt like a rocket ship after driving his 1968 Chevy pickup truck with the homemade mahogany cap on the back. Ninety or a hundred in the Kia was no problem until he hit the first of the snow.

It fell thick and wet, sticky on the wiper blades, accumulating on the outer edges of the windshield.

Leonard would be making good time, too.

As the snow got deeper, the Jeep would be a lot better than the Kia.

This far into the Front Range, the interstate was almost empty. The long-haul truckers and mountain residents, really anyone with any sense, had gotten off the road well in advance of this weather. The radio said it was a big storm system coming down from the Pacific Northwest. Even in late September, a big rain in Denver could be a blizzard in the Rockies.

When he left the city, Peter was soaked to the skin, shivering and still bleeding from the half round of flesh missing from his right triceps where a stray round from Leonard's MAC-10 had grazed him.

He'd cranked the heat and it made a difference, but he knew it would be a lot colder where he was headed. He'd spent a lot of time in the mountains, had seen powerful storms blow in again and again, but he still hadn't thought it would turn this ugly in late September.

He should have stopped earlier for better gear. He should have found a gun shop in Denver for more ammunition, at least. But he'd felt strongly that he had only a narrow window of time. Leonard would want to get to the cabin to take what he could, but he wouldn't stay too long. He'd know Peter was coming behind him, and he'd want to deal with Peter. But Leonard also had to know the police would come soon after.

The storm would delay that, Peter was now sure. The police in every jurisdiction would have their hands full without organizing a manhunt for one freaky shithead.

Past Lawson, he stopped at a lonely commercial strip. He'd seen a sign for a gun shop, but it had closed early because of the weather, a handmade paper sign taped to the door glass behind the steel grate.

Almost every other place was closed, too. They knew what was coming. Four inches of snow were already on the ground.

He filled the Kia's tank at an off-brand gas station attached to a taco stand and antique shop. He wolfed down five tacos loaded with green chili carnitas, standing at the front window, watching the snow, thinking that he hadn't actually cooked himself a meal in days. Hadn't even made his own coffee. There seemed to be something wrong about that. He wondered if he'd ever cook for June again. For anyone.

The taco man watched impassively as Peter dampened paper napkins under the water dispenser and cleaned the clotted blood from his upper arm.

He made a quick run through the antique shop, hoping for another weapon, or at least some ammunition—this was Colorado, after all. Turned out it wasn't that kind of place, mostly tattered quilts and rickety chairs and chipped tin cups.

But among all the knickknacks he found a glass-fronted case of old tools, including a decent Hart framing hammer with a straight claw and a long hatchet-style handle. It was a duplicate of a hammer Peter happened to own already, in a wooden box in the back of his old Chevy, parked outside McSweeney's grow.

The Hart wasn't an antique, but Peter thought it might be useful.

The balance was perfect.

He went back to the gas station and bought what clothes he could: an itchy blue Broncos T-shirt, a heavy hooded Broncos sweatshirt, an insulated Broncos hard-shell jacket that claimed to be waterproof, and a goofy Broncos stocking cap with the blue puffball on top.

As he changed in the bathroom, Peter smiled briefly at himself in the mirror, thinking that if his dad, a lifelong Packers fan, could see Peter now, he'd shit a brick.

Warmer now, Peter was more ready for what was ahead. His pants and boots were still wet, but there wasn't much more he could do about that. He bought fleece gloves and a half-decent folding knife he could open with one thumb. He bought ten feet of nylon rope, and a cloth Broncos flag on a two-foot wooden dowel. He bought a roll of paper towels, a can of 3-in-1 oil, four Snickers bars, and two giant coffees. It was amazing what you could find in a gas station.

Walking out to the car, he saw that another inch of snow had accumulated in the time he'd spent shopping.

He sat in the driver's seat with the defrost on high while he ejected the rounds from the Colt and the Winchester. He finished the first coffee while he dried the rounds and the weapons with the paper towels, cleaned and oiled each one using the flag's dowel for a cleaning rod, then laid it all out on the passenger seat with the framing hammer. Five rounds for the pistol, seven for the rifle.

It wasn't much, he thought, heading for the on-ramp.

No vest, no helmet. No extra ammunition. The guns were fifty years old, or older.

But they were good weapons. Durable in their design and well maintained, if you didn't count the abuse of the last few hours.

He was pretty sure they'd still shoot straight.

He got off the interstate at Silverthorne, heading northwest on a narrower state highway.

The snow was eight inches deep and getting deeper by the minute.

He saw only a single set of tire tracks ahead of him on the road.

Night was falling now, the clouds low and dark. Mountains rose on both sides, lit by frequent flashes of lightning, strange through the thick white flakes. Thunder rolled down the long, crooked valleys. Thundersnow.

It wasn't going to be easy to take Leonard out.

To kill him. The Marines had taught him that, among other things.

To destroy the enemy with any means at his disposal. No sugarcoating it, what Peter was going there to do. Erase that man from the earth.

Leonard would have the advantage, as long as his eyes had recovered from the pepper spray. He'd have gotten to the cabin first, a head start of thirty minutes to an hour, maybe more. He'd have McSweeney to tell him where things were, another weapon, maybe a scoped deer rifle. Any kind of ambush was possible.

Peter was still sure of where Leonard was headed. As sure as he'd ever been of anything.

And he knew he might not be the one who did the killing.

He'd seen Leonard move. He was as deadly a man as Peter had ever met, including any number of formidable killers he'd known.

There was no guarantee. Ever.

And that was the thing, right there. Not dumb risk, but real consequence. Depending for his life on his own heart and mind and skill. Because truly living meant the risk of truly dying.

He felt the thrill of it, rising up in him again. The static and the adrenaline become one powerful force shackled to his own will. Goddamn, he was alive.

It was possible, Peter thought, that he was kind of an asshole.

Could he truly not find another way to feel this vividly awake in the world?

This was why he couldn't be with June. This kind of behavior, courting his own death. It put her at risk, and Lewis, too. Best to keep going on his own.

He found the next turn onto a state road. Following the single pair of tire tracks ahead of him in the deepening snow.

The Kia didn't like the state road, steep and winding and climbing ever higher. Its tires were made for more polite weather. In this thick slop, they slipped at speeds over forty. Then over thirty. Soon Peter was creeping along uphill through the dark at twenty miles an hour, peering through the heavy falling snow.

Full night now.

The last time Peter was on that road, he'd been driving the red wrecker downhill with Henry dying behind him.

It looked different now, covered with snow.

Peter had seen too much to think it looked peaceful.

At fifteen miles an hour, he saw the wide pull-off where he'd steered Henry's stretcher off the road.

Where he'd shot the hijacker through the windshield and taken the wrecker.

A few miles farther was the embankment where Henry's truck had lain, broken and bleeding all manner of fluids into the drainage ditch. He saw where the hijackers had loaded Henry and Banjo and Deacon and Peter into the fake ambulance. Henry dying, Deacon already dead.

Where Leonard, dressed as a state trooper, had watched and smiled and waved the traffic past.

Remembering the hijackers, Peter felt a twitch in the long muscles of his arm, the tug of tissue parting under his blade. He took the turn onto the rough gravel forest service road that led to McSweeney's cabin.

The Jeep's tire tracks led the way.

The Kia didn't make it over the first hump. The wheels spun without purpose. But at least it blocked the road.

He got out of the car and left it there, unlocked, the key in his pocket.

Maybe he'd come back for the car. Maybe he wouldn't.

If Leonard wanted to get the Jeep past, he was going to have to take the key from Peter.

———

His breath steamed in the high, thin air. The cold seared his lungs, and the snow tangled his feet, twelve inches deep or more. Coming almost up to his knees in places.

The wind had stopped, although Peter knew that wouldn't hold.

His boots were dry but his socks were still wet. His pants were dry in the front where the heater had warmed him, but damp still on the backs of his thighs and ass, and cooling by the second in the high alpine air.

He used his new knife to cut the tips of the thumbs, index and middle fingers from the fleece gloves. He was going to need whatever dexterity he could manage.

He'd already reloaded the pistol and the rifle. Twelve rounds total. Not much.

Leonard's MAC-10 magazine held thirty.

But that shitty little stamped-metal machine pistol couldn't hit the side of a barn at fifty yards. Or twenty, on full auto. Whereas Peter's Winchester would put the round where he was pointing it, a two-inch group at a hundred yards if he was paying attention. And the lever action made it fast, too.

He did wish he'd found another box of rounds. Lewis had a box under the blanket on the back seat of the Jeep, but Peter figured it was long gone.

He tucked the long-barreled Colt into the deep left-side pocket of the big Broncos coat. He could get to it pretty well. He used the gas-station knife to cut a length of nylon rope to make a shoulder sling for the Winchester, fussing a little to get the length right so he could bring the rifle around quickly. He was planning to get off the forest road and would need his hands free for climbing through the trees. The knife went into the right pocket. The Hart framing hammer he jammed through the back of his belt under the coat, out of the way. It wouldn't be a quick-draw kind of thing, but he wasn't expecting a hammer duel. It was just insurance.

Despite the low, dark clouds, the night was lit from below, the thick wet snow luminous on the rocky slopes and the sky-reaching trees.

Standing still, it was so quiet he could hear the individual flakes land on his shoulders.

But he couldn't stay.

The Jeep tracks had two inches of fresh snow covering the tread marks.

Leonard was an hour ahead of him.

It was time to move.

The forest service road was only visible as a narrow lane of white where nothing grew and the snow had stuck uniformly to the cold gravel. The only evidence of humanity was the twin tracks of the Jeep leading him forward.

Henry had told him the cabin was two miles ahead.

The white lane kept close to the flank of the mountain, following the rocky contours around to the west. Snow-clad pines and firs climbed the slope above him and dropped down below, their slender tips level with his eye in places. Too dark for any view but the thickening cloud of bright falling flakes, fading to infinity.

After only a few minutes, he could feel his damp socks cooling. He picked up the pace, burning those green chili tacos as fuel, keeping himself warm and ready.

Was it just that morning that he'd run ten miles, leading Leonard to Lewis?

It was a good plan, it just hadn't worked. Leonard had seen it, somehow.

As he rounded the shoulder of the mountain, he felt the wind pick up. First a cool, feathery brush against his face, then a steady rising pressure. Then it was a shove in the chest, gusting hard, driving the wet snow into his face and coat and pants.

His boots had already grown an icy crust. The lane of white climbed steadily ahead of him. He couldn't focus on his mistakes or on the weather. He had to look ahead. Leonard would be setting something up. Some kind of surprise.

Peter hadn't wanted to get into the trees too early. It would be slower and harder going, and he'd get wet faster climbing around in the snow. But now he realized that wasn't even an option. He could see no place to get off the road where he could move at any speed at all. The terrain was too steep and rugged. And he was getting plenty wet anyway, the heavy snow blowing horizontally, soaking into his clothes.

He figured he was almost two miles in when the narrow road approached a broad mounded saddle between two rising rocky humps whose tops vanished in the swirling snow.

The twin tracks of the Jeep continued ahead, snaking through the trees and around fallen boulders before vanishing from Peter's line of sight.

He thought the cabin would be on the far side of the saddle, as far from the road as possible, with the best view of the peaks beyond and the valley below.

He heard a short mechanical rattle, softened by the snow.

Gunfire.

At the saddle, the terrain flattened enough on the left side for him to get into the trees. He felt the static sigh a little as he climbed uphill and away from the road. He skirted a rockfall and set a course parallel to the white lane below. It wasn't great cover, but he was off the expected path and moving forward at a steady pace. Working hard enough that he was relatively warm, and his core temperature hadn't dropped. He'd be fine as long as he didn't stop moving.

Below him, still marked with the twin tracks of the Jeep's tires, the road passed between two house-sized boulders, fallen aeons ago from some much higher promontory. A good place for an ambush. Slowly, carefully, he made his way around the boulders, a hundred yards out now, the Winchester in his left hand.

On the far side, he saw a faint white depression where the Jeep must have stopped for a time, the heat of its engine melting the snow. But no footprints, and no Jeep. The tracks rolled on ahead over the crest of the saddle.

Peter followed, a hundred feet above.

He came to a fence, simple split wooden posts and barbed wire marking the boundary. Rusted metal signs read PRIVATE PROPERTY. NO TRESPASSING. NO HUNTING. The white road ran along the fence, then away and back along the steep side of the mountain.

The tracks of the Jeep turned, passed between sturdy metal posts for a steel bar gate, standing open, rusty chain hanging down.

Peter stepped over the wire and kept moving forward.

49

June blinked her eyes, her vision clearing despite the pain of the windblown pepper spray. The rain worse now, lightning strikes every few minutes. Still no sirens.

Oh, she was pissed.

"I can't fucking believe you," she said to Lewis. "Better go now, you told him. What kind of shit is that?"

"He's crazy about you," Lewis said, his voice liquid and dark. A chunk blown out of his leg, staring right at her. "You know that, right?"

"Then why would he leave without me?"

"That Leonard is a serious motherfucker. Peter doesn't want you to get hurt."

June opened her mouth, then closed it again. She put Lewis's hand on the tourniquet, making sure he had a good grip. "Keep your hand right there," she said. "Let it loose every few minutes to keep some blood flow."

"June."

"Fuck you. I'm going after him."

Lewis watched as she went to look at the sleek green Volvo wagon parked at the back of the lot. It had a hole in the front grille and some kind of green slime puddled beneath it. And no keys. The only car in sight.

But there was a plastic water bottle inside, nearly full. She went back for the shotgun and broke the glass, reached inside for the water and sluiced it over her eyes. Better.

She walked back to Lewis. "What would be your advice about carjacking someone?" she asked. "I need a ride."

He gave her a tilted grin. "And you think that some kind of specialty of mine?"

"I've never done it before," she said. "If you don't give me some pointers, I'm gonna have to start from scratch, and I don't have much time before the cops get here."

He looked at her. "You're serious."

"As a motherfucker," she said. "Come on, Lewis. Help me."

He sighed. Then tilted his head toward the back fence. "I know you can climb that."

She nodded.

"Go get me my jacket. It's hanging over the bobwire at the top."

By the time June came back with his torn and soaked jacket, Lewis had levered himself to his feet, using the 10-gauge as a cane. "Shells in the pockets," he said. "Shotgun on the left, pistol on the right."

She looked at him.

"Peter's truck is parked out front," he said. "We had a towing company drop it earlier. We thought we might need another set of wheels."

"You have the keys?"

He shook his head. "Peter does. But I can teach you how to hotwire it."

"No need," June said.

The towing company had left the driver's door unlocked, so she didn't even have to break the window. She pulled back the seat and found a slender metal toolbox. Basic mechanical tools inside. She removed a large flathead screwdriver, a ball-peen hammer, and a pair of channel-lock pliers, then climbed into the driver's seat. With the screwdriver blade wedged between the ignition cylinder and the steering column, she gave the screwdriver handle a solid couple of blows with the ball-peen hammer until the cylinder popped loose.

"Um," Lewis said, looking over her shoulder. "Where'd you learn that?"

"My dad." She adjusted the jaws of the pliers and pulled the cylinder out of the socket. "He thought it would be useful information. You know, after the zombie apocalypse."

With the ignition cylinder free, she inserted the screwdriver blade into the slot, stepped on the clutch, and turned the screwdriver handle. The truck fired right up.

"I can drop you at the hospital," she said. "No embarrassing questions."

He pulled a giant revolver out of the back of his pants and handed it over, along with the shotgun. "Everything's wet," he said. He dipped into the jacket pockets and filled her hands with ammunition. "Dry these off, then crank the heat. It's gonna be cold as hell up there, but Peter's got spare clothes in the back. That shotgun, it's gonna kick hard. You gotta put it right into your shoulder and set your feet or it'll knock you over. The revolver, you gotta cock it with your thumb, it's not a modern weapon."

"Lewis?"

He was swaying on his feet now, his skin starting to look a little gray. He took a black phone from his shirt pocket, handed it over, and told her the access code and a forest service road number. "This map will take you to the right place. You'll figure it out from there." He looked to one side, listening. "Sirens coming. Better scoot."

June heard them, too. She reached out and took his face in her hands and kissed him softly on the lips.

"Dinah's a lucky woman," she said. "And you are a very good friend."

He took a step back, his eyes tight. "A better friend wouldn't have gotten shot," he said. "A better friend would be in the goddamn car with him."

"He doesn't have a better friend," she said.

Then closed the door, put the truck in gear, and drove out of there.

In the side mirror, she watched Lewis limp to the raised concrete loading dock, then sit and tighten the tourniquet around his leg.

She passed the ambulance on her way to the interstate.

Got the powerful old truck up to eighty on the freeway and never looked back.

50

Peter saw McSweeney's cabin in a broad clearing at the edge of a steep drop. It was a true cabin, a rough wooden structure with a steep roof and deep eaves, shutters over the windows. No power line coming in that Peter could see. Primitive and perfect.

Like it had been there for a hundred years.

A newer building stood at the far side of what must have been a circular driveway, with the same steep roof and deep overhangs, but smaller, the size of a two-car garage. A cigar-shaped propane tank sheltered under the eave on one side, a long pile of neatly stacked firewood on the other.

The black Jeep stood at the edge of the clearing, like a signpost Leonard had left behind.

He was here somewhere.

He'd pulled the Jeep in a loop so that it was facing out again, snow gathering against it. White exhaust spilled from the tailpipe. Newer cars could idle for hours on just a few gallons of gas.

Peter couldn't see anyone on the passenger side. The windows were unfogged, but maybe they were rolled down just enough to vent the moisture of respiration.

From this distance, he couldn't see any footprints leaving the vehicle, either.

He leaned against a tree and watched while the wind stole his heat.

The snow fell thicker, faster. The wind blew harder. The Winchester was no longer an advantage. Peter couldn't see for shit, and even if he could, he'd have to adapt his aim for the wind, which was gusting wildly. So much for a two-inch target grouping at a hundred yards.

He imagined Leonard sitting inside the Jeep, toasty warm. Polishing his guns, waiting for Peter, who could barely feel his feet and fingers.

He wondered if McSweeney was still in there, too, or if Leonard had thrown him off the mountain.

Fuck this. If Peter waited much longer, Leonard wouldn't have to fire a shot. The wind would do the job for him.

Peter circled back the way he'd come, crossed the Jeep's tracks by the gate, then climbed the slope on the other side of the saddle, creeping along, looking for movement, color, anything out of place.

Now he could see the Jeep from the driver's side. Closer in, because of the steepness of the slope, maybe a hundred feet.

He stopped behind the shelter of a shaggy evergreen and looked down at McSweeney lying in his green hoodie, a red mess in the middle of his chest, arms and legs splayed out as if making a snow angel. Maybe the gunfire Peter had heard.

McSweeney was no angel, Peter knew.

He hadn't done it on purpose, but he'd brought this on himself. On all of them.

Still, he didn't deserve to be dead here, snow on his eyes.

Peter guessed that meant Leonard had recovered somewhat from the pepper spray.

Enough to drive himself, enough to shoot.

How accurately, Peter would find out soon enough.

If the Jeep was a signpost, McSweeney's body was flashing neon.

Nobody here but us chickens.

From his perch on the slope, Peter could see that the snow by the body was all churned up. Maybe from a fight, maybe just the two men getting out of the car. But he could see a shadow line, what had to be a single set of footprints, heading around the near side of the cabin.

He couldn't see any sign of disturbance at the door. No evidence that it had been opened from the inside, either. The film of snow at the jamb was unbroken.

The secondary structure had a single door, also closed and snowed over. No foot traffic there.

Still on the slope in the clearing, Peter circled behind the secondary structure toward the cabin.

No Leonard.

But he could still see the Jeep, exhaust trickling from the tailpipe.

Peter made sure of the big Colt in his pocket. Accumulating snow, but dry enough.

He got behind a decent-sized Douglas fir. He raised the Winchester, steadied his aim. He might not be able to manage a two-inch grouping at a hundred yards, but he could sure as hell hit the damn Jeep at a hundred feet.

He put a round through the driver's-side window, spiderwebbing the glass.

Brought the lever down and up, ejecting the casing and bringing another round up. Six left.

He waited. No response. No movement from the Jeep or anywhere else.

He put a round into the front quarter-panel, hoping to hit some vital part of the engine. Cocked the lever, another round ready. Five left.

Fired another into the engine compartment. Four rounds left. Then another.

The Jeep made an odd high whine, coughed a moment, then died.

Leonard wasn't getting out that way.

If the body was a flashing neon sign, killing the Jeep was an invitation in skywriting.

Come and get it, asshole.

Keeping to the high ground, he followed the shadow line of footprints toward the cabin. Three rounds left in the Winchester, five in the Colt. He wasn't going to think about the possibility of more ammunition in the Jeep.

But something nagged at him. What was it? Something else in the Jeep?

The terrain got steeper, and he had to concentrate on his footing as he dropped down closer to the saddle. It was easier to see the footprints now, making a brief arc toward the cabin's front door before looping around the near side of the building. The slope was turning into a cliff, and Peter had to descend even more to track the footprints toward the back of the cabin, where a wooden deck spanned its width, cantilevered over the steep drop. The footsteps climbed the steps of the deck, then went to the edge.

As if Leonard had leaped off into thin air.

Those prints, so wide and sloppy in the thick wet snow.

Impossible to tell if he was coming or going.

Then Peter knew.

Leonard had turned and walked back in his own footsteps.

The oldest trick in the book.

There was a slender pine between Peter and the Jeep. He felt bark chips in his face at the same moment he heard the trio of shots, *pop pop pop*. The machine pistol set to singles now.

Peter turned sideways to improve his cover behind the skinny tree.

Leonard definitely had his eyesight back.

It was a good sign, though, Leonard being thoughtful with his ammunition. He might have been able to stop for a few more boxes of rounds, but if he hadn't found another magazine for the MAC-10, which wasn't something an average sporting goods store would carry, the added rounds wouldn't do him much good if Peter didn't give him time to reload.

Anyway, how would Leonard have stopped for anything at all, blinded by pepper spray, with McSweeney as his hostage and driver? Even getting gas would be difficult.

More wood chips, a few more shots. Peter wouldn't mind a wider tree. He peeked around the trunk and saw Leonard sheltered behind the Jeep's engine compartment, the densest part of the vehicle. Leonard's cannonball head peeked over the top of the hood.

Peter ran, feet slipping in the slop, the framing hammer in the back of his belt feeling strange and in the way. He slid behind a fat downed fir as Leonard fired again and again, the sound of the flat cracking shots oddly softened by the blowing snow. Was that nine total for Leonard, or ten? Peter laid the Winchester along the top of the trunk and sighted down the barrel. Leonard was nowhere to be seen. Reloading, maybe.

Peter ran again, trying to get in front of the Jeep so Leonard couldn't hide behind the engine block. Leonard popped up to fire, *pop pop pop*, and Peter came to a stop in the open. He raised the Winchester, so light and simple, truly an elegant weapon, paused just a moment to let out his breath, aimed, and pressed the trigger. *Crack*, a bright dimple appeared in the hood of the Jeep and Leonard disappeared again. Two rounds left.

Then Peter was up again, legs aching, feet slipping inexorably downhill but still closer to the front of the Jeep. Leonard up, too, aiming carefully, not that it would help him much, but even the worst marksman with a lousy weapon could put a hole in you, *pop pop pop pop*, Peter down now behind a rock, the Winchester raised and Leonard ducked down. Peter back on his feet without firing, running forward along the slope, legs burning, pants and gloves soaking wet, making progress before Leonard was up again, this time from the back of the Jeep, taking his time, knowing full well what Peter was doing. *Pop. Pop. Pop. Pop.*

Peter slid behind a tree and raised the Winchester, looking for feet in the snow or that round head through the glass of the cargo compartment, saw a shadow flicker and led the movement, and put a round through the back door, hoping it might punch through two layers of sheet metal into the man on the other side but knowing he'd missed as soon as he pulled the trigger.

One round left in the Winchester. Then the Colt.

Up and running again, he was head-on to the Jeep and there was Leonard slipping around the back. Peter stopped and stood and raised the Winchester and waited. The cold wind blowing, his fingers slow, his legs turning numb.

Leonard leaned abruptly from behind the rear wheel with the MAC-10 up, *pop pop pop pop*, ducking back as Peter pressed the trigger and the machine pistol leaped from Leonard's hands, the side of the ugly little gun bent inward.

No longer a weapon. Just dead metal.

Peter dropped the Winchester into the snow and worked the big Colt Army revolver from his side pocket. With his frozen bare fingertips, he cleared the accumulated snow from the trigger housing, the cylinder, the hammer. He was exposed, out in the open, maybe seventy-five feet from the Jeep.

Leonard poked his head out from behind the cargo compartment, saw Peter, and stood. He wore a hard-shell fleece camo jacket that must have come from Lewis's luggage in the back of the Jeep. His face was red and irritated from the pepper spray, but he didn't look like he was freezing. He looked warm and dry.

He really had been waiting in the Jeep. Fuck.

Leonard had a 1911-style automatic pistol hanging from his hand. The magazine would hold anywhere from seven to fourteen rounds, depending on the manufacturer and the caliber. The wind carried his laughter toward Peter, his harsh, powerful voice full of delight.

"Guess you really like the Broncos, huh?"

Seeing Peter in his blue gas-station clothes, cold and wet, legs and shoulders soaked to the skin, the rest of him not far behind. Warm enough from his adrenaline-fueled run that he hadn't started really shaking yet. He would soon enough if he didn't hurry up and shoot this guy.

"You're an old-school guy," Leonard called. "Believe me, I respect that. We should talk. Maybe work something out."

Watching Peter, seeing his wet clothes. Stalling for time. Letting Peter get colder.

"Or if you're going for some kind of duel, hell, we should get closer. So one of us can actually hit the other guy."

Seventy-five feet wasn't so far. Farther for the 1911 than the long-barreled Colt.

Peter turned his left side to Leonard, feet shoulder-width apart, felt a tremor in his shoulders, in the muscles of his stomach. The big .45 Colt Army twitched at the end of his arm. The static cold and crisp in his head.

He thumbed back the hammer, raised the revolver, took aim, and fired. The weapon leaped in his hand, the sound like a cannon.

Leonard stepping sideways with his own weapon up and firing.

Peter kept his eye focused on the other man. Center mass. Thumbed back the hammer again, aimed, fired. Again. Again. Again. He was empty.

Leonard was out, too. He held the automatic with the slide locked back, empty.

Laughing like a hyena.

Both of them cold, trembling from the adrenaline, not shooting for shit.

Neither of them so much as scratched.

Leonard stalked toward him, red around the nose and eyes from the pepper spray.

A wide smile split his round face.

"Guess we do this the truly old-fashioned way. One of us gonna die up here. And it ain't gonna be me."

He reached behind him and pulled up the back of his jacket and brought out something long and angular. "I was real happy to find this in your Jeep."

Peter remembered what was nagging him. Lewis's gun guy, retired to run his YouTube channel, had sold Lewis the two Colts, the Winchester, and the 10-gauge shotgun. He'd also thrown in something else.

The combat tomahawk.

A brutal and effective hand-to-hand weapon, a single piece of forged steel. A hatchet blade on one side of the head and a spike on the other.

Peter took in a breath and let it out. He looked around, trying to find the Winchester, thinking it would make a decent defensive weapon. But he couldn't find the rifle in the deep, trampled snow. So he reached under his own coat and pulled the Hart framing hammer from his belt.

The long wooden handle, a big checkered head, and twin straight claws for pulling sixteen-penny nails from thick lumber.

Leonard saw what Peter held and laughed again, a high hyena cackle. "Oh, I'm gonna have fun with you."

Suddenly, silently, the two men ran at each other.

The first contact was brutal, Leonard's attack fast and strong, a diagonal blow reaching in and down to chop at Peter's unprotected neck, Peter's sideways stutter-step saving him, the tomahawk blade slicing through the wide, thick shoulder of the Broncos jacket and cutting down the sleeve, a powerful impact, but none of the hot pain of ruptured skin as Peter swung the framing hammer up into the other man's body, landing a heavy but glancing blow into Leonard's ribs.

Their momentum carried them past each other, only to slow and circle and come together again. This time Leonard bent and scooped up a handful of snow, threw it at Peter's face as he came in with the tomahawk again, but Peter raised the hammer to block, the steel handle against the hard hickory, then gave a yank to pull the weapon from Leonard's hand. Leonard's grip was just as tight, and they came together, Leonard trying to butt Peter with his head, Peter jamming his stiff knuckles up and under Leonard's chin to crush his larynx, but neither man connected.

They separated and came together, again and again, fast and direct or slow and circling, feinting and slashing and parrying like dueling swordsmen, their thick layered clothing a kind of rude armor, the razor edges of the tomahawk's blade and spike against the raw, punishing power of the hammer's head and claw, their breath panting hot and hard in the blasting wind. Each tested his opponent's weaknesses, each man landing occasional blows, but no single impact powerful enough to do disabling damage, to change the balance of strength and speed and power.

But the weapons weren't equal. With each crashing parry, Peter watched the tomahawk's hard steel frame nibble away at the hammer's hickory handle. Even without a killing blow, Peter's simple carpenter's tool would never outlast Leonard's engineered weapon of war.

So Peter let himself be driven back, bit by bit, shortening his reach slightly, feeling for his footing in the cold, wet snow. The blade sliced at his knee, his neck, his face, closer each time.

On the attack, Leonard grew more confident, pushing faster. He swung the tomahawk a little bit harder each time, brought his arm back just a bit farther, leaving himself exposed for a single moment longer.

Peter watched the timing, saw the opening, but as he set his feet for the counterattack, a loose rock rolled and his boot slipped.

Leonard brought his weapon around backhand in a tight arc and buried the spike end into the outside of Peter's thigh, midway above the knee.

It felt first like a hard punch. Then like a red-hot poker.

Peter saw Leonard's smile widen, knew Leonard was thinking Peter's mobility was gone, this fight was over, just a matter of cleanup.

Until Peter grabbed the handle of the tomahawk and held it there, lodged deep in the muscle of his thigh. Maybe even into the bone. It didn't matter. The handle strap kept Leonard stuck there, too, just long enough.

Leonard's pepper-pink eyes widened as Peter brought the framing hammer around in a long looping sidearm blow. Claw-first into the side of the other man's skull.

The sharp twin wedge sank into Leonard's cannonball head like a ripe red melon.

Peter watched one-legged as the other man fell, staining the pure white blanket around them.

Then dropped beside him.

Peter lay in the soft pillowy snow, his jacket and fleece saturated with melt, his soaked pants beginning to freeze into a crusty shell. Sweat cooled rapidly on the rest of his beaten and battered body. He couldn't reconcile the cold on his skin with the heat on his leg, halfway above the knee, which was definitely on fire.

He felt the black exhaustion of the adrenaline draining from his system. His hands were shaking, a chemical reaction from the comedown. He'd haul his ass out of this snow in a minute or two. Get up and do something.

Do what, he didn't know. Something.

He'd already blown up the Jeep.

It was a long way down to the Kia.

The wind howled. He watched the trees swaying back and forth, the snow blowing sideways. He was pretty wiped. He hadn't had a good night's sleep in days. He'd fought and run and walked and climbed and fought again. The coffee was gone and the Jeep was dead and Peter was tired.

But he'd saved June.

Now the rest of him was beginning to shake, this time from the cold.

It wasn't a problem, though. The shaking was his body protecting itself, trying to keep his core temperature from dropping too low. He wasn't in trouble until his body stopped shaking.

Then he was screwed.

Then he was dying.

But he'd get up soon, he would. Get himself out of the wind, find a way to get warm.

Break into the cabin. Build a fire.

Any minute now.

In a few more minutes, anyway.

How had he gotten so tired?

He wasn't quite so cold anymore.

Hypothermia, probably. He was supposed to do something. Get moving, get warm.

Had the shaking stopped?

He wasn't sure. He couldn't tell.

The wind had died away again. Maybe that was it.

This wasn't a bad way to go.

Out in the open, on the side of a mountain. Trees and rocks and wildflowers waiting to bloom.

June was safe down in Denver.

He never did learn to sleep inside like she'd wanted.

No wind now.

The trees had gone still.

He looked up past the feathery branches into the infinite falling snow.

The fat wet flakes landing on his face.

Like looking into the future, he thought.

Like being at the front of a spaceship traveling a million miles a second.

The snowflakes like stars.

51

That old Chevy pickup was beautiful to look at, June thought, but it was a fucking sled going uphill in the snow. The rear-wheel drive sucked balls, and the heating system smelled like wet dog.

But the tires were good and the cargo bed was loaded down with all of Peter's shit, his backcountry gear and carpentry tools and that heavy mahogany cap, so the back end was nice and heavy. Those big tires dug into the snow pretty well, all told.

The roads were empty. Cell service hit or miss, mostly miss. There were places where the snow covered all evidence of human habitation entirely. It could have been two hundred years ago, June a woman on a horse, out looking for her missing man.

With a pit in her stomach, fear and worry.

She stopped at the turn to the state highway and beat the lock off the mahogany box with the butt of the shotgun to find some warmer clothes. Along with a neatly folded blue plastic tarp that she somehow thought might come in handy, Peter also had a set of actual old-school tire chains back there, which June's paranoid dad had taught her to install on the same day he'd taught her to break the ignition lock from an old car. The ignition lock was easier.

But twenty cold minutes later, she clanked forward wearing Peter's old fleece-lined Carhartt work coat going fifty miles an hour through a foot or more of wet, heavy snow.

Only two sets of tire tracks ahead of her.

The black pit in her stomach getting deeper by the mile.

Peter's truck didn't have a radio, so she sang to distract herself.

She knew a lot of pop songs, but she kept coming back to one particular hymn.

"From the halls of Montezuma, to the shores of Tripoli . . ."

Fucking Marine.

She was going to kill him.

As long as he was still alive.

It was well past dark by the time she saw the turn onto the forest road. The tire tracks stood out clearly on the white road, dark magnets pulling her forward.

The Kia sat high-centered on a rock only a hundred yards up the narrow track.

When she opened the truck door, the frigid wind hit her like a sledgehammer. She muttered elaborate obscenities as she scrambled to the Kia. It was unlocked. No key. No residual warmth left inside the car.

She popped the lid to that fucking trunk and found her suitcase and her backpack, pulled both out, and ran back to Peter's truck. She dressed in a hurry, the worry hole in her stomach gone bottomless now. Dry socks and T-shirt, long underwear under her thick polypro running tights, thin fleece sweater under her thick fleece jacket, then her wind layer, then Peter's heavy work coat over the whole thing. Revolver in the side pocket, shotgun on its wire over her shoulder, a thick wool hat jammed down low on her head and lined leather gloves on her hands and the folded blue tarp in her pack on her back, she ran up the road.

She's late, too late, she's too fucking late.

But her body did what she needed it to do, despite the beating she'd taken already that day, despite being locked in the trunk of a car. Her legs powerful from running and hiking and climbing, her heart strong and pumping, her lungs like bellows sucking oxygen from the thin mountain air.

She ran, following Peter's footprints up the long, narrow forest road.

But when his footprints left the road, she didn't. She stayed with the Jeep tracks, knowing that's where Leonard would be, where Peter would end up.

No sound but the crunch of her feet in the snow and that mournful howling wind.

She ran faster.

She found him there by the black Jeep, the snow gone a frozen red around his left leg. Some weird-looking tool jammed into his thigh. His eyes were open, his skin was cold.

But a white puff of breath still came from his open mouth.

"Hey," she said. "Peter. Hey! Marine!"

He blinked. His eyeballs rolled slowly in their sockets. Looking at her.

Now she could admit to herself why she'd brought the blue plastic tarp.

She laid it out on the snow beside him, weighed down the corners with snow, and rolled him on top. When she did, the tool came out of his leg, and she saw what it was, some kind of futuristic tomahawk, and she had to stop a moment until the shakes left her.

Then she saw that his leg was bleeding again with the tomahawk taken out, so she packed the wound with snow and got back to the job at hand. Laid him out on that blue tarp, gathered up the grommets at the bottom half, and tied them together with the wire sling from Lewis's shotgun. Bunched the top of the tarp in her hand and tied them in a rough knot, so she had a handle to pull on.

Then she stood up, and for the first time since she'd laid eyes on Peter, she looked around.

Saw the rodeo rider six feet away with the claw end of a hammer stuck in the side of his head.

She closed her eyes against the sight and ran to the shot-up Jeep. She was hoping to use the tarp to get Peter over the snow and somehow into the back seat. But no matter how many times she hit the button, the Jeep wouldn't start.

She couldn't pull him two miles down to his pickup.

He'd be dead by then.

She looked at the rough shuttered little cabin.

At the stovepipe poking through the steep roof.

"We're going on a little ride," she said. "Won't take long. Hold on, okay?"

She took the bunched top of the tarp in her two strong hands and pulled Peter to the front door. Used Lewis's revolver to blow the padlock off the hasp, and pulled Peter through the doorway and inside.

Left the door open behind her so she could see with whatever dim nocturnal glow came off the fallen snow.

Talking to Peter the whole time.

"Hey, a Coleman lantern, I grew up with these." She gave it a shake, felt the fuel slosh inside. "All gassed up, now I just need some matches." Took four steps to the rudimentary kitchen space. "Here we go, I remember this, adjust the wick, strike the match, look at that."

The little room filled with yellow light.

"Now we need some heat, right?" She closed the front door against the wind and went to the cast-iron woodstove in the corner. "First newspaper, then kindling." Another wooden match and flames flickered up. "And a big bin of firewood, nice and dry. Hot damn, we're in business."

She went to look at him, laid out on the blue tarp on the floor. He was still breathing, his eyes still open and following her. "I'll be right back," she said, and pulled the ancient plaid couch nice and close to the woodstove, then went to the bedroom in search of blankets. She found a folded pile in an armoire, along with a bonus surprise first-aid kit, a pretty good one. Expired Vicodin would do fine.

She spread two blankets down on the couch, fed some logs into the stove, and went to Peter, unwrapped him from the blue plastic burrito. His clothes were soaking wet.

"Now for the hard part." She stripped him naked and dried him off with kitchen towels. He was dead weight, skin cold to the touch, body pale and bruised and battered. The leg wound was a deep puncture, ugly, and bleeding again with her packed snow melted away. She hauled him up on the couch and under more blankets, then went to her backpack, fished around for a tampon, and held it up. His eyes were more focused now.

"I'm not going to lie to you, this is gonna suck," she said. "I'm gonna stick a tampon into your leg to stop the bleeding." She gave him a sweet smile. "This doesn't make you any less of a man."

Had his lips twitched? They were blue. She unwrapped the tampon, cut it down with shears from the first-aid kit, coated it with antibiotic gel, pushed it into the wound, and wrapped the leg in bandages. As she worked, Peter gave a deep groan and his body tensed under the blankets, which she took as a positive sign.

The woodstove was heating nicely now. It would take a while to make the whole cabin comfortable, but from five feet away, it threw off some heat. Peter's blankets were warm to the touch. She stripped off the old Carhartt coat and hung it over a chairback to dry by the fire. Peter's clothes hung dripping around the kitchen table.

She dug through the pantry and found decent supplies in mouse-proof containers, so she knew they wouldn't starve. She filled the pots and pans with snow and set them on the stove to melt. She loaded up an old blue enameled percolator and set that on the stove, too.

Peter had started to shiver again, which was good. She laid another blanket over him and fed the fire a few more logs. Soon she'd make some kind of broth and spoon it into him like a regular Florence fucking Nightingale.

He closed his eyes, then gave a sort of jerk, his arm tugging reflexively, and his eyes popped open again. Seeing something inside his head. Remembering it. Reliving it.

Every time he closed his eyes?

June wasn't sure she could ever come to terms with the things Peter had seen, the things he'd done.

The things he'd done for her. For all of them.

She knew her uncertainty didn't matter. She would hear everything he was willing to tell her, as many times as he needed to tell it. Whether she could come to terms with it or not.

But she was sure as hell about one thing.

She sat on the couch and gently raised his head onto her lap. He blinked up at her.

She put her hand on the top of his head. Twined her fingers into his hair.

"I'd like to register a complaint," she said. "You listening, Marine?"

His lips moved slightly, but nothing came out. They were a little less blue. She put her other hand on his bare chest.

"When a woman tells you she loves you? She's expecting a certain fucking response, you read me?"

He blinked again.

"Are you tracking, Popsicle boy? When I say *I love you*, you don't get to kiss me and leave. Are we clear?"

She grabbed his shaggy dark hair in her fist.

Tears running now down her cheeks. Raging at him.

"You don't fucking get to choose who I love," she said. "*I* choose, you fucking jarhead. *I choose.* And I choose *you*. I love *you*. Got me?"

His lips moved again. His voice soft and ragged, like something broken loose from the ice.

"Got you," he whispered.

She combed his damp hair with her fingers. Looked down at him, warming his face with her tears.

"And I've got you," she said. "I've got you."

He closed his eyes again, and this time he didn't jerk awake. His arm didn't tug reflexively.

His breathing slowed and deepened.

He was asleep.

She sat on the couch, felt his chest rise and fall under her hand, and stared into the fire.

Watched the logs, consumed by flame, settle into deep burning coals, warming the small rough cabin on the steep side of a mountain while the snow deepened outside.

EPILOGUE

Elle Hansen pulled into her driveway after a long and frustrating day, her three howling children strapped into their car seats, wild with hunger. They needed more than carrot sticks and apple slices.

She knew how they felt.

Her husband was still missing, along with her head of operations. The person she'd hoped to replace them with, Peter Ash, who'd stopped the hijacking in the mountains, wasn't returning her calls.

The insurance company was still dragging their feet. She was trying to arrange for a second mortgage on the house. Maybe that would see her through this, maybe it wouldn't. She had no idea if her dad had left her any money. Her lawyer had told her getting the will out of probate could take years.

Without Peter Ash, she was afraid her business would fail.

Although an interesting plan B opportunity had fallen in her lap the day before.

Maybe she could make them both work.

She was definitely grateful for the pair of Denver police officers who'd moved into her office during the big lightning storm two days ago, and for the other officers who followed her home from work and parked outside her house the last two nights. She'd baked them cookies, brought them coffee. Nobody had threatened to harm her or her children.

But on her way home today, the patrol car following her had peeled off on Alameda, and there was no new patrol car outside her house.

She had no idea what that might mean.

As she unpacked her ravenous children from the minivan, a big black American sedan pulled up in front of her house, followed by a little red BMW.

Three men got out of the black car. One of them was on crutches. A curvy blonde in a tight skirt climbed out of the red BMW and marched up the driveway.

"Elle Hansen?" She extended a hand with a business card. "My name's Miranda Howe. I've been hired to represent you as your attorney."

Elle took the card. "I already have an attorney," she said as she shooed the children toward the house. They milled around the front porch like badly trained dogs, waiting to be let inside. "What's this about?"

"I'm sure you have a corporate attorney for your business affairs," the blond woman said. "I'm here as a criminal defense attorney." She pulled a piece of paper from a leather folio and handed it to Elle. "This letter states that I have been retained by a third party to represent your interests for today and today only. Do you understand me?"

The three men had followed up the driveway more slowly, as if they might be afraid of her children. Sometimes Elle felt like that, too.

She already knew Detective Steinburger, who had talked to her about her missing husband, and Investigator Sykes, who was looking into the failed hijacking. The third man on crutches trailed farther behind, glancing up and down the street. She'd never met him before. Somehow he didn't look like a policeman.

"Sure," she said. "Whatever." She stuffed the letter into her purse, thinking her bad day had just gotten substantially worse. "Can we do this inside? I need to deal with my kids. If I don't get them fed, they're going to start chewing on the lawn furniture."

"Actually, we need to do this next piece out here." She skewered Elle with a glance. Her next sentence was crisp and clear. "Please listen carefully, and remember, Ms. Hansen, I am on your side here. The police believe that when you picked up your father's personal effects from the coroner's office, you accidentally took possession of an important piece of evidence."

Elle felt herself grow cold. "And what would that be?"

"A small plastic-wrapped package. It contains a leather cigar case. Inside the case is a plastic packet of cannabis seeds."

"I have no idea what you're talking about."

The blond lawyer, Miranda Howe, nodded at Steinburger. He stepped forward, pulling folded papers from the breast pocket of his horrible brown suit. "Ma'am, this is a search warrant for your home. Your attorney has verified that the paperwork is in order."

Elle looked at Miranda, who nodded.

"Then I guess you're coming in." Elle gathered her unruly pack of children around her, unlocked the door, and stepped inside, with Miranda, Steinburger, and Sykes following close behind. The house was a mess of kids' toys all over the floor and her work papers all over the table. Her stomach was a knot pulled tight.

"Sorry about the mess," she said. "It's been a really bad week."

Sykes looked at her with unnerving steadiness. "Where are your father's effects?"

"Oh," she said. "They're in an envelope on the shelf in my bedroom closet. I haven't really looked at it. Between the disappearance of my husband and the death of my father, I'm still a little stunned."

"Which bedroom, ma'am?"

She pointed, and Sykes stepped past her.

He returned a moment later with a large manila envelope. He undid the little brass clasp and set the items on the kitchen counter, one by one.

A leather wallet, a leather belt, a heavy wristwatch with a cracked bezel. A gold pen. A gold pocketknife.

No plastic packet. No cigar case.

Elle's two older children looked at her, quiet now, confused by the unusual activity. Her youngest child wailed.

Miranda said, "Elle, this is important. Please remember that I am your attorney. I am representing your interests today at no cost to you. But today and today only. You should know that the police have the coroner's inventory of your father's effects. Did you take anything out of that envelope?"

While Miranda was speaking, the third man had made his way into the house. His skin was brown, his hair was cropped short, and he wore a black tracksuit that fit him like a tuxedo, except for one leg, where it bulged around a big bandage or cast. Even on crutches he was somehow graceful, like a prowling cat. He looked Elle in the eye and she shivered.

She turned away and picked up her youngest. "Listen, I really need to feed my kids. Can't this wait until later?"

The man in the tracksuit said, "I thought your kids might be hungry this time of night, so I ordered some pizza. Plain cheese. The delivery man just got here, I hope that's all right." He leaned one crutch against the wall, pulled a sheaf of bills from the jacket of his elegant tracksuit, turned to the door, and limped back with a pair of large pizza boxes balanced on one hand.

As he made his way toward Elle, she could see that, even injured, he held himself in a certain way. Like Leonard had, like her father. Like Peter Ash.

As though he was always ready, no matter what might come.

She realized that he hadn't introduced himself.

He stared directly at her now. His face was calm and open. But his eyes somehow seemed to look right through her. As if he could see every action she'd ever taken, with every motivation, good and bad. And he was weighing them up at that moment on an old-fashioned set of scales, to see which way the balance might tip.

"Here's what I think," he said, his voice deep and liquid. "I think you took something from that envelope. Something you thought might have a certain, ah, sentimental value. But you forgot. Until just now."

She could feel those old-fashioned scales somehow, with the measured weights piling up on each side. Just in the way he looked at her.

She thought about the search warrant.

And the attorney, paid to represent her for this single day. Maybe paid by this man.

"Oh," she said. "A cigar case? Leather? Maybe I do have it. Let me think, where did I put it?"

"Probably the freezer," the man said. "It's almost always the freezer."

Elle felt an acute disappointment mixed with an equal amount of relief.

Sykes stepped past her and opened the top compartment of her fridge, surveyed the contents, and reached inside.

The cigar case, her accidental opportunity, her possible plan B, lay snug beneath two bags of frozen peas, just where she had left it.

It was made of two sections sleeved together, one slightly larger than the other, to accommodate cigars of varying lengths. Sykes tugged the sections apart, revealing an oblong clear plastic packet of small round green seeds. He examined the packet and found the vacuum seal intact.

Sykes nodded to Steinburger and returned the plastic bag to the cigar case, reassembled it, tucked the case into an evidence bag taken from his coat pocket.

The three men thanked her, shook her hand, and left. Miranda was the last to leave. "Good choice," she said. "I'm sorry about your husband. But something tells me you'll be just fine."

Elle scrambled for plates and paper towels as her children tore into the pizza.

Standing in the street by the cars, Miranda said, "That could have been much worse."

Steinburger nodded. "When you gotta call Social Services? Worse for everybody."

"You're still her attorney until midnight," Sykes said. "What about the insurance payment?"

"I already talked with the state's attorney," Miranda said. "He's agreed to expedite her case with the insurance commissioner. And he's not filing any charges. Against anybody."

Lewis snorted. "There's nobody left to prosecute. The feds want Russell Palmer more than ever, but right now they can't even find him, let alone charge him with anything. He's probably in Moscow or Rio or any of a dozen developing kleptocracies without extradition to the U.S."

Steinburger said, "I thought there were supposed to be rules against taking off in a lightning storm."

"Not everybody plays by the rules." Lewis smiled, his teeth gleaming under the streetlight. "Miranda, you'll send me a bill for Peter and for tonight with Elle, right?" She nodded. "Then I got a flight to catch. Any chance I can get a ride to the airport?"

"My place isn't far from there," Sykes said. "But we'll have to swing through downtown so Steve can get his car."

"I can drive Steinburger." Miranda looked at the tall, shambling detective with a gleam in her eye. "He'll have to buy me a drink for my trouble, but he looks like a man can handle his liquor."

Steinburger turned to Sykes. Looking for help, or maybe permission. "Paul?"

Sykes shook his head. "Don't say I didn't warn you."

AUTHOR'S NOTE

This Peter Ash book, my third, was meant to be set in Detroit. I spent the better part of a week there, driving around and talking to people, and found city and citizens both welcoming and utterly captivating. I spent four months trying to get the Detroit book going, but for some reason, it never caught fire.

Margret Petrie, Sweet Patootie and font of all wisdom, suggested that I try writing about something else.

As it happened, something else was lurking in the back of my brain all along.

On tour for *The Drifter* in January 2016, I was in the Phoenix airport, unreasonably early for my flight. Killing time in the corner of a coffee shop, I found myself talking to a man who, in the course of our conversation, told me he was on his way to Portland, Oregon, to begin a legal cannabis growing operation.

The Oregon recreational cannabis law had been passed only recently, and the man—I'll call him Alex—hoped to be ready for cultivation by the first of June, when the law went into effect.

I asked him where he'd gotten the experience for this project. Alex paused a moment, then smiled and said, "This will be my first *legal* grow."

I'm a curious guy, so I asked Alex several thousand follow-up questions. He proceeded to tell me the story of how he got started growing cannabis twenty years before in California. His story is much wilder than McSweeney's invented backstory—you wouldn't believe me if I told you. Alex helped immeasurably with the details in this book.

The other catalyst for *Light It Up* was an article in the *New York Times* about several Iraq War veterans who ran a thriving company, protecting those in the business of growing and selling legal cannabis in Colorado, and the challenge of the cash cannabis economy.

Drugs, money, and guns. What could go wrong?

One of the best things about being a writer is that you have an excuse to call up smart people and ask them dumb questions, and Hunter Garth of the Iron Protection Group was kind enough to share some insights into how various security companies work with the cannabis industry.

Hunter was understandably extremely tight-lipped with specifics—he obviously cares deeply about protecting his clients, and the details I've invented for this book do not come from Hunter—but "Grandma's Attic" was Hunter's term of art for a client's unknown stash place, and one piece of jargon too good for this writer not to steal.

The cannabis economy is evolving quickly, and at least one company is using Bitcoin to help allow growers and retailers to access the banking system. I hope this book isn't obsolete before it makes it into paperback.

One last note: In *Light It Up*, Peter is still grappling with the aftermath of his war, but he's making progress. For any readers out there still coping with your own experiences, I hope you're making progress, too.

ACKNOWLEDGMENTS

Thanks as always to the many veterans who have shared their stories either in person or online. As I've noted before, I'm not a veteran myself, and the Peter Ash books are much better for those conversations. If you have a comment or a complaint or a story to tell, you can most easily find me on Facebook—see my website, NickPetrie.com, for a link.

The *New York Times* has done a great deal of reporting on the consequences of the wars in Iraq and Afghanistan, including much on posttraumatic stress and veterans' lives. These stories continue to provide information and inspiration, and I'm grateful for the work of these wonderful reporters and this great newspaper. I've posted some links on my Facebook feed. For news on medical and social progress with posttraumatic stress, the *NYT* is a great place to start.

Thanks to Andrew Jones for his friendship and insight into attorneys and law firms. Andy is only slightly less steely-eyed in real life than his fictionalized doppelgänger.

Thanks to the cheerful folks at the Denver Crime Lab and Denver Police District 2 for answering my numerous questions. Anything I got wrong is my fault, not theirs.

ACKNOWLEDGMENTS

Thanks to Hickok45, whose YouTube channel got me started on Peter and Lewis's historic weaponry. Again, any errors are mine, not his.

Thanks to John Dixon for the bulletin board and index cards. Thanks to Graham Brown for telling me the third book is the hardest—I sure as hell hope you're right. Thanks to Jon and Ruth Jordan with *Crimespree Magazine* and to the Murder and Mayhem in Milwaukee crew for welcoming me with open arms and open beers. Thanks to the Mystery Writers of America and the International Thriller Writers—they write about terrible things, but crime writers truly are the nicest people you'll ever meet.

Thanks to the excellent Sean Berard, Steve Fisher, and Christine Cuddy in Los Angeles for their efforts on my (and Peter's) behalf.

Thanks again and again and again to the astounding Barbara Poelle at IGLA for getting Peter in print; to Sara Minnich, Putnam Editor Extraordinaire, for her sharp eye and her sharper red pencil; and to Stephanie Hargadon and the rest of the Putnam publicity team for getting me out into the world and talking to readers.

Thanks to the designer, Pete Garceau, who made this book so beautiful, and to Allison Hargraves, the talented copy editor who keeps my commas Oxford and otherwise prevents me from looking like an ungrammatical eejit.

I remain grateful every day for the heroes at Putnam sales who put the books in the hands of the booksellers, for the wonderful independent booksellers who put the books in the hands of the readers, and especially for you readers—you're the ones who truly fuel the fire and keep my butt in the chair and my fingers on the keyboard. Thanks for reading!

Last but not least, I am so lucky to have such a supportive family. I am especially grateful every day for Margret, who put up with so very much insanity during the writing of this book, and for Duncan, whose boundless curiosity and thirst for adventure remains an inspiration and a call to action.

ACKNOWLEDGMENTS

For all those readers addicted to facts, please note: this is a made-up fictional novel that is, in addition, untrue. I have bent the world to suit my needs, including the use of an antique gurney as a steerable alpine escape vehicle, as well as geographical liberties with Metro Denver and Colorado in general.

Also, weed that can cure all your problems isn't real.

If you believe that, you're probably smoking too much weed.